Kitty Kendall is a bucket list achieving, junk jewelry collecting, hopeless romantic who loves great wine and a good adrenaline rush from time to time. She also collect classy shoes and expensive perfume. But her greatest thrill in life is writing romance and the steamier the better.

Bring It On!

She's travelled extensively, some 37 countries and counting and she's addicted to experiences that make her scream… white water rafting, scuba diving with sharks and hang gliding are just a few. Her stories reflect her sense of adventure and her love affair with her very own hero.

Kitty also writes romantic suspense under the pen name of Kendall Talbot. She's won numerous awards including Romantic Book of the Year, Best Romantic Suspense and Best Continuing Series. Several of her books are Amazon bestsellers. Check out www.kendalltalbot.com to find out more.

Read more at www.kittykendall.com

BOOKS IN THIS SERIES

Rise of Memphis Box Sets:

Rise of Memphis Touch Me (January, February, March)
Rise of Memphis Tempt Me (April, May, June)
Rise of Memphis Tease Me (July, August, September)
Rise of Memphis Tame Me (October, November, December)

Rise of Memphis Monthly Chronicles

Rise of Memphis January Chronicles
Rise of Memphis February Chronicles
Rise of Memphis March Chronicles
Rise of Memphis April Chronicles
Rise of Memphis May Chronicles
Rise of Memphis June Chronicles
Rise of Memphis July Chronicles
Rise of Memphis August Chronicles
Rise of Memphis September Chronicles
Rise of Memphis October Chronicles
Rise of Memphis November Chronicles
Rise of Memphis December Chronicles

Rise of Memphis Tease Me

This three book box set contains:

Rise of Memphis July Chronicles
Rise of Memphis August Chronicles
Rise of Memphis September Chronicles

KITTY KENDALL

DEDICATION

This book is dedicated to all the women out there who need a little escape.

1ST JULY
SEX FOR BREAKFAST
Room 4 – Hot Horizon Hotel

Today was not only Friday, it was the first day of July, which meant I was officially halfway through my challenge. It was difficult to comprehend what I'd done so far this year, and my heart fluttered as I contemplated what wonderful surprises were yet to come.

I didn't have to wait long. The first surprise was Needledick actually walking through the front doors prior to his shift. It was the first time he'd been early in more than a year.

The second surprise walked in right alongside my boss. Mr. Hunter McCall, my perfect stranger from a couple of months ago, who made exquisite chocolates. He wore a tiny pair of shorts and jogging shoes, and based on the fine sheen of sweat covering his body, he'd been outside doing an exercise regime, probably similar to the punishing one I'd witnessed him doing the last time he was here.

Needledick and Hunter laughed together, sharing a private joke as they walked toward me, and I quickly tugged my hair out of my bun and tousled it around my face in some lame attempt to avoid Hunter recognizing me. In the back of my brain I knew my panic attack was foolish because Hunter only knew me as Memphis, yet I couldn't help it.

As the men neared the reception counter, I swallowed the lump in my throat and tried to ignore my thundering heartbeat as I studied them. They were complete opposites in every way. While Hunter could be the lead actor on some kind of outdoor reality show, Needledick had sickly white skin, a physique that showed his lack of attention to his body, and a smile that verged on a grimace.

Hunter said goodbye, tossed me a cursory wave, and then headed toward the elevator. I was torn between watching his sexy butt and turning my attention to my boss.

How could Hunter have stayed here and yet I'd missed it altogether?

"Morning," Needledick said, as he opened the top drawer to toss his keys in.

"Morning." I had to find out which room Hunter was staying in without my boss watching me. All I needed was two seconds on the computer. Normally, as soon as Needledick arrived, I escaped as quickly as I could.

"Has it been busy?" He put his hands together above his head and stretched as if he'd just woken up.

"Just a typical Thursday night. Nothing special." *Except for one of my previous sexual partners popping in unannounced.*

Needledick went into the staff room with his lunch, presumably to put it in the fridge, and I jumped straight onto the check-in screen on the computer and typed in Hunter McCall. The fact that I even remembered Hunter's surname was not only a miracle given that there'd been about a dozen men since him, but it also showed how much it suited him. Hunter McCall had it all going on, and his name was just the beginning.

"What're you doing?" Needledick's accusatory tone was like nails up my back, and I jumped.

"I was just finishing off some stuff." The name Hunter McCall was like a blazing hazard symbol in the search button on the screen.

"Want me to do it?"

I just about fell off my chair. This was a first. He never offered to do anything for me. "No. No. It's okay." I pressed the enter button and after a millisecond the screen changed to Mr. McCall's details, and I quickly scanned the computer. He was in room four.

"What are you looking for?" Needledick was right behind me.

"Oh, ummm." I cleared my throat. "Mr. McCall wanted a wakeup call for tomorrow and I hadn't had time to do it yet." I cringed at my terrible lie.

Needledick mumbled something under his breath, and as he watched over my shoulder I recorded a wakeup call on Mr. McCall's room for six a.m. tomorrow. *How had I become so evil?*

I clicked off the screen, said goodbye to Needledick, and then headed up to my room.

The usual niggling doubt that plagued my mind when I prepared my Memphis disguise had taken a backseat this morning. In its place was sizzling anticipation as I transformed myself into a sexy minx for my perfect stranger. The idea of going up to him kick started a lovely purring through my insides. It was like he was already calling to me, telling me to hurry up.

I tried to picture what I wore with him last time, in particular, which wig I chose? In my mind I went back to that night with him. We'd gone to the bar, and later in his room we'd played a guessing game with his delectable chocolates. I closed my eyes and had perfect recollection of him undressing me and placing his lovely hands on my hips. By the time I reopened my eyes, I knew I'd worn my red dress and my cute blond wig. It was amazing how much recall I had. Maybe I had a photographic memory.

That'd be nice. For the rest of my life I'd have a perfect recollection of all the wonderful men I'd met this year.

I chuckled at that thought and as I watched my reflection, despite being halfway into my transformation, I liked what I saw. Plain Jane wasn't so plain anymore.

My diary would help me remember too. Although I had no idea what I'd do with it once the year was over. The things I'd written were sacred. For my eyes only.

God help me if anyone got their hands on it.

Turning my head, I checked my love bite again. Although it'd been six days since my sexy red-headed sports physician had left his mark, it was still noticeable. Thanks to my Nars Luminous Foundation, it was now sufficiently concealed. I tucked my hair up into my blond wig and examined the finished result thoroughly to ensure my dark hair didn't peek out anywhere.

The last time I'd gone to Hunter was at night, and the dress I'd chosen was perfect for an evening on the town, but now, this early in the morning, I was torn over what to wear. On the Gold Coast, most people wore barely anything at all. Last week I'd worn my bikini and it'd felt just right.

A cheeky little idea popped into my head. I could wear one of my fancy-dress costumes. The French Maid, Poison Ivy, or the nurse outfit. I giggled as I tugged each of them out and tossed them onto the bed. Black, green, or white. Hunter had seen Memphis as a normal, supposedly sane woman. Little did he know just how far that was from the truth.

It felt so weird thinking of Memphis as another woman, and yet it had become so natural. How would I cope next year? I huffed and quickly moved on from that thought. I didn't even want to go there. Not while there was a hot guy waiting for me just two floors away. As I picked up each costume and held it against my body to look in the mirror, I tried to picture the look on Hunter's face when he opened the door.

An idea formed in my mind, and although the French Maid costume had already received more than enough outings it was perfect for my plan.

I put on red French knickers and a matching red bra, and tugged the costume over the top. The edge of my bra peeked above the white lace at my bust. Once upon a time this would have bothered me. Not anymore; I kind of liked it. I matched my sexy lingerie with a pair of killer red stilettos with an eight-inch silver-spiked heel.

Continuing the red theme, I selected my cherry red Gucci handbag. Then I opened the zipper on my black bag to transfer my emergency supplies to my new one and was shocked to discover I had just one condom left. Lucky last.

Mental note to self: Buy more condoms. And soon.

With a bunch of butterflies dancing about my stomach, I put my coat on to conceal my dress, then walked out my door and headed to the elevator. By the time I reached Hunter's room I was actually jittery with excitement. The idea of spending the morning with the hunky fitness fanatic who made exquisite chocolates was the best way to kill a few hours.

Standing outside his door, I removed my coat, plumped up my boobs to ensure there was a sufficient amount of red lace showing, and then knocked. "Housekeeping," I called out.

I heard him groan, and I giggled as I waited for the door to open. A couple of heartbeats later the door swung wide, and the scowl on his face vanished in a flash. His eyes lit up, and his cute smile dominated his face. My perfect stranger was at the top of the sexy-hunk food chain.

"Just Memphis!"

"Housekeeping at your service, sir?" I tugged at the layers of lace in my skirt and did a little curtsy.

He chuckled and stepped aside. "Quick, come in before someone sees you."

I laughed as I wriggled past him, strolled to his table, and tossed my bag and coat aside.

"Oh, wow. You look incredible."

"Thank you." I swung my hips from side to side, swishing my skirt around my thighs.

"How did you find me?"

I didn't have an answer for that, so I shrugged, acting all coy. "I have my little spies."

He walked from the now closed door toward me. "Well, I'll be forever grateful to them." Hunter had taken off his shoes and socks, but he was still wearing the shorts he'd been in when I saw him downstairs.

"I waited up all night, hoping to continue our chocolate guessing game."

I put on my best sad face. "I'm sorry I missed it. But I'm here now."

He scrunched up his nose and ran his hands down his sides. "If I'd known you were coming, I would've had a shower."

"Mmmm." The idea of watching him shower had my insides curling. "You can still have a shower. As long as I can watch." I'd become devilishly brazen, and my pussy pulsed at how good it felt.

His eyes bulged, and the movement in his shorts was unmistakable.

He closed the distance between us, curled his fingers around my neck, and brought his lips down to mine. Our mouths molded together, and our kiss was soft at first, but it quickly grew heated, demanding, making me delirious with primal want for him. His hand weaved into my dress and lowered the stretchy fabric down my bust to reveal my bra.

His fevered passion demanded my attention and I opened my mouth, allowing his tongue to explore mine. Our breaths mingled, our tongues danced, and our hands groped.

I squeezed his nipple. He massaged my breast. I reached around, pushed my hand into his shorts, and squeezed his tight butt. His fingers curling across the back of my neck had my hairs standing up to meet him.

Just feeling how much he wanted me had my heart racing, and I wanted to touch every inch of him, to taste him, to feel him inside me. Heady scents of deodorant, perspiration, and hot-blooded man invaded my nostrils.

I put my hands above my head, and he didn't need an invitation. In a flash, my costume was off, and he tugged my bra down, reached in and curled one of my boobs out so it popped over the top of the lace. It was uncomfortable, but when his fingers pinched my nipple and a moan tumbled from his throat, the discomfort evaporated in a flash.

He released from my lips and turned his attention to my neck and drew his tongue from the base of my neck all the way up until he licked my earlobe. A delightful shudder rolled through me, and a sense of urgency drove my fingers to explore his sculpted torso. I glided my fingers up and down his heated flesh, pausing only to squeeze his hardened nipples.

His tongue flicked just below my earlobe and my eyes shot open as I suddenly remembered my love bite. I gasped and wriggled out of his embrace.

He blinked at me, and I grappled for inspiration to explain my abrupt release. I put my hands on my hips and forced assertiveness into my voice. "You said I could watch you shower."

A smile curled at his lips, and his chest rose and fell with powerful breaths. "Okay then." He turned and walked toward the bathroom. At the entrance, he stopped and glanced at me over his shoulder a devilish grin lighting up his face. In a flash, Hunter bent over and whipped his shorts down around his ankles.

I gasped at the glorious sight. It wasn't dirty or disgusting. It was easily one of the hottest moves a man had ever made for me. His butt cheeks were perfect round globes, the skin paler than his shapely legs. The show was over in a second, and he laughed as he stood back up and kicked his shorts aside. He again looked at me over his shoulder, but this time he grinned like a man on top of the world. "Sorry about that. I don't know what came over me."

I knew exactly what he meant.

Laughing at his loss of control, I examined the contours of his back. Muscles bulged in all the rights places, from the tops of his broad shoulders down to his narrow hips. "Don't be sorry. You can do that for me any time." I wanted him to shift toward me so I could commit other glorious parts of his body to my memory. But he didn't. Instead, he turned his attention to the shower and played with the taps. In an erotic haze, I followed him into the bathroom.

Naked, he stepped into the cascading water, and I was eternally grateful that the cleaners kept the shower screens pristine. As I leaned back against a hung towel, Hunter rubbed soap over himself. Somehow, I'd fallen into a wickedly erotic dream. I was officially in heaven.

My insides squirmed, and my clit pulsed as I slipped into voyeuristic heaven. My subject was one of the hottest men in the world. He pushed open the door, smiled at me, and wriggled his eyebrows. "Coming in?"

My eyes shot open wider. My head said no; my body said "hell yeah." I must've looked confused or something because before I knew it, Hunter stepped from the cubicle and stood before me. My hands had a mind of their own as they reached out and glided over his dripping wet body. His skin was hot; he smelt divine, and my mind went crazy.

I slipped out of my shoes and unclipped my bra in one move. Hunter reached into my lacy panties and slipped them down my legs. No sooner had I kicked them aside than he reached for my bottom and hoisted me onto his hips. I wrapped my legs around him and hooked my ankles. Our lips latched together and I forced my tongue into his mouth, devouring him in every sense of the word as he carried me into the shower.

Luckily, all my wigs were top quality, or I'd look like a crazy witch in no time. The woman in the shop told me I could even swim in them. Not that I had that on my agenda any time soon.

Warm water tumbling over our bodies added to the heat already coursing through me. Hunter pushed my back up against the cold tiles, but the shock was only brief when he reached down between my legs and slipped a finger inside me. I gasped at the thrill of it and squeezed my thighs around him. As his tongue flicked in and around my mouth, his finger plunged into my throbbing pussy. All I could do was hang on and take the glorious onslaught. My body was alive, both inside and out.

I smelt the soap on his skin as the heat of his body caressed mine. Our breaths were ragged and as our lips parted, I leaned forward to lick his neck, tasting his salty skin. When I opened my eyes, I took in everything from the tumbling water and the light mist in the air to his wet, wavy hair and his slick, tanned skin. I was in an erotic movie, and I wanted to stay there forever.

Hunter's second finger found the first, and my insides clenched around them like a fist as he drew out my orgasm. A shiver rolled through me, and

I gasped as I came in a long, rolling shudder that matched his thrusting fingers. As I wrapped my arms around his neck, gasping for air, he wrapped his arms around me.

The head of his penis nudged at my opening, and I so wanted it to go farther. "Do you have a condom?" My voice was a ragged whisper.

Silently, he carried me from the shower and sat me upon the bathroom counter. At my side was his wet pack. He delved into it, removed a condom, and tore open the pack. As he rolled it on, I glanced at myself in the mirror. I expected to see panda eyes from smudged mascara, but to my delight I was pretty tidy. Then I just about yelped as I saw the unmistakable line of the damn love bite. I tried to turn to see it better, but I had no time, because suddenly I had my legs around Hunter's hips again and we were back in the shower.

Once my back was against the wall and his hands dug into the flesh of my bottom, I was lost to a lust-fueled world. With my arms around his shoulders and my legs around his hips, opening me wide, he entered me. I gasped as he filled me right to the hilt. Hunter's rapid breathing matched his fervid thrusting, and I was at his orgasmic mercy as I held on. The angle of this sexual position had him plunging deep inside me with rapid-fire thrusts. My orgasm ripped through me. It was sudden; it was explosive; it was bloody amazing, and I clawed at his back as I cried out.

Hunter groaned and cried out too. His fingers dug into my flesh and his hips shoved all that he had into me, over and over. He hugged me to his chest, and his breathing was that of a man who'd run a marathon. I squeezed him tight, never wanting to let go.

After a long while, Hunter let out a huge sigh and I pulled back.

He blinked at me and smiled. "Who are you, Just Memphis?"

I searched for an answer, but I had no idea either. To avoid responding, I leaned forward, kissed his cheek, and then released my grip on his hips. Standing before him, I placed my hands on his pecs and looked up into his lovely blue eyes. "You don't want to know."

He curled his hand around my neck. "As a matter of fact, I do. Will you join me for breakfast?"

I think I shuddered or something, because he blinked at me and frowned. Then his eyes drilled into mine. "I saw a nice-looking coffee shop outside the hotel. How about we meet there in half an hour?"

Fear, shock, disbelief, and a variety of other horrid emotions had me frozen to the spot. I could barely breathe. I could barely think. "I umm, I . . . I . . ."

He leaned over and kissed my forehead. "You're a fascinating woman, Just Memphis." Then he stepped back under the tumbling water again. I took this as my opportunity hop out and dry myself. With one of his towels around me, I went back into the lounge area, and in a daze, I gathered my clothing from the floor.

By the time Hunter emerged from the bathroom, I was dressed in just my coat and red shoes and had my bag over my shoulder. The towel looked perfect as it hung low on his hips just below his navel. He ran his hand through his wet curls and sighed.

With that lasting image firmly locked in my brain, I turned and walked toward the door.

"I'll be down in the café in half an hour, Memphis. Waiting for you."

I swallowed as I debated over whether or not I should go. The angel and devil in my brain were about to break into a fist fight when I decided it was just too hard. I turned to look at him over my shoulder. "You may be waiting a long time."

I strode out of his room. By the time I was in the elevator, my chin dimpled. By the time I made it to my apartment, tears pooling in my eyes made it impossible to see.

At my bathroom sink, I yanked off my wig, and as I scrubbed off my makeup, tears streamed down my cheeks, yet I had no idea why I was crying. With trembling fingers, I wiped my eyes and then as I gripped the basin, I bawled my eyes out.

I turned the shower taps to hot, and as I allowed the hot needles to pummel my flesh, my emotions rolled through me like thunder, but for the life of me I couldn't figure out why I was so upset.

After I stepped from the shower, I wrapped a towel around me, grabbed my phone, and sat on the bed with my knees tucked up to my chin.

Lolita answered on the second ring. "Hey babe, what's up?" It made sense that she'd responded that way, as it seemed the only time I rang her was when I was in trouble.

I was an ugly crier, and when I burst into tears, words refused to release from my throat. Lolita's panicked voice on the other end of the line was the only thing that made me settle down a bit and suck in a few deep breaths.

"Are you hurt?"

"No. It's nothing like that."

"What happened, babe? Tell me."

Tears spilled over my cheeks at her concern. I told her about me dressing in the French maid outfit again, and the incredible sex in the shower, and everything else in between. A sob released from my throat. "He asked me to breakfast," I blurted out, before another ugly sob gripped me.

"What?" She giggled. "I'm sorry, but did you say he asked you to breakfast?"

It sounded so stupid. "Yes." I sniffed.

"Oh Jane. Why does that upset you?"

"I don't know. I guess . . . I guess it's because I actually like him, but he doesn't even know the real me."

She sighed. "Babe. You listen to me. Memphis is you. She's every bit you."

"No she's not. I'm not. Oh God, see how stupid it is?" I wiped a tear that'd tumbled down my cheek.

"Jane, Memphis comes from you. Putting on a wig and makeup doesn't change who you are. Somehow, somewhere in you is Memphis. When you let her, she's gradually sneaking out."

"What do you mean?"

"I've seen a change in you. You're much more confident. You're finally seeing a sexy side to you that's been buried for too bloody long. You're having fun, and that's a good thing."

We sat in silence as I stewed over what she'd said.

"Tell me what you like about Hunter."

I found myself smiling at the thought of him. "He's kind. And funny. We laugh together. He just seems like a really nice man."

"He sounds like a good guy."

"He is a good guy, and I feel dreadful for deceiving him."

"Alright, here's what you're going to do." I imagined her crossing her legs in a traditional yoga pose. "You're going to put your wig back on and dress in something normal—something Jane would wear. Tone down your makeup a bit too, but not too much. Then you're going to have coffee with him and get to know him more."

"I don't know . . ."

"Babe. You've done nothing wrong. You're a single woman having fun. Besides, Hunter is doing the same thing. He's just had sex with a complete stranger too."

I blinked at that. "Yes, that's true."

"Exactly. So if you think you're doing something wrong, then he is too."

"I hadn't even thought of that." I rubbed one eye. "Except I'm in disguise."

"A disguise that he thinks is smoking hot. I bet he'd want you to do it all over again too."

I giggled at that. "It was fun."

"Of course it's fucking fun. Now go and have breakfast with him, and find out who this hot guy really is."

My stomach did little flips at the prospect of getting to know Hunter better. "Okay."

"Good, and ring me later and tell me all about it."

I slipped off the covers and sat on the edge of the bed. "I will. Thank you. Love you."

"Love you too, babe."

I clicked off my phone and placed it on the bedside table. The time on the clock indicated I had ten minutes to meet Hunter's deadline.

I strode to the bathroom, a new woman on a new mission.

With the hair-dryer on full blast, I dried both my hair and my wet wig as best as I could. Then I tucked my hair up again and styled the wig to its former cute style. I applied foundation, ensuring all my freckles and my blasted love bite were hidden. I played with my eyeliner and mascara until they gave me the cat-eye look that I liked, and I finished my makeup with a touch of eye shadow.

Considering the amount of crying I'd done, my eyes only had a small amount of the redness and puffiness that I usually had after tears. I squeezed in a couple of drops that I'd bought with my colored contact lenses and they instantly felt better. Satisfied that my disguise was sufficient to hide Jane and yet simple enough that Memphis didn't look like a lady of the night, I walked out to my closet.

I chose a pair of white jeans that I rolled up at the cuff to show off a pair of stylish caramel four-inch heels. I matched the stilettos with a similar-colored knitted top that tended to slip off my shoulder all the time. I switched into a strapless bra to solve that little dilemma, because although it was annoying, the off-the-shoulder thing was kind of sexy, but showing one bra strap was not.

At my jewelry collection, I scrounged through the bits and pieces and decided on a chunky set of long-string fake pearls and pearl-drop earrings.

I stood before the mirror. Although I didn't look like Jane, I didn't look like Memphis either. But I did like what I saw. The woman in the mirror was confident and sexy, and about to go on a breakfast date. My stomach fluttered at the thought of Hunter waiting for me.

With that notion in mind, I grabbed my phone and purse, and headed out the door.

As I crossed the marble lobby expanse, Needledick looked up from the desk. I was a second away from saying hello when I realized I was Memphis, and put my head down and kept on walking. It wasn't until I was out in the sunshine that I let out the breath I'd been holding.

With my sunnies on, I walked along the path and tried to calm my racing heart. The Blue Haven Café was the one Lolita and I went to every Tuesday after our morning workout, and we knew all the staff there. This would be yet another test of my disguise.

Hunter was seated at one of the outside tables, looking every bit as sexy as he had naked. He wore a simple white shirt with a couple of buttons undone at his neck. His blond hair was tousled in a messy, wavy style that had a few bangs falling near his eyes, and he wore glasses that looked as if they'd been made especially for him.

His jaw actually dropped as I approached, and my heart galloped at his cute reaction. He jumped up and pulled out a chair. When I reached him, he leaned in to kiss me, and I smelt a lovely mix of cologne, soap, and masculine man.

I sat, and when he sat opposite me he smiled. "That's twice this morning you've surprised me, Memphis." He kept his sunglasses on, so I did too.

I cocked my head at him. If he wanted surprises, I sure could give him one. "Twice?"

"Yes. I didn't expect you to come here. Just like I didn't expect to see you upstairs."

"I like to keep my men guessing." *Oh God.* I inwardly cringed at my stupid comment.

But to my delight, Hunter laughed and then raised his eyebrows. "Is that right? I'll keep it in mind."

He picked up a menu. "Shall we order?"

I didn't need the menu; I knew exactly what I was having. But in keeping with my persona, I lifted it up and pretended to scan the breakfast selection. All the while, hidden behind my glasses, I stared at the sexy man opposite. The sun caught on his wavy hair showing touches of brandy amidst the blond. His teeth were perfect, and every once in a while he ran his tongue over his lips. I wondered if he knew I was watching and did that for my benefit. Not that I was complaining.

Matt, the dour waiter, arrived at our table with a bottle of water and two glasses. "Are you ready to order?" His enthusiasm was non-existent.

"After you," Hunter said.

"Hi Matt. Can I have savory mince on toast and a large cappuccino?"

Matt crinkled his nose at me, but I ignored him. He was prone to acting weird.

But when Hunter also looked at me a little strange, I wondered if it was my choice of meal that caused that reaction, then I realized my error. I'd called the waiter by his name. I inwardly cringed, and as Hunter placed his order I contemplated how I'd explain that away.

The waiter left, and Hunter leaned back on his chair. "So you've been here before?"

I nodded. "A few times. So tell me, how did you go with introducing your chocolates to Queensland?" I was determined to divert the conversation away from me.

"Not too bad actually." He sat forward and steepled his fingers together. "I've secured half a dozen restaurants and a few cafés are interested."

"Oh, that's excellent. Is that why you're back?"

"It is." He tilted his head. "And I'd hoped to bump into you again."

I smiled, and my stomach fluttered at the way he looked at me. "I'm glad I did."

"You never did answer my question on how you knew I'd be there."

I frowned as my brain searched for an answer. "Yes, I did. I told you I had my spies."

He huffed. "You're an interesting woman, Just Memphis."

"Thanks. I've been called worse."

Our coffees arrived, and I used the distraction to work out what question to ask him next. I needed to dominate this conversation. I ran a spoon around my mug, catching the chocolate sprinkles that lined the edge. "So I never did get a chance to ask you last time if you've ever been married?" So much for idle chit chat.

"Nah. I got close once, but like your ex, she turned out to be a lying cheater."

My eyes widened. "I'd forgotten I'd told you that."

"Oh yes, you just about broke up telling me."

I frowned at him, and upon noticing his cheeky smile I rolled my eyes. "I did not. I'm well and truly over that bastard. What about you? Why haven't you moved on?'

"I don't know." He shrugged. "Hurt feelings. Insecurity."

"Pfft, I doubt it. The man I saw upstairs wasn't insecure."

He took his glasses off and raised his eyebrows. "What can I say? You bring out the best in me, Memphis. So . . ." He cocked his head. "How old are you?"

"Twenty-eight. And you?"

"Guess." He wriggled his eyebrows.

I gasped. "That's not fair; I told you. I'm not guessing."

"Oh come on. I'm curious how old you think I am."

"Okay, forget I asked. It doesn't bother me anyway."

"Really? You don't want to know?"

I shook my head. It was true—based on the men I'd had so far this year, age was no longer important.

Matt arrived with two plates. "The three-egg omelet?" he asked in his usual uninterested drawl.

"That's mine." Hunter's meal was placed before him and the savory mince before me.

"Is there anything else you're waiting on?" Matt should already know the answer to that question. Sometimes his ineptitude really got on my nerves. "No, we're all good."

Matt left and I removed my sunglasses, placed them aside, and forked some mince into my mouth. As usual, it was full of flavor. I rarely had breakfast here, often choosing a sweet treat instead, but whenever I did, it was this dish. My grandmother had been the queen of savory mince—before Alzheimer's stole that recipe from her, that was.

That gave me an idea. "Tell me about your family."

"I already told you about Mom and Dad, remember? They're both chefs."

"That's right, that's how you grew to love chocolate."

"Tell me about your family."

I put a forkful of mince in my mouth as I debated what to say. In the end, I decided the truth wouldn't hurt. "I grew up in Mildura, with Mom and Dad and a brother, who's now a professional football player."

"Oh really? What's his name?"

Oh God. I coughed on my mince. I'd totally walked into that trap. As I held a napkin over my mouth and coughed up a lung, Hunter reached around to gently pat my back.

"Geez, are you okay?"

I nodded and wiped a tear away from my eye. "Sorry about that. I think it went down the wrong way." I gulped at the water. Damn, this dating business was hard work.

Hunter resumed eating and as I sipped my coffee, I hoped he'd forget what he'd asked. The best way to help him do that would be to ask him something. "So do you have children?" Good one, Jane. Straight to the jugular.

"No, you?"

I shook my head. "No." I scooped another mouthful of mince into my mouth. "Do you like travel?"

His eyes lit up. "I love to travel. How about you?"

"I haven't done any yet, but I will one day. Where've you been?"

"Being a chocolatier, I've had to visit some of the most magnifique places in ze world." He slipped into a terrible fake French accent, and I burst out laughing. Hunter feigned horror at my teasing, and then we giggled together.

The rest of our breakfast was a lovely mix of laughter and curiosities. It was relaxing too, as he regaled me with stories of all the wonderful places he'd been to in his search for the finest ingredients in the world. His passion for travel was equaled by his passion for The Sweet Spot, his chocolate business. We laughed and chatted for so long that when I looked at the time on my phone, I was shocked to see that somehow I'd lost four hours with my perfect stranger.

When it was time to stand, Hunter placed his hand on the small of my back and leaned in to kiss my cheek. "Well, Just Memphis, it's been a delight."

A giddy flutter danced across my insides. "I agree."

"Would you like me to walk you to your room?"

Oh God. I'd love that so much. Thankfully, my brain kicked in just in time to stop my wish being blurted out. "No, that's okay. I'm catching up with a friend for lunch, so I'll just keep going." I felt rotten lying to him again.

He touched my elbow. "May I ask for your number?"

My heart skipped about a thousand beats. "My number," I repeated, like the complete fool I was.

"Yes. Your phone number."

"Oh, oh um . . ."

"You don't have to."

"It's not that. It's um . . . just that I work shift work and I . . . ummm . . ."

"You never told me that."

"What?"

"That you work shift work. What do you do?"

Oh shit. This was getting messy. "I'm a croupier at the casino." I had absolutely no idea where that lie came from.

"Oh wow, that's interesting." He tapped his temple with his finger. "Mental note never to challenge you to a game of Blackjack then."

I put on a fake chuckle. "Yep, that's right." That's me, a card shark from way back. Not.

"Okay, if you don't want to give me your number, can I at least give you mine?"

I grinned and nodded.

"Have you got a pen?"

I reached into my bag and removed a Hot Horizon Hotel pen.

Hunter twisted the pen in his fingers. "Ha. I pinched one of these too." He scribbled his number on a napkin and handed it to me. Then he leaned over and kissed my cheek. "I'll be waiting for your call."

Hunter turned and strode away, and I watched his sexy butt until he climbed the stairs of the hotel and disappeared.

It was a long moment before I dragged myself from the Blue Haven Café. I decided to go for a walk to clear my head. The sun was nearly directly above me, but thankfully the winter weather kept it quite mild.

I walked along aimlessly, enjoying my scenery and replaying every wonderful moment of my morning with Hunter. For the first time in my life, a man, and a sexy man at that, had asked me for my phone number. That one simple move had me grinning like a crazy woman.

My wandering led me outside the pharmacy, and I went inside to buy condoms. Unlike last time, today I had a fair idea of what I was doing. I grabbed the same brand I'd bought before and strode to the counter. The creepy guy at the checkout didn't eyeball me like he had last time, and the purchase took less than two minutes.

I made my way back to the hotel, put my head down and charged across the lobby in attempt to avoid Needledick. I needn't have worried though he was on the phone at reception.

The first thing I did when I entered my room, was take the napkin with Hunter's number out of my bag. I kissed it. I had no idea why I did that, but for some reason this simple token made me feel like a silly seventeen-year-old girl who'd just been asked to the prom by the hottest guy in town. I secured his number to my fridge with a surfboard magnet and stood back to admire it.

After brushing my teeth, I stripped off and put on a floral cotton pajama-set. As I sat on the bed, I reached for my diary, turned to the 1st July and wrote *Mr. Hunter McCall Room 4.* There was something about Hunter that made him special and he in turn made me feel warm and fuzzy, as if I was falling under a magical spell. I detailed our amazing sex in the shower and our breakfast afterwards. That's when I wrote *Sex for Breakfast* beneath his name.

I put the diary aside and crawled under the blanket. Hunter's lovely scent was still on me and as I closed my eyes, I pictured the two of us lying side by side, him with his arm around my neck, and me with my leg curled up over his thigh, capturing all the warmth of his exquisite body. As I allowed sleep to take me, I drifted into another perfect world.

7TH JULY
MY BAD BOY
Room 24 – Hot Horizon Hotel

Running out of staples was one of my pet hates. What was even worse was when someone else used the last one and was too lazy to replenish them. I huffed at the inconvenience, stood up from the reception counter, and wandered into the staff room. The stationery cupboard was immaculate; thanks to my endless hours of boredom, I was prone to ensuring every item was in its rightful place.

I plucked the box of staples from the shelf at eye level and proceeded to open it as I strolled back to reception.

"Hey gorgeous."

My jaw fell to the floor at the drop-dead hunk with his Schwarzenegger arms resting on the counter. "Corben!"

"That's me."

Frozen to the floor, I tucked a slip of hair behind my ear and played my eyes over the muscles bulging from his tight singlet top. The rose tattoo on his left bicep caught my eye. It was stunning. I couldn't remember seeing it last time. Surely I wouldn't have missed a masterpiece like that.

"So," he said, snapping my attention back to his lips. "What would you like to do first . . . fuck or go for a jog?"

The staples launched from my fingers and tumbled to the floor like scurrying ants.

"Are you okay?" A frown marred his beautiful face.

I nodded, dumbstruck, then shot to the floor to pick up the mess, hopeful the distraction would release me from the mind scramble I'd fallen into.

"Jane, are you there?"

I swallowed hard, tossed a couple of staples in the bin, and reluctantly sat up on my knees to look at him. "Hi." I actually waved. *I'm an idiot.*

"So, which is it . . . fuck or run?"

My eyeballs practically launched from my sockets as I gasped. "Corben! Shhh."

"Argh, don't worry." He waved his hand around the empty foyer. At least, I hoped it was still empty. "Nobody's around. So, what's your answer?"

"I . . . I . . ." *I'm a blubbering idiot.*

"I'll decide then. Shall I?"

I nodded so quickly my eyes couldn't keep up.

"Right then. You finish at six thirty, right?"

Nodding was about the only body movement I could manage.

"Okay, so I'll meet you out the front at seven. Don't be late."

He turned, and I dragged myself up onto the reception desk just in time to watch his cute butt in the tiniest gym shorts seconds before he disappeared into the elevator.

"Holy shit." I crumbled into the leather chair and wiped the sweat beading on my forehead with the back of my hand.

My pounding heart took an eternity to settle and when it did, I returned to the floor to collect the remaining staples. As I scrambled around on my hands and knees, I stewed over Corben's forthright request and couldn't decide if I should be mad or thrilled. Last time I was with him, I'd noted him as being a man of few words. Maybe the direct approach was the only one he knew. A guy as hot as Corben could get any girl he wanted; it seemed all he had to do was ask.

I'd fallen for it, too . . . hook, line and sinker. If he'd asked me to remove my underwear, I probably would've had them around my ankles before he could blink. I giggled at the thought. Thank God my theory hadn't been tested.

I glanced at the clock over the filing cabinet and was relieved to note I had just twenty minutes until the end of my shift. Then I'd have to wait out the customary delay until Needledick arrived to take over from me. With a bit of luck, my boss wouldn't be too late today, although I didn't hold much hope.

My thoughts drifted back to Corben with his broad shoulders and tight buns that begged to be squeezed. I pictured his chiseled physique jogging along the golden sand, striding out with those perfect muscular calves bulging with each step. A wave of anxiety ripped through me as I wondered how the hell I was going to keep up with him. Running with Corben! *What was I thinking?*

Fear of failure gripped me.

Not only did I worry about keeping up, but what if I couldn't concentrate with that hunk of spunk at my side and I landed face-first on the pavement? I fought the negative vibes by gritting my teeth and forcing positive affirmations into my brain. *I can do this.* Damned if I was going to look weak. It was suddenly very important for me to show him just how fit I was. The extreme workouts I suffered at the hands of Lolita were about to pay off. *I hope.*

Needledick arrived fifteen minutes late, which allowed me just fifteen minutes to get ready for Corben. Ten, if I included the ridiculously slow elevator rides. When the door pinged open at my floor, I ran to my room. As I dashed about, stripping off and redressing at breakneck speed, I threw in a few stretches as I went. Last of all, I did up my shoelaces and stretched my hammies at the same time.

If I'd had time, I would've rung Lolita and told her about going for a run with Mr. Universe. I giggled as I imaged her sprinting from her place to my hotel in an effort to join us.

I whacked on sunscreen, grabbed my sunglasses, shoved my room key into the discreetly hidden zip pocket in my Nike gym shorts, and headed out my door.

The elevator took forever to arrive and by the time it reached the lobby, I'd managed several decent stretches. I was late by three minutes. My tardiness distressed me, but then as I thought about it, I wondered why. I had no obligation to Corben, and if he wanted me, then he'd have to wait.

Yeah, I'll show him who's boss.

My newfound fortitude shattered to a gazillion pieces at my first glimpse of him. He faced the cresting sun. Bolts of yellow sunlight silhouetted him like he was a prize-winning portrait. Corben was a man of muscle, from his bulging calves to his outrageous shoulders. I was in for trouble. How on earth did I think I could keep up? As I contemplated running back to the elevator, he turned.

"'Bout time, Jane." His voice was loaded with authority.

"Sorry." *No I'm not.* I yelled that in my head

"Come on, sexy. Let's go."

Sexy! . . . *Okay, he's forgiven.*

He trotted ahead of me in a smooth, practiced gait and I fell in behind, enjoying his stunning derriere as it bulged and flexed with each move. The muscular globes were like some kind of hypnotist trick, guaranteed to make me do whatever he wanted.

"Come on, catch up." He waved his hand, egging me forward.

I caught up to him and we fell into a comfortable stride. It was hard to decide which one of us was setting the pace. Together we left the path, crossed the raised wooden platform, and hit the sand. We remained side by side even once we reached the part where the sand was firmer from the outgoing tide.

"You're good, Jane."

"Oh, thanks."

"Most women can't keep up."

"I'm not like most women." My quick statement shocked me, but I feigned confidence by raising my eyebrows at him.

He smiled at me, and the sun must've caught on those pearly whites or something because they positively dazzled. "No, you're not, Memphis."

We carried on in silence. The crashing waves and our shoes crunching in the sand were the only sounds. It felt good, basking in the glorious winter sunshine and breathing in the crisp morning air. *I really should do this more often.*

If Corben and I actually hooked up, would this be something we did every day? I just about face-planted at that outrageous thought. As if a guy like him would want a girl like me. I shook my head and concentrated on the red and yellow flags in the distance.

It wasn't until we neared the Mermaid Beach Surf Club that my breathing became ragged. I knew from experience that we'd run a distance of two miles, a run that usually took me fifteen-or-so minutes. I was sure we'd done it much quicker today.

As if some bell had sounded we both slowed to a walk at the same time, right next to the lifesaver's Jet Ski parked on the shoreline. The surfers were out in force today, smelling of suntan lotion and capturing me with their lithe, tanned bodies. They looked amazing, but next to Corben they resembled underdeveloped teenagers.

"Ready to head back?" Corben spoke his first words in about five minutes.

"Sure." We turned around and Corben walked toward the chair built out of surfboards near the beach shower. Curious, I followed. He sat and began undoing his laces. Taking his lead, I did the same. Then, with our shoes dangling in our hands, we walked past the mingling surfers again and down to the water. We skirted tumbling waves as we strolled back toward the Hot Horizon Hotel.

I tried to take glimpses at him without being too obvious. In the glorious morning sunlight he was a rough diamond, with dazzling facets in all the right places and muscles in all the rest.

He was more than six foot of male perfection, and as we walked along, every person strolling toward us ogled him like he was Channing Tatum.

"So what's your story, Memphis Jane?" His voice was a deep baritone.

I raised my eyebrows. "Story?"

"Yeah. What makes you pretend to be someone you're not?"

"Who says I'm not?"

Even Corben's mirrored glasses suited the scene. Yummy. "Me."

"Oh." A wave crashed over my ankles and I angled up the beach slightly, pushing him aside as I went.

"The woman who stands behind the reception desk at that hotel is nothing like the woman who sneaks into men's rooms to get her jollies."

I gasped at him, ready to retort, but then realized he was right. "I don't sneak into rooms," I finally said, half-hearted.

"No, you're right, but the rest is true. So why do you do it?"

Oh God, did I really want to have this conversation? Several more waves tumbled at my feet as Corben silently waited for my response. Eventually, I shrugged. "Because it's fun."

He nodded, as if my answer made perfect sense. "Jane doesn't have fun?"

"No."

Next second, he yanked his singlet top off and scooped me up, one arm around my back, one beneath my knees.

I squealed as he turned toward the ocean. "Oh no you don't."

He raised his eyebrows. "Try and stop me."

My screams were mixed with giggles as I beat his chest, but his cast-iron arms and square jaw showed his determination. "Throw your shoes on the sand or they'll take a dunking."

"No," I screamed.

He took another step, and when I tossed my Nikes as far as I could up the beach, he carried on into the water and I carried on slapping and squealing.

My butt was in the water now as the waves hit Corben's hips. He walked like a robot, and I had visions of him being the Terminator, carrying on his mission until it was complete.

"I'll kiss you if you stop." Desperate measures were required.

He slowed and lowered his mirrored glasses down toward me. "Go on then."

I giggled, then wrapped my arms around his neck and drew my lips to his. He may have been a muscular rock, but his lips were soft and delicate. It caught me by surprise. I glided my fingers through his buzz cut and pulled him closer to me, wanting more. As he opened his mouth and I pushed my tongue in to explore, I realized this was my first ever public kiss.

It was exhilarating, wild. Free.

None of the men I'd had relationships with had ever shown affection to me beyond closed doors. This was yet another Jane milestone, and as our kiss deepened, I wanted to thank Corben in the only way I knew how . . . with the best sexual romp ever. My clit purred at that wonderful decision.

He pulled back and I smiled at my casual sex partner. "Thank you."

"You're welcome." A cheeky grin lit up his face, and I screamed as he tossed me away.

Desperately clutching at my sunglasses, I plunged beneath a wave. Freezing water attacked me from all angles as I planted my feet and pushed for the surface.

"You bastard," I yelled, and giggled as I shoved my annoying fringe from my eyes.

He stood, his legs spread wide, statue-like, as a wave tumbled into him. His chiseled abs glistened in its wake and I saw the 'trust' tattoo beneath his left nipple.

"Trust, huh." I pointed at it. "I'll never trust you again."

"I didn't actually agree to your negotiation."

"But I kissed you." I curved a wall of water over him with my arm.

It didn't faze him one bit. "And what a lovely kiss it was."

He knew all the right things to say. Again, he was forgiven. I raced at him in a lame attempt to tackle him down. My brother had taught me this move many moons ago, and whilst I'd managed to overthrow Tyler on many occasions, Corben didn't budge. Instead, he threw me over his shoulder, my butt in the air and my fists pummeling his perfect derriere as he carried me out of the water.

He paused to pick up our shoes and his singlet before he carried on walking up the beach. I was a caveman's woman being manhandled to the love den. Yay me!

My fiery battle against him petered out quickly, and soon I was a soggy sack over his shoulder. He carried me all the way up the sand and over the wooden boardwalk, and didn't set me down until we were on the path that ran parallel to the beach.

I shoved my wet hair from my eyes and tugged my shirt down over my exposed belly.

"Well, that was interesting," I said.

"That, Jane, was fun." His teeth dazzled in the sunshine.

"Really?"

"Don't tell me you didn't have fun."

I gave him a sad face. "It was cold."

"Yes, and now, when you come up to my room, I'll warm you up."

Suddenly, Corben had a lot to say, and every word cast a magical spell, enchanting me.

"Okay," I said like a horny teenager on a first date. My purring insides hit inferno mode, heating me from the inside out . . . which was good, because my teeth still chattered from the freezing water.

He handed my shoes over. "I assume you don't want us seen together." With a quick flick of his wrist, he smacked me on the butt. "So get moving, sexy. I'll be waiting for you in room twenty-four."

He strode away, leaving me to watch his perfect ass yet again.

My shivering was what finally got me moving.

I scooted across the lobby, trying not to drip too much on the marble tiles. Needledick was at reception, and thankfully he was on the phone. He nodded at me and I prayed he didn't finish the call before the elevator arrived. I made it across the lobby in record time and pressed the button.

Corben must've sent it back down for me, as the doors opened right away. I stepped in and jabbed the button for my floor. As I shivered in the elevator, I studied my reflection. My hair was scrambled in all directions, my freckles were out in plague proportions, and my lips were a shade of blue from the cold. I turned away, disappointed with the view.

When the doors pinged open, I made my way to my room, peeled off my soggy clothes and hopped into the shower to wash my hair. As I lathered up, my attention switched to Corben. He was an interesting man. If I'd had a year to think about it, I would never have predicted him throwing me into the ocean like that. His serious demeanor had just shown a slight crack, and I liked what I saw.

After I toweled off, I blasted my hair with the blow-dryer for a couple of minutes, then gave up and tied it into a band instead. I put on a touch of makeup—just enough to cover my freckles and darken my lashes.

At my closet I chose an ankle-length skirt, colorful in design, full in fabric and with a rouched elastic waist that was perfect for easy removal. I matched the skirt with a simple white off-the-shoulder top. The last time I'd worn this was when Henry had made my body sing while I lay naked before the full moon. I loved that some items in my closet now had wonderful memories attached to them.

This time, however, I decided against a bra. My nipples showed as circular disks with tiny lumps beneath the sheer white fabric. It was naughty and sexy, and totally titillating.

I slipped on flat sandals, grabbed my bag and room key, and headed to the elevator. Anticipation had my insides quivering with every step. I knocked once, and a couple of thumping heartbeats later, he opened the door.

Naked.

His erection pointed right at me. "You're late."

Holy hotness on a hotplate. "Umm, sorry I—"

He let the door go, and I just managed to palm it and push on the heavy wood before it closed in front of my face.

I stepped through in time to admire his bare butt as he walked to the kitchen. The door clicked closed, and I nearly tripped over my tongue as I followed him into the room.

"You hungry?" He picked a wooden spoon off the counter.

"Pardon?" I placed my bag on a dining chair.

"I hope you like eggs."

"Huh." My brain couldn't function as my clit pulsed out a crazy beat that reverberated through my body and rendered my mind useless.

"Eggs," he said, as he stirred a pan on the hotplate. "Do you eat them?"

I mentally pushed my tongue back into my mouth and forced it to work. "Ahhh, yes."

"Good, 'cause you're going to need some protein with what I've got planned."

"Oh." *Please tell me . . . before I self-combust.*

He turned side-on to the stove, and his cock stood large and proud as it protruded from his groin. I certainly didn't have to worry about hair in my food because other than his buzz cut, he had none.

To improve my view, I stepped up to the counter and instantly wondered if I'd taken the elevator to heaven. The eagle tattooed on his back came alive as he stirred the eggs and flipped bacon. The muscles of his ass, much whiter than his legs, were perfectly formed, and all I wanted to do was clutch them and squeeze my fingers into that yummy flesh.

He turned with a stern look on his face and cocked his head at me. "Well, get your gear off!"

My eyes bulged. "Pardon?"

"Strip off, woman. The eggs are nearly ready."

My jaw actually dropped, and I blinked at him, dumbfounded as he turned his focus back to breakfast.

I did as he commanded and stripped out of my clothes. Naked now, I shook my damp hair out of the band and tousled it a bit.

Not sure what to do next, I returned to my spot at the counter to watch the show.

He turned to me, frying pan in one hand, wooden spoon in the other, and an enormous erection between his legs. My eyes hit frenzy mode as I tried to take it all in.

I'd never had a man cook for me before, and certainly not a naked one. Including the kiss on the beach, that was three firsts in one morning. I wasn't sure I could handle it.

Corben divided the food between two dishes, and then pushed a plate and cutlery to my side of the counter. "Enjoy."

I'd launched into some kind of kinky cooking show as we ate our breakfast stark naked in his kitchen. The sun shone in through the window as laser beams that caught on his shoulder and bicep, giving life to that already impressive rose tattoo. I tried to be discreet with my glances at him.

Corben, on the other hand, was not so subtle, and my hardened nipples grew even harder under his gaze.

The eggs were good and the bacon was exactly how I liked it—crispy—but I resisted eating too much, fearful that I may be in for some acrobatics in a few minutes.

Neither of us spoke, and as voyeuristic heaven hit a whole new level, shudders started between my legs and rolled through me.

His erection remained rock-hard through the entire meal, and I made a mental note to ask Lolly if she'd ever heard of that before. Maybe Corben had swallowed a bucket of Viagra before breakfast, and I was in for a marathon session. The thought convinced me to stop eating.

"That was delicious." I pushed my plate aside and gulped down water. I swirled it around, trying to ensure no bits of breakfast were left in my teeth.

He smiled, and wow, the muscle god in the kitchen became even hotter. Corben had it all going on. No wonder he'd been a finalist in the Mr. Universe competition. As I committed the vision to memory, I prayed I'd remember it for the rest of my life.

Corben tossed our plates into the sink, turned to me, wrapped his hand around his cock and pumped it once. "Ready."

It wasn't a question, it was a statement, and I just about passed out at the sexy command in his voice. "Uh-huh." Words were no longer important.

He came around the counter and reached for my hand, and for a second I thought he was going to lead me in a dance. With one hand curled around my waist to rest on my lower back and his other hand cupping my neck, he eased me back and sucked my breast into his mouth. The unexpected move had my clit pulsing out a heady beat.

I tilted my head back and felt completely safe in his arms as he flitted his attention from one breast to the other. His cock was a hard rod, nudging against my hip and I reached for it, wrapped my fingers around him, and trailed my hand up and down his length. Silky-smooth skin glided over solid muscle as I pumped from the base of his cock to the swollen crown.

Corben groaned and as I groaned with him, tingles shuddered through me.

I rolled my finger over the head, capturing a drop of semen that pooled there, and I used it to lubricate him. He smelt incredible, a potent mix of spice, soap, and hot-blooded man.

As he eased me upright, I continued my attention on his erection. He turned me sideways, so I positioned one leg between his parted legs. His probing fingers came at me from both angles. While his left hand pleasured my clit, teasing it with tight, pressured circles, his right hand glided past my bottom and drove into my vagina from behind.

I gasped at the onslaught and bent my knees, opening myself up to give him more. It took all my focus to continue pumping his jackhammer as he explored me with glorious precision. I savored the intensity. My body froze, every muscle rigid, and seconds later an orgasm ripped through me, fast, furious, and fantastic. Fearful I'd crumble to the carpet in a quivering mess, I gripped his thigh for support.

In one powerful movement, he swept me off my feet, and as I clutched my fingers around his neck he strode to the bed and tossed me onto the covers.

It wasn't delicate by any means, more like caveman mode, but the sexiness of it had me at his mercy. As I shoved my damp hair from my eyes, a sudden realization rocked me to my core. Corben was having sex with Jane. Plain Jane, not the sexy minx Memphis. My brain rocketed to overload. This freakin' hot guy wanted me—the Jane me. I just about came again at that mind-blowing thought.

Corben spread my legs, and with fierce dark eyes watching what he was doing, the muscles in his jaw clenched as he glided a finger into me, first one, then two. My pussy throbbed out a crazy beat matching the crazy beat going through my mind. He wanted me. He wanted all of me. And oh my God, if that wasn't the sexiest thing ever.

I put my feet on the bed and raised my hips, giving him a new angle to penetrate, and oh, what a good angle it was. His eyes, slightly glazed and darkened with concentration, proved he enjoyed this as much as I did.

I clutched at the bedsheets as he plunged my pussy, driving those fingers with splendid repetition. He watched every move and I in turn watched him, enjoying every bit of his ultimate concentration. His tongue flicked out and trailed across his lips, leaving a faint sheen.

My second orgasm hit me by surprise, and I gasped as I snapped my knees shut, securing his fingers inside me. Wave after wave of ecstasy barreled through me and I was trapped in an erotic coma, unable to move, yet I wanted to stay there all day.

It was a long while before I opened eyes that I hadn't realized I'd closed. A glorious smile lit up his face.

"My turn." He wriggled his eyebrows, and I opened my legs to release my clamp on his fingers.

Corben reached toward the pillows and came back with a condom packet that I hadn't noticed before. The guy sure knew how to prepare. In a flash, it was in position.

He wrapped his fingers around my hips and flipped me over to my stomach. My brain went crazy as I feared he was about to attempt something I didn't want him to do. I knew this sexual journey was about me stepping out of my comfort zone, but that was not on my agenda. The last few hours had been so perfect that I didn't want to ruin it, but I had to say something.

"Corben, I don't do anal," I blurted out.

"Relax."

Relax? Relax because he wasn't going to do it, or relax because it'd hurt otherwise? *Oh God, please don't ruin a perfect morning!*

I tucked my elbows to my sides, ready to kick him should this go wrong. His fingers weaved under my thighs and he tugged me toward him so I had one leg on either side of his legs. With his hands just in front of my knees he lifted my legs off the bed and held them apart, spreading me wide.

I fisted the sheets, gritted my teeth, and prepared to make a snap decision should he ignore my request.

I just about wept with relief when his penis touched my opening. As I hovered there, completely at his mercy, I pictured him staring at my ass and hoped like crazy that he'd find my butt wobble sexy when he pounded me. I smacked that untimely thought away as his penis, hot and hard, nudged my vagina.

Forcing myself to relax, I readied myself for another new position.

I had no control whatsoever over the depth of his plunge, putting me one hundred percent at his orgasmic mercy. He went deep, very deep, farther, I was sure, than any man had ever gone inside me before. He thrust away like a jackhammer going at full-blown speed and the ultimate depth.

The angle was glorious, grinding over my clit and hitting that part inside me that loved and hated it at the same time. His thrusts grew faster still, driving relentlessly into me, and my original thought of him consuming a bucket of Viagra flashed into my mind. Corben groaned with each plunge, but as his speed increased his moans grew louder as if gearing up for the grand finale.

I clawed at the sheets as another orgasm hit me. It was huge, cataclysmic. I saw stars and shot toward them. Every nerve in my body sizzled.

Corben cried out. His fingers dug into my flesh with his final gasps. Soon his rhythm slowed, and I listened to his ragged breathing. Unlike during our earlier workout, he was now panting for breath.

He pulled out of me for the last time and as I rolled to my side, I watched him walk to the bathroom. My insides pounded out after-sex blues as I crawled to the edge of the bed and sat with my wet hair over my shoulders.

A couple of seconds later, I stood and on wobbly legs, I gathered my clothing from the floor and dressed.

Corben came out of the bathroom, still naked, but no longer with the erect masterpiece between his legs. The guy sure was confident in his own skin. And with a body like that, he had every reason to be.

He put his hands on his hips as he stopped a few feet away. "Did Jane have fun?"

I giggled. "Yes, Jane had fun."

"Good."

Taking that as my cue to leave, I plucked my bag off the chair and swayed as I made my way to the door.

"I'll be back, Jane."

"I know you will, Corben."

He laughed, a deep, throaty laugh that suited him perfectly.

As I listened to that wonderful sound, I walked out his door and headed to my room.

I stood for a very long time under the shower, allowing the warm cascade to massage my weary body.

Afterwards, I brushed my teeth and slipped into flannel pajamas.

At my bed, I sat cross-legged on the quilt, plucked my diary from the bedside table and turned to the 7th of July. At the top I wrote, *Corben Willis Room 24, My Bad Boy*. I giggled at that. Corben sure did play the bad boy well. I'd never thought I'd like a guy like him. He was a man who took what he wanted, but there was something very sexy about it.

As I wrote about my first, very public kiss on the beach I described how alive that had made me feel. To show the world that somebody liked me, wanted me, and I in turn wanted him, was exhilarating. I decided that the man I ultimately fell in love with would need to be comfortable with public displays of affection. After today, it was now very important to me.

I wrote about the naked cooking session and the new sex position I'd experienced. Today was by far one of the most interesting days I'd had this year.

After I closed the diary and crawled beneath my quilt, I rolled onto my side. As I closed my eyes and breathed in nice and deep, I had perfect recall of my bad boy standing rock-solid in the waves as the water tumbled over his glistening body. I played it over and over in my mind in slow-motion, taking in every glorious tattoo, every bulging muscle, and every inch of his taut skin.

It was a magical way to drift off to sleep.

13TH JULY
KISS AND TELL
Hot Horizon Hotel

Needledick strolled through the front doors of the Hot Horizon Hotel as if he was walking in a funeral procession, rather than to the start of his shift. He was twenty-five minutes late, as usual. I tried not to glare at him, but with each step he took I increased the clamp on my jaw. I hoped he didn't think I'd cover for him today so he could go back to bed. Although I'd done it once before, I had no intention of doing it again. Especially after the night I'd just had—all I wanted to do was flop into bed.

"Morning." He sounded as if he'd just finished his tenth cigarette for the morning, though I was pretty sure he didn't smoke.

"Hi." I reached for my purse under the counter, ready to race out of there, and when I stood up he snapped his eyes away. *Oh my God!* Needledick had just checked out my butt. I squinted at him and a red flush blazed up his neck.

He cleared his throat. "How was the night?"

I backed away and edged around the counter in a weird backwards stride. "It was crazy, actually."

"Oh, really. You didn't see that prostitute, did you?" The excitement in his eyes made him look a little psycho.

"No, I didn't."

He clenched his jaw. "I'm going to get her. You watch." He rubbed his right fist in his left palm, no doubt attempting some kind of "I'm in charge" stance.

That simple move got me angry. For a man in charge, he sure didn't act it. "Why do you even think she's a prostitute?"

"She walks like one."

"Oh, and how many prostitutes have you seen?"

His mouth gaped and he blinked a few times. "Well, none in person. Only what I've seen on television."

"Excellent. So, how exactly did this woman look?" I thrust my chin at him, showing him who was boss.

"She had on a trench coat and—"

"Oh, well then." I rolled my eyes and flipped my hand. "She's obviously a prostitute."

"No . . . it was more than that."

"What? Pink hair and killer stilettos?"

"No." He frowned and shook his head so fast it was possible it could fall off. "You'll know when you see her."

I waved my hand in a dismissive move, turned on my heel, and headed toward the elevator—then, at the thought of him perving on my bottom, I turned and walked backwards. "I think you're making a mistake with her," I yelled across the lobby.

"Mark my words, with all these men asking for Memphis, she'll be back and when she does, I'll make her regret she ever came here."

Thank God the elevator pinged open. I stepped in and collapsed against a wall as I jabbed the button to my floor a million times. *How many men have been asking for me?*

I glared at my reflection and a little bit of dread glared back at me. Shards of ice traversed my back as the elevator made its slow crawl upwards and in the silence, the angel and the devil in my brain kicked off a fierce debate.

You are not a prostitute.

But you do sleep with random strangers.

That doesn't make me a prostitute—just horny.

Yes, but your horny inclinations are making you take uncharacteristic risks.

But the risks are worth it.

Worth losing your job over?

By the time I'd reached my room and opened the door, my head was spinning. Round and round the debate went until I wanted to squeeze my temples so hard my brain might burst from the top. I put the kettle on and strode to the bath. With the taps on full, I dumped the entire contents of the bubble bath Marjorie had given me for Christmas into the tumbling water.

With the angel and devil in my head about to break into a fist fight, I strode out onto my balcony, clutched at the railing, and sucked in the fresh ocean breeze. *In through my nose, out my mouth.* With my eyes closed, I repeated the meditation and let the glorious sunshine warm my flesh. Even though the sun was shining, winter still had a slight chill in the air.

"Jane."

I opened my eyes and blinked at the glare.

"Jane."

I peered over the railing and couldn't believe my eyes. Mr. Henry Addison, my suave tutor, stood next to a sleek black car and waved up at me. Even from this distance, I saw the huge smile on his face.

Giggling, I waved down at him.

"Want to go for a ride?"

Hell yes. He held two arms above his head as if ready to catch me.

"Okay." Henry didn't know it, but he'd already caught me many times over. "Give me ten minutes."

"Excellent. I'll wait right here." He patted the car's rooftop.

I squealed as I raced back inside, peeling off my clothes at frightening speed. Thoughts of flopping into bed evaporated, and my heart entered a playful gallop as I shut down the bath taps, pulled the plug, and turned on the shower. The hot water started immediately, and I jumped in and lathered up in my favorite mandarin-scented soap.

The angel and devil debate I'd had just minutes ago was long gone, replaced instead with brilliant images of Henry with his magical hands all over my body. He really did know exactly how to save me.

After I toweled off, I applied just a touch of makeup to cover my freckles and darken my lashes. I brushed my teeth and dabbed some Pinky Promise lippy on. Now to choose what to wear. It occurred to me that I should've asked Henry where we were going. I tried to picture what he had on downstairs, and after a moment's pause, I was fairly certain he'd been in jeans. That convinced me that casual was the way to go. At my closet, I chose denim jeans and a blue-and-white striped T-shirt. I tugged on a dark blue blazer and wrapped a navy silk scarf around my neck, then matched it up with a fake pearl earrings and matching necklace.

Glancing at my shoes, I mulled over which ones to choose. So many of them had never been worn, and I loved giving them sexy memories. Reaching to the back of my closet, I plucked a pair of caramel-colored Splendid Jayla sandals. The wedge cork heel was only three inches high; hopefully, it'd be suitable for whatever Henry had planned.

I glanced in the mirror. Grinned. Chewed on my lip and grinned some more. I was positively glowing. Something about Henry made me look good.

With a skip in my step, I grabbed my bag, sunglasses, and room key, and in the elevator, I fiddled with my hair until it arrived at the lobby. I wiped the smile away as I strode past Needledick with a scowl.

My smile was back once I entered the sunshine, and my insides flipped over the prospect of a couple of hours with my suave tutor.

Henry strolled up to greet me and placed his hand on the small of my back when he kissed my cheek. He smelt perfect; spices of the orient drifted off his skin as he kissed my other side. If my memory served me correctly, he was wearing the same aftershave as he had the first time we'd met. Maybe it was his lucky scent. It sure was mine.

He guided me to his car and opened the door for me to step in. I wriggled into the seat and inhaled fresh leather odors as he came around the driver's side.

"New car?" I asked the second he sat beside me.

"Rental."

"Oh." It suddenly occurred to me that I had no idea where Henry lived. Actually, I barely knew anything about him. I'd just jumped willingly into a car with a near stranger. Yet somehow, that bothered me very little. In fact, it inspired me to learn more about this sexy older man at my side.

As he accelerated away, I decided that now was the ideal time for it. "So, do you live near here?"

"No. Sydney."

"Oh. Did you fly up for another conference?"

He slowed down to stop at a red light. "No . . . to see you." He turned, and the intensity in his dark irises caught in the light through the sunroof.

My jaw dropped, and I nearly needed my palm to slot it back into place. "Oh." Words were impossible to form.

Thankfully, the light turned green and he turned his attention back to the road. He reached up, and at the flick of a button the glass panel in the roof glided open. Sun streamed in, bathing me in a lovely warm glow.

"Is that okay?" His voice was equally warm.

"It's perfect."

We drove in silence for a while with the ocean on my left-hand side and him on my right. Everywhere I looked, my vista was magnificent.

Henry had a comfortable yet intriguing aura about him. I didn't think I'd ever felt so relaxed next to a man and as the miles rolled on, I reminded myself of just how lucky I was to have met him. It never would have happened without Memphis, and I'd be forever grateful to her for that.

"What are you thinking about?"

He caught me off guard. "Oh ummm . . ."

"There's no need to keep secrets from me. We don't really know each other."

"It's . . . it's not that, it's—"

"Tell me quick, or I'll think you're fibbing."

I gasped at him.

"Quick." He laughed and lightly slapped my thigh.

Giggling, I adjusted my position on the seat so I could see him better. "Okay, I was just think how lucky I was that Memphis found you."

He nodded. "You're fibbing."

"No, I'm not."

"You are. It was me who found you—once when you were eating Iced VoVos, and the second time when you were pretending to be Memphis."

I huffed. "Okay, you're right about the Iced VoVos meeting, but I wasn't pretending to be Memphis—I was Memphis."

He turned onto the main highway and accelerated. "Do you still pretend to be Memphis?"

Oh, God. Did I really want to have this conversation? I reached up under my sunglasses and rubbed my left eye, stalling for a response.

"It's okay. It's none of my business."

I blinked at him. That was true, and yet for some reason I felt terrible for not answering. But then, I guessed by not responding I was in fact giving him an answer. Either way, I'd lost.

"I hope you're still doing it."

His comment jolted me back to the present. "Huh?"

"I imagine the confidence boost must be exhilarating."

I blinked at him, taking in every aspect of my sexy silver fox.

"How long have you been doing it?"

Dammit. I was supposed to be asking him the questions. I sighed, and decided I might as well get this over with. "My first time was the first of January."

"Oh, wow. Are you keeping tabs or something?"

I inwardly cringed. "Something like that."

He glanced at me, and it was his turn to drop his jaw. "You are keeping tabs. Tell me."

I shifted my legs straight on again, all of a sudden uncomfortable with kissing and telling.

"Come on, Memphis Jane. I'm an old man; I want to hear all about your sexual escapades."

His Memphis Jane label had me squirming because that was exactly what Corben had called me just last week. All of a sudden, the men in my life were becoming very interested in me. It was vastly different to what had happened during the last three years. And my entire life, for that matter.

"First of all," I said, "you're not old."

He waggled his head. "Well, that's all relative."

"Okay then. I don't think of you as old."

His grin lit up his face. "Thank you."

"Secondly, a lady doesn't kiss and tell."

"Ahhh. Memphis has morals. I like that."

It was my turn to slap him, and when he laughed, I laughed right along with him.

At the top of a large hill, the spectacular view took my breath away. Down below was dark green vegetation dotted with the occasional rooftop, and beyond that was a strip of golden sand skirted by dark blue ocean for as far as I could see. We wound down the other side of the hill and crossed a bridge over a large expanse of the Tweed River.

On the other side, four lanes curled around to the right and carried on along the highway. We, however, turned off onto a much smaller road.

The water was still on my left-hand side but now it was the Tweed River rather than the ocean. Henry slowed and at the flick of a button he wound down our windows. The breeze caught in my hair and scarf, and I tugged on them to keep them in place.

"Too cold?"

"No. It's perfect."

"You're perfect."

His comment had my insides launch into party mode. I turned to him and chewed on my bottom lip.

"It's a compliment, Jane. Say thank you." He didn't say it in a bossy or mean way, and as I considered his comment, I realized he was teaching me again.

"Thank you."

"Good. Now take your top off."

"What?" I burst out laughing.

He pointed up. "This's a deserted road. Take your top off and stand up through the sun roof."

"Are you crazy?"

"I'm serious.

"I can't do that."

"Of course you can."

I glanced at the road ahead. It was empty. I turned around to look behind. Again, empty of cars. In fact, empty of everything, no houses, no people, nothing but bitumen and grass edges. My heart skipped a beat as I actually considered his challenge.

"Go on." He raised his hand, indicating that I should get up. "This has been a bucket list item of mine forever, and you're the only woman I know who'll do it."

As my layers of doubt shredded away, the smile on my face must've bordered on insane, just like his request.

I looked up through the roof then glanced back at Henry. His eyes were alive with anticipation. How could I let him down? Especially after all he'd done for me?

I unbuckled my seatbelt and Henry slowed down a tad as I removed my coat.

My heart was a thumping gallop as I raised my T-shirt up over my head and let my pearls tumble down my chest. Before I changed my mind, I whipped my bra off, climbed onto the seat, and stood up.

The breeze blasted my hair and hurled my scarf and pearls around to my back. I clutched onto the front of the sunroof, and as I leaned forward with the wind in my hair, a wave of euphoria hit me. I raised my arms above my head. "Woohoo," I cheered.

My boobs wobbled in the glorious sunshine as we rolled along the deserted road. Henry's hand was suddenly on my right breast, and I giggled as I tried to absorb every aspect of this crazy, exhilarating moment. Laughing, I tried to push his hand away, but that only made him squeeze more.

I bent down, laughing. "Oh my God, you crazy man."

"Me? You're the one jiggling those sexy boobs through the roof." His smile was brilliant, and I leaned over and quickly kissed his cheek before I stood up again.

The sunshine, the breeze, the freedom—it was wild. It was wonderful. I put my arms above my head and screamed.

A shape in the distance caught my eye, and I squealed when I realized it was another car coming toward us. I dropped back into my seat and tugged at my shirt to cover my nudity.

"Happy now?" I said to Henry.

"Very. You?"

"Absolutely. That's the most fun I've had in ages." My mind suddenly shifted to Corben and how he too had shown me—the *Jane* me—how to have fun. This year, life was so bloody good. I didn't want the year to ever end.

As I put my clothes back on, Henry carried on driving, right to the end of the road where it met with the mouth of the Tweed River.

"Want a coffee?" he said.

"Oh, I'd love one." As if on cue, my stomach rumbled. "I'm hungry too."

"Good. So am I." He pulled into a parking lot opposite a small rundown café and turned off the engine.

I stepped out, and we met at the back of the car. He pulled the trunk lid up and removed a large red-and-white-striped plastic bag.

"What's in there?"

"It's a surprise."

"Oh, yay. I love surprises." My insides did a little jig.

"I know."

I tapped his forearm as we crossed the road together. "Really? How could you know?"

He shrugged. "Okay. I guessed. Did you have any other plans for your day off?"

"Pfft, no." I'd said it quickly and when he turned to me, I couldn't quite read the look on his face. Was it sorrow, pity, or disappointment? Either way, it didn't matter because the second we entered the café and I smelt caffeine, my attention was diverted.

I ordered a cappuccino and a breakfast bacon and egg wrap, and Henry ordered the same. After a brief discussion in which I was unyielding, I paid for the bill. I was grateful when he gracefully backed down. It was too early in the morning to make a scene, but I would have.

He turned and I watched the sway of his shoulders as he walked toward the fridge. My view was improved when he bent over to select a bottle of water off the bottom shelf. For someone in his early fifties, Henry had a physique that most men should aspire to.

Our coffee orders came in polystyrene cups and our breakfast wraps were sealed in waxy paper. The lady behind the counter put our order into a molded cardboard box and handed it over the counter. I reached for the box, along with a few napkins, and together Henry and I headed outside toward the seats in the sun.

But he didn't stop where I assumed he would. Instead, he stepped onto the road. "Where're you going?"

"Down to the beach."

"Oh, okay then." I caught up to his side. "So you've been here before?"

"My family used to come here when I was a kid. We spent nearly every Easter for about fifteen years camping at the Fingal Holiday Park up the road."

"Sounds wonderful."

"It was. Some of the best years of my life." He said it wistfully, and I thought I detected sadness in his voice.

As we traipsed over the sand, covered in long spindly grass, I tried to nominate the best years of my life. I didn't have to think hard. Without a doubt, this year was the best year ever. I could only hope that my future years didn't fade in comparison.

The vegetation encroached in on us as we navigated up a narrow track over a small hill. At the top, Henry turned sideways, left the main track, and followed an even narrower trail that skirted along the top of the sandbank. At a gnarly old tree, he stopped and turned to me, grinning. "I can't believe it's still here."

"What?" I frowned.

"This tree. I used to spend hours sitting in it, just watching the boats come and go."

I felt privileged to be sharing this moment with him. Turning toward the ocean, I glanced across the sandy beach that was about a hundred feet wide.

In the near distance, a small boat with a couple of fishing poles angled off the back motored out to sea.

Henry continued to look out across the sand, but by the cheeky grin on his face, I wondered if he was seeing something I wasn't.

It suddenly hit me. "You weren't just watching boats from this tree, were you?"

"Huh?" He raised his eyebrows, but continued smiling.

"You were spying on people." I playfully slapped him. "Who?"

"Nobody." He turned his attention to the bag and pulled a large picnic blanket out from within. He ripped a tag off it, and I frowned at him.

"Did you buy that today?"

"Yeah. I did a bit of shopping before I hired the car."

He indicated to me to sit by patting a corner of the blanket.

I put the cardboard carry-tray down and then, trying not to get sand on the blanket, sat with my butt on the edge and then peeled off my cork heels and wiped the sand away. Soon we were sitting side by side under the shade of the ancient tree, glancing out across the water.

He reached forward and handed me a coffee. "Cheers," he said, and we thumped our takeaway cups together. The coffee was now the perfect temperature to take a decent sip, and I did. It was good and strong—exactly how I liked it.

Henry handed me my breakfast. I unwrapped the wax paper and practically salivated as I took my first bite. Considering the dubious-looking little café we'd bought it from, the wrap was fabulous. It was loaded with bacon, lettuce, tomato, avocado, egg, and my favorite sauce, barbeque. I couldn't have done a better job if I'd made it myself.

"So tell me," I said, halfway into my wrap, "who were you watching?"

He turned with a look that said he'd expected me to ask again, then he licked his lip, lowered his wrap, and reached for his coffee.

"As I said, my family came here every year for about fifteen years. But we weren't the only families to do that. Over the years, we got to know the regulars. There was a family with three girls that had an annual trip here every Easter, too."

"Ooooh, I'm thinking you were sweet on one of those girls."

He chuckled. "You could say that."

"So what was her name?"

"Kimberley Tucker. Kim."

"What'd she look like?"

He frowned at me. "What is this, the Spanish Inquisition?"

"Nope. It's the Memphis Inquisition."

He laughed and as he bit into his wrap again, I assumed he was stalling.

I took a few more bites of mine. I could wait all day if I had to. It wasn't like I had anything else to do.

Henry wrapped up the remainder of his breakfast into the wax paper and tossed it into his bag. He reached for his coffee and changed his position on the blanket so he looked more toward me than the beach.

"Kim had long, dark hair, silky smooth, and in the sunlight, little streaks of copper would shine through, just like yours. Her eyes were incredibly green, like freshly podded peas. Again, like yours."

I couldn't help the smile curling on my lips as the expression on his face changed during his detail of Kim. Obviously, she'd meant a lot to him.

"Kim's lips were this lovely shade of soft pink, like fairy floss, and her skin was milky white. So white that she spent most of her time at the beach hiding from this sun."

"Ahhh, like under this tree."

He nodded. "Yes."

I tilted my head. "Was she your first girlfriend?"

He nodded, and I waited for him to continue his trip down memory lane.

I tossed my unfinished wrap into the bag and nestled my coffee in the sand so it didn't fall over. Then I turned to Henry and placed my hand on his thigh.

He blinked at me, then shook his head. "We weren't exactly dating. But . . ." He put his hand over mine. "Would you be interested in ticking off another bucket list item for me?"

"Do I have to get my shirt off?"

He burst out laughing. "Well, technically no."

"Technically? Sounds cryptic."

Henry had the most beautiful smile. Maybe as an older man, he'd mastered how to show a genuine smile, utilizing all his facial muscles. His smile melted my heart.

"Okay," he said. "I'm just going to say it. I've never told anyone this before."

"Sounds interesting."

He rolled his eyes. "Kim and I lost our virginity to each other. Right here under the tree."

"Oooh, you naughty boy." I slapped his thigh.

He shook his head. "Well, that's just it. I was a boy, just sixteen, and I had no idea what I was doing. I didn't do the right thing by Kim, by any means, and well"—he cocked his head—"I always felt guilty that her first sexual experience was terribly unsatisfying."

"Sounds exactly like my first experience."

"Really?" Concern drilled onto his features.

I shrugged. "Unfortunately. We were both drunk. To be honest, I'm not one hundred percent sure we even did it."

He laughed. "I bet many people have had that experience."

"So what's this bucket list item then?"

He held his palms wide, taking in our scenery. "I'd like to give this spot a better memory. Would you let me take you to the limit, right here, out in the open?"

My insides turned to jelly at his proposal. I put my finger to my cheek and rolled my eyes to the tree canopy, acting all coy. "Hmmm, let me think about that . . . okay."

He laughed and pulled me in for a hug. "You're amazing."

I listened to his steady heartbeat. "We haven't done it yet."

"I already know you're amazing."

"Thank you."

He let me go and looked into my eyes, right into my soul. "That's better."

I crinkled my nose at him. "So, how do we do this? Want me to take my top off?"

His eyes lit up, and he chuckled. "I'd love you to."

Crossing my legs to sit upright, I shrugged out of my blazer, scarf and T-shirt, then reached behind my back and flicked off my bra. The pearls flopped between my breasts, and I went to remove them, but Henry clutched my hand. "Leave them."

The air was cool, and my nipples tingled and hardened in the slight breeze. Henry reached over and cupped my left breast, embracing it with his warm palm. The expression of pure concentration on his face made him look as if he'd never caressed a breast before, and I wondered if he were reliving a childhood memory.

He leaned forward and wrapped his lips around my nipple, sucking it into his mouth, first one, then the other, paying impeccable attention to each breast equally. His breathing intensified, as did mine, and I was both delighted and amazed at how swiftly he produced my arousal.

A sweet shiver rolled over my clitoris as he eased me back onto the picnic blanket. Henry knelt at my side, his eyes driven with desire as he slotted the pearls back between my breasts, then he trailed his finger from my left nipple to my right, down to circle my belly button, and back up again. Tiny goose pimples prickled my skin as my nipples grew so hard they hurt.

I arched my back, and he leaned forward again, and I ran my fingers through his thick salt-and-pepper hair as he licked, nipped, and sucked my breasts, giving them a truly award-winning tongue lashing. My head rolled to the side, and through my lust-filled gaze I saw another boat in the distance, puttering past, completely unaware of the erotic show going on in these bushes.

My clit throbbed, wanting his attention, and I dug my toes onto the soft picnic blanket and raised my hips higher, silently willing him to touch me. He obliged and with his mouth still on my breast, he rubbed his hands over the thick denim between my legs. I wanted to tear every scrap of clothing from my body, to lay myself bare for his approval, but I forced myself to

wait, savoring every exquisite second, willing to ride out the anticipation.
He weaved his fingers into my jeans and I reached down to undo my zipper, but he playfully slapped my hand away. My breathing grew deeper, as did his, and I sucked in my belly and parted my legs, giving his fingers room. The clothing restriction was as excruciating as the anticipation, and I could actually feel my pussy growing wet even before his probing fingers reached their destination. *Why the hell did I wear jeans?*

Henry groaned, and I groaned with him as I writhed on the blanket. His fingers found my clit, and I just about shot right out of the bushes. The pressure of his hand beneath the denim was delicious agony. I gasped as he flicked my delicate nub, and at the same time he drew my nipple out with his lips, stretching it until my hardened flesh snapped from his grasp.

He did it again, concentrating on two of my erogenous zones with mature professionalism. My orgasm was greedy, growing larger with every movement he made.

I clenched my jaw and sucked my breath through my teeth, resisting the climax that threatened to wet my jeans at any second.

"Please, Henry, take my jeans off."

"Shhh," he whispered. "Soon."

He glided his hand farther between my legs, and the squeeze of my jeans placed the ball of his hand against my clit. His finger glided into me. My world tilted. I heard nothing; I smelt nothing as every inch of my body was ravaged by desire.

I raised my hips, reached out, and fisted the blanket. "Oh God," I yelled, as an orgasm tore through me.

I snapped my knees shut. I opened them. I was trapped in another world where my body was in control and there was nothing I could do. His finger plucked my clit, his mouth devoured my breast, and my pussy pulsed out my climax over and over.

I snapped my knees shut again, trapping his hand in my jeans, and I clenched my jaw as every muscle in my body rode out the miracle that rolled through me. Warm sensations caressed me like a big fluffy blanket, filling me with a massive dose of contentment. I'd officially found Heaven and was prepared to stay right where I was all day.

It was an eternity before I heard the crashing waves again and felt the whisper of breeze across my moistened breasts. I opened my eyes to see the most incredible sight. Henry had his eyes closed, and the look of pure satisfaction and serenity on his face was glorious, though it was in direct contrast to the ragged rising and falling of his chest.

I waited for him to look at me, and when he did, a beautiful smile curled on his lips. When our gazes met, it was like a sense of knowing crossed between us. Something unique had just happened. I didn't know quite what, but I didn't really need to know either.

I tried to ignore the moisture between my legs as I propped up on my elbows. "How did we do? New memory created?"

"Oh yeah."

"Good."

"Good? More like magnificent."

He eased backwards and helped me to sit. The first thing I did was look at my jeans, but instantly wished I hadn't. "Oh my God. It looks like I wet my pants."

"You did wet your pants."

I slapped his arm. "Thanks to you."

"Are you complaining?" He cocked his head in a cheeky grin.

I shook my head. "No. But what am I going to do?"

"You can wrap the blanket around yourself."

"Great. I'll look like a hobo."

"A gorgeous hobo."

I tugged on my bra, T-shirt and jacket and wrapped my scarf back around my neck.

"Want an Iced VoVo?"

"What?" I giggled as he handed over a packet of cookies. "I know they're you're favorite."

He tore the packet open and I accepted one.

"Tea? I brought green tea. That's right, isn't it?"

I curled my legs to the side as a warm sense of appreciation flooded through me.

He held the mug up as he handed it to me. "Cows."

My jaw dropped. The mug had little black-and-white cows dancing across a green paddock. No man had ever given me such a thoughtful gift, and I had to force back a swell of emotion that threatened to produce tears. "Wow," I finally said. "You sure know how to please a woman."

He wriggled his eyebrows. "Thank you, Memphis Jane."

Henry was very observant, more so than any other man in my life had ever been, and yet we'd only been together for probably five hours, maximum. I nibbled on the cookie and drank the tea, and at every opportunity I snuck glances at my suave tutor, taking in every laugh line and every gray fleck in his dark hair. Henry was the epitome of the sexy older man. If I wasn't careful, I could probably fall in love with him.

Was that such a bad thing?

I had no idea.

I needed to get my mind off that subject, quickly. "So," I said, placing my cup on the blanket, "what happened between you and Kim?"

"They just stopped coming." He shrugged. "No idea where she went."

I bulged my eyes. "You didn't get her pregnant, did you?"

"No. No, I saw her the Easter after that, but then never again. By God, we were lucky though. Damn foolish, what we did."

I had vivid memories of my panic after I lost my virginity to Will Appen. Yes, we'd been drunk, but that was no excuse for unprotected sex. To this day, I still wondered whether or not Will and I had perhaps not had sex after all, and if that was the reason why I hadn't fallen pregnant. Otherwise, it'd just been dumb luck.

"Come on." Henry climbed to his feet. "We better get you home so you can get some sleep."

His comment had weariness gripping me in a flash. I allowed him to pull me upright and I stood aside, trying to ignore the discomfort between my legs as he packed up our things. He dragged the blanket away and shook the sand off it, then he wrapped it around my shoulders.

I followed his lead back to the car and wrapped the blanket around my legs as I wriggled into the passenger seat. He hopped in beside me, started the car, and reversed out.

"Thank you for a wonderful morning."

He ran his hand up my leg. "Thank you, too."

We drove in silence, and I must have fallen asleep because it seemed like only minutes before we pulled into the drop-off zone at the Hot Horizon Hotel.

He came around, opened the door for me, and helped me out.

I suddenly realized my dilemma. How the hell was I going to get past reception without showing my wet patch?

I must've screwed up my face or something, because Henry adjusted the blanket over my shoulders. "I think you're going to need this."

I blinked at him. "You don't want it?"

"No. It's all yours. Looks sexier on you anyway."

"Ha ha."

He kissed my cheek, grabbed my shoulders, turned me towards the front steps, and smacked my butt. "Go on. Off to bed."

I waddled away. "Sounds like you're sending me to the naughty corner."

He laughed. "Maybe I am."

I tried to look elegant as I walked up the stairs with my legs apart and when the sliding glass doors opened, I was horrified to see Needledick walking from the elevator on his way to the reception desk. I inwardly cringed as I scurried toward the elevator.

"Hi Jane."

"Oh hi." I faked a shiver. "It's freezing out there."

He frowned. "Oh, really? I hadn't noticed."

I jabbed the elevator button. "Yeah, sure is. I'd advise against going out."

He looked toward the glass doors, and I turned to see sunshine, not a whisper of breeze to move the palm fronds, and five girls walking along in bikinis.

Needledick turned back to me, frowning.

I shivered again. "Brrr."

The elevator opened and I jumped in and attacked the button for my floor. I let out a huge sigh when the doors closed and it made the slow trip up.

At my room, I undressed, showered, brushed my teeth, and put on winter flannel pajamas, then strolled to my bed and reached for my diary.

I turned to the 13th of July, and wrote *Mr. Henry Addison*. As I thought about our wonderful morning and what I'd learned about him, I wrote *Kiss and Tell* beneath his name.

Once again, I lined the pages with details about Henry's miracle hands and how he could make me orgasm while barely touching me.

Why was that? Was it because I trusted him completely? Was it because he really was a skilled master? Was it because he was no longer a stranger and I knew what miracles he could perform?

I had no idea.

But there was one thing I did know. If Henry came back, I'd be ready and willing to see him again.

I put my diary aside, crawled under the quilt, grabbed my spare pillow, and hugged it to my chest. As exhaustion lulled me to sleep, I imagined the pillow in my arms was a man. A man who would hug me every night and allow all my dreams to come true.

24TH JULY
MY SIZZLING SURPRISE
Room 46 - Hot Horizon Hotel

If one more thing goes wrong tonight, I'm going to scream. Usually I liked to keep busy, but that didn't mean having everything breakdown in the one shift. With all the tiny bits of shredded paper that I'd pulled from the printer now in the rubbish bin, I put the toner back into the machine and pressed the power button again. Holding my breath as I waited for it to complete its usual start-up process, I prayed that the paper jam was now fixed.

With a pretty little jingle, the printer finally announced it was ready, and I sighed with relief as I returned to my computer and hit 'print' for the fourth time.

When the reception phone rang, I glanced at the clock and cringed. A call from a guest at two in the morning could only indicate trouble. I forced friendliness into my voice and picked up the handset. "Hello, Mr. Harper, this is Jane Nichols, Night Manager, how can I help you?"

"Jane, I have no electricity up here."

"Oh, that's strange. Okay, I'll be right up."

I put the 'back in five minutes' sign on the counter, grabbed my master key card, and took the elevator to the eighth floor. All the lights were working in the hallway, which was a good sign. I knocked on the door to room forty-six and a middle-aged man in checkered pajamas opened the door. His glasses sat on his head in amongst his scrambled dark hair, and despite the lack of room lighting, the scowl on his face was unmissable.

"It went out about half an hour ago. I'm still working here." He pointed to a laptop screen that glowed in the dark.

I flicked the light switch near the entrance, and after the change in his stance I instantly regretted it. With his hands on his hips, he stepped closer to me. "And . . . do you believe me now?"

"Of course, Mr. Harper. I have an electrician on the way," I lied.

"Well, how long's that going to take?"

"He'll be here soon and—"

"It's not good enough. I need to have this PowerPoint finished before morning and my bloody laptop battery is pathetic."

I shook my head. "Okay. I'll move you to another room."

He threw his hands in the air. "Great. Just great."

I held up my index finger. "Give me a moment to check the vacant rooms and I'll be right back up."

"So . . . I guess I'll pack my things then."

"That'd be great. I'll help you when I come back."

To the sound of his grumbling, I dashed to the elevator. It opened immediately and as I travelled down to the lobby, I wondered how I'd get an electrician at this time of night. The hotel was fully booked tomorrow, with most of the guests coming early in the morning. I need this fixed ASAP.

The doors opened and I raced to the desk, checked the room vacancies, and noted room forty-three was empty, just three doors up from Mr. Harper's room. I scurried back to the elevator and returned to the eighth floor. I went to room forty-three first and confirmed that the lights worked. Satisfied, I strode to Mr. Harper's door and knocked.

He was dressed now, but that was all that had changed. His clenched jaw and furling fists highlighted his anger.

"Room forty-three is vacant down the hall. Let me help you, and we'll have you settled again in no time."

He shoved a small pack at me. "Here, take that. I've packed everything up."

He had his laptop under his elbow and rolled a suitcase with his other hand. I led the way to the new room, opened the door, and flicked on the lights.

"There you go. I'm so sorry for the inconvenience." I placed his backpack on the dining table.

He rolled his suitcase in and hurled it onto the bed.

"Can I help you unpack, Mr. Harper?"

He sighed. "No, it's fine. I just need to get this done." His anger dissipated before my eyes.

"Okay. I'll make sure we discount your room for you. I'm so sorry."

"It's not your fault. I'm sorry I yelled."

"Thank you for your understanding. I hope you get your PowerPoint finished."

"No choice, I'm afraid. The boss needs it in"—he glanced at the clock on his laptop—"five hours."

I knew what it was like to be under ridiculous pressure and felt for him. "Can I at least make you a coffee?"

He nodded. "Sure, that'd be great."

Pleased that I could help, I strode to the kitchen and turned on the coffee machine. Mr. Harper sat at the table and instantly began tapping away on his computer. I watched him in silence as I waited for the coffee to drip into a china mug. Unsure how he liked it, I placed a sugar satchel, pod of milk, and a teaspoon next to the steaming black coffee and brought it to him. I sat the cup on the table at his side. "Good luck."

He blinked up at me as if he'd forgotten I were there. "Thanks."

I walked out the room and as I rode down in the elevator, I vowed that if I were ever under that kind of pressure in a job, I'd quit.

Back at reception, I focused on my new dilemma. I needed an electrician, and quick.

I scrolled down the list of emergency numbers pinned to the back of the reception desk and next to electrician I saw a card that read Jackson Kane, 24/7 Electrician. Exactly what I needed at this time of night. I dialed his number and was surprised when he answered on the third ring.

"Hello, I'm sorry to bother you. My name is Jane Nichols; I'm from the Hot Horizon Hotel."

"Yes. Yes. I'll be there."

I did a double-take. "But I haven't told you what—"

"It's okay. I'll be there in thirty minutes." The phone purred, and it took me a few seconds to realize he'd hung up. As I stared at the handset, I wondered what the hell had just happened. I put the phone down and went to the kitchen to make a cup of tea and wait his arrival.

A man came barreling in through the sliding glass doors twenty-five minutes later. He was short and stout but built like a footballer, and had a wild mop of black curly hair and flushed cheeks. As he juggled his equipment, he nearly tripped over his own feet on his way to the reception counter.

"Hi." I couldn't help but smile at his eagerness. "You must be Jackson Kane."

He put his hands on the counter. "Yep, at your service." He winked at me, and I nearly burst out laughing.

"Thank you for coming."

"No. No. Thank you for calling. To be honest, I never thought I'd get the call."

I frowned. "What call?"

"The call from the Hot Horizon Hotel." He was breathless, and as he ran his hand through the unruly mop of hair, I noticed the fine sheen of sweat on his forehead. It looked as if he'd run a marathon to get here.

I tried to ignore his cheesy grin as I placed the 'back in five minutes' sign on the counter for the second time that night. "This way please."

He hoisted a heavy-looking metal box with one hand and carried a burdened tool belt with the other. I had no idea why he wasn't wearing it, but didn't bother asking. They jingled in time to his steps as he fell in at my side.

As I pressed the button for the elevator, I turned to him, but he snapped his eyes away and fidgeted with the strap on his tool belt as we waited.

Maybe he sculled a coffee or something before he got here.

The tool belt tumbled from his fingers, and the thundering sound echoed off the polished surfaces of the lobby. "Sorry. Sorry."

As he bent down to pick it up, I studied his broad shoulders. Clearly Jackson worked out.

"Are you okay?" I asked as he returned upright.

"Yep. Just excited." His smile was model-worthy, with perfectly straight white teeth and lips like plump raspberries. His tongue flicked out as if he knew where I was looking.

I cocked my head. "About what exactly?"

The elevator pinged open and we stepped inside. He put the tool box down, then caught my gaze. His lips curled at the sides and when he winked again, I changed my stance, ready to karate kick him in the balls should he do anything weird.

"My mate Mickey was here a few months ago. He's a plumber . . ." he trailed off.

My heart leapt to my throat as I remembered that smoking-hot plumber with the stunning model looks. I feigned confusion. "And?"

Jackson wriggled his eyebrows, and his fingers trembled as he tugged at his shirt. "You know . . ."

My clit purred as I pictured my top-model gorgeous plumber and the amazing orgasms I'd had by his hands. I squirmed at my clenching insides and I shook my head. "Umm, no I don't."

Jackson squirmed too, and a quick glance was all I needed to see the bulge in his shorts. This guy was horny as hell. And cute. And sexy, in an unassuming, guy-next-door kind of way. He obviously wanted Memphis soooo badly, and all of a sudden, I felt obliged to give her to him. After all, he did race over here at three o'clock in the morning.

The elevator pinged open, and I strode ahead of him to room forty-six. "So, here we are." I pushed the door open. "See? No lights." I flicked the switches a few times for his benefit.

"Righty-ho." He squeezed past me, and I inhaled the musky cologne that he must've recently splashed on. "So, I'll leave you to it. Just press the reception button on the phone if you need me."

"Okay. I'll be right in here then." He turned from me and most of his body was consumed by the darkness. "Can you tell Memphis where I am, please?" He said it louder than he needed to.

I nearly giggled at his boyish eagerness as I shook my head. "I'm sorry. I have no idea who you're talking about."

"Okay." He shrugged. "I'll stay right here. Room forty-six."

I sucked my bottom lip to stop from giggling. It was a bit hard to critique in the darkness, but I think he wriggled his shoulders in some kind of sexy, come-hither move.

To stop myself from bursting out laughing, I turned. "I'll be at reception if you need me."

But I didn't go to reception. I went straight to my room, stripped off, put blue contact lenses in my eyes, plied on my makeup, plaited my hair, pinned it, and shoved it into the black wig that the sexy plumber had seen me in. I decided on my blue satin panties, but for a little cheekiness, I went without a bra. I wouldn't need it anyway. From the state I'd seen Jackson in, this was going to be over in a flash, which was a good thing, considering I should've been downstairs at reception.

I chose the French maid outfit again, as that was what he'd be expecting. In lightning speed, I'd transformed from Jane to Memphis and with my trench coat on and master key card clutched in my hand, I was on my way back up to the eighth floor in seven minutes flat.

My insides clenched in anticipation of red-hot sex as I made my way in the excruciatingly slow elevator. The doors pinged open and I strode with all the confidence in the world to the cheeky electrician.

I removed my coat and only knocked once before Jackson sprung the door open.

"Well hello." He stood naked except for his work boots and tool belt. Exactly like my sexy plumber had.

I chuckled. "Hello there. What have we here?"

"I'm your sizzling electrician."

The sizzle rolled off his tongue, and I laughed at his ridiculously corny yet incredibly horny announcement. This funny, awkward guy with the tousled hair and trembling fingers wanted me. That in turn made me want him, too. Jackson had broad shoulders, a narrow waist, and a chest full of dark hair, more hair than any man I'd been with so far, but not so much that he was Sasquatch-worthy.

I strode past him into the darkness. "Do you know the rules?"

"Yes. No sex. Just watch."

I giggled at his caveman-like voice. "Correct."

The dull glow from the open curtains gave enough light to make out basic shapes. Normally, I'd stride to the dining table and toss my bag over the back of a chair, but in my haste, I'd completely forgotten everything, including condoms. All I had was my master access key and I slung this onto the table, put my coat over the chair, and turned to Jackson.

"Okay, I'm ready." He flicked on a flashlight, and I burst out laughing. But when he shone the light on his cock, my laughter turned to a gasp. His erection was enormous, and totally out of proportion to his body, or maybe the concentrated beam of light gave that illusion. The head of his penis was a swollen crown, begging to be explored.

"Oh, you are ready." I strode to him, put one hand on his shoulder—managing the distance between us—and wrapped my other hand around his solid muscle.

Jackson sucked the air in through his teeth and reached for my breast. He squeezed hard, treating my boob like a stress ball. He was an overexcited schoolboy, and if his marathon-like breathing was any way to judge, he'd ejaculate any second. If I wasn't careful, he'd lose his load before I'd even had a turn.

"Take my dress off," I commanded, easing back from him.

His tools jangled as he stepped toward me, and in two seconds flat my dress was up over my head. But to my horror, my wig came with it, too. I snatched at my lacy costume before it hit the floor, seeking the hair trapped within.

As I fumbled to find it, he fumbled for my boobs, groping and groaning with overzealous fingers. The wig wasn't there. Faaark.

This called for drastic measures. As Jackson continued his attack on my boobs, I racked my brain for a solution. The darkness was my only savior.

An idea hit me, and I snatched the flashlight from his hand and stepped back. "Okay, bad boy, you need to calm down a notch."

He rubbed his hands together. "Sorry. Sorry. It's just I've been dreaming of this for months. I never thought it'd actually happen."

"And if you don't calm down, it'll all be over before we've had any fun."

"Yes. Yes. Mickey told me you'd be like this."

I frowned at that. "Like what?"

"You know. Take charge. He said it was so fucking sexy. Sorry, sorry, I didn't mean to swear."

"Hmmm," I mumbled. *He wants me to take charge.* "Turn around."

His tools clanged in his belt as he turned his back to me. I shone the flashlight on his butt and was delighted with what I saw. Two perfectly formed muscular globes, hemmed in by the tool belt. Before I'd even thought about it, I lightly smacked him on the ass. "Don't swear again."

He gasped, and I grinned at the wobble to his glorious white flesh. I couldn't believe I'd done that. It was weird yet fun and sent a firecracker through my already purring clit. He bent over slightly, showing me more, and I shone the pool of light on his derriere. It was something to behold— perfectly round, milky white, and devoid of any blemishes. My cheating bastard, ex-fiancé's butt was covered in coarse black hairs that sprouted at random and tiny pimples, on account of him always sitting on his ass. It was ugly.

This sizzling electrician, however, had a lovely bottom. So lovely in fact that I giggled and smacked him again. His firm flesh wobbled just the tiniest bit, and when he clenched the muscles together they bulged in such a nice way that I smacked him once more. Finding my wig was no longer a priority. This whole new experience was.

"Spread your legs."

He stomped his boots apart, changing the shape to his butt again. I smacked once more and God damn if that didn't make me horny. With the light shining on his white ass, I reached between his legs and cupped his balls. As I juggled the full weight of his scrotum in my hand, Jackson bent his knees and groaned.

"Oh God." The words whispered off his lips. "That feels so good."

"Hmmm." The hum in my throat matched the hum through my insides. Jackson was putty in my hands, and the absolute control of it had a delicious pulse throbbing from my clit and rocketing through my whole body.

I let go of him, and standing at his side, I reached around with the flashlight to shine it on his mighty erection. The pool of light lit up his cock, giving it center stage. And oh, what a star it was. My clit positively purred at the sight of it.

It was time for the attention to be turned to me. I shone the flashlight on one of my breasts.

"Suck."

He needed no further command. Jackson bent forward and latched his lips around my nipple. The flashlight illuminated down his back and highlighted his butt again. His lovely butt cheeks bulged and flexed as he gave my breasts attention. My nipples quickly became hard, bursting with lust as his lips sucked one and his fingers pinched the other.

I parted my legs, grabbed his hand, and guided him to my sex. He sure was eager and his fingers fed into my panties, glided over my clit, and plunged into my pulsing hole, lightning fast. The speed with which he did it had me gasping. Jackson's greedy fingers fought for my attention and so I gave it to them. A sharp tearing sound confirmed another pair of my underpants were ruined, but holy hell, it was worth it.

As his fingers ground over my clit, punishing it with delicious repetition, his mouth devoured my breast. An orgasm shuddered through me, ferocious and fabulous as a cry burst from my throat. My hot juices sprinkled down my legs as he continued to plunge my pussy. Over and over. Again and again. And again. I came once, twice, and I clawed his back as yet another orgasm ripped through me.

My weakened knees threatened to crumble me to the carpet and I gasped for a breath, certain he'd do this all night if I let him.

I stepped back. "Wow!" The word was a gross understatement. Jackson's fingers should be cast in gold.

The flashlight beam shone between us, and I spied my wig. It was right there, sprawled between us like a dead black cat. My already racing heart hit a whole new level at the sight of it. Its disheveled shape confirmed his heavy work boots were no match for the fine synthetic.

This called for some serious creativity.

"Come." I grabbed his hand, and the calluses on his palm rubbed against my hand as I led him farther into the dark room, the flashlight shining the way.

Trying not to illuminate anywhere near my head, I pulled a chair out from the table. "Sit." It was my turn for caveman talk.

Jackson did as he was told, and the tools on his belt jingled as he sat down. His erection looked even bigger now, protruding up between his legs like a powerful tool. I shone the flashlight on it, bathing it in a pool of light. This cute, funny man sure was a surprise.

"Stay," I commanded, and then using the flashlight as my guide, I went to the closet and plucked the waffle weave bathrobe that I knew would be there from the hanger. As I walked back to him, I undid the belt and let the rest of the fabric fall to the floor.

Threading the belt between my fingers, I returned to my plaything.

"Put your hands behind you."

Jackson didn't hesitate, and in a flash his wrists were visible through the bars in the back of the chair. His excited breathing filled the room as I tied the belt to his wrists and then secured him to the chair.

"Okay?" I'd only tied up one guy before, and it'd been a pathetic attempt to hold back that Casanova. Hopefully I did a better job this time.

"Yes." Jackson wriggled his fingers, maybe showing me I hadn't cut off his circulation.

I stepped around to the front of him, shone the flashlight on his groin, and trailed my fingers up his masterpiece. His cock bounced, and he sucked the air in through his teeth. My insides curled with his reaction. I twirled my finger around the head of his penis, and a small bubble of semen bulged from the slit.

Gathering his juice in my fingers I spread it around his crown, giving his cock a glorious sheen. A deep, manly groan tumbled from Jackson's throat, and his cock swelled even larger.

The pool of light intensified my focus, drawing my attention to just one aspect of this horny man. It was exquisite pleasure to offer it my undivided attention. Yet I wanted some of that action, too. I was torn between doing the sensible thing of distracting him while I fixed my wig situation and satisfying my greedy clit by driving my fingers into myself.

Maybe I could do both.

I wriggled out of what was left of my panties, and for a little tease I dragged them across his face. Jackson inhaled sharp and quick, and that simple move set an explosion through my insides. I flung my underwear aside and using the flashlight as a guide, I spread my legs and drove my finger into myself, grinding it over my clit with ferocious intensity. The light beam flickered up and down over my horny prisoner as I bobbed up and down in time to my thrusts. An orgasm came quick, and I cried out as it shuddered through me like a launching rocket. My juices spilled onto my hands and down my legs as I bent my knees to draw out the final shudders.

This flashlight thing was brilliant.

"Holy crap." Jackson's comment brought my attention back to him. Even in this minimal light his smile was magnificent, cutting through the darkness like a beacon.

"Your turn," I said.

"Yes please." His eagerness was an incredible aphrodisiac.

I eased forward, wrapped my fingers around his giant muscle, and pumped up and down just once. He moaned and his cock throbbed in my hand. I couldn't recall ever feeling that before. It was magnificent. I did it again, gliding my fingers over the soft skin and squeezing the solid tool beneath. It bulged again, and oh my God, if that didn't set my insides off a second time. I twisted my hand slightly as I manipulated from the base of his cock to the tip of his crown, and with each pump he bulged.

I increased my speed and seconds later a stream of white liquid shot from the slit in his crown. Holy smokes—*that* was the sexiest thing ever . . . it almost looked luminous in this light. I continued pumping as he shot his semen again and again over his upper thigh.

Soon he softened beneath my touch, and I removed the light's beam from his groin. But I wasn't finished yet; my pulsing clit wanted attention now. I swapped the flashlight over and using my left hand, so I didn't get his semen near me, I parted my legs and drove my finger into my wet folds again.

It was awkward and uncoordinated with my left hand but it didn't matter; I was so ready to burst that seconds later I screamed as I tipped over restraint and into heaven. Driving shudders shot through me like firecrackers as my juices pulsed onto my hand. It seemed like an eternity before the ecstasy that gripped me let go. I was still gasping for air when I opened my eyes again.

In the glow from the window, I could barely make out Jackson's features yet the smile on his face dominated, showing off perfect white teeth that practically glowed in the dark.

"Wow." His voice was a throaty whisper.

"Wow." I agreed. My sizzling electrician sure was a lovely surprise.

I suddenly remembered my wig and realized my mistake; I should've put it on while he was pre-occupied. A cheeky idea hit me and using the flashlight, I searched the darkness for something to cover his eyes.

The beam of light on the carpet highlighted my satin underwear. They'd be ruined now anyway. I picked them up, twirled them in my hand, and stepped toward him.

"Ready for more?"

His already amazing smile broadened. "Sure."

I gradually draped my panties over his eyes. "Don't move."

"I won't."

Once completely across his eyes, I let go, but the silly things fell right off his face.

"Woops," I said, as I gathered them from his groin. "Close your eyes." This time, I opened the underwear and, thankful they weren't completely torn apart, I fitted them over his head. It took all my might not to burst out laughing as I tugged the blue satin down to cover his eyes.

"No peeking."

"I won't."

Quick as a flash, I tugged on my trenchie and plucked my wig and costume off the floor. I tossed the flashlight onto the bed, and the circle of light bounced up and down the wall a few times as I strode away. I opened the door, then turned to Jackson. The glow from the glass doors confirmed he hadn't moved. He looked ridiculous sitting there naked except for his boots, tool belt, and my blue panties over his head. "You were incredible."

"Oh, Memphis, don't do this."

I strode through the door and was amazed to hear him laughing as I raced to the elevator.

"Come back, Memphis." He was way too loud for this time of the morning. The elevator pinged open, and I jumped in and jabbed the button for my floor a dozen times.

Back in my room, I giggled as I stripped, removed my makeup, and showered in record time. I redressed in the same clothes I'd worn earlier, and with my diary in my handbag, I made my way back to reception.

I held my breath as the elevator doors opened at the lobby floor, but sighed with relief when all was calm.

At the desk, I flopped onto my chair and waited for my heart to return to normal. As I wondered if my sizzling electrician had managed to get out of my ropes, I pulled my diary from my bag and turned to the 24th of July.

At the top I wrote, *Jackson Kane, room 46*, and as I thought about how his groin had been totally out of proportion with the rest of his body I wrote, *My Sizzling Surprise* beneath his name. I detailed in great length my horny session with the flashlight, and about smacking his bottom and the thrill of tying him up. I thought it was strange that he'd let a complete stranger do that to him. There was no way I would have. I giggled as I wondered if he were still secured to that chair. I doubted it; I'd deliberately tied that belt loosely.

But as the hour rolled on, I considered the chance that he may well still be trapped. I was torn between going up to him and staying right where I was and pretending I had no idea what had happened.

I decided to wait thirty minutes and if there was still no sign of him, I, Jane Nichols, hotel night manager, would go up to investigate how the electrician was going.

With each ticking minute, my insides clenched with indecision. Five minutes shy of my self-imposed deadline, Jackson stepped out of the elevator. I sighed with relief at his cheeky smile and smooth, confident swagger. He was still an overexcited schoolboy, but he wasn't as jittery as he'd been when he arrived.

"How did you do?" I played the concerned hotel manager to perfection.

He strode right up to the counter and when he ducked down behind it, I assumed he'd put his tools on the floor. He stood up again, and with his hands sprawled on the counter, he smiled at me.

"I was tied up for a little bit there, but I managed." He chuckled, and it was a wickedly contagious sound.

It took all my might not to burst out laughing. "So you got the lights working."

"Oh yeah, of course." He spread his fingers wide and rubbed them over the black marble. "Thank you."

"No, no, thank you for coming out at this time of night."

He wriggled his eyebrows. "It was my pleasure. When you see Memphis can you tell her the knots didn't hold?"

I shook my head. "I told you, I don't know who you're talking about."

He tapped his nose. "Yeah right. I know that you know how to find her. But don't worry; your secret's safe with me."

I screwed up my face. "Okay, whatever you say." Shaking my head to imply he was a little crazy, I backed away from the desk. "So I guess you'll email your invoice to me."

He waved his hand. "It's okay; this one's on me. Just remember you can call me anytime."

I was about to argue, but seeing the glimmer in his eyes, I conceded defeat instead. "Okay. Bye then."

He bent over, and a jangle of metal indicated he'd picked up his tools again. "Bye. Don't forget to call me."

I watched him stride all the way out the door and waited a couple more minutes before I burst out laughing.

It was always the men that I least expected that surprised me the most. I flopped back into my chair and spent the remainder of my shift flicking back through the entries in my diary and smiling at all the wonderful memories. So many different men. So many unique experiences. Each one had shown me something new.

Thirty sexual encounters in thirty weeks. It was hard to comprehend that I'd succeeded this far. It was even harder to comprehend that it was still so enjoyable. Before this year, I hadn't found sex enjoyable at all. Now, though, I couldn't imagine going a week without it. I laughed aloud and it echoed off the marbled lobby surfaces. Lucky me. I still had twenty-two more weeks in my challenge.

But what then? What would next year hold?

I didn't even want to think about it.

28TH JULY
TITILLATING TANGO
Room 50 - Hot Horizon Hotel

The alarm sounded and I rolled over to press the button to stop Lady Gaga blaring from the speakers. When silence returned, I flopped back onto my pillows to try and shake sleep from my brain.

Today was my birthday. I was one year off thirty and for some reason that triggered a starter gun in my brain. I was officially on a race to the finish line, although what the prize would be when I got there was still a mystery to me.

I stood up, opened the blinds and blazing sunshine lit up my room. Squinting against the glare, I stepped out on the balcony and breathed in the crisp ocean air. It was another beautiful winter's day on the Gold Coast and despite being a Thursday, people were everywhere. I put my hands over my head and stretched from side to side as I inhaled through my nose and out through my mouth. The serenity was a magic potion and with each breath I felt more alive.

Wide awake now, I pondered the next couple of hours with my lunch date. It didn't take rocket science to figure out how Clayton had learned it was my birthday . . . Lolita. As much as I'd wanted my birthday to slip by unnoticed, she'd insisted on the opposite. Lolly had been beside herself with worry over not being able to celebrate with me today. I could just picture how furious she would've been at the doctor who chose today to do minor surgery on her son's obviously painful ingrown toenail. I shuddered at the ugly memory of it.

Lolita had 'fixed' the problem of missing my birthday, though. She'd contacted Clayton and no doubt pleaded with him to take me out for lunch, and as he would've had to take time off work to do it, I felt quite guilty about that.

As I stood on the balcony, though, and marveled at my magnificent vista, I grew grateful that Lolita had made plans for me. The weather was perfect for a long lunch with a nice guy. And now I was really looking forward to it. I went back inside, poured strong, hot coffee into my new Friesian cow mug from Henry, and carried it to the bathroom. As I showered, I wondered where Clayton was taking me this time. Somewhere with a view, I hoped. I blow-dried my hair and ran the heating wand over it to make soft curls. After a dab of makeup to eradicate my freckles, I darkened my lashes and blushed my cheeks a bit. For a dose of color, I touched some Bobbi Brown Retro Red lipstick to my lips. I rubbed them together and smiled. I was happy with my look. Hopefully Clayton would be happy, too.

I paused at that thought. Of all the men I'd met this year, which one would I truly like to have my birthday lunch with? There were so many, it was impossible to narrow it down to one. As I spun the options around my brain, I walked to my closet.

With my lippy as my inspiration, I pulled my red knee-high boots from the closet. Red boots for the birthday girl. *Perfect choice.* I plucked my black wrap dress from the hanger and put it on, weaving my arms in and wrapping it around my waist almost twice to tie at my hip. It had short sleeves, and as it was a bit cool outside, I found a colorful woolen scarf with cute little knotted fringe and curled it around my neck a few times to hang loosely. I was tempted to put my trench coat over the top but settled on a black jacket with leather trimmings instead. I tugged on socks, then my boots, and checked my reflection in the mirror. This was good. Just enough to make me feel special, yet not so over the top that I'd stand out in a crowd.

Five minutes before Clayton was due to pick me up, I grabbed a red Michael Kors tote from the top of my closet. It had a pair of gold zips that could be maneuvered by cute soft leather tassels. I tossed in my sunglasses, lippy, cash, and credit cards, and with one last glance in the mirror, I headed downstairs.

Clayton waited for me at the hotel drop-off zone, and he waved as soon as I walked out of the sliding glass doors. He looked stylish in dark blue slacks and a white business shirt rolled up at the cuffs. His shoes and belt were a matching brown leather. For the first time with him, I felt like my outfit was suitable.

He greeted me with a glorious smile and a kiss on my cheek. "Happy birthday, gorgeous."

"Thank you." Clayton smelt divine. Floral and spice and everything nice.

He guided me to his car and held the door open for me to climb in. Seconds later, he slipped into the driver's seat. "Did you have a nice morning?"

"Nothing special. A few hours' sleep was good though." I buckled up.

"I'm glad you had some rest."

"How's work?" I asked.

"It's good. It's even better to sneak away with you though." He grinned at me, and a lovely tingle rolled through my body.

"Do I ask where we are going? Or is it a surprise?"

He pulled out into the traffic. "Hmmm. I think I'll keep it as a surprise."

"Okay." I relaxed into the seat and studied the eclectic mix of people enjoying the beautiful day outside. People from all walks of life came to the Gold Coast. Young. Old. Families. Singles. Groups of girls. Groups of guys. And businesspeople, treated to the sun and surf amidst their conference sessions.

Clayton followed the road that ran parallel to the beach heading toward Sea World. It was the same direction we'd gone last time we'd had lunch at that fancy restaurant where Dontrel, my sexy Jamaican drummer, had been performing. I hoped we weren't going there again. Without Lolly to help me, I wouldn't know what to do if I ran into Dontrel a second time.

My brain scramble settled when we drove straight past the marina. Four minutes later, Clayton pulled into a parking lot that overlooked the ocean. A long wooden jetty led out from the shoreline like an outstretched arm.

"Come on then." He popped the trunk, unbuckled, and climbed out.

The gentle ocean breeze blew a wisp of hair across my face, and I tucked it behind my ear and hopped out. I shut the door at the same time as Clayton slammed the trunk. I met him at the back of the car.

"I hope you like picnics."

I was grateful for my sunglasses because tears sprung to my eyes as I recalled my special picnic with Henry. "I love picnics."

"Good. Here, can you carry this?"

He handed me a tartan picnic blanket and a padded carry bag, and I was instantly reflecting further on my morning with Henry. My insides curled at that lovely thought, but I smacked my horny memories aside and forced my undivided attention to the wonderful man at my side.

He reached for my hand, and with a picnic basket curled over his other arm, we walked together across the grass towards a large shady Pandanas palm. A picnic table conveniently positioned in the shade was vacant, and I had the ridiculous feeling that Clayton had planned that, too.

"Give me a moment," he said as he put the basket on the wooden bench seat.

I shared my gaze between the magnificent scenery and Clayton's attention to the table setting. He tossed the picnic blanket over the weathered wood, and proceeded to pluck one item after another from the basket.

"What can I do?" I asked as he secured a stack of napkins with a couple of knives.

"You can get the champagne out, if you like?" He pointed at the padded bag I'd carried.

I unzipped the bag and the second I removed the bottle of Veuve Clicquot Champagne, I had a flashback to the first day of January when I'd opened this exact same brand of bubbles and sipped it all alone in my bathtub.

Wow. My life had changed a thousand-fold since then.

I peeled off the gold foil and twisted the metal tie to wriggle it off the cork.

"Here, allow me." Clayton took the bottle from me, and a loud pop preceded the cork flying into the palm's branches. It landed in a sandy patch amongst the grass, and I giggled as I fetched it.

Clayton poured the golden bubbles into two long-stemmed crystal glasses he'd placed on the table, and then handed one to me.

"Happy birthday, gorgeous."

Afraid that my chin would dimple with my swelling emotion, I sipped at the champagne. It was sweet, cold, and absolutely perfect, as was his choice for my birthday lunch. I'd never pictured Clayton as a picnic guy, yet I wasn't entirely sure why I hadn't.

He indicated for me to sit, and together we wriggled into the bench seat and sat side by side facing the ocean. "Isn't this magic?"

He must've read my mind. "It truly is. Have you been here before?"

"Quite often, actually. Telitha and I sometimes bring Clancy here for a run."

I frowned, and he aimed a finger down toward the shoreline. "It's the only beach around here where dogs are allowed."

Now that he'd pointed them out, I saw several dogs running along the water's edge. "What sort of dog do you have?"

"He's a caramel and white Beagle—a little pocket rocket. He and my daughter are inseparable. You should see them go crazy on the beach. It's exhausting just watching them."

"You sit here and watch?" I was curious why he didn't run around with them too.

"Yeah, I usually read the Sunday paper while they run amuck."

"Hmmm, sounds nice."

I tried to picture how I'd fit into that scenario. I was not a 'sit and read the paper' kind of girl. Was that because I'd never done it? I was more likely to run around on the beach. But would that be weird with someone else's child? Would Telitha even want me there?

"The dog was a lifesaver, actually." Clayton interrupted my tumbling thoughts.

"Oh, how's that?"

"He helped Telitha take her mind off her mom."

I nodded, and unsure what to say, I sipped the champagne.

Clayton opened a Tupperware dish and held it toward me. Inside was a selection of sandwiches. "I made chicken, lettuce and mayonnaise, beef with mustard, and turkey and cranberry."

"Wow, you've been busy."

He laughed. "Not really. Telitha helped."

"Oh." It took all my might not to gasp at him. "She knows about me?" I reached for a turkey sandwich and set it onto the red plastic plate he'd supplied.

"Yes, of course. She met you at Savannah's birthday party. Remember?"

"Uh-huh." I wouldn't exactly have said that she'd *met* me. It was more a fleeting glance than anything. All of a sudden this 'thing' with Clayton was becoming serious, and I wasn't exactly sure I was ready. Everything about him was amazing, except for the instant family. A man with a daughter and a dog was a huge commitment.

Is that what I want?

"Happy birthday." His grin was enormous.

My heart leapt to my throat at the tiny box, wrapped perfectly in red paper with a gold bow, that he held toward me. My fingers trembled as I reached for it.

"Oh Clayton. You really didn't have to." I trembled both inside and out as I pulled on the gold ribbon. *Please God, don't let this be a ring.*

The ribbon fell aside and I clenched my teeth as I flipped up the lid. Relief drained the blood from my body as I stared at the beautiful silver pendant centered in the black velvet.

"It's Saint Christopher, the patron saint of travel."

"It's beautiful." I lifted the silver disk onto my finger and ran my thumb over the raised figurine in the middle.

"You told me you wanted to travel; I didn't know what else to get you."

I smiled and leaned toward him, and as our lips met for a brief kiss my mind flipped with my swirling emotions.

He stepped out from the bench seat and stood up. "Can I put it on for you?"

"Yes please." I handed the case toward him and watched as he unclipped the chain from the velvet inlay. His hands were immaculate, with neatly trimmed, clean nails, and supple skin, devoid of calluses from manual labor. A delicious shudder rolled through me as he unraveled my scarf and draped his fingers across my neck to clip the chain in place.

"It's white gold. I wasn't sure which you prefer, as you don't wear any jewelry. But with your coloring I thought this would suit you."

White gold! Oh my God.

"Here, take a look." He held his phone toward me, and as I glanced at my reflection in his camera, he clicked off a few shots with him leaning over my right shoulder.

Our first couple photo. I smacked that silly thought aside. "It's too much, Clayton."

He wriggled in beside me again. "Don't be silly. I manage a jewelry store. You'd be stunned at the markup. Another sandwich?"

As I reached for a chicken sandwich with one hand, I fiddled with my new piece of jewelry with my other and realized that, excluding my extensive shoe and bag collection, this just became the most expensive thing I owned. How could it be that at twenty-nine, I owned nothing? That thought struck me from nowhere.

I had nothing else of value.

No car. No home. No shares—hell, I didn't even own a computer. Wow. I should consider myself lucky that a man as gorgeous and established at Clayton was even interested in me.

"Cheers." Clayton held his glass toward me and I raised mine, interested in what he'd be toasting to this time. "To the birthday girl. May all your wishes come true."

I sipped the delicate bubbles and thought about the only wish that meant anything to me. I wished to find the man of my dreams. As I glanced at Clayton and he in turn stared out over the ocean and munched on a sandwich, I wondered if I already had.

As the afternoon rolled on, we moved on from the sandwiches to a cheese platter he laid out with three cheeses, pâté, crackers, nuts, and dried apricots. Our conversation flowed easily, and we laughed together as he told stories about crazy customers and his daughter's funny antics.

The breeze picked up, producing tiny goose bumps that dotted along my arm. Clayton must have noticed, because he gathered my scarf from my lap, wrapped it around my neck, then put his arm across my shoulder and tugged me to him. I nestled into his chest and listened to his steady heartbeat.

"It's getting cool now." He ran his free hand up and down my arm. "Come on. I'll get you home so you can have a sleep before your shift."

I placed my hand on his leg and pulled back to look at him. "Thank you for a wonderful birthday."

He smiled and when he leaned toward me, our lips met. It was a soft kiss that had my insides dancing.

Together, we returned everything to the car and hopped in, and within twenty minutes he pulled up at the drop-off zone at Hot Horizon Hotel.

He came around to open the car door for me and when I stood up, we kissed again. "Thank you for a wonderful day and this beautiful necklace." I ran my finger over the pendant.

He cupped my cheek. "You're welcome. Have a good sleep."

I strode up the stairs and turned to wave as he drove away.

The little happy dance inside me put a spring in my step and as I crossed the lobby, I waved at Marjorie who was on the phone at reception. I hit the call button on the elevator and it opened immediately, which was a nice change. I stepped in and pulled my scarf aside to look at my new necklace in the refection. White gold really did look good on me.

The second I stepped into my apartment, my phone rang. It was Lolita.

"Hey, babe. So . . . how was it?"

I strolled to my bed and flopped back onto the covers. "It was wonderful. He's really nice."

"I told you."

"He made a picnic, and we sat near the beach and just talked for a few hours. He bought me a white-gold necklace with a Saint Christopher pendant. It's beautiful."

"Awww, I'm so happy for you two."

Us two? I wasn't sure I was happy with that reference. "Hmmm."

"Hmmm, what?"

I contemplated hiding my stupid turmoil from her.

"Tell me!"

Avoiding the question was pointless; Lolita would get it out of me anyway. "I think he's moving a bit faster that I am. He has a daughter, and I'm not sure I want an instant family. He's ready to settle down, but I want to travel the world before I have kids . . ." I blurted it all out, every stupid doubt I had about Clayton. "He's amazing and I should be so lucky to catch a man like him but . . . but. . ."

"Oh, babe, you have every right to have those doubts."

"Really?"

"Of course. Kids are hard work, and they'll impact greatly on a new relationship. Hell, they impact on every relationship. I understand exactly what you mean."

I sighed. "I'm still not ready."

"There's no need to hurry. He's not going anywhere. Just keep doing what you're doing and see what happens. You still have twenty-one weeks left of your challenge." It didn't surprise me that she knew how many weeks were left. Lolly knew everything.

"But I feel like I'm cheating on him."

"Bullshit," she blurted. "You're not. You haven't committed to him yet. He's just one of the guys you've met so far this year. You're not cheating on any of them."

Was that true? I went silent as I thought about the men I'd already seen a few times. Henry, Corben, Billy, Hunter, and Clayton. They were all so different; it was no wonder I was confused.

"Now," she said, grabbing my attention, "what're you doing tonight?"

I frowned. "Tonight? Working of course."

"Right. Well, I have a new challenge for you. You need to find a man and have wild, crazy, mind-blowing birthday sex. You, Jane Nichols, will have the best birthday ever. That's an order."

I laughed at her unbridled enthusiasm. "I've already had the best birthday ever."

"And that's a little sad. This new challenge is going to shoot it out of the stratosphere. Promise me you'll do it."

"I can't promise that. There are too many variables."

"Variables schmariables. I don't want excuses. I just want to hear all about your birthday sex when I call you tomorrow. Promise now. Quick."

I laughed along with her and before I thought a second longer, I promised—although I had no idea how I was going to keep it.

* * *

Five hours later, I made my way downstairs to start my shift.

"Happy birthday." Marjorie held a floral-wrapped package toward me and pulled me in for a hug.

"Thank you." I tore open the wrapping to reveal a pamper set with bubble bath, scented oil, and body lotion. All the gifts she gave me were similar— not that I was complaining. Anything to do with a bath was perfect for me. "This is lovely. I just finished the bubble bath you gave me for Christmas. Thank you."

"I know you like your baths. Now I've gotta dash. I hope you have a peaceful night."

I don't. I nearly giggled as I thought about Lolita's new challenge.

Exactly one hour later, the perfect variable strolled through the glass doors. As he walked across the marble tiles toward me, I studied my stunning potential birthday present. He wore a black waistcoat, buttoned up over a white long-sleeved shirt. Black slacks hugged his very narrow hips, and his black shoes were polished so highly that they flashed in the lobby lighting as he glided across the floor. I was probably grinning like a silly teenager by the time he arrived at my counter.

"Welcome to the Hot Horizon Hotel."

"Bonjour. I'm Sebastien De Marco." He held up two long, slender fingers. "Checking in for *deux* nights." His French accent oozed sexuality.

"*Bonjour.*" I couldn't believe I'd tried to emanate his sexy inflection. A red flush burned up my neck as I turned to the check-in cards and flicked through to find his name. Sebastien De Marco—it sounded as exotic as he looked.

"What brings you to the Gold Coast, Mr. De Marco?"

He tugged on the dark ponytail positioned neatly at the back of his neck. "I'm competing in the dance audition at the casino tomorrow." His accent was an aphrodisiac.

Trying to ignore my uncontrollable libido, I plucked a blue pen off the desk and twirled it in my fingers. "A dancer? I've never met a dancer before." That would explain his smooth stride and incredible physique. "I hope you're successful."

"*Moi aussi.*" He flashed a delightful smile, and hints of gold lit up his green eyes.

"Are you checking in alone?"

"Yes, everyone else is errr . . ." he looked to the ceiling, "*habiter* at the casino. But the noise . . . it drive me *dingue.*" He rolled his finger around his ear.

I nodded, completely understanding. "Yes, it's very noisy at the casino."

He nodded. "The beach is more *tranquille.*"

My birthday boy and I shared a common sentiment. "Yes. Yes, it is."

Sebastien had flawless skin and a trimmed three-day growth that perfectly matched the sexiness of his slicked-back hair. He had it all going on, and if things played out well he'd be getting it on with me very soon.

I passed his registration paperwork toward him. "Well, I'm glad we could help. You're staying in room fifty. It's a penthouse suite; you'll have a wonderful view of the beach from there."

"Perfect. Exactly what I need to clear my mind." He twirled his left hand in the air in an elegant expression of grace and poise, and when I noticed no wedding ring on his finger, I decided this was an invitation.

I have some ideas to clear your mind. Maybe we could do our own little tango. I shoved that delightful idea aside and tried to remain professional despite my libido doing a little jig inside me.

As I watched his graceful glide toward the elevator, I flopped back into my chair. Sebastien ticked all the right boxes—sexy, handsome, excellent body, no wedding ring.

I checked the clock. It was only ten thirty. It was going to be a long eight hours if I spent the whole time picturing my birthday present dancing around upstairs wearing nothing but a black bowtie.

Oh shit . . . I bolted up straight. If he was going to be my birthday present, I had to do this in the next ninety minutes.

I glanced around the empty lobby. Thursdays were unpredictable—sometimes quiet, sometimes crazy busy. I grabbed the check-in cards and flicked through them. Nobody else was scheduled to arrive today, so unless there was some kind of catastrophe, I could sneak away for a little bit.

Couldn't I?

Hell yeah. It's my birthday.

I threw the 'back in five minutes' sign on the counter and practically ran to the elevator. Up in my room, I fiddled with my makeup and chose the blue contact lenses to go with my long, blond wig. Suddenly, Memphis was back. Rather than wearing a bra and panties, I selected a little black lace teddy that I stepped into, eased over my torso and fixed in place with thin shoulder straps. The lace was so sheer that my nipples and belly button were easily visible, and it gave me about as much support as my pajamas. *Oh well.*

I couldn't waste time on my dress choice, so I decided on the same one I'd worn today. The dress had no zips or buttons; he could simply untie the knot and roll me out of it. Perfect for a quickie. I giggled at that wonderful thought.

The boots I wore today weren't right for the French man though, so I searched my closet for the sexy black stilettos with a gold trim that I'd bought online sometime last year. I found them and pulled them into the light. The heel was high—too high, really. But it wasn't like I'd be dancing in them or anything. All they needed to do was get me up to his penthouse and into his lounge. Once there, I'd have them off in no time.

Over one of my coat hangers I spied a sheer, lacy black shawl that was woven with slivers of gold thread into a complex cobweb-like pattern. Aunty Ann had bought this for me for my twenty-fifth birthday. When I'd unwrapped it, I'd been both overwhelmed at how beautiful it was and saddened that it would probably never see the light of day. On impulse, I grabbed my phone and with the elegant shawl draped over my shoulders, I smiled for the camera. I checked the photo and was delighted at how lovely my outfit looked.

Except it wasn't me in the picture. It was Memphis.

Disregarding the idea of sending the picture to Aunty Ann, I grabbed my black bag with the emergency supplies of money and condoms, dropped my phone into the pocket, grabbed my master key card, and headed out my door. I had an epiphany in the elevator and knew exactly how I was going to greet Sebastien at his door.

By the time I wiggled my way in my eight-inch heels to his door, my insides were curling with a greedy need to be satisfied. I hoped like hell he was ready to be ravished.

At his door, I plumped up my boobs in the non-existent support of my teddy, rubbed my lippy to smooth it out and silently sung 'happy birthday to me' as I knocked twice. I was nearly all the way through the song when the door swung wide.

The song vanished as I stared at the sexy Frenchman. He was still wearing the same clothes he'd had on downstairs, but now his hair was out. The dark tresses tumbled around his shoulders taking the sexy man he'd been downstairs to a whole new level.

"*Bonjour.*"

I had to force my mind to work and quickly licked my lips. "Hello. I was wondering if you could help me?"

"*Oui.* What is the *problème*?"

Oh my, that accent . . . My insides were liquefying.

I gripped onto my shawl and swallowed. "I . . ." I closed my eyes, hoping the blank canvas would help me focus. "I overheard you checking in downstairs. And, well . . . it's my birthday, and I was wondering if you would have a dance with me."

I opened my eyes.

Sebastien hadn't moved. He stood, his feet slightly apart, knees locked in place, one hand up holding the door open, and the other hand resting on his non-existent hip.

I licked my lips and my breath trapped in my throat as I waited out the silence.

Ever so slightly, the miracle happened. A small smile curled at the edges of his mouth as he unfolded his right hand toward me.

"*S'il vous plaît madame puis-je avoir cette danse?*"

I had no idea what he'd said, but every word of it sounded perfect. I allowed him to take my hand and guide me into the room. His other hand caressed the small of my back and the next second we were together, facing each other, joined at the hips—literally. My breath left me as I looked up into green eyes that devoured me with their intensity.

Before I knew it, Sebastien had my bag on the floor and one arm around my shoulder. His hips manipulated me in a move that I'd never experienced before, and we glided into the room. Our feet were as one as he twirled me around, the whole time keeping us glued together.

I was transported to another world, swallowed up by the tangible sexuality of this gorgeous man. We crossed the room, moving as one, keeping pace to music that only he heard. Near the spiral staircase, he paused, eased over to one side, and dipped me back. The swiftness of the move had me gasping, yet I felt completely safe in his arms.

As I looked up into his eyes, he reached toward my neck with his free hand, and with fingers as soft as a lover's touch, he gracefully removed the shawl from around my neck. Every inch of my body tingled with desire. It wasn't just the way he held me, the way he touched me—it was the way he looked at me, as if he could really, truly see into my soul.

I didn't get to savor that moment though as he raised me upright again, gripped me in his magnificent arms, and whisked me around the room. I pressed my palm to his back and felt every defined muscle with his movements.

I had no idea how he was doing this as I was a terrible dancer. The only way to get me to dance usually involved alcohol. Sebastien, however, was a skilled artist, painting the floor with his light-footed moves and guiding me along with him. My boobs jiggled in time to his steps, and the sensuality of the dance had my insides squirming for more. I forgot about my enormous heels and my uncoordinated legs and let him lead me around the decadent penthouse furniture with ease.

Together we crossed the room and near the front door he flicked off a few lights, casting us into elegant darkness. He caressed me again, and we twirled and danced, spinning around until I giggled with dizziness.

Suddenly, he dipped me back, and this time he raised one finger, touched it to my lips, and then glided it over my chin and down my neck. I tilted my head back and closed my eyes as he trailed it down between my breasts. My breathing quickened as he held me there, exploring my torso with excruciatingly slow precision. Next second, he tugged on the knot at my hip and before I knew it, my dress fell away.

I snapped my eyes open and Sebastien rose me to my feet and spun me around. Two seconds later my dress was off, and I didn't know whether to giggle or gasp.

He twirled his hand in the air. *"Il est magique, oui?"*

I blinked at him. I had no idea what he'd said, but if Sebastien kept talking to me like that, I'd let him do whatever he wanted.

When he frowned, I thought that maybe he needed a response.

"I . . . I'm sorry, but I have no idea what you said."

"Oh, of course. I said it was magic."

I did laugh this time, and his smile just made this incredibly sexy man even more so.

He stepped forward and stood barely two inches away. As I studied every aspect of his handsome face, he in turn studied me. We were no longer strangers; it was as if we'd known each other a lifetime. I reached out to undo the buttons on his vest and he let me. Our breaths fell in time to each button I released. Free now, I reached into the vest and placed my hands on his chest. The bulging muscles beneath the cotton fabric were everything I'd anticipated.

I glided the vest off his shoulders and let it fall to the floor. Turning my attention to the shirt, I undid those buttons too, eager to see what new surprises were in store for me. As I undid the last button and peeled the shirt apart, I was not even close to prepared for what I saw.

This was male perfection. Every possible muscle was defined with intricate detail. An artist could not have created a more magnificent specimen.

I eased his shirt off and gasped. Sebastien had his left nipple pierced, and dangling beneath the tiny ring was a diamond stud. As I reached up and glided my finger beneath the jewel, I felt his gaze upon me. I'd never been with a man with a body piercing and I had no idea what I could do with it. Embarrassed by my naiveté, I stepped back to take in the full picture of the man before me. He reached out and glided the thin straps off my shoulder, first the left, followed by the right. Then, using both hands he guided my teddy down my body, revealing my nakedness with measured control.

My breathing increased as my breasts were exposed. My breaths hit a whole new level when Sebastien leaned over and rolled his tongue around my right nipple. He curled his arm around my back, eased me over and held me there as his tongue and lips savored my hardened buds. To be held in his arms like that was easily one of the most erotic moments of my life.

We stood again and he returned to my teddy, lowering it over my hips to reveal my sex. He paused, leaning in, and as he inhaled I drove my fingers through his long hair. His fingers trailed down my legs, drawing the flimsy lace with them until it was off completely.

Sebastien held onto my hand, and warmth crossed between our palms as he stepped back to look at me. I was wearing nothing but my killer stilettos. They were meant to be the first thing I removed. His gaze was intense, his lips slightly parted as if he were about to say something. His chest rose and fell with every breath he took, and the bulge in his pants was unmistakable.

He ran his tongue over his lips. *"Oh mon dieu, tu es belle."*

My legs turned to jelly. If he'd continued talking, I would've had an orgasm right there and then. With the silent clock ticking in my head, I knew I had to get this going. As much as I'd rather stay here and do this all night long, I couldn't. I stepped toward him and reached for his belt. Without the grace he'd exhibited, I undid it along with his pants button, and his zipper, and yanked the final pieces of clothing from his body.

It was my turn to step back and inspect the male perfection before me. Sebastien was truly a masterpiece. His cock, protruding from his body and pointing right at me, was the central showpiece, and I wanted that work of art inside me right now.

I reached for that glorious muscle, wrapped my fingers right around it, and glided my hand over the smooth skin. Sebastien put his arm around me, and next second the two of us were dancing across the carpet again. Our hips weren't wedged together this time—that would be impossible with the extra bulge he now had. Instead, we were side by side as we waltzed toward his bed.

With an arm beneath my back, he guided me to the covers and laid me down with my head on the pillow. I dug my heels into the quilt and raised my hips, showing I was ready, oh so ready to receive my birthday present.

Sebastien knelt beside me and I reached for his cock. As I threaded my hand up and down his shaft, he wrapped his hand around my breast and squeezed. His other hand curled down my body and glided between my legs. I raised my hips higher and spread my thighs apart. He didn't waist a second and his finger glided into me, first one, then another.

His cock grew in my hand, and as I continued my own manipulation I studied every muscle in his torso which now glimmered with a fine sheen, enhancing his already amazing body.

I raised and lowered my hips in time to his thrusts and with his other hand working its magic on my breast, my insides created their own magic and I cried out as an orgasm pulsed through me.

Sebastien continued to rub until every last ounce of my lust was finished. It was sensational. On his knees, he wriggled around so he was between my legs.

"Wait." I propped up on my elbows to look down my body at him. "You need a condom. Bring me my bag."

He glided across the room as if floating on air, and when he bent over to collect my bag from the floor I was treated to a truly magnificent sight. The term 'buns of steel' was made for Sebastien De Marco.

The diamond below his nipple caught in the dimmed lights as he walked back to me. When he crawled up from the end of the bed it jiggled and glimmered with his movements. I looked down my body at him and as he paused between my legs, Sebastien raised up on his knees and made a show of tearing open the condom packet and rolling it onto his rock-hard shaft. This usually discreet act was now a grand spectacle commanding my attention.

He crawled forward, positioning his narrow hips between my knees, then fell toward me, planting his hands on either side of my breasts so he hovered above me. The bulges in his biceps held him in position. His hair tumbled around his face, framing him in a dark, messy halo. His nipple ring was right there, and I reached up and tugged on it but he winced and I quickly let go.

"Non, non, le faire à nouveau, il est bon."

I wished I hadn't touched his piercing and with no idea what he'd said, I rose my hips, showing him I was ready.

"It's good. Do it again." He spoke in English this time.

"Oh." I reached up, and with the diamond between my finger and thumb, I gently tugged on it again. He groaned, his eyes rolled, and the head of his penis nudged my opening.

I parted my legs, ready for his glorious masterpiece to give me my birthday present. Hovering above me like a god, and maintaining eye contact, he entered me. He plunged slow and deep, allowing me to feel every throbbing inch of him until he was right up to the hilt. He paused there, our eyes still locked, our breathing mingled, and deep inside me his cock bulged. It was an exquisite move that had my insides tingling.

He pulled out, pausing when his cock was right at the very tip. The heat of his crown nudged my pussy and I adjusted my hips, silently begging him to drive that jackhammer into me again.

And he did. All the way in, fast and hard, once, twice, three times. Then he stopped, pulled out to the edge, closed his eyes, clenched his jaw, and sucked the air in through his teeth. His torso was as hard as his swollen cock. Every magnificent inch was loaded with tension. His long, dark hair cascaded over his shoulders and tickled my breasts.

This time, when he entered me he rotated his hips as he penetrated, and that simple move touched something unique inside me. He pulled out and did it again, pivoting his hips, and with each stroke I grew more sensitive. *Is that my G-spot?*

I didn't know and I didn't care. Whatever he was doing, he could go right on doing it.

And he did.

Over and over he corkscrewed into me, increasing his pace with each plunge. I pulled my knees up, raising my bottom off the bed, and that set off a firecracker.

My birthday orgasm was everything it should be. Out of this world. Epic.

I clawed at the sheets. I clawed at his back. I was at his orgasmic mercy, and he drew out every ounce of my lust.

Sebastien cried out. His final thrusts were fast. Hard. And performed like a perfectly choreographed dance.

He fell onto my chest, and as I drove my fingers through his hair we remained as one until our breathing returned to normal.

It was a very long time before he rolled off me. With a jolt, I remembered where I should be and pushed up from the bed.

"Wow," I said as I rolled my legs off the side and planted my heels on the floor. Then I stood on wobbly legs and set about finding my bits and pieces scattered around the penthouse.

Sebastien propped up on an elbow and pulled a pillow down to cover his groin. "So is it really your birthday?"

Not bothering with my teddy, I pulled my dress on, and as I did the knot at my hip, I turned to him and smiled. "Yes, it is. Thank you for the dance. You dance beautifully."

He tilted his head, and his hair fell to one side. "You're the one who is beautiful."

"Pfft." I waved him away. "I bet you're surrounded by much more beautiful women than me every day."

"True." The certainty in his voice was undeniable, and I wanted to slap him. "But," he said quickly, "they are so obsessed with *leur apparence*, they've forgotten how to feel." He thumped his chest with his fist. The sound was like punching a board. He reached out for my hand and I stepped forward and took it. "The beauty within you allows you to feel, and that's what makes you beautiful. Don't ever lose that magic."

Okay, he's forgiven. His words set my heart fluttering, and when his green eyes drilled into me, I wondered if the enchanting Mr. Sebastien De Marco was caressing my heart.

A flush of heat flamed my neck and it took all my might to pull away from him. I made my way to the door, ready to dash for the elevator.

"Please." He stopped me with the pleading in his voice, and I turned back to him. "Please tell your name."

I clutched the folds of my dress and curtsied. "I'm Memphis. It was lovely to meet you."

He inclined his head. "Happy birthday, Memphis."

I stepped through his doorway, raced for the elevator, and after jabbing the button a million times, I plucked my phone from my purse to check the time. It was eleven forty. I'd been away from reception for more than an hour. My ride took forever to arrive, and with every ticking second my heart elevated a notch.

By the time I reached my room, I was just about having a heart attack. I dived into the bathroom, stripped off, plucked out my contacts, scrubbed off my makeup, pulled off the wig, and jumped into the shower.

Within five minutes, I was redressed in what I'd worn earlier. I grabbed my bag, shoved my diary in, and raced out the door again.

Back in the elevator, I fixed my hair and took in a few really deep breaths in an attempt to ready myself for whatever was waiting for me downstairs. I closed my eyes and actually prayed for the lobby to empty.

The doors pinged. My eyes shot open and an overwhelming sense of relief just about had my legs vanishing beneath me. I poured myself onto the reception chair, plonked my head down on the desk, and counted the seconds until my heart had a regular beat again.

It was midnight when I opened the diary and turned to the 28th of July. And as I thought about my highly erotic dance with *Mr. Sebastien De Marco in Room 50*, I wrote, *Titillating Tango* in the top margin. I detailed the start of my day with the wonderful picnic with Clayton and how pleasantly our conversation had flowed and the perfect white-gold pendant he'd given me.

I then went on to write about my other birthday present, my sexy Frenchman who'd had me gliding across the floor as if I were in slippers, not ridiculously high heels. Everything about him had oozed sexuality. I thought about what he'd said about the beauty within in me and smiled.

Two men in one day. Two magical experiences.

Best birthday ever.

5ᵀᴴ AUGUST
PASSIONATE PROMISES
Room 37 - Hot Horizon Hotel

I had a love/hate relationship with Friday nights. I loved them because they were usually busy with people coming and going through the lobby, which meant the hours whizzed by quickly. I hated them because I was working, while it seemed everyone else in the world was having fun.

Tonight, it had settled down a little after midnight, and I only saw about ten people until three a.m. At quarter to four, my night changed. For the better. Five people tumbled into the foyer, three men and two women. The girls were scantily clad despite it being winter and the early hours of the morning. Tattoos covered their arms and chests—actually, nearly every visible part of their flesh except for their faces. Each girl had her arm around a man. The fifth guy hung back from the other two couples.

It took me a moment to realize they all wore eyeliner, the men and the women. They looked mean or angry or something, and as they waltzed right past my counter without even a glance in my direction, I wondered if they were in a band.

The last guy was different from the other two men. He was slightly shorter, more square in the shoulders, and his hair was styled, short at the back and sides, with a side part that led to longer hair that swept from left to right with a high top. Unlike the rest of the group, he appeared to take pride in

73

his clothing. He wore black like the others, but his skinny jeans didn't sag around his thighs, and the button-up shirt with square gold buttons looked expensive. His leather jacket was such a good fit that I wondered if it had been custom made.

At the elevator, one couple started kissing and it wasn't just a little peck. Even from this distance I saw their tongues. They weren't shy with their hands either, and within seconds his hand was up her skirt, and based on the amount of ass cheek I saw, I doubted she was wearing underwear. The other three seemed oblivious to the action.

The fifth man turned to me, tilted his head toward the sexed up couple, and scrunched up his face. I waved, a timid little hand-in-the-air move that said I saw them but I wished I hadn't. The woman raised her knee, giving the tall man even more of her to play with, and thankfully the elevator pinged and the five of them disappeared from view.

The second they were gone, I pulled the check-in cards off the back counter and riffled through, trying to find the five mysterious strangers. There were fifty-two rooms in the Hot Horizon Hotel and tonight forty-four of them were occupied. At this time of year, it was mostly businesspeople here for conferences or international guests enjoying our glorious winter weather.

I found one of the tall men first. Zenon Justice. I huffed. With a name like that he was destined to be in a band. He was twenty-four years old and visiting from Melbourne. The second tall man was Dallas Cole, same age as his mate and also from Melbourne.

The last guy, the one who'd held back from the others, was Mason Cole, also from Melbourne but twenty-six years old. I slid over to my computer and Googled their names. Within a couple of searches, I'd discovered that three of the five strangers formed the band Empire Angels that consisted of two men and one woman. I recognized the men as the two taller ones, and the woman in the band had to be one of the two I'd seen, however I couldn't tell which one. According to their website, there were four members in the band, but the fourth guy was not with the men who'd walked through my hotel. Ten more minutes of searching revealed that the bass guitarist who usually played with the band was currently in rehab after a near-fatal drug overdose.

It was a search on their Facebook page that put the final piece of the puzzle together. Mason Cole had agreed to fill in until their usual bass guitarist recovered. I shuffled the check-in cards back together, leaving Mason out.

"Well hello, Mason."

I'd rolled in the hay with a lead guitarist before. Literally. When I was seventeen, Joel Parkinson and I'd spent an evening in the hay barn situated right above the room where the Blue Light Disco was held. The fact that he was a lead guitarist in a band, and that he'd picked me over every other girl in Mildura, had me as horny as a virgin on prom night. We'd kissed until my lips were bruised, but other than him manhandling my previously untouched boobs, that was where the barnyard romp had stopped.

As I thought about that night in the hay—uncontrollable breathing, feverish, groping hands, the smell of his leather jacket, the taste of rum on his tongue—I realized this was my chance to improve my claim of having slept with a guy in a band.

I giggled as I decided that Mason Cole, the fill-in bass guitarist for Empire Angels had just become my thirty-second sexual challenge.

I spent the final hours of my shift searching Mason Cole on the web, but the man was an enigma. Unlike the other members in the band who had pages and pages of pictures, usually with women hanging off them, Mason was a virtual unknown. By the end of my shift all I knew was Mason's age, address, that he played bass guitar, and that he was about to meet Memphis. I just hoped he wasn't too tired.

The end of my shift came and went with no sign of Needledick. Half an hour after he was due to start, I rang him.

"Hello." His groggy voice confirmed my assumption.

"Are you still *asleep?*"

"Oh, shit. What time is it?"

"It's seven. You should've been here half an hour ago."

"I'm sorry I've had—"

"I don't want to hear it, *John.*" His name snapped off my tongue like a whip crack, and I couldn't believe I'd spoken to my boss like that.

"I'll get in there as quick as I can."

"You better." I hung up the phone. My anger had me standing and pacing behind the reception desk. My boss was paid more money than me and had better hours than me, but he had no commitment to his job whatsoever. My blood continued to boil as I paced out the minutes until he arrived.

It was quarter to eight when he finally crawled through the door.

"I'm sorry, Jane," he said halfway toward reception.

I flung my bag over my shoulder, put one hand up, and shook my head. "Please don't talk. I'm so angry I'm worried I'll say the wrong thing. I'm tired, and I'm going to bed." I strode away, and with my back to him I waited for the stupid elevator to arrive and jumped in the second it did.

As it rolled slowly upwards, I furled and unfurled my fists. When I looked in the mirror, my flushed cheeks dominated. I looked as angry as the Empire Angels had looked. My mind flicked to the fifth guy. Hopefully he was ready for some action, because I had a bit of fury I needed to work off. Lolita had once told me that sex was the best medicine for anger. I was about to test that theory.

After I'd showered and toweled off, I stood before the mirror and reached for my eyeliner pencil. Just like the band members must've done, I glided it both above and beneath my eyes and smudged it into the corners with my finger. It was a completely different look for me, although maybe a little too dark. Fishing through my makeup I found an eye shadow set, and after a moment's hesitation, I applied sparkly gold eye shadow to the top of my eyelid and a touch beneath my eyes, too. I darkened and lengthened my lashes, and if ever there was a time to try out my violet contact lenses, then this was it. I reached for the box, and within a minute or so I had the purple disks in. The finished result was stunning. I was truly amazed at the whole new style I'd created for myself.

My black wig was the obvious choice for my sexy rocker look. I pulled the sorry sight off the shelf. I hadn't actually had a good look at the wig since my sizzling electrician had stomped all over it. The hairs scrambled in all directions, and a good chunk at the back stood up like it'd been slept in. But as I turned the wig around on my hand, I realized that this was probably the ideal hairstyle for a groupie.

I plaited my hair, pinned it up, pulled the black wig on, and burst out laughing. I looked as if I'd already had a wild romp, which, I realized, was exactly the kind of look I was going for. Rather than smoothing it down, I tipped my head over, tousled it more, and attacked it with hairspray.

I stood up and laughed long and loud. *Tina Turner, eat your heart out.*

Now for my outfit. I scanned my closet, looking for something suitable. As I tugged the clothing aside, disregarding each one, I paused at the very last item in the closet. It was a stretchy black dress with a square neckline and capped sleeves, hemmed just above my knee. It was what most women called a little black dress.

I called it a disaster.

Last time I'd worn this dress was three and a half years ago. I remembered the night distinctly because I'd worn spanks underneath, which hadn't been that unusual for me. But the second I'd sat down to dinner, the damn elastic had rolled from beneath my bra strap to my waist. Throughout the evening, as I'd pretended to enjoy the conversation with my new Hot Horizon Hotel work colleagues, I'd fought with the damn elastic that'd crawled down my body to form a hideous roll the size of a tire at my waist.

I'd stayed in that seat all night, dreading the moment I had to stand, and I remembered my agony as my bladder grew to mammoth proportions. It was a wonder I hadn't passed out as my growing stomach was strangled in a death-like grip by the industrial-strength elastic. When I'd eventually waddled my way to my room, I'd just about wet my pants in the frantic struggle to get out of the straitjacket. It'd been a life-changing experience as I hadn't worn the torture devices labeled as shapewear since.

People could take me as I was, or not take me at all. *Yeah.*

Thanks to Lolita and her obsession with exercise, I'd lost weight, which hopefully meant I wouldn't need spanks to make this dress look good. I eased the stretchy material over my head and pulled it down. It molded to my figure like a glove, but wasn't too tight that I'd be trapped like I had been in the silly sequined dress I'd worn for Billy, my sexy cowboy.

I looked in the mirror and turned sideways. It didn't look too bad. Actually, that was an understatement. The dress looked pretty darn good. After today, it was going to have a much better memory and would return to the center of my closet.

I stepped into a pair of black chunky heels that sported a one-inch platform at the front, but scowled at my big toe poking through peephole. My nail polish, as usual, was a disaster. With my stilettos still on, I strode to the bathroom, fished out the same nail polish I already had on, and painted my toenail right through the peephole. Once finished, I smiled at my ingenuity.

With my bag over my shoulder containing my master key card, emergency cash, condoms, and phone, I headed out the door. The second I stepped into the elevator, I giggled. This wild hair made me look crazy. Given my life this year, maybe I was.

I strode to Mason's room, did my usual final check, involving plumping up my boobs and rubbing my lippy, and then knocked. A minute or so later, I knocked again. Two minutes later, I reached into my bag and pulled out my master key card. With one last deep breath that I let out in a big gush, I scanned my card, pulled down on the handle, and walked into his room like I was meant to be there.

As I'd thought, Mason was asleep, but I didn't expect him to be naked, facedown and spread-eagled on the bed. My first thought was that he must've been cold—my second thought was yum! Mason Cole looked pretty darn sexy lying there, and I was tempted to pull up a chair and absorb every inch of his nakedness until he woke up. But as if he'd sensed he was being watched, Mason rolled over onto his side and opened his eyes.

I stepped up and sat on the edge of the bed. "Hi."

He pulled back. "What the—"

"Sorry to scare you, but I was wondering if you could help me."

"How the hell did you get into my room?"

"Oh." I waved my hand. "I told that guy downstairs I'd lost my room key and he gave me one." I felt dreadful for implicating Needledick in my devious plans, but only for a couple of seconds. Mason commanded much more of my attention. With his eyeliner gone, he looked just like any normal guy, only way over to the good side of sex on a stick.

Mason tugged the sheet over his groin and scrunched his face at me. "Ummm, why?"

"Well . . ." I stood up and slipped my heels off. "I'm really horny and I've never masturbated in front of a guitarist before." Masturbate was so easy to say these days.

"Ummm, what?" He frowned. "And how do you know I'm a guitarist?"

"I'm staying in this hotel too, and I saw you check-in yesterday." I shrugged. "And I couldn't believe my luck when you played at The Avenue last night. I was there with a bunch of girlfriends." I wiggled my head and hoped like hell my lie was convincing. "Yep, I'm a groupie." I'm also a bloody idiot. I giggled, hoping he'd laugh too.

He blinked at me. Blinked some more. Maybe he thought he was dreaming or something.

To help him along, I tugged my dress up my thighs. "Is it okay if I start? You can watch if you want."

His jaw dropped, but other than that there was nothing.

I pulled the dress up and eased it off, careful to leave my wig intact. Tossing the dress aside, I now stood wearing just a black bra and panties. Mason still hadn't moved, but the bulge beneath the cotton sheet had. That was the sign I needed.

"Want me to continue?"

He nodded and shifted on the bed so he lay on his side and was propped up on an elbow.

I reached behind my back, unclipped my bra and flung it toward my dress. As Mason licked his lips, I reached up and caressed my breasts. I imagined it was him doing it. As I recalled my frenzied barnyard romp with Joel Parkinson, I wondered if Mason would be more gentle or harder than Joel had been. I parted my legs and rolled my hand down my body, fed it into my panties, and touched my clit.

But there was nothing. I wasn't quite ready and the touch that usually set off rockets was uninteresting.

Continuing to rub, I tried to produce the arousal that often came to me in an instant. But for some reason, today I was flat. Maybe the anger I'd accumulated earlier was still there, stifling my libido.

I stopped and looked at him. Mason's groin was a flagpole beneath the sheet, but other than that he hadn't moved. My shoulders sagged. This was too hard. It wasn't meant to be hard.

I removed my hand from my underwear and stood up. "I'm sorry. This isn't working." I reached for my dress and turned it over, searching for the entrance.

"What? Don't stop. I'm sorry. It's me, isn't it? Please keep going."

I paused, my arms threaded into my dress, ready to curl it over my head.

He wriggled to the edge of the bed and sat with his feet on the floor and the sheet draped over the erection between his legs.

"Are you married?" I asked.

"No."

"Girlfriend?"

"Recently separated."

"Oh." I took my arms out of the dress. "How recent?"

"Three weeks."

"Hmmm." That was recent. "Do you still love her?"

He cocked his head and looked up to the ceiling. "Yes and no."

"Well that's cryptic." I held my dress against my nakedness.

"It's a long story." His shoulders sagged as if burdened by the weight of the world.

For some inexplicable reason I felt sorry for this complete stranger, and after a deep sigh, I put my therapist hat on and strode to the bed. "May I?" I indicated to his side.

"Sure." A small smile curled at the sides of his lips. His totally kissable plum-colored lips.

I felt ridiculous sitting there in just my underpants, but resisted covering myself and forced confidence into my demeanor. "Want to tell me what happened?"

"There's not much to tell. She wants to get married. You know, settle down, have kids, get a dog, a home, and a huge fucking mortgage. I don't."

Hmmm, he was talking my language. "What do you want?"

"I'm only twenty-six. I've spent my whole life doing what everyone else wanted. Got a degree in engineering—my parents' passion, not mine. Got engaged to my high school sweetheart—her idea, not mine. Helping my brother in his band from time to time—his idea, not mine."

"You don't like the band? But you're so incredible." It always surprised me how good I was at lying.

He shifted in his seat to look directly at me, and I too shifted his way. His eyes were stunning, as blue as deep sea ice.

"Thanks. I love playing guitar. But not like that."

His voice was soft, melodious. I could listen to him speak all day long. "Like what then?"

"I hate the noise of those places and I hate that you play an entire set and not one person in the crowd listens."

"I listened." My naughty lie had me glancing down at his groin. The flagpole was no longer there, but a bulge was still prevalent.

"You're not like the other girls."

"I'm not like any other woman." That was an understatement.

"Hmmm. You know my brother, Dallas?"

I nodded, hoping he didn't ask me to describe him for clarification.

"He convinced me to come on this tour. Told me it was the perfect way to get over my breakup with Dawn. He said the women would be hanging off me every night." He ran his tongue over his bottom lip. "I didn't believe him. But also, I wasn't interested. The women I've seen hanging around the band . . . well, let's just say they're not my type. Until now."

He moved his hand and when he rested it on my thigh, I was certain the earth moved.

"You sure are easy to talk to. What's your name anyway?"

"Memphis."

Suddenly Mason was on me. Our lips locked. In one move his leg rolled over my hip and he pushed me back. Our tongues mingled in a greedy fight to taste each other. His hands were on my breasts, firm and confident as he squeezed and caressed them. I drove my fingers through his hair and pulled him down onto me, wanting the heat of his body against mine.

The fire in me ignited. Flames licked up my insides, feeding a burning desire for this confused young man. His flagpole was back and the firm rod nudged against my pubic bone as his hips writhed over mine. He rolled his body to one side, yet we kept kissing, our breaths mingled as our tongues explored.

The hand that had been on my breast glided over my belly and fed into my panties, seeking the heat between my legs. Every bit as eager as he was, I raised my hips and parted my knees. He didn't miss a beat and plunged his finger inside me. His breathing deepened, as did mine as he thrust his finger in and out with frightening speed. The fine lace of my underwear was no match for his excitement, and the sharp ripping sound confirmed yet another pair gone.

It was totally worth it.

From this angle, his palm ground over my clit with each plunge of his finger. I cried out, releasing my lips from his. Every muscle in my body pulsed to an orgasmic beat and I pulled his hair, holding his head in position next to mine as my climax tore through me. It was hot. It was explosive. It totally rocked my world.

I released the fistful of hair I still had so he could move, and he pulled back. "Holy fuck, that was hot." His eyes were enormous.

"Uh-huh." Words were not a priority for me right now.

"No, I mean, like hoooooolllllly fuuuuuck."

The way he said it had me wondering if he'd never helped his ex-girlfriend to orgasm. If it were true, the thought horrified me. To be in a relationship for all those years and never bring her to an explosive climax was a sad, sad story. I needed to show this puppy exactly what a woman could do.

Without a second to waste, I flipped him onto his back and straddled him. His cock, still rock-hard, prodded at my bottom. "Put your hands above your head."

He did as he was told and I pushed up to my feet and stood above him like a mighty warrior about to conquer my disciple. Maybe I was. I stepped my feet together and wriggled out of the ruined underwear and tossed them aside. Then I looked down at him, waiting until our eyes met. "We're only getting started."

His Adam's apple bobbed up and down, and as his eyes bulged I stepped back over him. The deep blue in his eyes flared as his gaze fell on my vagina. His lips parted, and the rise and fall of his chest increased. His reaction had every nerve in my body tingling. I glided my finger over my pubic hairs and with a bend in my knees, I drove my finger into myself. Mason's eyes widened. His tongue flicked out to wet his lips, and he reached up and rubbed his thumb over my clit. The sensation had my insides shooting skyrockets. Within seconds, all control was gone and I plunged that finger into myself over and over. He joined in by pushing a finger inside with me, too.

It was a whole new sensation, and together we drew out a most glorious orgasm that had me bending my knees until I thought I'd collapse. My juices pulsed from me, trickling over my hand and down my legs. Mason grabbed my hips and pulled me down, and using his hand, nudged his penis at my opening.

My head screamed at me, and I managed to launch off him in a flash. "Hold it right there, big fella. Don't move."

I raced over to my bag and plucked a condom from the side zipper. "Put this on. Quick."

He snapped it from my fingers, peeled it open with his teeth, and rolled it onto his erection in ten seconds flat. I straddled him again. "Now, where were we?"

He wriggled his eyebrows and I reached down between my legs, wrapped my fingers around his cock, and guided it to my pussy. Once in position, I put both hands on his chest and as I glided that glorious muscle into me, my eyes rolled. Mason filled me completely, like the final puzzle piece slotting into place.

With my hands on his chest, I rose up and down, taking charge of the speed and depth. Mason's hands clutched my breasts, gripping them firm and tight as he squeezed over and over. Each plunge produced another layer to my building orgasm. But this one was different—deeper, more intense, growing slowly, slowly as it reached every nerve in my body.

Mason clenched his teeth, making the muscles in his jaw bulge. I pushed back from his chest and drew my feet and knees up so I squatted above him. His cock was deep, deep inside me and it felt so good. He reached up, and as he thumbed my clit, I clutched his arm for support and rode him like there were no tomorrow, in and out, up and down. With every plunge, his cock thumped that wonderful part inside me that demanded attention.

"Fuck yeah," Mason yelled. His eyes shot open, but he didn't seem to be seeing. He shut them again, and as he dug his fingers into my hips I rode him up and down until my hot juices flowed again. Gasping for breath, I fell to his chest, and he clutched me to his body. As I lay there, listening to his galloping heart, his cock gradually shrunk inside me.

Soon I eased off him, nestled into the crook of his arm, and let out a huge sigh of contentment. A couple of minutes later, I rolled over to the side and stood up. As I gathered my bits and pieces from the floor, Mason wriggled to the end of the bed and draped the sheet over his groin.

One look at my panties was enough to know they were ruined. I stepped over them and picked up my dress. I threaded my arms into my dress, and not bothering to put on my bra, I pulled the stretchy black fabric over my nakedness.

He cleared his throat. "You've convinced me."

Ready to put my foot into my shoe, I frowned at him. "About what?"

"That I should be happy that Dawn left me. There's a whole world out there I haven't explored. You're just the beginning."

I liked that, and when Mason's smile lit up his face I knew he meant every word of it. I inclined my head. "Glad I could help."

With my underwear in my bag, I slung it over my shoulder, strode to his door, pulled down on the handle and stepped through. As I tugged on the sides of my dress, strolled to the elevator and pressed the button, I pondered what he'd said. How many people were in marriages purely to please someone else?

It was a horrifying thought. I was ready to find the man of my dreams, yet I wasn't ready to settle down with kids and a mortgage. Thank God Alexander and I hadn't had children. That would've been a disaster. There was still so much I wanted to do. I wanted to travel, I wanted . . . The doors pinged open and Needledick was right there.

My heart exploded as his eyes bulged. I couldn't breathe. I couldn't move. My feet were frozen solid. I forced my body to walk and stepped into the elevator and turned my back to him. The doors closed, trapping me with a monster.

"I told you we don't want people like you in this hotel."

I turned to him and with these heels on, our eyes were level. "Pardon. I don't—"

He clutched my arm.

The anger that I'd successfully eradicated was back in a flash. "Let go of me," I hissed through clenched teeth and tried to pull my arm away.

He cocked his head. "Or what?" His grip increased.

I stared right at him. "I'll kick you in the groin, karate chop your throat, and take your knees out from under you."

His fingers dug in like pincers. "Pfft, yeah right."

And that's exactly what I did.

Within seconds, Needledick was on the floor clutching at his balls and groaning like he was giving birth. The doors pinged open, and I stepped over him and scurried across the lobby. My heart was an earthquake as I strode up the street, eager to put serious distance between me and the hotel.

Ten minutes and five or so blocks away, I did the inevitable and rang Lolita. "Hey babe, what's up?"

"Feel like picking up Memphis again?"

She burst out laughing. "Hell yeah. Where are you?"

"I'm at the playground parking lot at Currawa Beach. Do you know it?"

"I'll find it. I won't be there for about twenty minutes though, is that okay?"

I screamed on the inside. "Yeah, that's fine."

She laughed as she hung up. I scanned the area, looking for a place to hide. Wanting to put some distance between the playground and myself, I chose the trunk of a gnarly old tree that looked as if it'd withstood centuries of coastal wind. From my vantage point I'd be able to see Lolita drive in. As I counted out the minutes I tried to ignore the disgusted looks from the young women pushing over-decorated baby carriages toward the swings.

My thoughts turned to my boss, and soon the anguish over what I'd done had my heart right back into earthquake mode. I was in trouble. Memphis had gone too far this time. It suddenly occurred to me that what I'd done was assault.

I was a quivering mess by the time I spied Lolita's enormous Jeep Grand Cherokee. Leaving my shelter, I strode toward her, but she didn't slow down. I ran toward the car, and as she sped past I yelled out but she must not have heard. Frantically waving above my head, I stood in the middle of the parking lot in a desperate attempt to catch her attention.

The brake lights went on, and her car lurched to a stop in the middle of the road. I ran as fast as my heels could take me, and the second she stepped from the driver's side door I heard both her thumping music and her raucous cackle. She came around the back of the car and the cackle hit hysteria. Her perky boobs threatened to bobble right out of her low-cut top as she folded over in fits of laughter.

I rolled my eyes as I slowed my approach.

"Fucking hell, babe, who are you?"

"Can we just get in the car?"

"Look at your eyes. Is that purple? Ooooh, I want some. Wow, you've even got eye shadow—"

"Lolly, please."

She hugged me to her chest and her shoulders jiggled with her excitement. "You're a scream, babe." She pulled back. "Now get in. I want to hear all about it."

We slipped into our seats and as I did up my seatbelt, she shut down the music and turned to me. "First, are you hurt?"

"No." I rolled my eyes. "But Needledick may be."

Her perfectly trimmed brows shot up her forehead. "Needledick? What happened?"

I debated for about three seconds over telling her to move from the middle of the road, but knowing it was pointless, I told her what I'd done to my boss.

"Holy shit. I wish I'd seen that. Fucking bastard deserved it."

I scrunched up my nose. "Not really. All he did was clutch my wrist."

She pointed her bright pink fingernail at me. "No. It was more than that. He tried to restrain you. Silly bastard shouldn't have done that. He doesn't know who he's messing with."

A car horn beeped behind us, and Lolita simultaneously gave them the finger and put the car into gear.

As she drove from the parking lot, I pulled off the black wig and let out a huge sigh. "I'm in trouble."

"No, you're not. Memphis may be, but not Jane. You remember that."

That was true.

"You just need to be more careful."

"I am careful, but what am I supposed to do when I run into him in the elevator like that?"

She started to chuckle. "Kick him in the balls of course."

Her giggles were contagious, and soon we were both well and truly belly laughing.

The drive to her house took less that twenty minutes and by that time, I had my hair unpinned and thanks to her travel makeup kit, I removed most of my makeup.

As I plucked out my purple contacts, Lolly asked me where I got them from.

"The optometrist at Pacific Fair. They were really cheap."

"Wow, I want some."

I didn't bother asking what for, afraid of what she might say. I wrapped the lavender disks up into a tissue. The paper would ruin them, but I wasn't too worried; I couldn't see myself wearing that color again anyway.

She pulled into her driveway and I felt like I'd been hit by a Mack truck as we made our way inside. "Is Calvin home?" I dreaded that he might be.

"No. Poor bastard is going to be so pissed that he missed this."

Lolly led the way, and at the kitchen table she pulled out a chair and urged me to sit. "Now I want to hear all about the sex and don't miss even one thing."

I groaned, sighed, and then, determined to get it over as quickly as possible, I replayed every sordid detail.

"Holy shit, babe. That sounds fucking awesome."

"Yeah, it was pretty good."

"Pretty good? Sounds way better than that."

I closed my eyes. As a result of the adrenaline rushes I'd experienced this morning, I felt like I'd climbed Mount Everest.

She clicked her fingers. "Oh, I get it."

I snapped my eyes open. *Oh no, here we go with the lecture.*

"You're having doubts, right?"

I nodded, then plonked my head on the table and stared at a tiny little speck in the white marble as I waited out her impending speech.

"Here we go again. Don't worry about Needledick; he deserves everything he gets. Was he late today?"

"Yep, didn't get in until a quarter to eight."

"What? Fucking hell. Jane should've kicked him in the balls."

I huffed and sat up.

She touched my arm. "Nothing has changed. Jane's still safe. Jeez, I didn't even recognize you—there's no way he would've."

That was true.

"Just carry on like nothing happened and see what he does about it."

She was right, and when I started to nod she clutched me around the shoulders again. "There you go. All better again. Now, want a champagne?"

I shook my head. "I just want some sleep."

"I'm not surprised, you horny little bitch." She roared with laughter and as I giggled along with her, my final threads of tension melted away.

By the time she dropped me back at the hotel, wearing yet another one of her ridiculously tiny outfits, it was nearly midday. I waved her goodbye, breathed in deeply, planted a smile on my face, and strode up the front steps like I normally would.

The gods were on my side, because not only was Needledick serving someone but he had eight people hovering around waiting their turn. It was checkout time, and I made a mental note to utilize that more often. I arrived at my apartment without incident.

I showered, put on my winter PJs, had a bite to eat, brushed my teeth, and pulled back the covers of my bed and wriggled in. Sitting with my diary on my lap, I turned to the 5th of August, and at the top I wrote *Mason Cole Room 37.*

I didn't bother writing about Needledick and the disaster that had happened after; instead, I wrote about Mason and the incredible sex I'd had with the confused bass guitarist.

As I thought about his dilemma and how easy it would be to agree to marrying someone just because you'd been with them for a long time, I vowed that I'd never do that.

I made a promise to myself that the man I married would be the one I truly loved, deep down in my soul. Our love would be so strong it'd be a living, breathing thing, making our hearts ache when we were apart and piecing them together every time we were clutched in each other's arms.

With that thought, I wrote, *Passionate Promises* beneath the guitarist's name.

I closed the diary, slid down the bed, and rolled onto my side. My body was weary but my mind flipped around from one crazy thought to another. I shut my eyes and forced myself to think about a man holding me, our hearts beating as one as we shared the rest of our lives together.

14TH AUGUST
GIFTS FROM GOD
Room 7 - Hot Horizon Hotel

It was Wednesday. *Yay.* My favorite day of the week, and my only day off work. I didn't have huge plans for today. In fact, I had no plans at all. But that was fine with me. I was actually looking forward to a day of lazing around my apartment.

Even though it was still dark outside, I grabbed my cup of green tea and strolled from reception out the sliding glass doors. I was surprised to see it was raining. I hadn't even realized. I eased onto the seat and inhaled the freshness in the air. It was like cleansing my soul, which, considering my crazy, unconventional life, was a miracle.

Other than the downpour there was very little movement outside. I sipped my tea and watched as the sun gradually illuminated the horizon. Spears of light shot up from the waterline to pierce the black clouds, offering some hope of a sunny day.

I'd nearly finished my tea, and the sun still struggled against the black clouds when a taxi pulled into the drop-off zone. A couple of seconds later, both the driver and another man climbed out and met at the trunk. Assuming they were removing the passenger's luggage, I took the opportunity to return to my desk and grab the check-in cards.

The doors slid open and a man walked in wearing jeans and a knitted sweater that opened at the collar to show hints of a checkered flannel shirt beneath. He dragged a small suitcase across the marble tiles toward me with his eyes lowered, as if he were assessing each step. The poor guy looked as if he'd come from a funeral or something just as depressing.

"Good morning, welcome to the Hot Horizon Hotel."

"Thank you. I'm Cameron Jax, checking in."

I shuffled through the cards, looking for his name. "Sorry about the weather."

He huffed. "Yeah, I hope it's not like this tomorrow." His dark eyes intensified, becoming almost black.

"Oh? What's on tomorrow?"

"A sunrise beach wedding."

The way he said it made me think this was some form of torture, rather than the joy I'd expect for a wedding. "Oh." I winced. "That would be bad."

"Bad? Pfft. That's an understatement. The bride will seriously lose her marbles, and she's already nutty enough."

"Is she a friend?"

"Client." He rolled his eyes and ran his hand over his rough stubble.

"A client?" I tilted my head.

"I'm a wedding planner."

"Oh, I've never met a wedding planner. How exciting!"

"Yeah." His answer was loaded with sarcasm. "As long as bridezilla doesn't come out to play."

"I'm sure it won't be that bad." I slid his paperwork across the counter. "Can you please check the details and sign here?"

"You'd be surprised. I get to see one of the worst human emotions pretty much on a weekly basis."

I frowned as I stewed over which emotion that could be.

Our eyes met. "Jealousy," he said, deadpan. "It can make a woman very ugly."

"Oh dear."

"Yep. It's my job to make the wedding the most incredible day in a bride's life, but if she's loaded with jealousy, no amount of makeup or rose petals will fix it."

I frowned. "Hmmm, I can see how that would be a problem."

He frowned with me, and despite the concerned look marring his features, Cameron was handsome, in a guy-next-door-who-you-always-dreamed-of-hooking-up-with kind of way. *The knitted sweater helped.* I just wanted to jump into his arms and twirl around like they did in those romantic-comedy movies. I shoved the lovely thought aside and forced my brain back into work mode. "Here's your key. You're in room seven."

He reached for the card, and I noticed he wasn't wearing a wedding band. Maybe he didn't believe in marriage anymore.

"I hope you have perfect weather tomorrow."

His shoulders sagged even farther. "Me too. I was the one who convinced the bride to have a beach wedding."

"Oh." I had no idea what to say.

He pulled his lips into a thin line, sighed, grabbed the handle on his suitcase, and headed toward the elevators. I felt for him. To have so much pressure based on something that was completely out of his control was awful.

The phone rang, and I picked up the handset. "Welcome to the Hot Horizon Hotel, this's Jane, how can I help you?"

"Hey, baby-cakes. How'd you like to go on a date with me on Saturday the twenty-fourth of August?

Henry? It sounded like Henry, but what if I'm wrong? I clutched at the counter as the names of all the men I'd been with this year whizzed around my head.

"Jane, are you there? It's Henry."

"Henry! Oh jeez, you had me worried there for a minute."

"Really? Who else would it be?"

Oh god, don't make me answer that. "Ummm . . ."

He chuckled. "You don't have to tell me. But you do have to answer my first question. So what do you think? Fancy a hot date with a senile old bugger in two weeks?"

Relief came as an ice bath that flooded through me as I slipped into the office chair. "I told you, you're not old, and yes, I'd love to go out with you."

"Perfect. I'll pick you up at eight-thirty on Saturday the twenty-fourth."

I smiled as I remembered our last date, and then I caught myself. Was that a date? He'd just asked me to another hot date, too. *Did he think we were dating?* The question confused me.

"Jane? Jane, are you there?"

He dragged me back from mental despair. "Sorry, what did you say?"

"I said, wear something comfortable."

"Oh, okay."

"Perfect. See you then."

He hung up the phone, and as I mulled over Henry asking me on a date, Needledick entered through the sliding glass doors. I'd been so distracted with Henry that I hadn't even noticed my boss was late. I finished up the paperwork for Cameron, the wedding planner, as Needledick approached the counter.

"Crappy weather out there." He ran his hands through his wet hair.

"Yeah, do you know if it's going to let up?" I reached for my bag under the counter in a manner that ensured he couldn't check out my bottom.

"Apparently, although it doesn't look like it at the moment." He tossed his keys into the top drawer.

We did our usual handover and after I said goodbye, I headed for my room. I loved the sound of the rain, possibly because we didn't get it too often on the Gold Coast. For breakfast, I made eggs on toast and a strong coffee, and I stared out to the gloomy sea as I sat at my small dining table to eat. Beneath the clouds, the ocean looked like molten steel. White caps punctuated the grey, showing just how choppy it was out there. I shuddered at the thought of being on the water today. I didn't like it at the best of times, but on a day like today, it'd scare the crap out of me. The idea of curling up in bed and reading a book or watching a movie was much more appealing.

With sleep beckoning, I finished my breakfast, and as I was washing up the dishes, my phone rang. I quickly dried my hands and tugged my phone from the side pocket of my bag.

One glance at the number on the screen had my stomach flipping. I forced a smile into my voice and jabbed the green button. "Hi, Mom."

"Hi Jane, how are you?"

"I'm good. How about you and Dad?"

"We're both good, too."

And, as usual, that's where the conversation ended.

Mom cleared her throat. "We've decided to have a birthday party for your father's sixtieth."

"Oh." *Oh crap, here we go.*

"Your father and I would love you to be there."

"Oh Mom, it's really hard. You know I work weekends."

"That's the reason why we're giving you plenty of notice. It's on the twenty-second of October. That gives you two and a half months to arrange the time off."

Acid bubbled in my stomach at the thought of going back there. "I'll see what I can do."

"Jane, if you love your father you'll come home for his birthday. He misses you."

"Of course I love him, Mom, but it's just not easy to arrange time off."

"When was your last vacation?" she snapped the question down the phone.

"Oh . . . ummm, I don't know."

"Have you had a vacation since you took that job?"

"No."

"Exactly. They owe you time off. I don't want to have to explain to your father that his only daughter can't even make an effort on his special birthday."

The acid in my stomach stirred and I sighed. "Alright, I'll talk to my boss."

"Good."

"Okay, Mom, I've just finished my shift so I'm going to sleep—"

"There's . . . one other thing." The hesitation in her voice had me dreading what she was about to say.

I moved to my bed and sat on the edge. "What?"

"Alexander will be there."

"There . . . there where?" I was pretty sure she didn't mean just in Mildura, but there was no way she'd invite my cheating bastard ex-fiancé to my father's birthday. Would she?

The silence on the phone was like a funeral parlor and it hit me. "You've got to be kidding me. You invited that bastard to Dad's birthday?"

"Xander and your father are friends."

"Friends? What the hell?"

"They go fishing together. He's changed, Jane; you should give him a chance. He's been though such a terrible time."

"*He's* been through a terrible time? What the hell . . . he cheated on me."

"Yes, and he's really sorry for that."

"Sorry! How can you even talk to him, let alone be friends?"

"Jane, listen to me. You and Xander—"

"His name is Alexander."

"Anyway, you two were together three years. We got to know him. We liked him and, well, after you broke up, we continued to have him over to dinner and . . . now Xander and your father go fishing quite a bit."

"Argggghhh," I screamed. "I can't believe this. How long has this been going on?"

She cleared her throat. "It never actually stopped."

"Let me get this straight. Alexander had sex with dozens of women while we were engaged to be married, and after I broke up with him and left town, you continued to be friends."

"Yes, and now after what Chelsea-Lea did, he's just so broken."

I wanted to launch down the phone and claw her tongue out. Instead, I clenched my jaw until my teeth hurt. "You're unbelievable."

"Jane, please don't. Your dad wants to see you. Don't ruin his birthday."

The acid in my stomach was a full-blown volcano as I seethed over how to respond.

"We love you, and we miss you." Her affirmations seemed so shallow.

I remained stunned into silence.

"Okay, you must be exhausted. Have a good sleep. I'll ring you again next week."

"Yep. Okay."

"Love you."

After a pause, the phone went silent, and I flopped backwards onto the bed and rubbed my temples, trying to suppress the thump that hammered across my brain.

As the stupid conversation rolled around my head, I picked up my phone again and opened messenger.

'Hey, r u busy?'

'Nope.' Lolita responded immediately.

'Good. I need some dojo time. R u keen?'

'Hell yeah. U ok?'

'No. Just got off the phone from Mom.'

'Shit. Ok, I'm free. I'll pick u up in 20 mins.' She signed off with a smiley face that sported a huge cheesy grin.

I brushed my teeth, dressed into my gym gear, grabbed my Karate Gi and my bag, and made my way downstairs. Needledick waved at me as I crossed the lobby, and I reluctantly waved back.

His eyebrows drilled into a straight line. "Are you going for a run? It's raining."

"No, going to karate."

"Oh, I didn't know you did karate."

My heart nearly stopped as I realized my mistake. My mind flashed to the incident in which I'd brought Needledick to the floor in the elevator last week. Before I'd incapacitated him, I'd told him I was going to karate chop him in the throat. *And now he knows I do karate.*

Damn, why did I open my big mouth? "Oh, well I've just started." *Lies upon lies upon lies.* My once simple life had become very complicated.

When he squinted at me I had a terrible feeling he'd seen right through my deception.

"Bye." I picked up my pace, and as I raced across the lobby my sneakers squeaked on the marble tiles.

I stepped through the sliding glass doors, and the tumbling rain perfectly matched my tumbling emotions. With a squeal of tires, Lolly pulled up in her Jeep Grand Cherokee. She was my knight in shining armor, and I had no idea what I'd do without her.

I climbed in, and she leaned over to hug me. "What'd the bitch do this time?"

It was just like her to get right to the point.

Unclenching my jaw and forcing back the emotion that made it near impossible to speak, I told her everything.

"Jeez, what's wrong with them?"

I shook my head. "I have no idea. They don't seem to realize how much this hurts me."

She squeezed my knee. "Well, I can. Let's go kick and punch some of that anger out. Then we'll make a plan." We eased out of the drop-off zone, and the rain sounded much heavier as it pummeled the roof of her car.

We arrived at Kamoto's Karate dojo twenty minutes later and dashed through the rain to the front door. In the reception area, I slipped into my

Gi and within a minute, Master Kamoto was admonishing us for not coming every week. We waited out his speech in silence. It was a ritual we went through every once in a while and after a brief discussion, he once again seemed to give up on converting us, turned his back, and walked away.

Lolly and I weren't perturbed; we did karate purely for self-defense, not to win any competitions. I was happy with my green-belt status, and I was sure Lolita was happy with her purple belt, two levels above me.

Odors of pine and disinfectant invaded my nostrils as we entered the large room surrounded by floor-to-ceiling mirrors. About twenty-or-so men were already in there, and Lolita and I found our own space at the back of the room, dropped our bags and started with a warm-up. After a series of stretches, Lolita led the routine and we launched into a punishing workout of punches, kicks, strikes, blocks, and stances.

Lolita paused after she'd just kicked the crap out of a body bag I was holding and when her eyes bulged, I braced for the announcement I knew was coming. "Okay, I have a plan." *Damn she was loud.*

Everyone in the room turned to us.

"What?" I whispered as I chuckled at her outburst.

"Come on." She plucked our bags from the corner, then grabbed my arm, and I personally apologized to nearly everyone as she dragged me through the crowd and led me outside. The rain was easing, and a flock of rainbow lorikeets struck up a chorus as Lolita indicated for me to sit on the bench seat at the front of the dojo.

She stood, rubbing her hands together. "Alexander is a cocky asshole, right?"

"Understatement, but yes."

"He probably thinks he's done nothing wrong."

"Well obviously my parents think that."

"True. Here's what you're going to do. You're going to go to your father's birthday."

I rolled my head back. "Oh, Lolly, I don't know if—"

"Shhh, hear me out."

I cocked my head at her bossiness.

"You are going to that party, and you're going to look so fucking hot they'll hardly recognize you. That bastard is going to regret ever cheating on you."

"I don't think he knows what regret is."

"He will when he sees the sexy, confident woman you are now."

It had been more than three and a half years since I'd left Mildura, and Lolly was right; I had changed. For the better, too. But could I confront Alexander? Just the thought of seeing him again had an inferno of anger flooding through me.

She jiggled from foot to foot. "Oh my god, this is so exciting. We need to go shopping and buy you the sexiest fucking dress ever. His eyes will pop right out of his head."

I couldn't help but grin at her enthusiasm.

"Oooh and you know what? If you get close enough to that bastard, you can knee him in the balls, too. You're getting good at that."

We both roared with laughter, and as I pictured doing exactly that, her phone pinged and she tugged it from her bag. "Shit, Cal says Savannah's been throwing up. Sorry, babe, I'll have to take you home."

"Of course. I'm sorry." We started toward her car.

"Don't be sorry. You know you can call me anytime."

"Thanks, Lolly. I don't know what I'd do without you."

"Pfft. Stop it—this's what girlfriends do."

As I buckled up, I thought about the friends I'd had before I'd moved here and met Lolita. Chelsea-Lea had been my best friend, and she'd turned out to be the biggest back-stabbing bitch ever. "Not all girlfriends."

She shot me a glance. "Oh yeah. When you see that slut, slap her across the face from me."

As I laughed aloud, I wondered if Chelsea-Lea had given birth yet, and then I wondered who the father was. Suddenly, the idea of going back to Mildura was appealing. Maybe it was time I went home and showed them just who Jane Nichols was.

Lolita drove into the drop-off zone at the Hot Horizon Hotel. We said our goodbyes, and I made my way to my room. After a quick shower, I crawled into bed, and as I tried to predict how my next encounter with Alexander would play out, I drifted off to sleep.

* * *

Seven hours later, I woke feeling completely refreshed. I'd had a surprisingly great sleep, considering the morning I'd had. I jumped into the shower and washed my hair. After a quick blow-dry, I made a simple meal of grilled salmon and a salad that I tossed out of a packet.

With a sneaky glass of wine and my wholesome meal in hand, I moved out to the balcony. The rain had stopped, and the setting sun cast an interesting sepia color over my view. People were out in droves on the beach again, enjoying the mild breeze and the final gasps of sunshine. I hadn't realized how hungry I was, and I finished my meal in about two minutes flat.

As I sat back and sipped my wine, I considered Lolly's idea. With each mouthful of Shaw & Smith Sauvignon Blanc, the concept of going home grew more appealing. I truly had changed since I'd moved to the Gold Coast. And not just in looks. I was now a strong, independent woman . . . who was having sex on a weekly basis. I giggled at that.

Alexander may have cheated on me with nearly every woman in Mildura, but at least the sex I had didn't hurt anyone. In fact, it did the opposite. I always felt better afterwards, and I was pretty sure the men I fooled around with did, too.

As if on cue, a man strolling from the shoreline with his pants rolled up and shoes in his hand caught my eye. His knitted jumper alerted me to his identity. It was Cameron, the wedding planner. I was pleased for him; it looked like the weather was going to be nice tomorrow after all. As I tried to picture him without the worried scowl on his face, the idea of going to him and having a rollicking good romp before my shift snapped into my mind.

Before I knew it, I'd taken my dishes inside, tossed them into my sink, and with another top up of my wine, I headed to the bathroom.

Cameron and I had conversed for some time this morning, so a change of eye color was imperative. I chose brown today and popped the contact lenses in with my newfound skill. I proceeded to convert myself into Memphis, applying more than enough makeup, and today I selected the cute blond bobbed wig.

At my closet, I debated what to wear. I wanted to make this a bit of fun. He needed cheering up, and I also wanted to show Cameron that not all women were bridezillas. The poor man needed fixing.

With that thought, I lunged at my naughty nurse uniform. I giggled as I plucked the miniscule outfit off the hanger and held it against me. This was exactly what Cameron needed.

Last time I'd worn this, I didn't wear any underwear. It was wonderful to now have clothes with fabulous memories to go with them. This time I chose a white bra, and a G-string that was made from barely any fabric at all. I put on my lacy stockings and secured them at the top of my thigh with the decorated elastic trim. I weaved my arms into the nurse uniform, curled it around my back, and pulled it together to do up the zipper.

I chuckled as I stood in front of the mirror. It sure was sexy. Now for the shoes.

I tugged my boots from the bottom of my closet, slipped into them, and did up the back zipper. By the time I was dressed and ready, my insides curled with excitement.

With my trench coat covering my naughty Memphis outfit, I grabbed my bag with its trusty supplies and headed toward Cameron. I just hoped he was ready and willing for a little bit of fun. As I rode the elevator down to the next floor, I fiddled with my wig in the mirror. The pep talk I'd had with Lolita this morning had me feeling amazing. I was invincible. Life this year was incredible, and I couldn't wait to show all the people back home the new me.

In the meantime, I had a sexy man waiting for me in room seven who needed cheering up. And I was in exactly the right mood to do it.

I strode to his door, removed my coat, fiddled with my boobs a little, and then knocked. After a couple of heartbeats, the door opened and his jaw dropped.

"Hi." I did a silly wave thing. "I, ummm, saw you downstairs, and you looked a little sad. I thought you'd like some cheering up." I bobbled my head like a ditzy teenager.

"Oh, well, geez. This's a little embarrassing."

"What is?"

"Ummm, well, I've never had a . . ."

Oh god, he thinks I'm a hooker. I guess in this costume, he could be forgiven for thinking that. "Oh, it's nothing like that. I'm not a prostitute or anything. I'm just a single woman who's horny and," I leaned in to whisper, "I like to masturbate in front of complete strangers."

It's official. I've totally lost my marbles.

His already lowered jaw dropped even farther and his eyes bulged.

I crinkled my nose. "I know, it's a little weird. But it's the truth." I shrugged. "So, can I come in?"

He looked past me to peer up and down the hallway, then ran his eyes over my costume. "Okay." He sounded so skeptical, I was amazed when he stepped aside.

I inhaled his lovely aftershave as I walked past. It was earthy and masculine and totally yummy. The door clicked closed as I tossed my jacket and bag over the back of the chair. I turned to him, and he'd stopped halfway between the door and me and still wasn't showing even an inkling of excitement. In fact, he looked even more worried.

"First . . ." I held up a finger. "Are you married?"

"Oh God, no."

I nearly burst out laughing at his assertion. It sure was ironic given his line of business.

"What about a partner? Are you attached?"

"No and no."

Excellent. "Are you okay with this? All you have to do is watch."

"Is this a joke?"

Why do men continue to ask me this? "Do I look like I'm joking?"

"No. You look amazing, but this . . . type of thing never happens to me."

"Then this is your lucky day." It was time for Memphis to take over. "So, you can sit over there if you'd like." I pointed at the bed, and Cameron sidestepped over and sat without taking his eyes off me. He ran his tongue over his lips leaving a delicate sheen in its wake.

I strode to him, and as I went to put the toe of my boot on the bed between his legs he quickly shuffled back. The whites of his eyes were visible, and for a horrible second I realized I'd scared him. With my sexy red boot now just inches from his groin, I offered him my most seductive smile. "Can you help me out of these please?"

As if mesmerized, Cameron guided his hands around my boot, like he was about to caress it. With one hand guiding down the zipper, his other hand was warm and soft against the back of my knee. Just that simple touch alone had my heart skipping a beat.

When the zipper was all the way down, he cupped my ankle and eased the boot off my foot. His fingers were so delicate, like a lover's stroke, that my insides began quivering. This very brief touch had me eager to have his hands all over me.

I swapped feet, keen to have my other boot removed, too. Cameron had the hands of an angel, and thankfully took his time taking this boot off as well.

After my shoes were removed, I stepped back slightly to stand before him. He looked up at me. His pupils were wide, almost swallowing up his brown irises. Our eyes met, and it was as if something familiar crossed between us. Burning desire lit up my insides.

Wanting to capitalize on that hunger, I reached for the zipper nestled in the valley of my breasts and gripped the clasp between my fingers. I kept my eyes on him as I lowered the zipper. His chest rose and fell with ragged breaths, and the bulge in his jeans grew.

My skin-tight fabric practically burst open as I eased the zipper down my body and my breasts bulged from the white material, happy to be free from the constraint. I pulled the zipper right to the bottom, and after a little tug the dress unhooked from the hem and parted. With the nurse uniform now open and hanging loose at my sides, Cameron had a sneak peek of my lingerie.

He devoured me with his gaze, and it made me so damn horny. Shivers charged through my body at the intensity in his eyes. Primal instinct kicked in, and I guided the dress off my shoulders and let it fall to the floor. I reached around and unclipped my bra, and it too fell at my feet. His already wide eyes grew wider as I stepped forward. My breasts were the perfect height for his mouth and as my breathing increased, Cameron eased forward on the bed and cupped his warm hand beneath my left breast.

The shivers charging through me became skyrockets. I had no idea how, but Cameron must have been some kind of magician as his touch had me lost to another world. His hands were soft cushions, treating my breasts like precious gems. He leaned forward and as he continued to caress my left breast, he took my right nipple into his mouth and sucked, drawing it out until my hardened bud snapped from his lips. Cameron was a boob expert, and I was prepared to experience his professional touch all night if he wished. All year if he'd let me.

It occurred to me that he was still fully dressed and I reached for his sweater, greedy to see what hid beneath. He put his hands over his head, and in a flash both his sweater and flannel shirt were off, and the torso I'd hoped was there totally was.

Broad shoulders tapered in to narrow hips and in between, every muscle was perfectly formed. I had estimated Cameron was in his late thirties, but after seeing this incredible body, I wondered if I was out by about ten years. Either that, or he knew all the right moves at the gym.

Cameron returned to my breasts, and I let him. With his hands manipulating one boob and his mouth savoring the other, I willingly slipped into another world. A world where my mind took a back seat while every sensation in my body took over.

As he flicked from one breast to the other, I clawed my fingers up his back and drove them into his thick hair. The sexual coil deep inside me pulsed out a tribal beat that had my pussy begging to be played with. I reached down and threaded my hand into my G-string, and the very first touch of that oversensitive bud nearly had me launching off the carpet.

I sucked air through my teeth and flicked my clit again. A fire ignited within me, starting deep inside and blazing along every nerve in my body.

For some reason I was really sensitive today.

As Cameron continued his onslaught on my breasts, I drove my finger over my throbbing clit and into myself. I was wet and hot, and so close to climax that I squeezed my insides around my fingers and bent my knees. I must've groaned or something because Cameron stopped his exquisite manipulation and lowered his eyes to my hand and its unbridled exploration.

The look of pure rapture on his face was a lethal aphrodisiac, and I hooked my thumbs into my G-string and dropped it to my ankles. I parted my legs and pushed my fingers back into my velvet folds, rubbing deeper, faster and harder over my clit. Every delirious probe stacked another quivering layer of lust onto my orgasm, and soon my climax was of mammoth proportions.

Cameron stood up and whipped his jeans off in a flash. His cock was a mighty flagpole lunging from his body toward me. He wrapped his hand around that glorious muscle and pumped it fast and hard. The gentle hands that'd been on me were long gone—only wild abandonment endured.

His eyes were sealed shut. His mouth wide open. His legs apart, clenched into place as his hand pumped his cock like there was no tomorrow. Standing barely a foot apart, the two of us performed the most natural, wild, explosive act.

It was erotic; it was mind-blowing. It was liberating.

White liquid shot from his crown, once, twice, landing in a long stream on the carpet. The primitive joy of his ejaculation had me at the very edge. My legs threatened to buckle beneath me as I bent my knees even farther. Everything around me blurred into obscurity so I closed my eyes and allowed my body to take over.

I tipped over that glorious edge and screamed as my hot juices trickled over my hand again and again. The sensations that had gripped me in a vise came apart, launching me into the blissful place that I'd come to love.

Sounds soon returned, and I heard both of our ragged breaths along with his television that I hadn't noticed was on earlier.

He let out a big gush of air. "Holy . . . wow." His eyes bulged at me. "Women don't surprise me very often."

I grinned at him. "Glad I could help."

A frown drilled across his forehead. "You said you saw me downstairs. Where?"

"Oh." I cleared my throat. "I watched you stroll up from the beach. You walked straight past me." A truth and a lie mingled together—was that bad?

He lowered his eyes. "Hmmm, sorry about that. I don't normally miss beautiful women."

With that lovely comment, I pulled my wet G-string up my legs and although it felt disgusting, I tried to ignore it. I gathered my trench coat off the chair and pulled it on. I collected my bra and nurse uniform and shoved them into my bag. Then I reached for my boots.

"Here, let me help you." Cameron fell to floor and reached for the back of my heel.

To have a naked stranger put my shoes on for me was both surreal and incredibly erotic. His hands were a gift from God.

Once he had both boots on, he eased back onto the bed and sat again. Before I did something silly like tear my clothes off and dive on him, I strode to the door.

"Oh wait. Please tell me your name."

I was glad he'd asked. "I'm Memphis." I'd like him to remember me the next time he was dealing with a bridezilla. His smile was incredible, and with the vision of the naked man grinning at me permanently etched into my mind, I walked out his door.

My legs were jelly as I made my way to my room. I stripped off and stood under the hot shower for ages. As I reflected on my day, I sighed. It'd been twenty-four hours of tumultuous emotions. But what'd started out horribly had ended fabulously.

After dressing for work, I grabbed my diary and sat at the dining table. I turned to the 14th of August. At the top I wrote *Cameron Jax Room 7* and as I thought about his wonderful hands, I wrote *Gifts from God.*

Cameron had made me feel like I was the only woman in the world. And not just with his hands—with his eyes, too. He'd mastered the art of truly looking at a woman. Maybe in his line of business, his gift ensured his success.

I lined the diary page with vivid details of what he'd done and in particular how we climaxed at the end. To watch a man ejaculate and know I'd caused that unbridled reaction was the most amazing thing in the world.

With that wonderful thought, I closed the diary, grabbed my bag, and headed out my door, ready for another night managing the Hot Horizon Hotel.

18TH AUGUST
TOP OF THE BUCKET LIST
Room 14 - Hot Horizon Hotel

I was looking forward to the conference that was currently setting up in my hotel. Wine was something I'd like to know more about, and some of the finest vineyards in Australia were showcasing their products here for the next two days.

According to Marjorie, about six tons of alcohol had passed through the lobby today, and I couldn't wait to taste a few of the wines. I put the 'back in five minutes' sign on the counter and strolled into the conference room. Dozens of people milled about, setting up their stalls, unfolding tables, hanging signs, and stacking up rows of plastic cups, and some were even sampling wine.

They were a noisy bunch and based on their laughter and smiles, they were excited about the impending couple of days, too. I strolled from stall to stall, introducing myself, checking out the wine labels, making idle chit-chat and ensuring the stall holders were all happy with our facilities.

The conference room was set up with three rows of display tables, and halfway along the middle row, a man caught my eye. He was a beacon, drawing me in like a sex magnet. Slivers of copper reflected in his dark hair that fell across his forehead with just the right amount of bounce. Broad shoulders tapered down to thin hips that moved with a fascinatingly smooth rhythm.

As I pretended to glance from stall to stall, my eyes were continually drawn back to him as he set up the booth around him. A ring on his finger flashed in the light, and it took a few heartbeats before I established that the circular ring of gold was on his right hand.

His eyes were large, almond-shaped, and framed with the longest, darkest lashes I'd ever seen. I imagined he was born from a mix of cultures. Italian, maybe, based on his dark hair, or something exotic like Brazilian. He moved with a confident grace, and the way he fingered the wine bottle captured me in ways that had my kinky insides purring.

Suddenly, he looked in my direction, and the way his eyes devoured me had a hot flush barreling up through my insides and burning my cheeks in about three seconds flat. He smiled, a gorgeous broad smile that lit up his eyes as much as his face, and had my feet firmly planted on the carpet.

He waved, indicating that I should approach. I convinced my feet to move and suddenly I stood before the sexiest vintner I'd ever met. Actually, he was the only winemaker I'd ever met, but his looks suited his career choice perfectly.

"Good evening."

"Hi." I forced my brain to act professionally and scanned his setup. "Is everything to your liking?"

"Yes." His gaze travelled up my body. "I like everything very much." His Italian accent had me pondering if my first guess at his bloodline was correct. "Would you like to taste?" He glided his finger along a dark bottle and trailed around a gold circle at the top showing off the award-winning label.

Before I'd even thought about it, I nodded like a child agreeing to dessert. Red wine and I were not exactly friends, and more than one glass usually rendered me legless. But how could I resist his delightful request? Drastic measures had been called for.

He turned, and I admired the jeans that molded perfectly to his derriere as he reached with one foot off the ground and plucked a pair of real wine glasses from a box at the back of his booth. I tried to calm my racing heart as he turned back to me with a smile.

"I'm Luca, by the way."

"Hi, Luca. I'm Jane Nichols, the night manager here."

He held his hand toward me and when I reached out, his cozy, soft palm enveloped mine. "Lovely to meet you."

I cleared my throat and blinked. *Is he flirting with me?*

With expert skill and bulging biceps, Luca guided a corkscrew into the top of the bottle and pulled. The cork released with an elegant pop, and he held the bottle to his nose. With his eyes closed, he inhaled, and the expression on his face was the epitome of concentration as ever so slowly, the edges of his mouth curled with obvious satisfaction.

"*Perfecto.*" The word whispered off his lips like an angel's song.

He poured the wine into the glasses and I was struck by how deep red it was, like freshly picked pomegranate. The light caught in the liquid as he swirled one glass around, capturing shades of red in the downlights. He held it up, squinting to examine the glass closely, then nodding his approval, he offered it to me.

As I reached for it, he cupped his hand around mine and showed me how to hold the glass properly. "You must caress the glass. Hold it as if it were your lover."

The blush already burning my cheeks bathed me in lava. Sweat prickled my forehead as he guided my hand in slow, mesmerizing circles that had the wine swirling around the inside of the glass. His body emitted a warm hum that spoke directly to my libido.

"See? The wine, it coats the inside of the glass. It's a lovely full body. You will see."

"Hmmm." Words were my enemy right now.

"That is good." He nodded with conviction.

As I nodded with him, I feared I may fall under a hypnotic trance if I watched the swirling wine much longer.

"Okay." He let go of my hand, and it was akin to having my womb removed. "Now, we sip." He picked up his own glass and brought it to his lips, puckered, and tipped up the rose gold.

I copied, pouring a generous quantity onto my tongue. It was liquid heaven, and I imagined sitting by a fire with Luca, both of us naked as we savored his delectable nectar.

"And?" He raised his eyebrows and glided his hand from high up on his chest, down over his abs and let it rest on his non-existent belly. "Do you feel it here?"

I copied him, matching the slow trail of his hand over my own body and did indeed feel the wine warming my insides. "Yes. It's wonderful."

He smiled a truly fabulous smile, and I knew without a shadow of a doubt that Luca would be my next sexual adventure. We sipped the remaining wine in silence and as I devoured him with my gaze, I was certain he in turn was examining me. Every breath he made matched mine. We were already in sync, and I couldn't wait to continue that journey in the bedroom.

The anticipation was going to kill me.

It suddenly occurred to me that he was flirting with Jane. Plain Jane. The very idea had a hot flush blazing through me so quickly it was a wonder I didn't self-combust.

I had to get away before my cheeks and neck matched the color of the wine. Swallowing the dryness from my throat, I held the empty glass toward him. "That was delicious. Thank you. But I must keep moving."

"You're welcome." Our fingers touched as he took the wine glass from me, shattering my ability to utter another word, so with my heart in my throat, I spun on my heel. Leaving his booth was like escaping wet concrete, and I had to force my brain into that of Jane Nichols, the night manager.

I continued around the remaining booths, introducing myself and assuring the other delegates that if they needed anything, then I'd be at reception, ready to help.

By the time I returned to the front counter and removed the sign, it was close to ten-thirty. During the course of the next half an hour, many people left the conference room and disappeared into the elevator. When Luca left, he was chatting with another woman but the distance they stood apart suggested they didn't really know each other, which was a relief.

When the bar closed at one-thirty, a flood of people left about twenty minutes later, and I overheard several debates over where they'd go next. People came and went; conversations carried on around me. Nobody glanced in my direction. It was as if I were invisible.

All of a sudden, I was back to the insecure woman I'd been last year. I flopped onto my office chair and felt immensely insignificant in the large, marbled foyer.

For the first time in three and a half years, I was beginning to dislike my job. I wanted to go out partying like these people. I wanted a social life that crept into the small hours of the morning.

What's wrong with me?

I didn't do partying. But now, for some inexcusable reason, I wanted to try it. With a jolt, I realized I was jealous.

As I observed people crossing the lobby, I began to contemplate my future. My brain quickly skipped from me being single to me being attached. That in turn flipped to how difficult any relationship would be with my stupid job.

It was with a sinking heart that I also realized that my career choice may have contributed to my relationship status. That was a shocking thought, and I sat up and wanted to mentally slap myself. I shouldn't have been thinking like this. Especially not while I had a challenge to complete. This year was supposed to be fun.

But come the new year, maybe it'd be time to look for a new job. I brightened at that thought, and as the early hours of the morning crawled along, my mind drifted from what type of job I'd look for, to all the different people I'd met at the conference this evening. Within seconds, my brain snapped to my sexy winemaker upstairs.

A quick flick through the check-in cards revealed that he was staying in the room next door to mine, and from that second onward I was consumed. I pictured going to him, all dressed up and ready for sex. I pictured him naked and imagined every inch of his exquisite body. I pictured his gorgeous hands caressing my boobs, and I pictured our writhing bodies glistening with sweat as we teased each other into a carnal frenzy.

The remainder of my shift was consumed with these erotic thoughts, and by the time my boss came and relieved me of my shift, I was practically jittery with excitement at the prospect of going to Luca.

As I rode the elevator to my floor, I contemplated going to the sexy winemaker as myself, but realizing it would be inappropriate after I'd demonstrated my professionalism as the hotel's night manager, I quickly cast the silly thought aside.

In my room I showered and applied my Memphis makeup, complete with blue contact lenses and the long blond wig. Luca and I had spent some time gazing into each other's eyes so it was imperative I looked nothing like Jane. I chose a simple black dress that crossed over at the front to meet at my waist and flared out to a full skirt that stopped just above my knees. For a little spice I chose my zebra print Nilenia Givenchy stilettos and tugged the matching purse from the shelf in my closet. These stunning shoes and clutch had cost me a whole week's pay, and it was a thrill to be finally wearing them. Thank god I'd stockpiled all these accessories or my outfits would be positively boring.

With a touch of my favorite Bobbi Brown Retro red lippy on, I glanced at my reflection. My conservative dress was jazzed up just the right amount with the shoes and perfectly suited my planned meeting with Luca.

It was going to be a little weird coming out of my apartment and walking just ten feet to his. Without a second thought, I grabbed my bag, planted a smile on my face and crossed the short distance to his room and knocked.

The door opened a few moments later, and I was treated to a wonderful greeting. The man I'd met downstairs had increased in sex appeal in the space of just eight hours. He wore tan slacks and a white T-shirt that was tight enough to show off his bulging pecs. Yummy.

"Can I help you?" His accent was yummy, too.

"I hope so. I noticed you last night; you were setting up a table near mine, and . . . as we have a few hours to kill before we start today, I thought we could get to know each other a little better." I offered him my sexual diva smile.

His thick brows drilled together. "I beg your pardon?" His accent wasn't so sexy now, and I blinked up at him.

"I, um—"

"You've got the wrong door, lady. I don't do things like that."

I felt as if I'd been punched in the gut and slinked away.

"I didn't see you last night? What's your name?"

I turned, walked away and was forced to keep walking right past my door.

"I'm calling hotel management. I bet they'd like to know about you."

My chin dimpled as I waited through the humiliation for the elevator to arrive. I just about shattered into a million pieces when it finally pinged open. Tears stung my eyes as I jabbed the lobby button. As I stared into my own eyes, a bolt of horror hit me. If he called reception, there was every chance Needledick would be waiting for me.

No . . . not me—a blond-haired bimbo.

I yanked my wig off and shoved the long synthetic locks into my purse. Scrambling at the pins that held my hair in place, I then tousled it out around my shoulders. I plucked my contacts from my eyes and flicked them on top of the wig and forced the clutch to close. Using the underside of my hem, I scrubbed at my lippy, grateful my dress was black. Then I licked my thumbs and careful not to touch my lashes, I desperately wiped away as much blue eye shadow as I could. The thick mascara would have to stay.

For the first time ever, I was grateful for the slow elevator.

By the time it did a little jig announcing its arrival at the lobby, I was back to Jane. Well, Jane in a stylish dress, classy high heels, and an abundance of mascara.

The door pinged open, and Needledick was right there. His arms were folded across his chest, his legs apart, and a deep scowl was drilled onto his face.

"Oh, hi John. Are you okay?"

He blinked at me, his jaw ajar. "Did you see a blond woman?"

"Yeah." I frowned. "She got out on the first floor." Holy shit I'm clever.

His eyes bulged. "Shit." He jumped into the elevator, and I stepped out.

"What's wrong?"

"It's that hooker." He jabbed a button over and over. "I'm going to get her this time."

"Oh, do you want my help?"

"No. I've got this." As the doors closed, he clenched his jaw and nodded at me.

Ten seconds later, I burst out laughing as I crossed the lobby. But five seconds after that, the enormity of how close that was hit me. I stepped outside, crossed the road, and stood on the path looking out to the ocean.

Jesus. The adrenalin rush of the last ten minutes hit me like a thunderbolt, and before I crumbled to the pavement I moved over to the bench seat and sat down. The sun was a white fireball hanging high off the ocean, yet it was still cool. A gentle breeze drifted up from the water, cooling the inferno coursing through me.

What had gone wrong? Why didn't Luca want me? My first rejection was a slap to my face, and it stung like hell. I forced back tears as I tried to focus on the positive—my close escape.

I needed coffee and food, but most of all I needed Lolita.

It took all my effort to crawl to the Blue Haven Café. I sat at our usual table out the front, and when Matt arrived with his customary dour look, I ordered a cappuccino in a mug and a slice of chocolate mud cake with ice cream and extra cream. A sugar fix was imperative.

Once I'd sorted out my tumbling emotions, I rang Lolly.

"Hey babe," she answered on the first ring.

"Hey."

"Oh dear. What's happened?"

I swore the woman was a freak. All I'd said was one word and she knew I was troubled. I tumbled it all out, not even stopping when my sugar fix arrived.

"Jesus, that was close."

"I know."

"Hey, but you didn't get caught."

I spooned the rich cake into my mouth, rendering it impossible to answer.

"Oh, no you don't," she blurted out. "Don't you go stopping your challenge now!"

Sometimes it felt like Lolita was inside my head, because I had been thinking that this disaster may have been a sign that I should stop. Luca had been so flirtatious. Of all the guys I'd had so far this year, he was easily the one who'd given all the right signals. I'd thought he was a sure thing. After thirty-three sexual encounters, I still had no understanding of men.

"Jane." Lolly snapped me back to the conversation.

"I'm here."

"Tell me what you're thinking."

I sighed. "I just don't get it. Luca was flirting with me last night, and I swear he was so ready to jump into my pants. Yet when I did go to him, he rejected me. It hurt, Lolly. I thought I understood men."

"Pfft, babe, you'll never understand men. They're fucking off the planet when it comes to logic. You know that Mars/Venus thing. Well, it's more like Mercury/Pluto—that's how far apart we are when it comes to understanding each other."

"But how could I have got him so wrong?"

"Who cares? I'm amazed you've gone this far without a rejection."

I gasped. "Really?"

"Shit yeah. It's a testament to how fucking hot you look."

I grumbled and ate another bite of cake.

"Now you listen to me. You've had one rejection in thirty-four weeks. What's that? Like, point-zero-zero-zero-sixty-nine percent?" She laughed. Math was not her strong suit. "That's nothing," she continued. "Men and women would never hook up if we gave up after one rejection. This should just make you more determined."

"Umm, why?"

"To prove to yourself that you're fucking worthy, of course. That Luca guy was a loser, and he just missed out on the best sex in his life."
I chuckled.
"That's better. Now, it's Friday already. You have three days to find a man with a hard-on who can keep you on track."
We laughed together. "I'll see what happens."
"No, you fucking won't. You'll make it happen. Do you hear me?"
"Yes, Mom."
"Bullshit, I'm not your mom. I'm your mentor, and that's an order."
"Okay. Love you."
"Love ya too. Mwahhhh." She hung up the phone, and I forked a huge mouthful of chocolate cake smothered in whipped cream into my mouth.

* * *

Sunday morning came around quickly. Too quickly, and I was in trouble. If I didn't find a sexual partner in the next fourteen hours, my year-long challenge was over. I'd tried, tried heaps, but not one man who'd walked through my marble lobby had suited. It was as if all the single men in the world had suddenly gone underground.
The phone rang. "Welcome to the Hot Horizon Hotel, this's Jane, how can I help you?"
"Jane, it's John. I'm so sorry, but I'm going to be late in. Can you cover for me?"
My already despondent mood dropped even lower. "How much later?"
"I'm not sure, at least three hours, but could be as late as eleven o'clock. I'm at the hospital with Mom, and they need to run some tests."
I sighed. "Sure, okay."
"You're a lifesaver. I owe you."
Yes, you do. About a million times over. "Ring me if you'll be later than that."
"I will. I'm sorry." He hung up, and I put the handset down and slumped into the chair.
Great. I checked the clock. It was 6:15a.m. What was I going to do for the next five hours? I'd already shuffled things around in the stationery closet, and I'd cleaned the fridge out last week. Checkout wasn't until midday on a Sunday, so I didn't even have that little distraction to look forward to.
I tugged open the top drawer and pulled out the bundle of pens. Half an hour later, I'd tossed out the twenty or so pens that didn't work and then color coded the rest into groups that I secured with rubber bands. The job I'd once thought was interesting had become boring as bat-shit.
I laughed, and the sound echoed about the marble expanse. That was the saying Henry had used the day I'd met him. Thinking of Henry reminded me that my job wasn't boring—not all the time anyway. It was imperative

that I focused on the positive, or I'd begin to hate my job.

At eight-fifteen, two incredible positives strolled into the building. I sat up, touched my hair, and wished like hell I'd used some of the boring time at the desk to apply more lippy. I swallowed back my thumping heart as two fireman approached my counter.

"Hello, ma'am. Is John available?"

"Oh, um, no, he isn't. He's been delayed." *There is a heaven and I'm living in it!*

"I'm Jane Nichols, the night manager. Can I help you?" *Remove your clothes or something similar?*

The taller one ran his hand through his short dark hair. "We're here to do a routine check on your sprinkler system water tank."

"Oh. It's on the roof, right? I can show you the way." I put the 'back in five minutes' sign on the counter.

"You here alone, Jane?"

Was that a pick-up line? It sounded like a line. "Yes, always."

"Roger, how about you stay here, watch the counter for Jane while we go up to the roof?"

"Yep, no probs."

Roger put his hat on the counter, and the tall fireman turned to me. "Lead the way."

My heels clicked across the marble tiles in time to my beating heart. I pressed the button and sucked on my bottom lip in an attempt not to drool.

He held his hand toward me. "I'm Nathan Carmichael, by the way."

When our palms touched, the earth moved. Actually, it was more like a full-blown earthquake.

The doors opened and we stepped in, turned, and stood side by side, facing the mirrors. He wasn't even touching me, yet just being in this tiny space with him made the heat of his body like a blanket that smothered me with burning desire. An insatiable desire that started from deep within and raced through my entire body. Memphis was needy, and I was just about bursting from a lack of control.

Nathan was a good eight inches taller than me and built like I'd expect a fireman to be built, with broad shoulders and bulging pecs that featured beneath his high-visibility tight-fitting shirt. His nipples were hard lumps pointing at me like a couple of lethal weapons. The thick red braces holding up his florescent yellow pants brushed right alongside his nipples, and it took all my willpower not to reach over and snap those braces against his chest.

"Have you had a good night?" His voice was deep, throaty. Manly.

Not until now. "It was okay."

"Do you always work the night shift?"

"Uh-huh."

His eyes were light brown, like molten honey, and I wondered if he'd like to dribble honey all over me. I smacked that naughty thought aside. Remember, you are Jane. Memphis was clawing to get out, and I was grateful when the doors opened on the ninth floor.

I led the way along the corridor to the emergency exit at the end and opened the door. The glowing exit sign lit up the stairwell and the closed in space amplified Nathan's breathing. The emergency stairs went both up and down from this point, and as I climbed each stair to the rooftop my heart accelerated. Though, not from exertion.

Using my master key card, I opened the door, and as I squinted against the glare, I stepped out onto the rooftop. I stood aside and watched Nathan stride toward the water tower. His awkward gait was probably the result of his heavy-looking boots. He bent over at the water tower, and I once again thanked the stars for making Needledick late.

I sighed with contentment but then, realizing how weird it would look with me standing behind him, I strolled up to his side. "So what exactly are you looking for?"

"Just checking that the valves are working. These older units need to be examined every year. Shouldn't take too long."

"Take all the time you want."

He turned, and when he smiled up at me, my heart skipped a beat. With him down on one knee like that, it was as if he were proposing, and my giddy little brain was screaming hell yes. His long fingers worked quickly, flicking one valve after another, and I wondered what it would be like to have those lovely digits on me. *In* me.

Damn it, Memphis.

I needed to settle down. He was just doing his job. Like I was just doing my job.

After ten minutes or so, Nathan stood up, towering over me again. "Okay, all done."

Pity. I could've stayed here and watched him work all day.

"Lead the way." He indicated for me to step in front, and I retraced our steps back to the ninth floor and pressed the button for the elevator.

He glanced down at me with his molten eyes, and I was certain our breathing rose and fell in time. His hard nipples bulged through his red shirt and nudged against his braces. The angel and devil in my brain struck up a rampant debate over whether or not I should reach out and pinch them.

The doors opened, and we stepped in and once again we turned to stand side by side, facing the mirror. He turned to me and looked down. His honey eyes oozed over me with more sexual desire than I'd ever seen. Obviously, I was reading way too much into it. I was Jane, not Memphis.

Then the craziest thing happened.

One second I was standing at his side, the next I had my back against the wall, his mouth was on me, and somehow, in two seconds flat, he had my pencil skirt up around my waist and his hand in my underpants.

Our breaths mingled together, our tongues lashed each other, and with each bend of my knees his finger plunged deeper inside me. Together our moans tumbled from our throats and echoed about the mirrored cube. For the second time that day, I was grateful for the slow elevator. Our raging passion, however, was anything but slow.

As I groped his chest, feeling every exquisitely carved muscle in his torso, he tore my panties from my body. The sharp ripping sound ricocheted through my lust-fueled body.

Clutching his shoulders, I raised my knee and hooked it up over his thigh. He didn't miss a beat and two of his fingers plunged into me, rubbing over my clit and ramming me with ferocious intent. I gripped his high-visibility braces and cried out as an orgasm tore through me.

It was fast. It was incredible.

It blew my fucking mind.

He must've had ESP or something because he suddenly released me, and the ping of the elevator announced the doors were about to open. He smiled, and oh my god, if it wasn't the most glorious smile ever. I blinked, trying to comprehend what'd just happened.

"You might want to pick those up." His lowered his eyes to the floor.

I followed his gaze and spied my lacy black panties on the ground. As fast as lightning, I tugged my skirt back down and picked up my underwear.

The elevator opened, and he saluted me. "Thank you, ma'am."

The fireman strode casually across the lobby, his mate joined him, and they walked out the sliding glass doors. My jaw dropped when the two firemen high fived each other and carried on walking as if everything was normal.

Thank god the lobby was empty because I could barely breathe, let alone walk to the reception desk. I straightened my ponytail, and as I concealed my underpants in my hand and wondered what just happened, I somehow crossed the marble expanse to my desk and flopped into my chair.

How the hell did Plain Jane get an orgasm in the elevator from a mysterious firemen? That shit just didn't happen.

So much could've gone wrong. I gradually crumbled to a mess as I realized just how risky and stupid that'd been. I could've been caught.

I'd officially lost my fucking mind.

The minutes ticked along with me in a daze, and by the time Needledick arrived I could barely think. As I did the handover with him, I tried not to focus on the fact that I wasn't wearing underpants. It was more than a little distressing.

As I made my way to my room, my mind was like the giant pirate ship that swung back and forward at the showground, smashing through one emotion after another.

Somehow I made it to my room, and before my brain shattered like a smashed mirror, I dialed Lolita.

"Hey babe, what's up?"

I blurted it out, everything from the intense unspoken sexual tension to the mind-blowing orgasm with the fireman.

"Jesus Christ, Jane!"

I knew it. I'd crossed that imaginary boundary that put me in the fucking stupid category. A tidal wave of heat rose up, and I started to hyperventilate. Tears stung my eyes, and I feared I was about to vomit.

"I'm so jealous."

My brain snapped back to reality. "What?"

"That's another thing you've done that I haven't."

"What?" I said.

"What, what?"

I scrunched up my face as I tried to understand what she was saying.

"Oh god," she huffed. "Don't tell me you're second guessing what happened?"

"Ummm . . ."

"Jesus. So let me guess what's going through your brain. You had a mind-blowing orgasm with a fireman in a fucking elevator, for God's sake, and you think that's bad."

"Uh-huh."

"Are you kidding me? You just did the top three things most women only dream of, all in one go. A fireman. Holy shit. In the elevator. Mind-blowing orgasm in twenty seconds flat. And he tore your undies off. Jesus, I'm going to come in my pants just thinking of it."

"Lolly," I said half laughing, half shocked by her honesty.

"Shit, Jane, I've gotta go find Cal and fuck his brains out. Bye."

The phone clicked and I stared at the screen, hardly able to believe my best friend had just hung up on me.

I dragged my ass to the bathroom and showered. Afterwards, I cooked a bacon and egg sandwich and drizzled barbeque sauce all over it. Holding that on a plate in one hand and a green tea in my other, I walked out to my balcony to see what was happening in the real world.

A couple of bites into my delicious breakfast, I spied a pod of dolphins diving through the waves near the shore. Every once in a while one of them jumped from the water in a graceful display of agility and strength. That glorious sight reminded me of just how lucky I was.

The phone rang, and I dashed inside to grab it off my nightstand. It was Lolita.

"Okay, I'm back," she said the second I answered. "Cal says thanks."

"Ummm, what for?"

"For making me horny, of course."

I groaned. "Great," I said sarcastically.

"Anyway, let me give my little speech before you go off on some harebrained idea to give up your challenge. What happened today is at the top of every woman's bucket list. You got damn lucky, girlfriend. Half the women in the world would be cheering for you."

"And the other half?"

"Well, they'll be bitchy with jealousy of course."

I laughed at her. Lolly sure did have an interesting outlook on life.

"So, I've said this before and I'll say it again. You're a single woman having a bit of fun. That's it."

"Yes, but what I did was risky."

"So? What's the worst that could've happened?"

"Headline news telling the whole world about my slutty indiscretion?"

"Wow, you've actually thought about this."

"Of course."

"Good. So you know that's not going to happen. It'd probably only be third page news in the *Pics People* magazine."

I gasped, and she burst out laughing.

"I'm fucking with you, babe. Now stop this foolishness and be proud of what you've done. Okay?" She went silent. Lolita never did silent, and I let her stew as I mulled over my answer. It must've been torture for her, and I imagined her chewing on her knuckle to stop herself from speaking.

"Okay," I finally said.

"Okay what?" she responded in a flash.

"Okay, I'll be proud of what I did."

"That's better. Cal and I are happy for you."

"Thanks."

"Anyway, I've gotta go. Time to get my nails done. Love ya."

"Love you, too."

I put the phone on the bedside table and flopped back onto the pillow. Was Lolita right? Did half the woman in the world have 'sex with a fireman in an elevator' at the top of their bucket list? I knew I never had. Actually, I didn't have a bucket list, but even if I did I would never have thought to put that on it.

I reached for my diary and turned to the 18th of August. First I wrote about my failure in room fourteen and how much that rejection had affected me. What had actually hurt the most was how poorly I'd read his signs. The sexy winemaker had been making signals at me all night. At least, I'd thought they were signals. But I'd read him so wrong. Even after more than thirty sexual experiences, I still didn't understand men.

I shook my head at that thought and turned my focus to the firemen and my mind-blowing orgasm. For the second time in one day, I'd been grateful for that silly slow elevator, although it needn't have been that slow as that orgasm had hit me like a rocket. I've seen men get erections in ten seconds flat, but I'd had no idea my libido could be aroused at lightning speed, too. What had made it so exciting? Was it the fireman? Well, he had helped. He was hot, especially when he looked at me in an 'I'm going to devour you' kind of way. Was it the confinement of the elevator? Maybe. Was it the chance of getting caught? *Oh god, please don't let it be that.*

As I detailed how explosive that ride had been, I wrote *Top of the Bucket List* beneath my sexy fireman in the header of the page.

August sure was turning out to be an exciting month. Actually, every month this year had been exciting. And risky. I'd nearly been caught a few times now.

Was I dancing with fire? Probably.

Could I keep this challenge going? If it made me feel like I did right now, then hell yes, I could.

I closed my diary and stepped back out onto the balcony. Seconds later, a dolphin launched from a distant wave. I smiled as I clutched at the railing, and for the hundredth time this year I appreciated just how good life had become.

24TH AUGUST
SOARING TO NEW HEIGHTS
Room 10 - Hot Horizon Hotel

Saturday slipped into being without any fanfare, and as the small hours of the morning ticked by without any work to occupy my mind, my brain hit frenzy mode, skipping from one difficult question to the next. It'd been six days since my raunchy sexcapade in the elevator with the fireman and my emotions had been all over the place ever since. I just couldn't get it out of my head how lucky I was that I hadn't been caught. I'd never done anything like that. Until this year, that was. Was Memphis corrupting me that much? The answer was a resounding yes.

Did that upset me? That was where my dilemma came in. Maybe Memphis had been in me my whole life yet she'd been stifled. I huffed as I realized I was referring to Memphis as another person. *I really should be admitted to the loony bin.*

Needledick arrived the customary twenty minutes late, and after handover, I took the elevator to my room. I showered, dressed in my bathrobe, and made myself a simple breakfast of peanut butter on toast, matched it with a strong coffee, and strode out onto the balcony to eat.

A bunch of young kids were doing a surf school at the edge of the breaking waves. The boards were as big as they were, yet they handled them with ease. I guessed they'd be no older than ten. A group of adults hovering nearby faced the kids, and I assumed they were the parents. It had me thinking about Clayton and Telitha. He'd said he sat back and watched while his daughter played with the dog on the beach. Maybe that was what parents did. The only other couple I knew with kids was Calvin and Lolita, and they weren't the sit-back-and-watch kind of people. Not with anything.

It was a beautiful day. The sun was a golden ball high off the horizon and there was barely a whisper of breeze. It looked like thousands of people were already enjoying the fabulous last-of-winter weather. I finished my toast and held my warm mug in my hand as I reflected on the boring week I'd just had. It occurred to me that it may have been boring simply because I hadn't spent the entire week searching for my next passion partner.

Henry had kindly filled that role when he'd rung two weeks ago to invite me on a date today.

And that was when my next mental debate came barreling into my already tumultuous thoughts. Henry had called it a date. What would he think if he found out about my other 'dates' on this year-long challenge?

I shook my head, trying to free my mind of the unanswerable question, but my brain just wouldn't switch off. It was a wonder I was even functioning.

This double-identity thing was winding me up. I just hoped that when this year was over, I'd still recognize myself.

At eight o'clock, I strolled back inside, washed up my dishes, and as I brushed my teeth, I stood at my open closet and tried to work out what I'd wear.

Henry had said to wear something comfortable and whilst jeans instantly sprang to mind, that was what I'd worn the last time I'd seen him. A hot flush coursed through me at the memory of what he'd done to me in my jeans. Maybe he planned on more of the same. I diverted from the jeans and flipped past one dress after another in an attempt to make a choice. By the time I'd decided, my mouth was full of toothpaste foam, and I raced to the bathroom to rinse off.

The dress I chose was a long maxi with a simple line of elastic that secured it below my bust. The sleeves were fitted, three-quarter length and the dress was an interesting color—not quite olive, not quite steel grey. After I put it on, I went to my jewelry collection and chose a chunky set of wooden beads that was weighted down with a large orange crystal.

When the beads fell between my breasts, I was reminded of the last time Henry had played with the pearls I'd worn. This cemented my decision on the necklace.

I slipped into a pair of flat sandals that were decorated with hundreds of colorful beads. As I recalled how sunny it was outside, I reached up onto my toes and pulled down my large floppy white hat. I put it on and checked the mirror.

It amazed me how often I was happy with my reflection these days. Maybe Memphis was putting a positive spin on my opinion of myself. When she wasn't getting me into trouble, that was.

I grabbed my caramel leather tote and shoved in a colorful pashmina, along with all my other essentials. With five minutes to spare, I headed downstairs.

Once again, Henry waited beside a sleek black car in the drop-off zone, and I just about tripped over my skirt at his casual-yet-confident stance. Henry looked like a man on top of the world. Maybe that came with his age.

I felt a sense of relief as I moseyed down the steps toward him. Of all the men I'd met this year, Henry was the one who could help me through the tumbling doubts that'd gripped me this week.

When I arrived at his side he kissed my cheek, and I smiled at his now familiar scent.

"You look lovely."

 "Is this dress okay?"

"You're supposed to say thank you."

"Oh. Thank you."

"That's better."

He opened the car door, and I scooped up my skirt to sit. Seconds later he was in the driver's seat, and he nudged the car into gear and we pulled out into the busy weekend traffic.

"Do I get to ask where we're going?"

He nodded. "Sure."

"Okay, where are we going?"

He turned and grinned his beautiful smile at me. "It's a surprise."

"I knew you'd say that." I slapped his arm, and as I turned my attention to the surrounding scenery I reflected on the fact that Clayton had said exactly the same thing when he took me to lunch on my birthday. Other than their age, the two men were very similar in personality. I wondered what else they had in common.

"So, do you have children?" I couldn't believe I'd blurted that out.

He looked at me, weird-like. "Yes I do. A pigeon pair. My son is twenty-six and my daughter is twenty-three."

"Oh." I had no idea whether this additional knowledge influenced my opinion of Henry. It certainly had with Clayton.

"No, they don't know about you . . ." Henry said. "In case you were wondering."

"Ummm . . . no, I wasn't, actually."

"What were you thinking then?"

Oh god, why do I always walk into these difficult questions?

"Quick, answer or I'll think you're making things up."

"Really?"

"Yes, come on. Tell me."

I let out a huge sigh. "I'm not sure you really want to hear it."

"You're wrong. I want to know everything about you."

No, you don't.

"Whatever it is, Jane, it won't change my opinion of you."

"This might."

"Oooh, now you really have me intrigued. I tell you what. Let's have a marvelous day and then if you want, you can tell me this afternoon."

His calmness washed from him over onto me and diffused the dark clouds that'd billowed across my mind. "That sounds like a good idea."

He turned the car onto Sea World Drive toward the marina, and once again my stomach curled into knots. One of the restaurants at the marina was where I'd seen Dontrel, and at the end of this road was the beach where Clayton had taken me for lunch. I clenched my fists until my fingernails dug into my flesh as we approached the marina, but I inwardly breathed a sigh of relief when we carried on.

We drove past the marina, and just as I silently begged Henry not to take me near the dog beach Clayton had taken me to, he turned into the Sea World Resort parking lot.

"You're taking me to another hotel?"

"Nope." His quivering lip confirmed he was trying not to smile as he navigated the parking lot, looking for a spot.

As much as I liked surprises the suspense was killing me. So far every day with Henry had been wonderful, and judging by the glint in his eyes, I had every feeling that today was going to be just as enjoyable.

He pulled the car into a spot and touched my leg. "Ready?"

"Sure." By the time I'd grabbed my bag and hat, he was around my side with the door open and his hand held toward me to help me out.

The air was really still, not even a whisper of breeze, and the sun was hot enough that I tugged my hat on.

"It's my turn to be intrigued," I said as we walked side by side into the resort.

"It's exciting." His enthusiasm was contagious, and it was impossible to wipe the smile from my face.

I anticipated him walking toward reception, but he went the opposite way and led me through glass sliding doors, down a set of steps, and out to the enormous resort pool. Several people of all ages were in the water, and I assumed it was heated. Kids splashed about at one end, playing a game with a purple ball. Adults lounged at the other end on inflatable beds and despite it being just nine in the morning, several nursed cocktail glasses with fruit slices decorating the edges.

We skirted the pool and passed through a glass gate and onto the sand. The front of my hat tilted up, and that's when I saw where Henry was taking me. My heart lurched at the sight of a seaplane nestled in the shallow water. Henry turned to me. His brilliant smile lit up his whole face, and he did a little jig with his shoulders. "Excited?"

Tears sprung to my eyes. "Oh my god, yes. Is this another one of your bucket list items?"

"It sure is."

"Why didn't you take Helen when you were together?" Jeez, I'm nosy.

"The bitch doesn't like to fly."

I frowned at that. "But I thought she went to Vanuatu with your golf buddy."

"See what I mean? She's a bitch."

I burst out laughing.

"Come on." He grabbed my hand and led me across the sand.

Our pilot was the epitome of what a pilot should look like—fit, tall, and handsome. Crisp white shirt, navy shorts, and mirrored glasses finished off the look.

Henry held his hand forward, and the pilot took it. "Hi, I'm Henry and this is Jane."

"Nice to meet you. I'm Steven Donovan, Steve, your pilot for today."

Henry placed his palm on the small of my back and nudged me slightly in front of him. It was such a familiar move that felt oh-so right.

"Okay, I'll get you to take your shoes off, and Jane you'll have to lift your dress to get over the water," Steve said.

"Unless you want me to carry you," Henry whispered in my ear.

"I'll be fine." I giggled and squatted down to remove my sandals.

The pilot indicated for us to come with him, and he led me through the ankle-deep water toward the plane.

He reached up and opened the door. "Now watch your step. I'll get you to sit up in the front seat next to me."

"Oh no, Henry should sit there."

"I'll have it on the way back."

Henry was right behind me, and I turned. "Are you sure?"

"Yes, of course."

"Okay." I climbed into the cockpit and ogled the hundreds of knobs and dials as the two men settled into their seats.

Steve handed each of us headphones, and I slipped the large padded disks over my ears. Seconds later, they crackled to life.

"Okay, how's that? Can you both hear me?" Steve's voice sounded like it was a million miles away.

"Yes." I nodded

"Roger that, Captain." I couldn't decide if Henry's slightly high-pitched voice was from excitement or the headphones. Either way, I giggled.

The pilot helped me with my seatbelt, and then started flicking switches and turning dials. The propeller out of the front windshield began to spin and seconds later, the plane roared to life. I squealed as we left the safety of the shore and headed out to the middle of the seaway. Our speed picked up quickly, and the pilot turned the plane parallel to the beach.

The momentum increased as the water whizzed by, and it took me a few seconds to realize we'd lifted off. We rose quickly, and I squealed again as we flew over a couple of kids in kayaks and soared into the air. It was incredibly graceful, and within seconds we were high in the sky. Long golden beaches stretched as far as I could see and met with intense ultramarine ocean. Vegetation-covered deserted islands dotted the landscape, and giant tankers and equally large cruise ships populated the horizon.

"Oh wow. This's incredible."

"I know." Henry spoke as if he were in a trance.

Of all the wonderful things I *could* see, I couldn't see Henry. I wanted to hold his hand and squeeze my gratitude into his palm. As soon as I could, I was going to show him just how grateful I was. Emotion gripped me as I realized how lucky I was, and in that moment I was eternally grateful that I'd discovered Memphis.

We soared over dozens of tiny deserted islands surrounded with sand, and a series of sailboats with colorful billowing sails that skipped over the tiny whitecaps dotting the deep blue ocean. It truly was a magical experience.

About fifty minutes into the flight, the engine noise changed.

"What's happening?"

"It's okay, love. We're just coming in to land." Steve gave me a thumbs up signal and I repeated his move, showing him I was okay.

We gradually lowered toward the water, and I was on the verge of screaming when sea spray kicked up as we ricocheted off the ocean. We bounced a second time, and I was nudged back in my seat when a wave announced we'd touched down completely. We glided along for a couple of minutes before Steve twisted a dial, and the engine noise dulled and the propeller slowed.

The pilot angled the plane toward a sandy beach and we peacefully glided to a stop at the water's edge.

"Here we are." Steve unbuckled his seatbelt. "You two go and stretch your legs, and I'll get things set up."

Before I had a chance to ask any questions, Steve had left his seat and walked, hunched over between the seats to open the door again.

Henry hopped out first, and I grabbed my shoes, bag, and hat, and followed his lead. I stepped out onto one of the pontoons that kept the plane afloat. Henry stepped into the water and reached up to me. "Come on."

I tilted my head, ready to argue, but once I saw the pure thrill on his face I couldn't do it. I knelt over and put my arms around his shoulders, and with one arm beneath my knees and one around my back, Henry lifted me into his arms. As he carried me to shore, I kissed his cheek. "That was wonderful. Thank you."

He wriggled his eyebrows. "It's not over yet."

The dazzle in his eyes had me wanting to cartwheel up the beach, but I pulled him in for another kiss instead.

Henry set me down on the warm sand and as I lifted my skirt, I wished I hadn't worn such a long dress. He left my side to go and talk to Steve and I bent over and tied the fabric into a knot above my knee.

When he returned, he carried a large bag that looked the same as the one he'd had last time I'd seen him. As much as it was killing me to know, I resisted asking what was in there. I put my hat on, and he took my hand and led me away from the plane.

The view was spectacular. Gentle rolling waves lapped at the fine sand as we strolled along, and soon all the worry that'd consumed my thoughts this week evaporated and I felt the most relaxed I'd felt in days.

He let go of my hand and bent down to collect a small shell from the sand and gave it to me. It was a conch shell, caramel and white in color and about the size of my thumb.

"It's beautiful."

"Just like you."

I was two seconds away from objecting when I caught myself. "Thank you."

"Ahhh, we're making progress."

I wanted to ask what we were progressing toward, but decided against it, as I wasn't sure I was ready for his answer. Especially as Henry considered this a date. Lolly had told me dozens of times that my sexual encounters were all about fun. I hadn't pledged myself to any of these men. But maybe accepting this 'date' had me committing myself more than I'd anticipated. *Was that a bad thing?* I had no idea.

Henry was incredible; everything about him made him special to me. Although his age had never bothered me, the fact that he had grown children made me wonder if he'd want more. I wanted children, my own children—three at least. *Oh god, I'm totally over-thinking*—

"So how've you been?" Henry lurched me from my illogical landslide and when he turned to me, the concern in his eyes had me wondering if he'd somehow perceived my emotional rollercoaster.

"I'm fine."

"I'm sensing you're not."

I tilted my head at him. "I thought we were going to do this later, after our wonderful day."

"You're right. I'm sorry." Nodding, he guided us away from the waves and headed to the center of the island which was a vista of healthy green trees.

He touched the small of my back, just a gentle nudge of reassurance, and then moved in front of me to lead us up a small embankment. His impressive body enhanced my already spectacular view.

At the top, the grass was mottled patches of brown and green. Henry continued walking farther inland, and soon there was enough shade cover that I removed my hat and tousled my hair out.

I had assumed he knew where he was going, just like the last time he'd led me into the bushes, but when he started looking left and right, I wondered if he did. A dull roar caught my attention, and after a few seconds I realized what it was. I turned back toward the ocean, and my jaw fell as our plane took off.

"Where's he going?"

"Don't worry. He'll be back in a couple of hours."

"Oh." Trapped on a deserted island with Henry. *Yay me.*

"Here," Henry announced as he turned to me. "This looks like the perfect spot."

I glanced about the broad, grassy expanse. "Perfect for what?"

A small smile curled at his lips. "For us." He reached into his bag and pulled out a picnic blanket, very similar to the previous one.

"Did you buy these in bulk?"

Henry laughed, and it was such a deep, infectious melody that I joined him. "Maybe I should have."

The blanket billowed out, spilling across the grass, and Henry indicated for me to sit. Seconds later, he sat by my side.

"I hope you don't mind. I had so much fun last time, I'd like to improve on it."

"Oh." My insides did a little happy dance.

Henry placed his hand above my knee, just below the knot of my dress. "You make me feel alive, Jane."

The sun, filtering through the foliage, caught in his eyes, magnifying the intensity I saw in them. I chewed on my bottom lip and swallowed. "Henry . . ."

He touched his finger to my lips. "Shhh." His hand glided up my thigh, leaving a trail of goose bumps in its wake. "We'll chat later."

I nodded. "Okay."

He turned and kneeled to face me, the sun caught in his hair, highlighting slivers of silver. Our eyes met, and for a moment we just looked at each other. The intensity of that special moment had my heart thumping in my ears.

Ever so slowly, his hands glided up my thighs. Henry had a gentle smoothness about him that had my insides positively purring.

"You know I haven't kissed you yet."

"Yes you have."

"Yes, but not on your lips."

That was true. I tugged on my lip as the idea of him kissing me had my already happy insides dancing.

"May I?"

As I nodded, my tongue lashed out over my lips, offering him an invitation. He leaned forward, placing his hands on my cheeks, and the second I closed my eyes his lips found mine. His fingers glided down around my neck, and I tilted my head to the side, and as we moaned in unison, our lips parted. Our tongues forged across new territory, and it was an explorer's dream.

His kiss was soft yet eager. He tasted of peppermint, he smelt of spice, and he felt like heaven.

My insides purred a delicious beat as his tongue tangoed with mine. I melted under his touch as his fingers moved from my cheek to my breast. He cupped my boob in his palm and caressed it as if it were a delicate prize. I reached for his chest, found his nipple, and flicked my thumb over his hardened bud. His groan confirmed he liked my touch, and our breaths mingled in an inferno of lust as I alternated my attention from one nipple to the other.

Henry had mastered the art of kissing, and I was prepared to experience this glory until my lips were red raw. My clitoris had other ideas though, and the pulsing throb had me grinding my hips, begging him to touch me lower.

It was an eternity before we released each other, and Henry eased back. His large pupils threatened to consume the light blue in his eyes. His chest rose and fell, and the bulge in his groin was unmissable. He licked his lips and smiled. "Wow."

The word whispered off his lips like he was in a trance, and I grinned and nodded. "Wow."

He put his hand on my knee. "You do things to me that make me feel incredible. I haven't felt this way in a very long time."

"And you do things to my body that I've never felt before."

His smile was glorious, capturing every part of his face in the most magnificent of ways. "I'd like to kiss you again."

Hell yes. "Okay."

He lowered his eyes to my hips. "Down there."

Hell yes, a thousand time over. "Okay."

My heart galloped as Henry threaded his hands up my dress and tugged on my underpants. He drew them down slowly, and I raised my hips to help and pulled my dress up, allowing him to watch the show. His tongue lashed out over his lips, and his eyes glazed.

He curled the lacy fabric off my ankles and brought it to his nose, and when he inhaled, his eyes rolled backwards. Watching him do that was a potent aphrodisiac that had my building orgasm hitting a whole new level.

I raised my hips and parted my knees, and when his attention turned to my pussy a delicious shudder rolled through me. Henry's gaze was driven with intensity as he cast my underwear onto the rug.

I glided my hands up and down my thighs as I pumped my knees open and closed in a little game of peek-a-boo. The anticipation was excruciating. Yet I could wait for him all day. Henry was my suave tutor and when he was teaching me a new move, I was his ready and willing pupil.

Finally, he placed his hands on my knees and sucked in a shaky breath. His trembling fingers glided down my thighs and parted my legs. He licked his lips and leaned forward, and the second his tongue touched my pussy I clawed at the blanket and gasped.

He raised my right leg and I bent it when his left hand cupped behind my knee. His hot tongue glided up and down my velvet folds as the fingers on his other hand entered me. As his tongue licked my clit, hot, hard, and wet, his finger probed in and out of my pussy with fevered thrusts. Rockets shot through me that lit up every nerve in my body. My orgasm hit me, fast and explosive, and I screamed as I climaxed.

As I drove my fingers through his salt-and-pepper hair, Henry's head bobbed up and down as he lapped at my juices. His fingers continued to plunge, drawing out every last drop of lust from my body.

I heard nothing. I smelt nothing. But I felt every single exquisite sensation that rippled through me. He didn't just take me to the edge; Henry took me way beyond it. It was sensation overload, and a magical euphoria gripped me, eliminating everything else in the world except my body. He had a gift, and I was so willing to take it.

It was an eternity before he pulled up from between my thighs. His glazed eyes and partially opened lips had him looking drunk. Drunk on ecstasy.

He licked his lips. "Yummy."

"Thank you."

He chuckled. "You're getting better at this." He smiled that glorious smile that said everything in the world was perfect.

I propped up on my elbows and drew my knees together, and that was when I noticed the dark stain on his trousers. He looked down at his pants and then at me, but he didn't look embarrassed. In fact, he seemed pleased.

"You do that to me."

The look of pure satisfaction on his face had me smiling with him.

He reached into his bag and handed me a towel. "Excuse me for a second," he said, then he grabbed the bag and disappeared into the bushes.

Using the solitude to wipe myself, I once again marveled at how messy sex had become. I tugged on my undies and stood up in time to see Henry walk toward me. He'd changed his pants.

"Wow, you *are* organized."

"Yep, you should know that by now."

It was true. Every moment with Henry seemed to be perfectly choreographed. I wondered if I'd be able to keep up with that perfection.

I didn't get a chance to ponder that question because Henry grabbed my cheeks and kissed me, just a simple, fun kiss.

He bent over, grabbed the blanket and dragged it to the side to shake off the sand. "Hungry?" He asked as he folded the blanket into the bag.

"Always."

"Good." He grabbed my hand and with my bag over my shoulder and my hat on my head again, he led me back down to the beach.

We were silent as we strolled back toward where the plane had dropped us off.

"What's that?" I pointed at an umbrella in the distance.

"That's lunch."

Beneath the blue-and-white umbrella was a small wooden table and two chairs. A champagne bucket was nestled in the sand to one side, and the metallic-topped foil on the bottle inside reflected the water, giving it a blue hue.

The second we arrived, Henry pulled out a chair for me and I sat. He went straight to the champagne and had the cork popped in seconds. The bubbles fizzed as he poured it into the two glasses. He put the bottle back in the bucket, offered me one of the glasses, and held his own forward. "Here's to secluded beaches."

I giggled. "To secluded beaches." Our glasses chimed as we brought them together.

The champagne was cold, sweet and delicious.

Henry gave me a plate and cutlery and grabbed a set for himself, then he proceeded to remove the lids off the Tupperware and position them about the table. The selection was magnificent, and my stomach rumbling increased with every dish that was revealed. Once he'd finished, there was very little room left on the table.

He sat at my side. "Ladies first."

My first attack was on the prawns. I grabbed four of them and a dollop of pink seafood sauce from a small glass jar. Henry followed my lead, and we set about peeling the prawns.

"So are you ready to talk to me?"

I yanked the prawn's head off. "I am talking to you."

"You know what I mean."

"Ohhh, I'd hoped you'd forgotten about that." Our day had been perfect so far, and the last thing I wanted to do was divulge my crazy challenge to him.

"Come on, Jane. There's no need to hide anything from me."

As I dunked my peeled prawn into the sauce and bit into it, I tried to unscramble the thoughts blazing through my mind.

Yes, I didn't really need to hide anything from Henry, but did I want to ruin the special thing we had going on?

"Are you having an affair?"

"What?" I swallowed my prawn. "No! Is that what you think?"

"Yes, of course. You're sneaking around pretending to be Memphis, and you get jittery and evasive when I ask too many questions. Don't forget I've experienced a cheating partner before."

"So have I. And I'd never do that. Not to anyone."

"Good. Then whatever it is that's troubling you can't be as bad as you think."

"Pfft." I rolled my eyes. "Okay." I sighed. "I'll tell you."

"Good. Have another prawn."

I wrenched the head off the prawn and tossed the scrap toward a seagull that'd landed off to my side. Here we go. "After my fiancé cheated on me, I was so hurt by what he'd done that I couldn't stand the sight of him, or any of the dozen or so women who'd slept with him. In that small town, it was nearly impossible to avoid the daily confrontation. So I moved to the Gold Coast."

Henry sipped his champagne, silently listening to my sorry story.

"I spent the next three years consumed with my work and improving my fitness. But I didn't find time for me. No dates, no men, no sex. Not once."

"That's a shame."

"There were two problems. One is my crazy night shift, which means it's hard to go on dates. Believe me, my girlfriend had tried to hook me up many times. But the second problem was . . ." I cleared my throat, "I don't have sex with strangers."

"Ahhh."

"Ahhh what?"

"I assume this is where the costume came in."

"Correct. On the first of January, I did the craziest thing. I put on a French maid costume that I'd bought for the fancy-dress staff Christmas party, and pretending to be someone else, I used my staff access card to walk into a complete stranger's room and masturbated in front of him."

He clapped his hands. "I love it."

I blinked at him. "You do?"

"Hell yes. I bet it was one of the most erotic moments of your life."

I nodded. "Uh-huh."

"So you just kept on doing it?"

"Uh-huh."

He cocked his head. "There's more, isn't there?"

I nodded and gulped back the full glass of champagne. Henry reached for the bottle, topped me up, and then turned to me, waiting.

A big sigh rumbled off my lips. "My girlfriend, Lolita, challenged me to do it every week for a year."

"What?" He slapped his hand on his thigh and burst out laughing.

"You don't think that's weird?"

"Yes, it's weird." He continued chuckling. "But it's also fabulous. So how are you going with the challenge?"

I spread my hands apart. "This is week thirty-five. I haven't missed one yet."

"So what . . . you need to have sex fifty-two times in fifty-two weeks?"

I shook my head. "No, not sex. Just a sexual experience."

He raised an eyebrow. "So you haven't had sex with any of them?"

I plopped my elbows on the table and covered my face with my hands. "Please don't ask me that."

Henry wrapped his hand around my wrist and eased my left hand away from my face. "I'm only asking to see if there's hope for me."

I turned with my jaw dropped. "You're not grossed out?"

He reached for both my hands and held them in his. "No, I'm not grossed out, as you put it. I'm fascinated. I certainly don't see anything wrong with it. You're single; I assume the men are willing. It's not like you're drugging them before you have your wicked way with them."

I huffed and rolled my eyes. "Of course not."

"I actually think it's fantastic. You get to explore your sexuality, and you get to meet different men. It'd always bugged me why you'd picked an old bugger like me."

"I told you, you're not old."

His eyes bulged. "Have you had someone older than me?"

I gasped, and was two seconds off saying no, when I stopped. "I'm not going to kiss and tell."

"Awww, that's no fun. I'd love to hear all about them."

"That's a little weird, don't you think?"

"I'm weird? You're the one with the split personality."

I pouted. "I don't have a split personality."

"Well, I, for one, am truly grateful that you do. And to your friend and her challenge. Otherwise, I would never have met you. We wouldn't be having this lovely lunch on a deserted beach." He spread his hands at the view. "And I certainly wouldn't be experiencing you and your delicious body."

My heart fluttered. This conversation had gone much better than I could've expected. Maybe there was hope for me once this crazy journey was over.

"So what happens at the end of this year?" He must've read my mind.

I shrugged. "I have no idea."

We were silent for a while as we nibbled at the antipasti platter.

"I'm glad you told me this, Jane."

"Really?"

"Yes. Now I know I have until the end of the year to teach you a few more things."

I burst out laughing and reached for my champagne. "I'll drink to that."

We chinked our glasses together, and I drank back the delicate bubbles.

The following hour or so was consumed with eating and talking much more freely about ourselves. I learned more about his life, career, and children, and he in turn learned more about my life in Mildura, my job, and Lolita.

A dull roar had me looking to the sky. I spotted our plane and watched it come in to land and glide right up to our beachside picnic. We helped Steve pack up the equipment, and soon we all climbed back into the plane. Henry took the front position this time, and I settled into the seat behind him.

The flight back was much shorter as the pilot took a more direct route. We landed at Sea World Resort within twenty minutes.

Once we were back on the sand, Henry handed the pilot some money and shook his hand. A delightful sense of contentment washed over me as we strolled back to the car and hopped in.

"Thank you for a magical day."

"Thank you for fulfilling another one of my bucket list items."

"Which one? The plane flight or the sex on the beach?"

He laughed. "Actually, you're nearly right. It was a seaplane flight and sex on a deserted island."

"We didn't have sex."

"We had fun though." He raised his eyebrows, as if seeking confirmation.

"Yes, we had fun. Are you flying home now?"

"No, as a matter of fact I'm staying in your hotel, room ten."

I turned and frowned at him. "You're kidding?"

"No."

"When did you check in?"

"Around seven o'clock this morning. I must've just missed you."

"Yeah."

"But don't worry—I'll forgive you if you don't sneak into my room."

"I have work later."

"I know."

"And I need to get some sleep now."

"Jane, it's okay. I know."

"Oh."

When we arrived at the hotel, he used his room key to open the security gate, drove down to the underground car park, and reversed into his designated spot. We climbed out, and the sound of our doors closing echoed about the concrete space.

I didn't want to walk into the hotel with him and paused at the front of the car, unsure how to say it.

"So I guess this is where we say goodbye."

Wow, he really was intuitive. "Thank you."

It took all my might not to wrap my arms around him and hold my body to his. He caressed my cheeks and lowered his lips to mine for a brief kiss. "I'll be back, Memphis Jane."

"I'll be waiting, my suave tutor." A little bit of Memphis had instigated that comment, and I instantly regretted the ridiculousness of it.

"Is that what you call me?" Even in the dimmed lights of the parking lot, his grin was impressive.

I'm such an idiot. I nodded.

"I like it. Now off you go, or I'll have to tear your clothes off and teach you another lesson."

Before I did something stupid and allowed him to make good on that threat, I kissed his cheek and tossed my bag over my shoulder, and with my hat in my hand, I walked up the ramp to the front of the building.

Back in my room, I went to the bath, turned on the taps, and poured in a good slosh of the new bubble bath Marjorie had bought me. I undressed and removed what little makeup I had on and brushed my teeth.

I grabbed my diary and rested it onto the edge of the tub along with a fresh cup of green tea. Before the bath had filled, I slipped into the warm water. The muscles in my body quickly unraveled as the tumbling water raised the level higher with each second.

Sitting up, I reached for my diary and turned to the 24th of August. At the top I wrote *Mr. Henry Addison Room 10* and next to that I wrote *Soaring to New Heights.* That was exactly what today was, and not just because of that wonderful joyride.

I wrote in great detail about how Henry could produce orgasms that were unparalleled to any other. I'd had many orgasms this year, but somehow the ones with him were a level above the others. Was that because of what he did, or was it because of how I felt about him? I'd wondered if I was falling in love with Henry once before.

But was I prepared to fall in love with a man who may not want more children?

I snapped the diary shut and slipped beneath the water. With my toe in the faucet to stifle the flow of water, I pondered that question. Was I willing to sacrifice having children to marry the man I loved?

Love was about sacrifice, but was I prepared to sacrifice that?

As the warm water caressed me, the potent question consumed my mind.

.

2ND SEPTEMBER
DOUBLE TROUBLE
Room 33 - Hot Horizon Hotel

As the elevator crawled down to the lobby, I tugged my hair up into a high ponytail and tied a band around it. I checked my reflection and wished I'd applied foundation as my freckles were having a little party on my cheeks tonight. The slight bags under my eyes were a perfect representation of how tired I felt. I hadn't slept well today. For some reason, I just hadn't been able to switch my brain off for long enough to get a deep sleep. Hopefully tonight was busy otherwise I was likely to face-plant on the desk and stay there.

Before the elevator dinged, a dull noise emanated from the usually quiet lobby. The doors opened to dozens of people milling about. They appeared to be younger than me, in their early twenties or so, and I was instantly reminded of the twenty-nine rooms that had been booked by the Southern Cross University in Sydney. It looked like my wish for a busy night was about to be granted after all.

Marjorie looked up from her seat at reception and smiled at me.

"Hey, Marj, how was your day?"

She rolled her eyes. "It's been crazy."

"Everything okay though?"

"Yes, except for these bloody uni students. They're a noisy bunch. They've been coming and going all day. Oh and there's a couple of weirdos in the bar asking for Memphis."

A couple? I gripped the counter, fearing my legs would buckle beneath me. "Oh, really?"

"Yep. I don't know who this Memphis woman is, but I'm beginning to believe John. Maybe we do have a lady of the night lurking here."

Oh God. Lady of the . . . I'm going to be sick.

"Anyway." She opened the bottom drawer, removed her bag and slung it over her shoulder. "I'm off. Popcorn and movie night with the kids." She hugged me to her chest. "Have a good one."

"Thanks."

The second Marjorie toddled away, I collapsed into the chair.

A couple were asking for Memphis! Who could they be? And were they together? Or was it just a coincidence that they were both here on the same night? That could be messy.

I had to see who they were. After sucking in a few deep breaths to steady my tumbling thoughts, I put the 'back in five minutes' sign on the counter, pushed up from the seat and forced my wobbly legs to lead me into the bar. The noise from both the people and the music bordered on deafening. The university students outnumbered the other slightly older patrons I spotted in the dim lights. I had a flashback to the young virgin who'd experimented with Memphis months ago. He'd been a uni student. I scoured my brain, trying to recall exactly what he'd looked like. Sandy blond hair, a trimmed goatee. As I weaved my way through the gyrating throng toward the bar, I scrutinized all the blond men I could see.

Tania was busy serving drinks and both her and the bar manager, Pete, turned toward me as I stepped in behind the counter.

"Hey guys. Busy night."

"Sure is. This lot came in about an hour ago." From Tania's grin, I'd say she was happy with the crowd. Our usual demographic was much older than this, and I often thought Tania was out of place working in our bar. She was a pretty, petite blonde with a quick smile, and despite being just twenty-two, she had no problem handling unruly patrons who were often twice her age.

As her attention was diverted to a young man at the serving station, I scanned the crowd, searching for a familiar face, but didn't recognize anybody. Maybe they've gone. I wasn't sure if I was happy or not about that thought. The curiosity alone was going to kill me. I needed to check the booths at the back to be sure.

A brilliant idea hit me. "Would you like me to collect some glasses for you?"

Pete wiped his forehead across his sleeve. "That'd be great."

I pushed back through the swinging gate and proceeded to gather empty glasses dotted around the tables. With a row of empty beer glasses lined up my arm, I turned around, and the sight of the man in the corner booth hit me like a sonic boom. Bathed in a red hue from the fancy bar lighting sat the gorgeous magazine-worthy plumber from months ago.

Our eyes met, and a flood of fear ripped through me as recognition lit up his face. He waved and when the other person in the booth turned around to look at me, I wanted to evaporate into thin air. I was frozen, trapped in a mental frenzy as my trembling knees threatened to have me crumble to the floor.

The plumber and the electrician, sitting in my bar. It sounded like a bad joke.

It was bad news, that was for sure. I forced my feet to move, and in a blur I managed to offload the empty glasses and despite my race to get out of there, I didn't break any of them. After assuring Peter and Tania I'd pop in again a bit later, I scurried back to my haven behind the reception.

But seconds later, my already racing heart hit an explosive level as two of Memphis's past conquests walked toward me.

They were stunning representations of the male species. The plumber could grace center stage of any male revue show, while the electrician had that cute, you-can-trust-me-with-your-life look about him. They both grinned like drunken teenagers as they crossed the distance from the bar to me in long confident strides.

"Hello Jane," the plumber said. "Do you remember me?"

My stomach contents were seconds away from launching upwards as I shook my head and shrugged. "Sorry, no. Should I?" Hopefully those words actually came out of my mouth.

"I'm Mickey the fixer." His steely eyes drilled into me. "I'm the plumber you called a few months ago."

"Oh, hi." I waved. *I'm an idiot.*

"Yeah, and I'm Jackson. You remember me, don't you?"

"Um, oh yes. You were the electrician who came in the middle of the night."

"Yep, Jackson Kane. Your sizzling electrician."

Mickey scrunched his face at his mate, then splayed his fingers on the counter and pushed them toward me. "My mate and I are looking for Memphis."

I tried to ignore his intoxicating scent, even though it was the perfect blend of woody tones and hot-blooded man. "I'm sorry, but I don't know who you're talking about."

"It's okay." Jackson touched his nose in some kind of 'your secret is safe with me' move. "We won't tell anyone."

I shook my head. "Sorry, guys, but you must be mistaken."

133

"Right." Mickey pulled back and inhaled nice and deep, filling out his already broad chest. "Well, when you see her, let her know we're in room thirty-three. Waiting."

My head spun. *They're in a room. They booked a room. For me? Holy crap.*

Mickey turned and strode away, and I reverted my attention to the enormous grin on Jackson's face. He wriggled his eyebrows. "Tell Memphis her sizzling electrician is waiting."

I stifled a giggle as he spun and scurried across the marble tiles to his mate's side.

While Jackson jiggled from foot to foot as they waited, Mickey stood, his feet slightly apart, his hips rock solid, as rigid as a battle-hardened soldier. The second they disappeared into the elevator, I glanced at the clock. It was 11.10p.m. Being a Friday night, there was a good chance Lolita was still awake. As discreetly as I could behind the counter, I madly tapped out a text.

'Trouble. 2 men here.'

Her reply came in a flash. '2??? Cryptic.'

I huffed. 'Electrician and plumber.'

'What? Together?'

'Yep.'

There was a slight delay before her reply popped up. 'Holy shit, well get your gear off and go fuck those 2 puppies.'

"Hi."

I snapped my eyes up from the text to see two young women at the counter.

I quickly flipped my phone over. "Sorry. How can I help you?"

"Can you tell us where the nearest taxi stand is?"

"There isn't one nearby, but I can call a cab for you. Where are you going?"

"We were thinking about the Hard Rock cafe."

I tried to ignore my dinging phone. "Okay. I can call a taxi for you, but at this time of night it may take a while. The best thing to do would be to walk to the tram station, as it goes to Cavil Avenue and Hard Rock is right there."

"Is the tram station far?"

My phone started vibrating across the desk, and I palmed it in place. Obviously Lolly was trying to ring me now. "No, only about a ten-minute walk."

As I gave the women directions, my phone dinged again, and a hot flush blazed up my neck.

The second the ladies disappeared out the front sliding glass doors, I flipped my phone over and read the messages.

'Hello.'

'Jane, you there?'

'Oh don't be like that.'

'Want me to call you?'

'Okay, I'm calling.'

'Shit, babe, you're worrying me now.'

I glanced about, and deciding it was safe to text, I shot her a message. 'Sorry, really busy here. Can't call.'

'Okay. I thought you must have passed out.'

'I'm close.'

'With adrenalin?'

'Fear!!!!'

'Of what?'

Of what? Had she even read my message? 'TWO MEN.'

'Hell yes. Bucket-list tick. Go for it.'

I should've known she'd be like this. 'Have you ever done it?'

'Shit yeah.'

Thousands of questions ran through my brain, and I tried to sift out the right one to ask. '2 men?' I started with the obvious.

'Yep.'

Two men . . . I couldn't even imagine how that would work. It was tricky enough just having one man to concentrate on.

'And 2 women.' Her next text had me flopping into my seat.

I was dumbstruck, yet I should've known Lolly would have done that. She'd always been very open with her sexuality. Not like me. Before I'd met her, I didn't even talk about sex. Now though, she knew everything about my devious exploits.

My dinging phone dragged me back to the conversation.

'Have I scared you?'

'No.'

"What then?

'I'm not like you.'

'Memphis is!'

I couldn't stand texting anymore. I put the 'back in five minutes' sign on the counter and raced into the lobby toilets with my phone. But that plan was foiled by the six or so young women congregating in there.

"Hi, ladies, sorry for the interruption. I was just going to check the toilet paper situation."

"That one's empty." The dark-haired woman stopped applying lipstick long enough to point at the last cubicle along.

"Okay," I said. "I'll be back in a second."

Damn. I raced to the stationery cupboard, placed my phone on top of the filing cabinet, and tugged the bulk packet of toilet paper from the shelf. With six rolls in my arms, I crossed the lobby and pushed backwards through the doors.

"Here you go, ladies." The women were loudly discussing the benefits of lip-liner as I proceeded to replenish the toilet paper and added a spare roll to each cubicle. I took the opportunity to go to the toilet myself, and when I came out they'd gone. After I washed my hands, I returned to reception. The six women were now hovering between the Triple H Bar and the lobby, and as I waited for them to make a decision my phone repeatedly dinged.

The second the women disappeared into the bar, I dived into the back office and without even checking her messages, I rang Lolita.

"Jesus, babe, what's going on?"

I huffed. "It's nuts here tonight. Fifty or so uni students up from Sydney."

"Is that all? Okay, tell me about the dueling hunks."

I poked my nose out of the room and confirming all was clear at reception, I put my back against the wall and tried to calm my racing heart. "Do you remember me telling you about the plumber from months ago?"

"Yes. *Top Model* gorgeous, he fingered you from behind while you still had your clothes on."

My jaw dropped. "What the hell? Are you recording our conversations or something?"

"No, but that's a great idea."

"Lolly!"

"What? They'd be a hoot to listen to again."

"Will you stop it?"

"Okay, sorry. Carry on."

"So Mickey told his mate, the electrician, about me—"

"Memphis."

"Yes, Memphis. Well anyway, both of them are here together."

"And . . .?"

"They were in the bar, but they came out and asked me to inform Memphis that they were here."

"Ohhh, this's gold, babe."

"No, it's not gold—it's a disaster."

"This's the perfect chance to have a threesome."

I clenched my jaw, closed my eyes, and pictured naked bodies crawling all over each other. I snapped my eyes open, grateful to eradicate the images. "Lolly, I don't think I can do that."

"Sure you can. Two men pleasuring you—it's fucking hot."

I squirmed at the thought. "It's just . . . it seems a little slutty."

"Don't be silly. What's the definition of a slut, anyway?"

"A woman who has many casual sex partners."

"Oh, so I guess you're already there." She giggled.

"That's not helping, Lolly."

"Well it's true. You're—"

"Still not helping," I interrupted.

"Right. Okay. Let's be serious. Have you had sex with these guys?"

"No, neither of them, and when the electrician was here last time he said Mickey had told him the rules."

"Good. So the first rule of threesomes is that you must establish the ground rules."

"Hey, Lolly. You don't understand. I don't want a . . ." I cleared my throat and checked that the reception area was vacant. "A threesome," I whispered. "I want to figure out how to get rid of these guys."

"Now, now, let's not be too hasty."

I groaned.

"I do believe you once said you didn't do casual sex either."

"Awww, that's not fair."

"I'm just saying don't discount it so quickly."

I wanted to crawl into the stationery cupboard and shut the doors on my crazy world.

"Are you listening?"

"Yeeeees." I was about as enthusiastic as a prisoner on death row.

"Okay, let's just think about this. First off, you're the one in charge. So you set the rules, and if either of those guys break them, you can knee them in the balls. You're good at that."

"Ha ha. Funny."

"Actually, you don't even have to have sex with them. Just have a bit of fun. Tie them up or something and take turns having your way with each of them while the other one watches."

I moaned.

"Hey, remember that couple you watched having sex? That made you so fucking horny you grinned like a nutter for weeks."

"No I didn't."

"Hell yeah you did. Don't tell me you didn't like it."

I had instant recall of the Irish guy and his stunning mistress. It'd been incredible seeing the way they touched each other. Watching their unbridled passion had swiftly sliced another layer off my naivety.

"Oh, I know." Lolly launched me back to the present. "They could blindfold you and you could guess which guy was doing what to you."

I heard a cough, and my eyes bulged. "Oh my god!"

"What?"

"Was that Cal?"

"Of course. Say hi to Jane." She put me on speaker.

"Hi, Jane."

Oh faaarrkkk. I slid down the wall until my knees were at my chin. "Has he heard everything you've said?"

"Of course. But don't worry; he's cool."

"So he knows you've had a threesome?"

"Of course. You know we don't have any secrets, and it wasn't just one threesome."

"And he's okay with it."

"Shit yeah. It makes him randy, doesn't it, babe?"

I pictured Cal's cheeky grin. "Of course."

"Besides, Jane, what happens before you meet a guy is exactly that— something you did before you met him. You can't undo the past. It's what you do once you get together that counts."

"Well said, honey." Calvin's deep voice cut into her speech.

"Thanks, babe."

Subtle sucking noises drifted down the phone, and for the hundredth time I was given an open demonstration of their love for each other. Maybe their choice to share their past exploits, thereby eliminating secrets, had made their passion and love so strong.

"Anyway, babe, Cal and I think you should have the threesome."

"Sure do," Calvin weighed in on the conversation.

"So here's what you're going to do."

I huffed. "What?"

"Oh, cheer up. You've got men lining up to be with you. Six months ago, your vagina had almost sealed back over."

I am ready to die. "Oh great. Thanks for sharing that."

"You're welcome. Anyway, it sounds like you're in for a busy night at work, correct?"

I turned to check the counter and although no one was standing there, based on all the noise in the lobby, I assumed there were still dozens of people around. "Probably."

"So spend the night thinking about it. Those hunky hunks upstairs aren't going anywhere, and come morning, you can go up to them with a plan."

As I silently thought about it, she went silent, too. It would've killed her.

"Maybe," I finally said.

"I bet you do it."

"Really?" I forced sarcasm into my voice. "What do you bet?"

"Oooh, Memphis has a challenge for me."

"Cool." Calvin seemed to be enjoying this.

"Okay, I think a bit of reverse psychology is called for." She moaned. "If you do it, I'll eat cheesecake with my green tea on Tuesday."

That was a huge challenge for Lolly. I'd never seen her eat sweets. "Okay, that's a deal. But I'm not telling you anything until we're sitting at the coffee shop on Tuesday."

"Oh, what? You can't do that."

I pushed up from the floor, almost feeling normal again. "Yes, I can."

"Oh fuck, babe, you'll kill me. Anyway, all this talk about threesomes has made me horny again, so . . . gotta go."

She hung up, and I giggled as I returned to the reception desk.

The night flew by, and I was stunned when Needledick suddenly appeared at the counter. I'd been busy all night and was so engrossed in catching up with the check-out paperwork for today that I hadn't noticed the time.

"Morning, Jane, how was your night?"

"Crazy. I'm sure these uni students don't sleep."

He huffed as he tossed his keys into the top drawer. "I'd love a good night's sleep."

I was seconds away from asking him how his mother was when I caught myself and turned my thoughts to the handover process. "You have about nine guests arriving this morning. All the check-in cards are here." I patted the pile of index cards on the counter. "And fourteen guests are checking out."

"Okay." His enthusiasm was non-existent.

I grabbed my bag. "Alright, I'm off to sleep then. Have fun."

"Yeah, not likely. I need today like a hole in the head."

I had the impression he was dying for me to ask what was wrong, but I resisted with all my might. With his dour comment perfect for my departure, I turned on my heel and tugged my skirt down as I walked toward the elevator. Within five minutes, I was in my room and had both taps running full-on into the bath. I poured in a decent quantity of Marjorie's bubble bath and then went to the kitchen to make breakfast.

With my peanut butter on toast and a strong hot coffee in hand, I returned to the tub, stripped off, and hopped in. As the warm water hugged me like a true friend, my thoughts went to Lolita. The relationship she had with Calvin was special. Was it because they shared everything?

Would I be able to tell a future husband-to-be that I'd had a threesome? The concept of a discussion like that horrified me, and as I nibbled on my toast, I tried to force my brain away from it.

But I couldn't.

The more I thought about the two hot men waiting for me upstairs, the more it consumed me. But then I realized it wasn't me they were waiting for . . . it was Memphis. Memphis would be the one having the threesome. Strong, confident, sexy Memphis.

I really have gone mad.

I swallowed a large gulp of coffee and then grabbed my cotton washer and lathered it in soap. As I ran the warm cloth over my legs, my mind skipped over the never-ending positions three sexed up people could get themselves into. As much as I didn't think it would, my insides pulsed with pleasure at the images playing through my brain.

Could I do this? Could I share my libido with two men?

I'd be in charge. I could dictate who did what. And what went where. I giggled at that.

Suddenly, the decision was made. Memphis was back, and the two hunky spunks were about to meet one very curious woman.

I jumped out of the bath, toweled off, and applied my abundant Memphis makeup with haste and skill. My dilemma came at my choice of wig. The black one I'd worn for each of them before had been a mess after Jackson had stomped on it last time, but it was a total loss after my recent attack on it with the hairspray for my rock-chick look.

Without any other solution, I decided Mickey and Jackson were about to meet the blond-haired, blue-eyed Memphis

With makeup and hair done, I stood before my closet and scoured it for choices. The green satin in my Poison Ivy costume caught my eye, and I shoved the other clothes from around it and pulled it off the rack. Poison Ivy—beautiful, deadly, and she took what she wanted. I laughed as I declared this as the perfect outfit to wear while taking on my two crusaders upstairs.

I slipped on the green satin underpants, then, tugging the fabric together inch by inch on the boned corset, I gradually hooked the clips until it reached my breasts. With the corset in place my breasts were plump bulging mounds that threatened to burst from the top after any movement.

The green shoes that I'd worn last time hadn't been worn since. I slipped them on and then finished the outfit with the long green satin gloves that reached my elbows. With the costume in place, I glanced in the mirror. *Wow.* The transformation was both shocking and perfect.

I tugged on my trusty trench coat, checked my bag for emergency supplies, and before I changed my mind, I headed out my door.

With every second I rode in the elevator up to the sixth floor, my heart elevated a notch, too. Every sexual experience I'd had this year had taught me something, and I'd grown in confidence with them, too. What I was planning to do now though put me right back in the novice corner, and I was equally excited and petrified at the same time.

But I'd come this far. I was dressed. Ready. And more than a little inquisitive.

At the door for room thirty-three, I fitted my mask in place and after a quick glance up and down the hall, I removed my coat and knocked.

A little commotion erupted through the door, and I heard someone say, "I told you she'd come." Seconds later, a grinning Jackson greeted me. He wore the hotel-supplied bath robe. *Just the bath robe.*

My sizzling electrician whistled. "Holy shiiiiitt. You look hot."

"Move aside, Jackson." Memphis was here, and she was in charge.

Jackson stepped backwards and as I passed him, he smacked me on the bottom. I spun on my heel, and the cheeky grin melted from his face.

"Sorry."

"You will be."

He rubbed his hands together as the door swung closed and clicked into place.

I turned, crossed the room, and flung my coat and bag onto the table. "You two are very naughty, coming here and asking for me."

"Oh, we know." Jackson's growing erection and cheeky grin showed he was as horny as he was mischievous.

Mickey stood in the middle of the room, poised halfway between the bathroom and the bed. He wore steel gray track pants that matched the steel grey of his eyes. In fact, everything about him was like steel, from his steely abs to his rigid stance. The white drawstring on his pants was undone and fell either side of his groin, which wasn't as happy as Jackson's was.

"You've changed your hair." Unlike his excited sidekick, there was no inflection in Mickey's voice. Was that good? Or bad?

"Yes." Did he recognize me? By the blank expression on his face it was impossible to gauge what he was thinking. My heart hammered in my chest as I waited for a reaction. But there wasn't one. He remained statue-like, rooted to the floor. Jackson rubbed his hands together and stepped toward me.

I held my gloved hand up, making him pause. "Stop right there, Captain Horny."

"Okay." He nodded with enthusiasm.

I glanced at Mickey, and a small smile curling on his lips matched a slight twinkle in his eyes.

"Here's the rules." I stepped back so I could view both of them easily. "Number one, I'm in charge. Number two, like last time, we won't be having sex." My heart pounded as I waited out the silence. I turned to Jackson. "Okay?"

"Yes, fine with me." He rubbed his hands together as if agreeing to an ice cream.

"And you?" I turned my attention to the sexy plumber and noticed the bulge in his groin was pushing past the two white ropes dangling down the front of his pants.

He nodded. "Whatever you say."

"Right, now I need two chairs, over here." The second I pointed to where Mickey stood, Jackson began dragging two chairs over.

"Now get on your knees and bend over."

Jackson stripped his robe off.

"Did I say disrobe?" I raised my voice, confirming I was in charge.

"Oh shit, sorry. Sorry." He grabbed the robe off the floor and pulled it back on.

"Now on your knees and bend over the chair."

Jackson did as he was told.

"Come on, mate, what're you doing?" Jackson looked up at Mickey.

I couldn't read the expression on Mickey's face, but his groin was certainly talking to me. Mickey looked toward me and our eyes met. A strange sense of knowing crossed from him to me, and for a couple of heart-pounding seconds I feared the worst. He actually had recognized me. Or somehow knew I'd never done this before. Either way, my show was over.

But then, his rigid demeanor changed. Either he'd talked himself out of it or maybe into it, because he stepped around his mate and fell onto his knees at the second chair.

Jackson clapped him on the back.

Mickey spun to him. His clenched teeth squared out the muscle in his jaw. "Dude, touch me again and I'll fucking kill ya."

"Right. Sorry."

I nearly burst out laughing. These two were poles apart in sexuality. The plumber oozed it with every calm move; Captain Horny was exactly the opposite.

Stepping forward, I raised the bathrobe up over the electrician's ass, folded the fabric to keep it in place, and then gave him a whack on his bottom. "Don't ever come to this hotel again!"

"Okay."

I smacked him again. "Say 'yes, Memphis.'"

"Yes, Memphis." He grinned at his mate, and Mickey looked at him with what appeared to be mild disinterest.

I stepped behind the plumber. "Track pants down." This was going to be a test, as Mickey didn't seem to be interested in my little show of domination. But I didn't have to wait long. He hooked his thumbs into the elastic sides and whipped them down to his knees in a flash.

My breath caught in my throat as I admired this gloriousness. The two sexy bottoms were a sight to behold. Each of them was slightly different. Mickey's was more muscular with olive skin, whilst Jackson's was milky white and round.

I stepped forward and paddled my gloved hand across Mickey's bottom. He clenched after I slapped him, bulging those muscles perfectly. "Don't ever come to this hotel again."

"Yes, Memphis."

I slapped him again, just for the fun of it. "Good."

I moved side on to him, then curled my gloved hand over his ass, round, and down between his legs. Mickey shifted his knees apart, giving me room, and I cupped his balls in my hand. The weight of them surprised me, and as I caressed them in my fingers, Mickey groaned.

It was the first uncontrolled emotion he'd emitted, and it shot heatwaves through me. I adjusted my stance so I was able to smack him again. With his heavy balls filling my left palm, I gave him a whack with my right. Mickey groaned, and as his balls sucked upward, he pushed his hands forward and gripped on to the back of the chair. As my insides pulsed out a heady beat, I smacked him again and tried to memorize every raunchy millisecond of it.

I stepped from Mickey to Captain Horny and repeating the move, I cupped his balls and smacked his bottom.

"Oh yeah. Do it again?"

I whacked him harder. "Shhh. No talking."

"Yes, Memphis."

"I said no talking." That called for another smack, so I did.

I moved between them, Mickey on my left and Jackson on my right. They were the perfect distance apart to enable me to reach down and cup their balls at the same time. As I squeezed and caressed their scrotums, the two men reacted differently. While Jackson squirmed and gasped, Mickey clenched his jaw and gripped the chair. My insides positively purred at the control I had over these two hunks.

It was time to turn the attention to me.

"Okay, men. Up, strip, and sit."

They obeyed, and within seconds I enjoyed the most exquisite sight—two incredibly hot men, naked. The sun streamed in through the blinds, bathing their chiseled bodies in a delicious warm glow. Their cocks stood rigid, towering up from between their legs. What Jackson had in length, Mickey made up for in girth.

Mickey sat up straight, unmoving, with his hands at his sides, however the electrician wriggled constantly, as if a steady current coursed through him.

I pointed at the electrician's cock. "So," I said. "What do we have here?"

Jackson wiggled his eyebrows. "My pleasure-seeking missile."

I swallowed my laughter by turning to the sexy plumber. "What do you call yours?"

"My cock." He rolled his eyes at his mate.

I chuckled at that. I couldn't help it. These two incredibly horny men were funny. They were a comedy act and a male-revue duo all in one, and I was center-stage in the best show on earth. Until this year, I'd never realized sex could be so much fun. For the hundredth time, I was glad I'd stepped out of my comfort zone.

Using my teeth, I pinched the tips of my glove off my fingers, then I held the green satin fingertips toward their mouths. As if we were in a perfectly choreographed movie—a porno movie, maybe—the two men worked in unison to remove my gloves from my arms and cast them aside with perfect timing.

With my hands free, I plumped my boobs up over my corset. It was easy as they were just about ready to burst out anyway. I'd made this move with my sexy batman, and I remembered how it'd driven him wild. One look at Jackson was enough to know he was enjoying it, but Mickey was still a man of stone. Maybe he wasn't into this threesome thing.

With my boobs balancing over the top of my corset, I stepped toward Mickey and straddled him. With my legs either side of his, I eased forward. The head of his penis nudged at my vagina, teasing my purring insides. I placed my hands on his shoulders and lined my breasts up with his mouth. "Suck," I commanded.

And Mickey did. He closed his eyes and wrapped his lips around my nipple. The swiftness of his move had the already greedy orgasm growing inside me swelling. His hands found my ass, and as he squeezed my globes and sucked my nipple with lust-fueled intensity, I turned to look at Jackson.

The electrician was positively sizzling. His grin was huge, his eyes wide, and his hand glided up and down his cock with slow, measured moves. Just seeing him like that sent a rocket through me, and I moaned as I clenched my insides, trying to tame the beast growing in me. I ground my pussy over Mickey's cock, applying pressure to my clit with each movement. Showing my breasts undivided attention, Mickey's lips sucked. His teeth gently nipped, and his hot tongue glided across my hardened nipple over and over. Jackson alternated his hand from his cock to his balls, and it reminded me that I needed to alternate my attention between the two men.

Reluctantly, I snapped my nipple from Mickey's suction and eased back from him.

"Your turn," I said to Jackson.

"Okay." Jackson rubbed his hands together like he was rubbing a magic lamp.

I stood at the electrician's side so I could view both him and the sexy plumber. The second I nudged up to him, he wrapped his hands around my boobs and groped them like they were a couple of stress balls. His eyes were greedy with lust, and I was two seconds off telling him to settle down when I decided to let him have his fun. I reached down and glided my finger up his shaft.

Jackson bolted upright, as if I'd had acid on my fingers. He clutched the chair, and when he panted I realized that this bad boy was seconds away from blowing his load.

"Hey, mate, you need to chill." Mickey said what was on my mind.

"I can't. This's so fucking hot."

I glanced at Mickey and an incredible sexual beast looked back at me. The plumber was at the top of his game, and his looks and sex appeal set my body on fire. With him looking at me like that, and Jackson squirming before me with unbridled lust, I knew I was experiencing one of the erotic moments of my life.

I was torn between which man I should focus on. Mickey must've sensed my apprehension, because suddenly he was at my side. He swept me into his arms and I hooked my hands around his thickened neck. With each step he carried me to the bed, I inhaled his sexy masculine scent.

He lay me down, and as he ran his tongue over his lips, he bent over and unhooked my corset. Once it was undone, I planted my heels on the bed and raised my torso off the sheets, and he tugged the green satin free. His cock was in a perfect position for my outstretched hand, so I wrapped my fingers around him. As I glided up and down that smooth muscle, his chest rose and fell in time to my movements.

I raised my hips. "Take them off, too." My voice was barely a whisper, yet he moved to the end of the bed, reached up, and slipped my underpants from my body. As I opened my legs, showing Mickey all there was of me, I caught sight of Jackson. His eyes were wide and his lips were parted as if ready to speak.

"Do you want to see?" A blaze ripped through me at my sexy invitation.

Jackson jumped up and practically ran to stand beside his mate.

I reached down and touched my clit. That simple sensation sent rockets through me. Two of the hottest men in the world wanted to watch me masturbate and I was ready to give them the best show on earth.

I rolled my finger over my sensitive bud, applying pressure until it verged on painful before plunging into my already wet hole. My insides clenched, launching me into exquisite paradise. I was lost to another world. A world that blurred into a lust-fueled haze where I heard nothing and smelt nothing, but felt every single little movement.

Moments later, the two men knelt at either side of me. Four hands were on me, groping my breasts and doubling the attention to my oversensitive pussy. Glorious sensations ripped through me as they worked together, pleasuring my clit and plundering my pulsing hole.

I raised my hips; I lowered them. I raised them again, giving them more. I couldn't concentrate as every inch of my body sizzled.

At the point of no return I threw my head back, cried out, and let my body perform the most beautiful magic.

My orgasm was explosive. Cataclysmic even.

I saw stars, I saw rockets—I saw nothing, yet I felt every single thing.

I reached out with my hands and to my delight, two rock-hard cocks were right there. I wrapped one hand around each, pumping with the same ferocity they'd shown me. It was out of control. I'm out of control.

As they both continued to plunder me, drawing out another wild orgasm, Jackson cried out. My eyes shot open just in time to see him ejaculate. His hot semen flew across my stomach yet I continued to simultaneously pump both of them.

Mickey stiffened, his jaw clenched, but his eyes drilled into me as yet a third orgasm tore through me. I pumped Mickey's thick shaft until his hot cum shot across my belly too. Soon they both began to soften in my hands, and I let go.

I turned my head from one man to the next, and it was only then that I realized I still had my mask on. I didn't know whether to laugh or cringe at the ridiculousness of it. As the two men eased off the bed, I was suddenly in a hurry to get out of there. Droplets trickled down my belly as I wriggled off the mattress and before either man beat me to it, I made a dash for the bathroom as quick as my eight-inch green stilettos could take me.

I shut the door and using a wet face washer, I wiped all the incriminating evidence from my body. With each pass of the cloth, I grew more and more confused by what I'd just done.

After I was clean, I sat on the toilet and with my elbows on my knees, I covered my face with my hands. Within seconds, the angel and devil in my brain were having a heated debate.

Wow, that was incredible.

I just had sex with two men. What kind of woman was I?

No, I didn't have sex, just a little fun.

I can't believe I did that.

As much as I wanted to stay there until the men had no choice but to leave, I couldn't. I stood up and flushed the toilet.

As I leaned on the bathroom sink, I stared at my reflection. Whilst I looked funny in the mask, there was no missing the confusion in my eyes. I had a serious debate ahead of me.

Deciding to leave the mask on, I grabbed a still damp towel from a hook, wrapped it around myself, took a deep breath, and then opened the door.

They were both dressed in the clothes they'd worn when I first arrived in the room. Mickey was in the kitchen and Jackson sat at the dining table.

I felt completely out of place as I gathered my corset and underpants from the floor.

Jackson reached for my hand as I neared the table.

"That was incredible." The sincerity in his voice took me by surprise.

"Thank you."

He squeezed my hand in his. "I never thought I'd ever experience anything like that."

His impassioned honesty had my throat constricting. A smile soon lit up his face, and his eyes glistened as he looked up at me. I smiled back. I'd just made this man's dream come true and that made me feel wonderful.

He drew the back of my palm to his lips and kissed it. "I'll never forget this."

"Neither will I." And that was the honest truth.

As much as the concept of two men at the same time had had me feeling uncomfortable, it had also made me feel incredible and sexy.

When he dropped my hand, I looked over at Mickey. He stood in his custom stance, hips locked in place, jaw clenched. Then he blinked slowly, raised his fingers to his mouth and blew me a kiss.

I smiled at that. The simple gesture sent flutters of joy through me.

With my trench coat on, I shrugged out of the towel and let it fall to my feet. I pushed my costume into my bag and with it over my shoulder, I stood facing them. "I meant it when I said you can't ask for me again. You'll get me into trouble."

"Aww, but Memphis—"

"We won't," Mickey cut into Jackson's attempted rejection.

I backed away and headed to the door.

"Hey Memphis."

I turned to the deep voice.

Mickey held up his coffee mug. "I'm glad we met you."

"Me too." Jackson nodded and grinned like a love-struck teenager.

"Thanks, you too." With that wonderful departing comment, I left the room and pulled off my mask.

My wobbly legs safely transported me to the elevator and as I awaited its arrival, the devil and angel struck up a second feisty discussion in my mind. By the time I arrived at my room, my head was spinning. I went straight to the bathroom and turned the shower taps to hot. I let the powerful cascade pound my body as I allowed the debate to whirl around my brain.

Did I do anything wrong?

The answer was a resounding no. I'd had a consenting sexual experience with two smoking-hot adult men. What was wrong with that?

The more I dwelled on that answer, the more I decided that it was the truth. I honestly hadn't done anything wrong. In fact, it had been incredible. After the shower, I dried off and wrapped the bathrobe around myself. I walked to my bed, grabbed my diary and turned to the 2nd of September.

At the top of the page I wrote *Jackson and Mickey Room 33*, and I giggled as I wrote *Double Trouble* next to their names. In great detail I described what had happened in room thirty-three, and then I went on to write about my mental anguish over what I'd done.

My mind flitted to Calvin knowing about Lolita's threesomes. I honestly believed their openness to discuss their past relationships was what made their love for one another so strong. Secrets were what tore people apart. The inability to discuss with your partner what turned you on and what didn't could only lead to disaster, or worse, one person in the relationship being unsatisfied. This may be the root of many breakups.

At the bottom of the page I wrote, *I feel so good about this sexual experience that I'd feel comfortable telling a future partner all about it.*

147

Writing everything down was cathartic. I truly felt a weight off my shoulders having worked through that ethical debate.

This year was allowing me to become a confident, sexual woman. My only hope was that the man of my dreams would be willing to share his true feelings about our sex life with honesty and without malice.

I closed the diary, and as I strolled to the kitchen, eager to satisfy my grumbling stomach, I tried to picture who the man of my dreams would be. By the time I sat on my balcony with an egg and lettuce sandwich smothered in mayonnaise, a wonderful glow was whispering through me because I had no doubt that come Christmas this year, I would have found the man of my dreams.

Maybe I already had.

6TH SEPTEMBER
BREATHLESS ENCOUNTER
Room 20 - Hot Horizon Hotel

Lolly powerwalked from the gym to the Blue Haven Café, but after the workout she'd just put me through, I had no intention of trying to keep up. By the time I arrived at my usual seat she was impatiently tapping her long red fingernails on the tabletop.

"Alright, I'm ready," Lolly said the second I sat opposite her. "Did you have the threesome? I bet you did."

I flicked my ponytail over my shoulder and grinned. "You need to order cheesecake with your tea."

"Holy shit. I want to hear every fucking detail." Lolly was loud. Way too loud for a coffee shop at eight-thirty on a Tuesday morning. "Did you like it?"

I couldn't help but grin as I looked into her intense, inquisitive eyes. "It was . . . It was . . ." I gazed out to the ocean, searching for the perfect word to describe the experience.

"What can I get you ladies?" Matt's timing was impeccable.

Lolita's clenched jaw was enough to know she was seconds off tackling the grumpy waiter.

"What's the special today?" I saved him from Lolly's all-out attack.

"We have pavlova slice with fresh berries and a mandarin coulis."

"Sounds perfect. I'll have that with whipped cream and a skinny cappuccino in a mug." I pointed my finger at Lolita. "And she's having the New York baked cheesecake." Lolly rolled her eyes. "With extra cream, too."

She poked her tongue out as if she'd been poisoned.

"Do you still want green tea?" I ignored her exaggeration.

She nodded, and Matt jotted our order in his notebook and then silently slinked from our table.

"You made the bet." I grinned at Lolita.

"You're trying to kill me." She wriggled in her seat. "Now tell me all about your threesome before I explode."

She was hopeless with suspense, and as I contemplated teasing her a little longer, I adjusted my chair so I had a better view of both the walking traffic and the rolling waves.

"So I decided to wear my Poison Ivy costume. You know, the satin green one I wore for Batman?"

"Oh yeah. Green corset, long satin gloves . . ." She imitated pulling on long gloves.

"Yes, that's the one. I thought it was a cool way to show them who was in charge."

"I bet that drove them wild."

"It's funny—you have to understand how different these men were. Jackson was all fidgety and excited but Mickey was all cool and calm, a man in control."

"I can tell you loved it. Tell me about their cocks." She did a little hand clap.

"Wait a sec, I'm getting to that." I glanced around the café as I leaned forward. "I made them kneel down and bend over a chair . . ." I paused while a couple walked past our table. ". . . naked, and I gave them each a little smack on the butt."

She burst out laughing. "Holy shit, that's gold." She wriggled her perfectly formed eyebrows. "Memphis likes a little BDSM then."

"What? No. It's nothing like that. Just a quick smack. I told them it was their punishment for coming back."

"Yeah, yeah. I bet you liked it."

I giggled. "It was kind of fun. And I think they liked it, too."

"Are you fucking kidding? Of course they did. Cal loves it when--"

I stuck my fingers in my ears. "La, la, la, la," I sung loud enough to drown out her words.

When her lips stopped moving I took my fingers out.

"You're mean."

"I've told you I don't want to hear about what you and Cal do."

"And that makes you a terrible girlfriend."

My jaw dropped. Was I a terrible girlfriend? "It's just that you guys are in love. What you do is special and should be a secret between you and Cal."

"Well that's going to make our coffee sessions bloody boring next year."

"No it won't. We'll have all sorts of wonderful things to talk about."

She shook her head, not entirely agreeing with my comment. "Whatever. Anyway, get back to your threesome. I want every little detail."

I looked around at the nearby diners, praying her booming voice had gone unheard. As nobody was staring at us open-mouthed, I assumed all was good.

"Okay, listen to this." I started chuckling. "I got them both to strip off and sit on a seat each, and oh my god, they looked so hot. Anyway, I pointed at Jackson's"—I leaned closer to her—"penis and I said, 'So, what do we have here?'" I couldn't stop chuckling. "He said it was his pleasure-seeking missile."

Her hearty laugh showed off her perfect white teeth. "Shit, that's funny. What'd the other guy call his?"

"His cock."

Lolly rolled her head back and laughed so hard her boobs nearly wobbled right out of her bright pink sports top.

I caught sight of a man strolling toward us, and as the blood drained from my body, I lowered my eyes and prepared to slip under the table.

Lolita wrapped her hand around my wrist. "What is it, babe?" Her Spidey sense was on target again.

I shook my head, unable to speak as Billy the cowboy walked right behind my chair and into the coffee shop.

She increased her grip. "What?"

"Billy." I nodded in his direction. How she'd missed his cowboy hat, I'd never know.

"The sexy cowboy?"

As I nodded, I let my hair out of the ponytail and tousled it around my face. Lolita laughed loud, so loudly in fact that I realized she was putting on a show for Billy. "Oh Jane, you're a riot."

"Lolly," I hissed and shook my head. "Stop it."

She grinned at me, and I turned my attention to the ocean. As I prayed for a tsunami to swallow me up, out of the corner of my eye I saw the hunk in the cowboy hat stroll toward us.

"Jane?" His deep voice captured my name in the most alluring of ways.

"Oh, hi." I faked surprise and tried to ignore the Barbie-doll grin on Lolita's face.

"It's lovely to see you again."

Lolly tapped her nails on the table. There was no ignoring her intention.

I cleared my throat. "Billy, this is my friend Lolita."

He held his hand toward her, and for a second I thought she was going to jump up and kiss him. "I've heard all about you, you sexy cowboy." She actually winked at him, and I wanted to die.

"Really?" He turned his attention to me, and I was sure the smile I attempted looked more sinister than friendly.

Lolita indicated to the spare seats. "Why don't you join us?"

As I kicked her under the table, Billy pulled out a chair. "I'd love to."

Lolly put her elbows on the tabletop, sat her chin on her palms, and stared at Billy. "So," she said. "What's a hunky cowboy like you doing on the Gold Coast?"

I sucked in a deep breath and let it out very slowly, as if meditation was my only savior.

He took his hat off, and after he placed it on the spare chair at his side, he tousled his sandy blond waves catching shades of gold in the morning sunshine. "I'm a guest stunt rider at the Outback Spectacular."

Lolita licked her bottom lip. "I see . . . handsome and talented."

Oh god, where's my tsunami? I kicked her again but if she felt me, she didn't show it.

"How often do you that?"

"Roughly every eight weeks or so."

"Ah." She nodded and fluttered her eyelashes.

Matt, our dour waiter, arrived and placed our cakes and drinks down. Lolly cringed at the giant slice of cheesecake, which made me even more determined to make her eat it.

Matt turned to Billy. "Can I get you anything?"

"Sure. Can you tell me what cakes you have?" Billy's southern accent suited his attire perfectly.

While Matt went through the options, I studied my cowboy. Although he looked completely out of place in this surf location, with his button-up shirt tucked into his belted jeans, he also looked like he perfectly belonged. Actually, he'd probably look completely at ease anywhere.

Both Lolly and Billy turned to me at the same time. "What?"

Lolly burst out laughing. "Billy asked you if it was nice."

"What?"

"The pav."

"Oh. I haven't tasted it."

"Well eat some then." Lolly kicked me under the table, and I mouthed 'owww' at her.

I scooped a decent spoonful into my mouth. If a giant wave wasn't going to save me, then a giant sugar fix would. The pavlova seemed freshly made with a crunchy crust and a nice gooey middle. The fruit topping was sweet and delicious too. "It's excellent."

"Okay, good," Billy said. "I'll have that too please. Thank you."

Matt's droopy eyes lowered further, making him look as if he'd nod off at any moment. He left the table, and I turned my attention back to my sugar savior.

"So Billy, the Outback Spectacular isn't exactly close to here. Why do you come to Jane's hotel?" Lolly hit him with another question.

"Well, it's really different to back home, and I like to stroll along the beach each afternoon before I go to work. It relaxes me."

"So you like the beach then."

"Only to look at. I love the country better."

Lolita tapped the back of my hand with her red talon. "Jane's from the country."

"Oh?" His eyes dazzled. "Where?"

"Mildura."

"Animals or crops?"

"We had crops. Oranges and strawberries," I said.

"I'm an animal man myself."

"I bet you are." Lolly wriggled her eyebrows.

To avoid poking her eyeballs out, I ate more pavlova.

"So you have a farm?" She was an efficient interrogator.

"Yes, five thousand hectares, out past Roma."

"Wow." She said it as if he'd shown her a ten-carat diamond.

Billy's pavlova and coffee arrived, and as Matt positioned them on the table I tried to catch Lolly's eye, but the crazy bitch ignored me.

Lolly sat back, sipped her green tea, and stared at Billy as he began to eat.

I tucked into my sugar fix and tried to hide my embarrassment at her blatant ogling, but after a couple of mouthfuls I couldn't ignore it any more. "You'll have to excuse my crazy friend. She has no scruples." I clenched my jaw at Lolita.

"What, babe?" She fluttered her eyelashes.

"Stop staring," I whispered as quietly as I could.

"Sorry, I can't help it." She turned to Billy. "Jane's told me all about your glorious body."

Oh god, where was a random assassin when I needed one?

Billy laughed, and it was so fresh and contagious that I soon laughed along with him.

"I'm glad you like it," he said to me.

"Oh she does, don't you, babe?" Lolita answered for me.

I shoved a forkful of pavlova into my mouth and nodded.

"So you live on that big farm by yourself?" Lolita was relentless.

He swallowed a mouthful. "Sort of. My folks have a cottage on one of the boundaries, and I have another couple of houses a bit aways, where staff lodge from time to time, and then there's my place."

Lolly looked totally impressed with his situation. I, on the other hand, couldn't stand the thought of living within walking distance of my parents.

Billy pushed his half-finished meal away and dabbed his napkin to his lips. "I think I've intruded on your morning enough." He stood, reached for his hat, and pushed his chair in. "Will I see you later, Jane?"

"You will," Lolly answered for me again, and I smacked her arm.

Billy laughed and tipped his hat. "Well, if you're interested, I'm in room twenty. It was a pleasure to meet you, Lolita."

"Oh, the pleasure was all mine, Cowboy Billy."

He adjusted his hat, turned, and ambled away.

Lolly started giggling the second he left, and as we watched his sexy butt in his perfectly fitted faded jeans, her laughter hit a new crescendo. Soon, I couldn't help myself and roared with laughter, too.

I slapped her again. "You're out of control."

"You loved it."

I huffed. "I don't know about that."

"I do. Besides, I asked all those questions for you. At least now you know more about him."

That was true. I'd explored just about every inch of his body, but until now I knew next to nothing about the man in the cowboy hat.

"And?"

"And what?"

"What do you think of him now?"

I stirred my spoon around my coffee mug as I contemplated my answer. Whilst he certainly made my heart flutter, was he the man for me? For my future?

"Okay," she said. "Time's up. Tell me what you're thinking."

I took a sip of my coffee. "Billy is incredible. He's sexy—has an amazing body. He's gentle and kind and seems to know what he wants in life."

"He wants you."

I cocked my head in response.

"He does. Look at him—he was drooling over you."

"No he wasn't."

"Hell yes he was."

I lowered my eyes from her intense gaze. "Hey, you haven't touched your cheesecake."

She pulled a sad face.

"Eat, or you don't get another word from me."

She huffed. "Torturing me two ways. You really are mean." Lolly screwed up her face as she plunged her fork into the thick, creamy cheesecake and put it into her mouth. As I waited for her to swallow, my mind drifted to Billy. He had everything going for him and I was sure thousands of women would line up to be with him, yet I was still hesitating.

Lolita paused with another forkful of cheesecake at her lips. "Tell me what you don't like about him."

The answer, I realized, was easy. "He lives on a farm."

She chewed quickly and swallowed. "What's wrong with that? You're from the country."

"Exactly. I know what it's like to live in a small town. Since I moved here, I discovered there's so much more to life. I love living near the ocean and . . . well, I don't think I want to leave now." I was rambling.

"Maybe he'd move here, too."

I shook my head. "I wouldn't want him to do that."

"Look, you're jumping way ahead of yourself. Right now, that sexy bull wrestler is getting all steamy waiting for you. Go up there and fuck his brains out."

"Lolly!" I glanced around, and this time a few people were looking our way. I wanted to run and hide, but instead I just bulged my eyes at her.

"What? Don't worry about them. They're all jealous. Now, I'm serious. Go and have a jolly good ride, and don't worry about the serious stuff. It'll work itself out."

I took a large gulp of my coffee. "This's the fourth time he's been here. Don't you think that's serious enough?"

"No. He's smart enough to know when he's on a good thing. Just enjoy the ride." She giggled.

I finished the rest of my coffee and placed the mug down. Billy sure was exciting in the bedroom. My mind drifted to the last time we'd been together and how amazing I'd felt when I'd licked him. Maybe I could try that again.

"You're smiling. Tell me what you're thinking."

I giggled and leaned forward. "I was thinking about Billy."

"And . . .?"

"And . . . I licked his . . . you know."

"And . . .?" Her eyes bulged.

"And, it was nice."

"Nice? Pfft, you sure do play things down. Hey, that reminds me—you haven't told me about the threesome."

I glanced at her cheesecake, which she'd barely touched. "And you haven't eaten that."

"Okay, how about we go bite for bit? For every juicy piece of info, I'll eat a bite of this retched cake."

"It's not that bad."

"Sure is. I'll need to run to Brisbane and back to work off these calories."

I rolled my eyes. She'd probably do it, too. "Okay."

"Okay, so you had them naked on the chairs. Then what?"

"I tugged my boobs over my corset and let Mickey have his way with them. Eat."

She scowled and then put the tiniest spoonful in her mouth.

"While Mickey was working on my boobs, Jackson was watching. Eat."

"That's not enough info. Tell me more."

I rolled my eyes. "Okay, while I was with the plumber, Jackson was watching me and playing with himself."

"And, how did you feel?"

"It made me so freakin' horny. His eyes were really wide, and he kept licking his lips and stuff. So while he was watching me and I was watching him play with himself, Mickey was doing the most amazing things to my boobs." Just going back there in my mind had my insides curling. "Eat."

Lolly scooped another mouthful in. "So, how did you fuck? Were you sandwiched between their two cocks? One in your pussy, one up your ass?"

"What? No. Ewww, that's disgusting."

She flicked her hand like I was over-exaggerating. "So how'd you do it? Oh, let me guess—you gave one head while the other fucked you from behind."

"No—"

"Okay, rode one guy and gave the other head."

"No, Lolly, stop. It wasn't like that."

She pointed her fork at me and scowled. "You didn't fuck them, did you?"

I shook my head.

She shoved her plate away. "Oh my god, you made me eat that shit and you didn't even fuck them."

"Shhh."

"Oh pfft." She threw her hands in the air. "You tricked me."

"No I didn't."

She sat back and folded her arms across her abundant boobs. "So tell me then. How was it a threesome?"

God, she was loud. With trepidation, I glanced around. Thankfully, the café was nearly empty and the tables that were occupied were a fair distance away.

"We fooled around for a bit. In the chairs. Then Mickey carried me to the bed. I let both of them watch me, you know, masturbate." Lolly rolled her eyes to the ocean and sighed as if completely uninterested, so I carried on. "Then they came up and knelt at either side of me. They had their hands all over me and in me and it was amazing. And then I grabbed both of them and played with them until they both came all over me."

She didn't move. I had no idea what she was thinking. Lolly didn't do silent. "I still had my mask on."

She frowned. "What?"

"The green Poison Ivy mask. I'd kept it on the whole time. Right to the end."

Lolly clapped her hands and laughed. "Lucky you don't write porn, because you'd be terrible."

I laughed along with her, relieved that she didn't seem mad at me. "So do you forgive me?"

"No. You're in for a tough workout next Tuesday. I can't believe you made me eat that and you didn't even fuck those guys."

"You ate about five forkfuls."

"Yes, and I can already feel it making its way to my ass."

I smiled at her. Lolita had an incredible body that she worked so hard to maintain. I actually felt terrible now. "I'm sorry I made you eat that cake."

She waved her hand. "It's okay, I'll work it off on Cal later. All this talk about sex has made me horny." Her eyes bulged. "So are you going to fuck Billy now?"

I frowned. "I . . . I don't know. We haven't got that far yet. We do other stuff."

"What else haven't you done with him then?"

I pictured my sexy cowboy, his highly toned muscles, and those interesting molasses eyes.

"You're smiling."

"I was thinking about him. You know what I'd like to try again? I don't think I did a good job last time. I'd like to try a sixty-nine."

"Ahhh, there's definitely a skill to it."

"Yeah—avoid choking to death."

Lolita burst out laughing. "You're a hoot, babe. Okay, here's a tip. Both of you lie on your sides."

I blinked at her as I tried to picture how that would work. "I never thought of that."

"Or if you sit on his face, then you can lean down, and you manage how much of his cock you take into your mouth. Don't do it the other way, with him on top, or you'll need CPR in a few minutes."

I rolled my eyes. "I know what you mean."

She glanced at her phone. "Dammit, I've gotta go." She plucked a twenty-dollar bill out and sat the salt shaker on it to stop it from blowing away. "Tell me you're going to Billy."

"Yes, yes, I am." I didn't even need to think about it.

She hopped up and came around to draw me to her chest. "I'm so proud of you."

"Thank you." Though I had no idea what there was to be proud of.

She kissed my cheek. "See you next week."

"Okay. Bye."

As she jogged away, my thoughts drifted to Billy. By the time I'd left the café and made it to my room, I was so excited about going up to him that my insides positively purred.

First thing I did was strip out of my exercise gear, and jump into the shower. It was interesting, as knowing a man was waiting for me meant I didn't need to rush. I shaved my legs and when I washed my hair, I even did a five-minute conditioning treatment.

By the time I'd toweled off, blow-dried my hair, brushed my teeth, and applied minimal makeup to cover my freckles, it was already ten-thirty a.m.

As I stood at my closet, I realized that for the first time I'd be going to Billy as me, Jane Nichols. I had no idea what to wear. Billy was stunning, every bit the hunky male that loads of woman dreamed of standing alongside. As I tugged one dress after another along the hanging rack, I tried to picture what outfit would match Billy perfectly. I paused at my blue blazer. Last time I'd worn it I'd been with Henry. I'd paired the blazer with my striped T-shirt and wore it with jeans.

Jeans for my cowboy seemed perfect.

I tugged the clothing out and held it against my body, but soon decided that wearing exactly the same outfit was a little weird. So I swapped the striped T-shirt for a plain white one. This time, I'd tuck my jeans into my long red boots and tie it all together with a red scarf. The idea of Billy peeling the denim off me was suddenly very enticing. Or maybe he was just as skilled as Henry had been and could shoot me to the moon while fully clothed. My insides clenched at the delicious thoughts running through my head.

For my lingerie, I decided to skip a bra—I wouldn't need one for long anyway, not with how quickly the throb was growing inside me. I'd be lucky to have my clothes on for ten seconds.

I checked my outfit in the mirror. Other than my nipples being blatantly obvious through the white T-shirt, this was the type of outfit I liked to wear—the Jane Nichols side of me, that was. The clothing Memphis wore was sexy, and there was no doubt it made me feel sexy, but it didn't make me feel like me. I just hoped Billy was ready to see the real Plain Jane, or this could be a very short date.

My heart skipped a few beats as I realized I'd called it a date.

Before my tumbling thoughts ruined the excitement that pulsed through my pussy, I grabbed my bag, checked it had everything I needed, and strode out my door. As I rode the elevator up to the next floor, I rummaged through my bag, searching for lipstick. In my haste to leave, I'd forgotten it completely. The only thing I had was a nude gloss. I glided it on and rubbed my lips together.

The doors pinged open, and with each step I took toward Billy's room, I grew more nervous. He was about to see me for who I really was—Plain Jane. My heart galloped at an alarming rate by the time I reach his door and knocked. I closed my eyes and counted out the seconds.

At the click of the handle, I opened my eyes to the most glorious sight. Cowboy Billy was all man, a potent mix of brawn and calm. He was smoking hot and sexy.

I drank in his appearance, everything from his cute matching dimples to his narrow hips, so perfectly contained in his well-worn jeans. Billy literally took my breath away.

"Hi Jane." He held his hand forward. "It's lovely to see you again."

I nibbled on my bottom lip as his fingers enveloped mine, and I was fairly certain the earth moved at our first touch.

"You look incredible."

I just about melted under his intense molasses gaze. "Thank you."

He let go of my grip and reached around my back to guide me into the room, and as the door shut he turned to look at me. "Can I get you something to eat? Drink?"

"No thank you."

Normally I'd walk into a stranger's room, toss my bag and coat onto a chair, and start stripping. I suddenly felt very awkward. Very Jane-like, as I stood stranded between the front door and the dining table.

Billy may have sensed my trepidation as he stepped toward me. His hands glided into my jacket and rested on my waist. This simple touch had my nipples hardening and my breath quickening. "You're beautiful."

Billy was the one who was beautiful, but my knees were set to collapse beneath me over the sincerity in his voice.

His eyes were incredible. Long dark lashes framed the liquid honey. All the worry that'd gripped me earlier melted away as I succumbed to his enchantment. His tongue glided across his lips, and a shiver rolled through me as I tilted my head and closed my eyes, willing him to lower his lips to mine. Barely a breath passed before my wish was granted.

The world around me vanished into obscurity as the warmth of his tongue met mine. He tasted of mint and smelt of exotic spices. I curled my fingers up around his neck, drawing him to me, silently telling him to give me more. His hands curved up from my waist and he gently ran his thumb over my nipples, drawing out my hardened buds until the fabric that covered them felt like a straitjacket.

I inched my hands up his chest, feeling every steely muscle that languished there. His nipples were tiny pebbles, and I gently pinched them between my fingers. I pushed my tongue into his mouth, meeting his in a delicious duel. Our heated breaths grew faster, matching my racing heart. His gentle attention to my breasts was both exquisite and agony as a delicious pulse started at my pussy and throbbed right through me.

"Oh Billy." His name felt so right whispered off my tongue.

He pulled back, his eyes loaded with lust-filled intensity. Billy reached up with his hands and cupped my cheeks. I thought he would kiss me again, but instead he curled his fingers into my collar and removed my jacket. The fabric fell to my feet and as I kicked it aside, his eyes lowered to my chest. I looked down too and my nipples were lethal weapons, bulging from the white cotton.

He glided his index finger around my nipples, and as I rolled my head back and closed my eyes, my body sizzled. Every little node around my nipples hardened beneath his touch. He tugged my T-shirt from my jeans, and I raised my hands over my head. The shirt was off in a flash, and I felt so damn sexy standing there topless.

I reached for his shirt, wanting the same for him. His fingers trembled as he helped me with the buttons, and seconds later he was shirtless, too.

Billy was a muscle god, perfectly sculpted from years of hard work. This was the body every man should aspire to.

He leaned forward, and when he sucked my breast into his mouth, I just about climaxed right there and then. While his tongue and lips explored my left breast, his hand manipulated my right. I drove my fingers through his golden hair and gently tugged him closer.

He moaned, and I moaned with him. As much as I was enjoying his divine attention he was enjoying it, too. The orgasm building inside me was enormous, mammoth even, and as I scratched my nails up his back I fought the urge to let my body take over.

I reached for his belt, desperate to release the bulge that dominated his jeans. As I fumbled with the buckle, he stood back up and reached for the button on my jeans. We were in a race to undress each other. A race that I won, and within seconds Billy had his jeans around his ankles and his glorious cock pointing right at me.

I fell to my knees—I couldn't help myself. I needed to taste him, and with my fingers digging into his toned bottom, I sucked his solid rod into my mouth. My lips glided over the smooth skin, drawing him into my throat. Once he was all the way in, I held him there, ensuring maximum suction.

Billy moaned, and when he ran his fingers through my hair I gradually released. As I eased his cock out of my mouth, I rolled my tongue around his shaft, exploring every aspect of him. I paused at the tip, sucking hard until he slipped out.

I looked up at him. His eyes were closed, his lips slightly ajar as if words were about to be whispered across them. I glided my right hand around his hip, and as I curled it between his legs he stepped apart, giving me more to play with.

With my left hand wrapped around his shaft, I cupped his balls with my right hand, and I curled my tongue around his glistening crown.

Billy hissed, his entire body tensed, and I carried on rolling my tongue around and around, glancing up from time to time, to see if he were still watching. His fingers curled through my hair, and he groaned.

"Oh, Jane." To hear him say my name set off a firecracker in me, and the pulsing in my pussy hit a new tempo.

A bubble of semen twinkled at the slit in his penis, begging me to taste. So I did. It was salty yet sweet. I poked my tongue into the slit, wanting more, and Billy bent his knees and emitted a deep, primal moan.

He clutched my shoulders and pulled back. "Jane, wait." He reached for my hand, pulling me to my feet. The pupils in his eyes were large black discs almost swallowing his beautiful honey irises. He bent down and tugged his boots from his feet, casting them aside with little care. Then, using his feet, he pulled his jeans off too.

My smoking-hot cowboy stood completely naked and I devoured him with my gaze. Every inch of him was a work of art. Muscles bulged in all the right places, and his cock stood tall and proud, pointing up toward his perfectly formed navel. I could've stood there and admired him all day long. Our eyes met, and something wickedly delicious crossed over his. A heartbeat later his hands were on my hips, and as he ran his tongue over his lips, he walked me backwards. Under his guidance I sat on the end of the bed, and Billy knelt down, lifted my foot to his thigh, and glided the zipper down my boot.

The concentration on his face was as exhilarating as his glistening body, and I was once again reminded of how lucky I was. With the second boot removed, he sat up on his knees and placed his hands on my thigh. "Lie back, baby."

Baby! Oh my god, yes. I tugged my bottom lip into my mouth as I obeyed his wishes. His hands glided up my hip, and after he undid my zipper, I raised my bottom off the bed and closed my eyes as Billy glided my jeans down my body, taking my underpants too.

With my eyes closed, I pictured his expression, and imagined him running his tongue over his lips as he savored my nudity. The second my jeans were off my ankles I parted my legs, silently welcoming him to my body.

His warm hands curled over my knees, and I parted them farther. Barely a heartbeat later, magic happened. Billy's tongue glided up my pussy. It was hot, hard, and greedy, and I raised my hips, begging him to do it again.

Billy didn't need a second invitation, and as I succumbed to his charms I set my mind free and let my body take over. The throbbing pulse sizzling through me grew faster, quickly taking my body to the edge of mind-blowing release.

I threw my arms out, clutched at the sheets, and screamed as my orgasm tore through me. It was hot. It was explosive. It was out of this world. And the man between my legs continued to take me there.

I propped up onto my elbows just in time to see Billy look up. His eyes rolled slightly, as if lost in their own world. By the expression on his face, he was quite happy there. He ran his tongue over his lips, lapping up my juice, and oh my god, if that wasn't the most incredible thing in the world.

"Come here, you." I grabbed his hand and giggled as I dragged him up beside me.

We lay on our sides, facing each other. His mammoth erection prodded my pubic bone as his hand curled around my breast. "You're amazing." He reached up to push my hair over my shoulder. "And beautiful."

I leaned forward, and our lips met. The gentle kiss we'd had earlier was replaced with a needier one. His tongue thrust into my mouth, and I instantly regretted it. The taste was horrid. The realization that it was me I was tasting nearly had me gagging.

I pulled back, and the sixty-nine position Lolita had mentioned earlier flashed into my mind. Curling up onto my hands and knees, I flipped my body around so now his cock was in my face and my pussy was near his. I raised one knee up, and at the same time I clutched onto his butt cheek and pulled myself closer to him.

Billy didn't miss a beat, and before I'd had a chance to get comfortable his head was between my thighs and his tongue had found my hot-spot again. It was concentration overload because as I savored his rock-hard cock, licking, sucking, and gliding my tongue all over it, he showed my pussy the same exquisite attention.

A zillion glorious sensations ripped through me as another orgasm built at lightning speed. As he licked up and down my velvet folds he pushed a finger into me, first one, then two, and I raised my leg in the air, pointing my toes to the ceiling, opening myself nice and wide. Every part of me sizzled, yet I continued my feast on him.

I cried out as another orgasm ripped through me. This one surprised me, yet it was just as amazing as the last—fast, ferocious, and fabulous.

Billy thrust his cock toward me, and as I glided him into my mouth he shot his load inside me. I swallowed it back, trying not to taste it this time for fear I may gag again. His cock swelled inside my mouth, and with each pulse, hot semen pumped into the back of my throat. To feel that raw action was incredible. The taste, however, was still a little nasty. Thankfully, I'd swallowed most of it.

When he stopped thrusting, I glided my lips up his shaft and felt him soften beneath my suction. He pulled his head out from between my legs, and as I lowered my foot to the bed I swallowed a few times, ensuring the last of him was gone.

Billy rolled onto his back and flipped his feet off the side of the bed to sit up. I joined him, and we sat side by side.

He reached for my hand and our fingers entwined. That simple action felt so right, and I nuzzled against him. Billy kissed my forehead. It was sweet and loving, and yet it said so much more. Was this what falling in love was like? Two people feeling so comfortable with each other that actions told so much more than words?

I didn't want to analyze it for fear my twirling thoughts would ruin a perfect moment. Instead I focused on the wonderful after-sex feelings throbbing through my body.

It seemed like an eternity before Billy eased forward and stood. "Would you like a shower?"

I smiled up at him. "No thank you. I'll go home."

He nodded as if expecting my answer.

As I set about re-dressing, Billy disappeared into the bathroom. By the time I had my jeans and boots on, he'd stepped back into the room wearing just a towel. It sat low on his hips, showing off that sexy V-shape that was like a beacon pointing the way to his groin. Billy sure did know how to capture my attention, and before I stripped off again and tackled him to the bed, I pulled my shirt on. My nipples were still rock-hard, and I tried to ignore them as I pulled my jacket on.

Billy came toward me and reached for my hand. "Thank you for a wonderful morning."

"Thank you, too."

He brought my palm to his lips and kissed. "I'll be back in a couple of weeks. Would you like me to call you this time?"

Before I'd even analyzed his question, I nodded. His dimples studded his cheeks as his smile deepened.

He leaned forward and kissed me. Just a simple brush of our lips.

I reached for my bag and with it over my shoulder, I turned to take in one last look at my glorious cowboy. "See you soon, Billy."

As I rode a mountainous after-sex high, I made my way to my room and took a long, hot shower. By the time I crawled into bed I was both emotionally and physically satisfied. I reached for my diary and turned to the 6th of September. At the top I wrote *Cowboy Billy Room 20*, and as I thought about how Billy had produced an orgasm that took my breath away I wrote *Breathless Encounter*.

I detailed everything we'd done, from Billy's gentle touches of my nipples through my T-shirt, to the mind-blowing sensation overload of that sideways sixty-niner. With a contented sigh, I put my diary away and slipped under my quilt.

I tugged my spare pillow to my chest, and as I let sleep pull me into a beautiful world I imagined the pillow was Billy, hugging me in a warm, comforting embrace.

15ᵀᴴ SEPTEMBER
THE PERFECT LOVER
Room 2 - Hot Horizon Hotel

There was no denying I was nervous. From the very moment I'd agreed to Clayton's request, I'd been consumed with dread over how it would go. I was a bit annoyed with how he'd done it, too. He'd invited me to coffee. *All good there.* We'd decided on a day and time. *Easy.* Then he'd dropped the bombshell. It was school holidays, and would I mind if his daughter came? *What was I going to say?*

Now, as I waited for the minutes to tick along until he picked me up, my stomach wouldn't stop churning. The chances of getting any food down were diminishing by the second.

Whilst I loved spending time with Clayton, the idea of meeting his daughter terrified me. Dozens of unanswerable questions shot through my brain.

Was it too soon to meet her? I mean, after all, Clayton and I'd only had a couple of dates.

What if she didn't like me?

What if she did?

Would she ask me if I was going to be her next mother?

That last question had me pacing my apartment. I was too young to be the mother of a seven-year-old girl. Actually, no—that wasn't true. I was certainly old enough in years but I was too young in experience with children. I had no idea what I was doing.

The only kids I'd had any time with were Lolita's children, Savanah and Maddox, and those kids were amazing.

I glanced at the clock on my microwave. It was time. I sucked back a few deep breaths, ran my sweaty palms down my skirt, grabbed my bag, and strode out the door before I changed my mind.

As I rode the elevator I practiced smiling, and the more my lips trembled the more the acid in my stomach twirled. "Hi," I said to my pale reflection. "I'm Jane, a friend of your daddy's."

Friend. Yes, that was what I was. His friend. Not girlfriend. Just friend.

The doors pinged open, and with each step I made across the lobby I forced confidence into my stride and an upbeat attitude into my brain.

It was overcast outside, as gloomy as my thoughts. Clayton waited beside his Audi, and waved at me the second I arrived at the top of the stairs. As usual, he looked stunning—every bit the handsome, available professional he was. I arrived at his side, and he leaned in to kiss my cheek.

"Hey gorgeous." His cologne was lovely, with just the right amount of floral and spice.

"Hey, how are you?"

"I'm great." He opened the back door of the car. "This's Telitha." The little girl beamed, all blond hair and pink cheeks. She actually looked happy to see me.

"Hi Telitha. I'm Jane."

"Hi. You look so pretty."

"Oh, thank you."

I glanced at Clayton. He was beaming too, and it was easy to see the resemblance between the two of them.

He turned to me. "Are you hungry?"

"Always."

"Good. Let's get going then." He shut the back door and opened the passenger one for me.

I gathered my skirt and slipped into the leather seat.

"How old are you?" Telitha had moved forward so she was leaning between the two front seats.

"Oh." I cleared my throat. "I'm twenty-nine. How old are you?"

"I'm seven and a half; my birthday is in February. When's your birthday?"

"Mine was in July."

"Have you been married before?"

Clayton slipped into the driver's seat. "Telitha, sit back, honey."

Thank god Clayton had saved me. However, it looked like I was in for the Spanish Inquisition. He put the car into gear and pulled onto the deserted road. "How was your night shift?"

"It wasn't too bad. A bit quieter than I like it though. Did you work today?"

"No, Daddy and I took Clancy down the beach. She's my dog. It was fun.

You should come with us next time."

Clayton turned to me. The pride on his face was undeniable. There was an awkward pause before I realized he was waiting for my answer.

"Umm, well, that would be nice."

The questions didn't stop, and I was mentally exhausted by the time Clayton pulled the car into a parking space overlooking Mermaid Beach.

"I hope you don't mind going to the surf club. Telitha likes the playground here."

"Sounds great."

He stepped onto the pathway that weaved through the bush, and Telitha grabbed his hand. She then wiggled her fingers at me, and the second I stepped forward she clutched my hand, too. We looked like the perfect wholesome family as we walked along with the pretty little girl in the bright pink dress skipping between us.

It was both weird and cute at the same time. Every glance Clayton sent my way showed just how pleased he was with how things were going.

"The coffee here is excellent," he said as we reached the sign-in counter.

"Oh, good. I need a caffeine fix right now."

We entered through the glass doors, climbed the stairs and passed the poker machines, and he guided me toward a table alongside enormous glass windows that overlooked the ocean. The scenery was stunning and would perfectly suit any five-star restaurant.

Telitha grabbed my hand, and before I knew it, I was being tugged along by the seven-year-old. I glanced over my shoulder, but Clayton just smiled making it obvious he had no intention of rescuing me. She pushed through a glass door and we stepped onto artificial grass that was soft and spongey.

"Watch me." Telitha squealed and dashed off toward a bright yellow ladder. Several moments later she came tumbling down a spiral slide and rolled out at my feet.

"See." She jumped up and down in front of me as if I hadn't noticed her.

"Yes, I saw you."

"Hey you two. How about we order first?" Clayton's voice was a relief.

Telitha dashed back through the door, and Clayton reached for my hand.

"I'm sorry," he said. "She was a bit excited to meet you."

"Oh." I had no idea what to say. What had he told her about me that would make her excited?

We arrived at the cake counter, and the extensive selection was medicine to my eyes. My mouth salivated as I gazed over one sugar fix to the next, trying to ascertain which one would make me feel better.

I couldn't go past the hummingbird cake. I ordered it with extra cream and a large cappuccino. The three of us made our way back to the table, and Telitha sat between Clayton and I.

The little girl hit me with a thousand questions, everything from did I have a dog to why didn't I paint my nails. Clayton barely said a word until our food arrived. Grateful for the reprieve, I tucked into the cake. Between every mouthful, Telitha talked. It was exhausting, and by the time she ran off to the swings again I was ready for the silence.

He reached across the table and wriggled my hand into his. "I'm sorry. She can be a little overwhelming."

I dabbed my napkin over my lips and reluctantly pushed my cake away. "It's okay. I'm just not used to kids."

"Once she gets to know you she'll settle down."

Oh god. "Clayton . . ."

He must have heard the trepidation in my voice, as his shoulders slumped and the smile that'd been on his face since he picked me up evaporated.

"I'm sorry, Clayton, but I'm just not ready for kids. I mean, I'm ready for kids, but I don't know if I'm prepared for a seven-year-old."

He pulled his hand away and lowered his eyes. I wanted to cry at how dejected he looked. His silence was agony.

"She's adorable and you're . . . you're incredible and amazing and—"

"A single parent," he interjected.

I nodded, but he wasn't looking at me. "I'm sorry. I shouldn't have led you on."

"You didn't lead me on. We had fun. I've really enjoyed your company."

"And I've enjoyed every second with you too, but it wouldn't be fair on you or Telitha if we kept seeing each other." A huge weight lifted off my shoulders once I'd said that and it served as confirmation that I'd made the right decision.

He nodded and looked up at me. "I really thought you were the one."

My heart shattered to a million pieces. "I'm so sorry."

"No need to be sorry. You're right. It wouldn't be fair on Telitha." He sighed, a long, deep sigh and shrugged his shoulders. "I guess I should take you home."

"No, no. I'll catch a cab."

"I insist, Jane." His squared out jaw convinced me to give in.

"Okay, thank you."

"I'll go get Telitha."

He stood, and as he walked toward the playground my stomach churned so dramatically I thought I'd throw up. But when the little girl put her arms around her daddy and squeezed him tightly as she jumped off the slide, I knew I'd done the right thing. Telitha had already been through immense emotional turmoil when her mother had left—I couldn't put her through that again. It was better to let Clayton go now, before we grew too serious.

Clayton nodded at me once he stepped back through the door, and I grabbed my bag and followed him down the stairs.

Telitha had her arms and legs wrapped around him and as she stared at me with a beautiful grin, she snuggled into his neck.

Life could be cruel sometimes. Hopefully Clayton would forgive me.

The drive back to the hotel was as long as it was torturous, as Telitha barraged me with a dozen questions and Clayton remained stony silent. I'd never been so happy to see the driveway to the hotel, and it took all my might not to jump out before he'd even stopped the car.

I turned to the back seat. "It was lovely to meet you, Telitha."

"When can I see you again?"

"Oh, ummm . . ."

"Jane's really busy, honey. She's got to go now." Clayton saved me.

"Okay, Daddy."

I placed my hand on Clayton's arm, ready to speak, and he opened his side door. Taking his lead, I stepped out of the car too. We met at the back of the car.

"Can I at least have a hug?" He opened his arms to me, and I stepped into his embrace.

"I'm sorry, Clayton."

"It's okay. I understand." We pulled apart, and my hands fell into his. "It was fun while it lasted."

I nodded. "Yes, it was."

He leaned in, kissed my cheek, and then strode back around to the driver's side. Seconds later the Audi moved away, leaving me all alone on the front steps of my hotel.

By the time I arrived at my room, I was shattered, both emotionally and physically. I stripped off, put on my pajamas, and crawled into bed. It was impossible to suppress my quivering chin, and as I clutched my spare pillow the tears flowed.

* * *

The sound of my bedside alarm startled me, and I rolled over to cut off the news broadcast. I couldn't believe I'd slept, let alone for five hours. I yawned, stretched my arms above my head, and listened to my rumbling tummy. Rolling out of bed, I made my way to the bathroom to relieve myself, and then turned on the shower.

As the warm cascade tumbled over me, my thoughts went to Clayton. I played out what had happened over and over in my head, and as much as I knew I'd just let an incredible man slip through my fingers, I also knew I'd made the right decision.

By the time I'd showered and dried off, my rumbling tummy couldn't be ignored a moment more. With my bathrobe around my shoulders, I wandered to my kitchen. Without much hope of inspiration, I tugged open the fridge and sighed. If a complete stranger looked in here they'd think the apartment had been abandoned. Even my usual survival staples of peanut butter and eggs were absent.

My stomach roared in protest, and I made a snap decision to treat myself to a meal out. Tying my belt around my waist, I strode out to the verandah to check the weather. The sun was still high enough to cut through the gaps in the tall buildings and cast long bolts of golden light onto the sand. A cool breeze whispered up from the ocean and tickled my skin.

Leaning on the railing, I inhaled the crisp, clean air. It was like an elixir, filtering away all the angst that'd filled my morning. The evening weather was perfect to spend in a nice café overlooking the ocean, and I knew exactly the right place.

The idea of eating out appealed greatly, and I dressed quickly in jeans and a caramel knitted sweater. I pulled on ankle-high boots and grabbed my Michael Kors tote that matched them perfectly. With my bag swinging off my arm, I headed out my door with thoughts on a thick juicy steak waiting for me at Steakside.

Marjorie was all by herself at the reception desk, and as much as my stomach complained about the slight deviation from the plan, I headed toward her. "Hey Marj."

"Oh hey luvvy, how are you?"

"I'm good—hungry though. I'm heading out for a meal. Has it been busy?"

"Yeah, crazy busy. We're fully booked. Last weekend of the school holidays."

I huffed. "Yeah, I know. At least the hours go quickly."

"You're not kidding."

"Anyway, I'm off to eat. See you later."

"Okay, make sure you have a wine for me."

I laughed as I turned. "Okay then, just because you asked."

She chuckled with me, and the sound echoed around the marble expanse. I strode out through the gap in the sliding glass doors and down the front steps. Deciding to walk along the beach path, I strolled in the opposite direction to the abundant holiday crowds that were a standard feature on Cavill Avenue. People were everywhere, mostly families taking advantage of the setting sun. Down on the beach, dozens of people were in the water, which I imagined would still be cool. Too cold for me, anyway. The ocean needed to be like bath water for me to swim.

Unless a hunk like Corben tossed me in. The thought of my Mr. Universe contender raised my spirits. Life wasn't all doom and gloom—I still had a few regular men willing to see me, and I was willing to see them. And who knew how many more men I'd meet before my wonderful sexual challenge was over.

I took my time, enjoying the scenery and letting my thoughts flit from one sexy man in my life to the next. It was heaven, really, and a rare occurrence.

Normally, my brain was a crazy scramble of frightening thoughts.

A young family walked toward me. The father was fit, tanned, and utterly beaming as he carried a small toddler on his shoulders. The mother looked equally happy as she walked hand in hand with a little girl carrying a bright pink bucket and spade. With the beach setting in the background and their four beautiful smiles, this young family could easily be declared Gold Coast pin-up material. I actually felt blessed to witness their united happiness, and my contented feeling hit a whole new level.

Twenty minutes after I left my hotel, I arrived at Steakside and was greeted by a young woman with a petite frame and a big smile. "Good evening. Would you like a table?"

"Yes please. A table out the front would be nice."

She grabbed two menus and turned. "Okay, follow me."

Her choice of table was perfect to capture both the distant ocean and the walking traffic. She pulled out a chair and when I sat, she handed me a menu and placed the other one opposite me. "No need for the other menu."

"Oh, sure." She gathered it up again. "Can I get you a drink?"

"Do you have Shaw & Smith Sauvignon Blanc?"

"Of course."

"Excellent. I'll have a glass of that please."

"Okay, I'll be right back."

The second she left I grabbed the menu and scoured the selection. The eye fillet on the right-hand side was like a flashing beacon, and my mouth salivated as I contemplated which sides to choose with it. With my decision made, I flipped the menu closed and settled back in my chair to enjoy the scenery.

My vista was magnificent, and other than my hunger pains screaming at me, everything was perfect. A man at the neighboring restaurant caught my eye. He was side on to me, also looking out toward the ocean. His smooth, dark hair reflected in the flames dancing atop the Tiki torches dotted around his restaurant. The man reached for his wine and when he inhaled it, I was reminded of my disastrous encounter with the winemaker. I quickly cast that thought aside, determined to maintain my upbeat demeanor.

The man turned toward me, and my heart stopped. It was David Lawson, one of Memphis's repeat gentleman. I quickly looked away, hopeful he didn't recognize me. After a couple of frantic heartbeats, I glanced in his direction. He was still in his seat, looking out over the ocean again. I let out a long, slow breath.

"There you go." The waiter placed my wine on the cardboard coaster. "Can I get you something to eat?"

"Yes please. I'll have the eye fillet, medium rare, with mushroom sauce and blue cheese sauce, and I'll have the polenta chips and buttered greens."

"Okay." She finished writing down my order and lifted the menu off the table. "Thank you very much."

A quick check of David confirmed he hadn't moved. I in turn was tempted to switch seats, but then I realized he'd only ever seen me as Memphis. With each ticking second, I relaxed a little more, and before long, I realized that my already perfect view had become even better with David in it.

He sat alone, yet there was something about him that told me he was happy. I guessed, like me, he'd grown accustomed to sitting alone at restaurants. It wasn't everyone's cup of tea. Lolita would go stir crazy if she had to sit by herself at dinner, or anywhere for that matter. She'd die without someone to talk to. It was one of the reasons why I loved her. Lolita had a beautiful talent of making everyone feel welcome.

David captured my attention in so many ways. His movements were graceful, calming, and he looked every bit the confident, available man, which was so different to the David I'd first met way back in January.

I contemplated the idea that he may be back on the coast to see me. Well not me, but Memphis. My insides fluttered at that thought as my brain skipped to the last time we'd been together. He'd wanted me to teach him a few things.

As I watched him sip his wine and glide his fingers through his thick, glossy hair, I wondered if he'd returned for another lesson. My pussy responded to my pondering with a couple of delightful pulses.

If he was ready to see me, I was so ready for him.

My meal arrived, and as I devoured the perfectly charred steak I contemplated what I'd teach David this time. By the time I'd finished eating, I was both full and excited about what the next few hours would hold. Mr. David Lawson had just become my thirty-eighth sexual adventure. That was, as long as he was staying in my hotel. I'd be devastated if he wasn't.

At seven o'clock David was served another glass of wine, so I pretended we were dining together and ordered another one for me, too. I wouldn't normally drink before work, but what the hell? It'd been a tumultuous day.

When my wine arrived, I raised my glass to him. "See you soon, sexy." I giggled at my silliness.

About half an hour later, David stood up so I tossed back the last of my wine, grabbed my bag, and headed to the counter to pay. With one eye on him, and the other on the handsome guy behind the cash register, I was torn between which way to look. This year sure had changed me. I just about burst out laughing at how wonderful life was.

By the time I paid and walked out of Steakside, I spied David ahead of me, just about to disappear around the corner. I breathed a sigh of relief at the direction he'd headed in; it was toward the Hot Horizon Hotel.

By the time I reached the corner, I realized I had a dilemma—I had no idea which room David was in. And in addition to that, there was every chance he'd ask Marjorie about Memphis. Last time he'd visited my hotel, he'd come to reception counter and I'd just been lucky it was me working at the time and not somebody else.

A bold idea hit me, and as I quickened my pace, my heart was set to explode as I committed to going through with it. With one last deep breath to calm my racing heart, I reached his side and looked up at him. "Hi. It's David, isn't it?"

"Oh, hello." He blinked, maybe trying to remember my name.

"I'm Jane. The night manager at the Hot Horizon Hotel. We met last time you were there."

"Yes, I remember. We met out the front on Easter Friday. I'm heading there now."

"Excellent. Mind if I walk with you?"

"No at all; I'd be delighted."

And so it was that David and I fell into stride together like any normal couple would do. I looked up at him. "Are you working on the coast again?"

"No, not this time. I'm actually visiting someone."

"Oh, a girlfriend." *Holy shit.* I'm such an idiot.

"Um . . . well she's . . ."

"No, sorry, you don't need to answer that. It was very rude of me."

"Well, actually, maybe you can help me again. Her name is Memphis, and I left a message with you last time. If she comes in, can you tell her David Lawson is staying in room two?"

I silently sighed with relief. "Of course."

"Thank you. I've been a couple of times and haven't seen her. Maybe today's my lucky day."

Oh my god. My head spun at his comment. How many times had he been here? Who had he asked for Memphis? Marjorie or Needledick? I couldn't keep up with all these men requesting me. *No wonder my boss is so obsessed with Memphis.*

We arrived at the hotel and at the top of the stairs I decided I'd head toward Marjorie, rather than hop into the elevator with David. I didn't want him to see that I lived here, too. "Okay, have a good night."

"You too, Jane." David gave me a little wave and continued walking to the elevator.

"Hey Marj."

"How was your dinner?"

"It was great. Eye fillet, polenta chips, mushroom sauce . . ."

"Oh stop it, you're killing me." She lightly slapped my arm.

"Anyway, I'll see you in about"—I glanced at the clock—"an hour or so."

"Okay, I'll be ready."

I spun on my heel, and it took all my effort not to sprint to the elevator. Time had gotten away from me. The damn thing took forever, as usual, and when it arrived I jumped in and jabbed the button a dozen times. I utilized the slow ride to decide what Memphis would wear tonight.

Back in my room, I applied my makeup in record time, and even though I knew I hadn't used my colored contact lenses with David before, I decided that I'd need them this time. He'd looked into my eyes way too often on the way to the hotel, and I couldn't risk him recognizing me. I plucked the blue discs out of the compact case and popped them in one at a time.

My cheeks were already rosy, thanks to the rush of getting ready and the two glasses of wine I'd consumed. It would probably also explain the nice carefree feeling I had as I prepared for my next sexual adventure.

The contact lenses made the change in my appearance both instant and amazing. It was then that I realized my next issue—my black wig. It had well and truly past its use-by date.

I leaned over the basin, and as I stared into my eyes in the mirror, I tried to think it through. After a minute or so, I decided that David would meet redheaded Memphis. Hopefully I'd figure out a decent excuse for the different hairstyle by the time I arrived at David's room.

After plaiting my hair and pinning it up, I tugged on the fiery red wig. In a flash, Plain Jane was gone and Memphis was out in all her glory.

Satisfied with how I looked, I went to the closet and grabbed out the black wrap dress I'd worn on my birthday. I held it to my body, and the skirt flared out as I twirled around. I smiled at my reflection and clutched the counter when the room started spinning. Maybe I shouldn't have gulped that last bit of wine. Too late now—I had work to do. I strode to the kitchen and drank a quick glass of water.

Focus, Jane. You're running out of time.

At my lingerie drawer, I chose my leather and lace teddy that pulled on without any clips, zips, or fasteners. I stepped into it and pulled it up. The second it was on, I felt sexy, and I couldn't wait to see David's face when I stripped down to this.

My shoe choice for today was my Givenchy zebra-print eight-inch stilettos. They were so damn stylish, I just wished I'd had more opportunities to wear them.

Dressed now, I looked in the mirror. There was no way David would recognize me as Jane. With the final touch of Ciate Liquid Velvet lipstick, I smiled at my reflection. I was ready, and if the flutter in my stomach was anything to go by, then my body was ready, too. I tossed my supplies into the clutch that matched my shoes, and felt very seductive in my fancy stilettos and flowing skirt as I strode to the elevator.

David's room was two floors below mine, and the ride in the elevator seemed to take about twenty minutes to get there. My time with David was rapidly dwindling. It was going to require some swift movements to get this sexual romp on the go quickly.

At his floor, I strode straight to his door and knocked. Barely three seconds later, David opened the door with an incredible smile. It was such a lovely welcome.

"Oh." His eyes lit up. "Memphis?"

"Hello, David." I'd forgotten all about the fact I looked different this time and hadn't worked out a suitable reason for it. I decided not to elaborate and hoped he didn't ask.

"Wow. You look incredible."

I smiled up at him. "Thank you. May I come in?"

"Of course." He stepped aside, and as I strode past him, I ran my fingers over his chest, feeling all the lovely muscles beneath his linen shirt. I glided to the table as fast as my eight-inch stilettos could carry me, and as I placed my clutch on the glass I heard the door click closed.

"I'm so glad you came. I missed you the last two times."

"You need to stop doing that, David."

"What?" He paused halfway between the door and me, and a look of horror marred his handsome features.

"Asking for me at reception. You'll get me into trouble."

He gasped. "Oh no. I'm so sorry."

"It's okay. Just don't do it again."

"Well, that's why I wanted to see you."

"Oh?" I cocked my head.

"I wanted to say goodbye. You see, that woman I told you about? I'm going to ask her to go steady with me." His eyes lit up, and he looked so wholesome I wanted to give him a big hug.

"Good for you, David."

"Well, obviously I don't know if she'll say yes, but I hope so."

"I'm sure she will. She's a fool if she doesn't."

A red flush crept up his cheeks. "Thanks."

Now I felt foolish. Here I was, hoping to get my rocks off with David, and all he wanted to do was say goodbye. It dawned on me that I'd wasted all that time getting dressed for nothing. I reclaimed my clutch and tucked it back under my arm. "Okay then. I guess I'll be going."

"Going? No, wait."

I frowned at him.

"I . . ." He let out a big breath. "I'd like to learn more. I mean, if you don't mind, I'd like you to teach me how to make her feel special."

My heart melted at his request. "You'll know what to do."

"No. I may not." He stepped forward and reached for my hand. "You've taught me more than any crappy magazine did. And I don't want to look like a fool."

I squeezed his hand into mine. "You won't look like a fool. If you love her, then you need to talk to her about these things."

"I will, it's just, she's really beautiful, and I'm sure she's had more experience than me, so I need to . . ." He lowered his eyes. "I don't want to be embarrassed."

His pleading was genuine, but the idea of doing anything with him when his heart was for another woman was wrong. I released his grasp on my hand and stepped back. "I can't, David. Not now that you've told me you're interested in someone. It wouldn't be right."

"But you can show me. I want to know how to please her. Maybe you can describe it and show me, without us, I don't know, touching. Does that make sense?"

If only all men were as keen on satisfying their partners as David was. For some inexplicable reason, I felt a crazy obligation to his future partner to teach him.

He could look but not touch. Was that bad? It would be just like him going to a strip show, I guessed. Not that I'd ever been to one. I decided my moral compass would remain intact as long as he didn't touch me.

I nodded and hoped like hell I didn't regret this later. "Okay, I'll show you some things, however you need to keep your distance."

"Thank you." He rubbed his hands together. "Thank you."

I put my clutch back on the tabletop and pulled out a chair facing the bed. "You can sit here."

David strode over and plonked down like an obedient student.

As I tried to work out how to play this out, my brain whizzed around so fast that I regretted that extra glass of wine. Then again, maybe the alcohol was exactly what I needed to get me through this.

I started to slip out of my stilettos, but stopped. "See my shoes?"

He glanced down, nodding. "Uh-huh."

"See how sexy they are?"

He nodded again.

"Well, they make me feel sexy. If your woman wants to buy sexy shoes, you let her. Understand?"

"Okay."

"No amount of shoes is ever enough."

"Okay."

I was beginning to enjoy this. David was my putty, and I was about to manipulate him into the best a man could be. Undoing the belt at my waist, I twirled it around, and he watched it spin as if it were a hypnotist's device.

"The same goes for her lingerie. It makes a woman feel sexy." As I peeled my dress open, gradually revealing my racy leather and lace teddy, David's eyes widened. "Let her buy as much lingerie as she needs.

He nodded slower this time, as if absorbing every word I spoke.

I curled my dress off my shoulders and let the fabric fall to my feet. As David ran his gaze up and down my body, he wriggled on his seat. I eased the spaghetti strap off my left shoulder. "Make your movements slow and sensual, taking your time with every inch of her body." I curled the strap down, hooked my arm out, and repeated the move with the other strap. The firm elastic bodice remained in place despite the straps being gone.

"You should look her in the eyes from time to time. Devour her with your gaze. And whatever you do, don't always have sex with the lights off. You want to see each other. To see how your bodies move. Trust me, it's incredible."

"Okay, I will."

I hooked my thumbs into the lace at the top of my teddy and peeled it down, gradually revealing my breasts. My insides curled with anticipation as I stood bare-chested before him. He ran his tongue over his lips and tugged his knees together. Clearly, my show pleased him.

"When you hold her breasts"—I curled my right hand beneath my left boob—"you want to caress them. Treat them as if they were your most prized possession. Which they are, by the way. Do you understand?"

He nodded.

I squeezed my breast, massaging the fullness with my fingers. "Sometimes I like it a bit rougher, but start gentle until you work out what she prefers."

"How rough though?"

"Well . . . remember they're not stress balls, and they are attached to my body. Be guided by her; she'll let you know when it's too much. Listen to her. Her breathing will let you know what she's enjoying. As will her body." I stepped apart and twirled my hips around. "She'll move her hips, her pupils will grow, and she'll make certain noises. Listen and watch for these reactions—that's how you'll know to keep going."

"Okay. I will."

I stepped closer to him as I ran my finger around my nipple. "See how my nipples harden? This is a sure sign of arousal. Men are lucky—their erection shows us they're interested. Woman have less obvious signals. You need to look for them."

As I continued to twirl my finger around my nipple it grew even harder, and as much as David's eyes showed he was enjoying the show I realized I was enjoying this, too. I was performing a valuable duty for David's future lover, and it felt damn good to be imparting my wisdom.

I curled my hand over my torso and glided it over my sex. As I bent my knees, I rubbed a finger over my pussy. The fine lace provided the right amount of friction, and I sucked the air between my teeth at the gloriousness of it. David cleared his throat, and I snapped open eyes that I hadn't realized I'd closed.

With my thumbs hooked into my teddy, I peeled it down my body and tossed it aside. "Tell her how beautiful she is. But also show it with your eyes. Really, truly look at her. Glide your hands over her body, down the curves of her waist." I demonstrated with my own hands. "Over her hips. Whisper in her ear how beautiful she is. Woman are insecure creatures—we need to hear these things."

"Okay, I will."

I parted my legs farther and glided my finger over my pussy. The first touch of my clit sent rockets shooting through me, and I shuddered.

"What did you do then?"

"Oh." I'd forgotten my role as teacher. I glanced back at the bed, then at David. As much as it felt very clinical, if I was going to do this properly then David needed to see it all.

I strode to the bed and laid down with my legs dangling over the edge. "You can come closer if you want."

Quick as a flash, he was positioned in front of me. Before I changed my mind, I glided my hands down my thighs and parted my knees, showing David all of me. He sucked the air in through his teeth, confirming he liked what he saw.

I closed my eyes and concentrated on every movement of my body. With my index finger, I glided it over my clit, applying pressure as I dragged the length of my finger along it. At the very tip I pushed down and rolled the little nub around. My knees opened and closed as if having a mind of their own, and my insides curled inward, clenching in exquisite little pulses.

"Tell me what you're doing."

"Oh, sorry."

"Don't be sorry. It's amazing."

What was amazing for him was so incredibly erotic for me that it was impossible to concentrate. I closed my eyes again and returned my attention to my clit. "This's my clitoris." It felt so wrong saying that out loud, but I carried on regardless. "This little piece of flesh is probably one of the most sensitive parts of a woman's body."

"Okay." His voice sounded a million miles away.

"You can do all sorts of things. Roll your finger around." I showed him with my own finger. "Push down. Flick. Every touch sends little shudders right through me." I could barely talk.

I glided my finger lower and entered my vagina and after I dipped my finger into the wet folds and pulled it out, I ground it over my clit, stirring up lovely sensations inside me. I plunged again. And again. Each time becoming faster than the last. I brought my knees together; I opened them. I was performing the greatest show of my life, and I was out of control.

Faster and faster I plunged into my pulsing hole and over my super-sensitive clit. I raised my hips off the bed and parted my legs, showing David every move as I thrust in and out.

I screamed as my climax ripped through me. It was explosive, and as I continued my grinding over my clit, my juices squirted from my body and over my exploring fingers. I snapped my knees shut, trapping my fingers in my core, and the electric pulses continued to sizzle through me.

It was an eternity before reality returned, and I lowered my feet to the floor. I cleared my throat as I sat up. "Sorry. I got a bit carried away at the end."

He shook his head. "That was incredible."

The enormous bulge in David's pants was impossible to ignore, and when I lowered my eyes he cupped his hand over it. "Sorry."

That was my cue to get out of there. I gathered my teddy from the floor and slipped it on, then I grabbed my dress, and as I simultaneously slipped into my stilettos, I wrapped the dress around my body and tied it at my waist.

"Thanks for everything, Memphis."

"You're welcome. And David?"

"Yes?"

"The most important thing about a relationship is communication."

"I know."

"I mean about everything. Absolutely everything. Including sex. Make it your mission to find out what she likes and what she doesn't. Not everyone likes to talk about sex, yet it plays a huge part in every couple's life."

He nodded and his pupils darkened, making me wonder if he'd had some kind of revelation.

I stepped up to him, clutched his cheeks, and leaned over to kiss his forehead. "Goodbye, David. And good luck."

"Thank you."

I turned on my heel and headed for the door.

"I'll never forget you, Memphis."

At the door, I glanced at him over my shoulder. "Likewise, David Lawson."

His glorious smile lit up his face, and he raised his hand to wave at me. With that parting image, I strode out his door and headed to the elevator.

Back in my room, I noted I had just twenty minutes before my shift started. I dove into the bathroom, removed my wig and makeup, and showered in record time.

I put a frozen Thai chicken curry in the microwave, and while I waited for it to heat up, I grabbed my diary, turned to the 15th of September, and at the top I wrote *Mr. David Lawson Room 2*. I was impressed with what David had done, because I imagined many men were too proud to ask how to please a woman. Society made it seem that men should just know what they were doing—and women, for that matter. I giggled as I realized that that was one of the reasons why I was enjoying this year so much. It was teaching me more about myself than I'd ever imagined possible. David was going to make an amazing partner, and so was I.

As I ate my dinner, I contemplated what I had just done and with each mouthful I acknowledged that I didn't feel slutty or embarrassed by it. In fact, it was the opposite. I'd basically performed a show that would teach David how to please a lover. His partner would be forever grateful for what I'd shown him. I just hoped that the future man in my life was dedicated enough to want to learn what pleased me.

With that thought, below David's name, I wrote, *The Perfect Lover.*

After I finished my meal, I tossed the frozen dinner tray into the bin, drank a glass of water, and went to the bathroom to brush my teeth.

With my bag over my shoulder, I headed toward the elevator. When the doors opened, I stepped in and using the mirror, I applied a lick of lipstick. My reflection showed how happy I was. My cheeks had a lovely healthy glow, and my eyes dazzled.

But just before the elevator arrived at the lobby, a shocking reality hit me. In the space of twelve hours, I'd lost two wonderful men in my life.

23RD SEPTEMBER
UNCHARTED WATERS
Room 52 - Hot Horizon Hotel

Thursday nights were often unpredictable, sometimes slow enough that the minutes dragged by and other times crazy-busy with people coming and going all night long. Last night was the latter, and so it was a nice surprise when a sliver of golden sunlight pierced the horizon. I glanced at the clock and noted I had just one hour left of my shift. Rising from my chair, I headed into the staffroom and made myself a cup of tea.

With my favorite teacup in hand, I headed out to the sun lounge to welcome in a new day. The morning air was very still, not even enough breeze to ruffle the leaves on the Pandanus palms. A flock of rainbow lorikeets swooped from tree to tree in a noisy chorus of screeches and flapping wings. As I sipped my tea, a warm glow illuminated the distant horizon and I spied a handful of surfers out on the dark ocean, bobbing up and down like little black corks.

A taxi drove into the drop-off zone, and the second it stopped my heart skipped a beat. Mr. Henry Addison waved at me from the passenger seat, and my skipping heart fluttered in reply.

"Good morning," he said as he stepped out of the car.

"Well hello stranger." He was hardly a stranger anymore. In fact, Henry was the man I'd seen the most this year, and my insides purred at the thought of spending more time with him.

He removed his small carry-bag from the taxi trunk, and as he climbed the five steps toward me the car drove away. I shuffled over on my seat, and he put his bag down and sat beside me. His usual scent was as delightful as it was familiar.

He nudged his shoulder to mine. "No cookies today?"

"Sadly no, I've run out."

"Hmmm, that's a shame."

"I know."

"Have you had a good night?"

"Yes thank you. It was steady. Kept me busy."

"That's good."

We both turned back to the sunrise, and as we sat in comfortable silence I realized just how pleasant it was. The sun pushed up from the horizon and cast golden rays across the ocean. Not a single cloud dotted the sky and as the panorama unfolded, a flock of seagulls scurried across the sand at the waterline as if they were in some kind of race.

"It's beautiful. No wonder you like to sit here."

"It's calming to my soul." *Phew, that was deep.*

Henry turned to me. His lovely blue eyes were attentive. "Does your soul need calming?"

I scrunched up my nose. "I think you know the answer to that."

He nodded and turned back to the ocean. "Maybe I can improve on the therapy by inviting you up to my penthouse later."

"Okay." I didn't even hesitate. Going up to Henry in the penthouse would be like walking up to heaven.

He laughed. "Wonderful. What time shall I expect you?"

"Hmmm . . ." It was Friday and the idea of having fun on a Friday night, just like all the normal people in the world did, was very appealing. "Would sunset suit you?"

"Sounds perfect."

Little butterflies danced across my stomach.

He stood up and reached for my hand. "Would you care to check me in?"

"I'd love to."

His fingers caressed my palm, and he helped me to stand. Together we strolled inside, and I stepped in behind the counter and reached for the check-in cards at the back. When I plucked Henry's name from the pile, I noticed that he'd booked this room yesterday. He was lucky to get the penthouse—it was usually booked well in advance. Henry seemed to have some kind of lucky charm watching over him. Or maybe it was just that older men had that confident air about them that ensured all the important things in life slotted nicely together.

I moved over to the computer to check his room. "Hmmm, I'm sorry,

Henry, but your room is occupied at the moment. You won't be able to check in until two."

"That's okay—I'll come back later. Can I leave my bag somewhere?"

"Of course. We can keep it back here."

Henry came around the counter and followed me into the staffroom. He put his bag down where I indicated and then reached out to put his arm around me, nestling his palm at the small of my back. My heart pounded out a thumping beat as he molded his body to mine. His eyes were alive, glancing from my eyes to my mouth and back again.

My breathing quickened as I silently begged him to kiss me. I ran my tongue over my lips, inviting him. He lowered his mouth to mine, and I closed my eyes and melted into his embrace. At the press of his tongue, I parted my lips, tasting hints of peppermint and coffee. When I curled my fingers around his neck a moan tumbled from his throat. Our bodies moved as one, our hips rocking back and forth, and as our tongues curled together a delicious heat enveloped me. The bulge in his pants pressed into my belly, and I glided my hand down to touch it.

Henry pulled back, blinking. He rubbed his hands down his thighs.

I cleared my throat at the realization of where I was and what I was doing. Have I lost my mind? That question had been answered months ago and the answer was a resounding yes.

"Hey what's going on here?" Needledick's voice cut through the atmosphere like a chainsaw, and I jumped.

Oh god, did he see us? A blaze of heat flooded my neck as my heart exploded in my chest. I checked the clock and couldn't believe he was here early. Of all the days, it had to be today.

"Jane was just letting me store my bag here for a while." Henry strode toward John and offered his hand. "I'm Henry Addison."

John shot a glance at me before he took Henry's hand. "I'm John Karwatsky, the hotel manager."

"Nice to meet you."

My feet were rooted to the floor, and I hoped like hell John didn't talk to me because there was no hope of me speaking right now.

Henry walked around to the customer side of the lobby and placed his hands on the counter. "May I just say that Miss Nichols does an excellent job."

"Oh? Really?" John glanced sideways at me, and spikes of fear drove up my spine.

"I've stayed here a few times now," Henry didn't miss a beat, "and no matter what time of the day or night I arrive she's always very friendly and professional."

By the look of John's cagy eyes, he didn't believe a word Henry had said.

"Thank you," I said to Henry.

"You're welcome. Anyway, I'll return at check-in time for my bag. Thank you, Jane." Henry tapped the counter twice then turned and strode out the sliding glass doors.

I forced my feet to move me toward the counter. "Excuse me. I'll just grab my handbag."

Needledick stepped aside, and I bent down to collect my bag from the floor.

"Do you always take men into the back room?"

I stood up and gasped. "No, I don't always take men into the back room."

"Looks to me like you could've carried that bag yourself."

The fire blazing up my neck was a full-blown inferno. "Henry offered."

"Really?" His sarcasm was unmistakable.

"Yes. Really." I backed away and hooked my bag over my shoulder.

"You two looked pretty comfortable in there."

I swallowed back the bile that crawled up my throat and forced defiance into my voice. "What does that mean?"

He cocked his head and looked as sneaky as a criminal. "I'm onto you, Jane."

"Onto what, John?" I snapped his name off my tongue.

"I'm going to catch you, and when I do you'll be out of here so fast your head will spin."

"Look, I have no idea what you're talking about." Keen to put distance between me and Needledick, I walked around the counter and strode toward the elevator.

"The karate gave it away."

Faaarrrkkk. I jabbed the button a million times and every second I waited, Needledick's dagger eyes pierced right through me.

The doors opened. I jumped in and pressed the button for my floor. The second the doors closed again, I clutched at the railing, hyperventilating enough to become dizzy. Tears stung my eyes, and by the time I reached my floor I could barely breathe.

Through my blurry vision I made it to my room, opened the door, threw my bag on the table, and then flopped face-first onto the bed. I pulled my spare pillow to my chest and squeezed the life out of it as the tears flowed.

When I couldn't cry a moment more, I rolled off the bed, plucked my phone from my bag, and then lay back down again.

I rang the only person in the world who could help me.

Lolita answered on the first ring. "Hey babe."

"Needledick knows." A deep sob released from my throat.

"Oh babe, don't cry. What does he know?"

I told her everything from the wonderful kiss with Henry to the very last words Needledick had said to me.

"Oh shit."

"Yes. Oh shit. I'm in trouble."

"Okay, let's think about this. He has no proof, right? Otherwise he would have said so."

"He's going to watch me like a hawk now."

"And how's that going to change anything?"

"If he catches me as Memphis again . . ." My mind whizzed around at the endless possibilities, not one of them good.

"Babe, you know what?"

"What?"

"Even if he does catch you, what would be the worst that would happen?"

"Oh, you mean besides ultimate humiliation?"

"Yes, besides that."

I huffed. "I'd lose my job, of course."

"Really? I don't think so. You wouldn't be the first person to have sex with a customer."

I mulled over her statement. It was probably true. "But how does that help me?"

"I don't think they could fire you for it. Hell, even Bill Clinton didn't get the sack for screwing with that Lewinski woman."

"Ummm, I think he did."

"No. He got the sack for lying about it. Not for doing it."

"So, what're you saying? As long as I don't lie I'll be fine?"

"Oh my god, that's exactly what you should do. If he catches you, you tell that bastard that what you do in your spare time is your own business. He won't know what to do with that."

I rumbled my breath through my lips. "Lolly, I think it's time to give up this craziness."

"Like hell you will. Henry will be up in that penthouse getting all hot and horny for you."

Oh yeah. I'd forgotten all about him.

"Listen, Jane, if you give up now, Needledick wins. You don't want that, do you?"

The idea of Needledick beating me at anything was repulsive. "I guess not."

"Exactly. You're nine months into this, babe. Don't give up now." Her pleading sounded genuine.

I sighed, and as I thought about what she'd said my mind drifted to Henry. No matter what I decided, I knew I'd still go up to him. Just like I'd go up to Billy. And Corben. And Hunter, David, and Dontrel—hell, even the plumber and electrician would be impossible to resist, should they return. I sat up and wiped my eyes.

"You're right," I said. "That bastard will not beat me."

"That's my girl. Now have a good sleep so you're ready for that sexy beast in the penthouse."

I giggled. "Okay." An evening with Henry was exactly what I needed.

We said our goodbyes and I hung up the phone.

My grumbling stomach was what eventually got me moving again. I turned on the television and listened to the news as I set about making myself an omelet with bacon, feta, and cherry tomatoes. Once it was ready, I carried my restaurant-quality meal and a steaming coffee out onto the balcony.

As I ate my breakfast and breathed in the crisp ocean air, my mind spun around in endless circles. Over and over, I replayed both my heart-stopping discussion with Needledick and my equally heart-stopping kiss with Henry. I could still feel Henry's lips upon mine, and if I closed my eyes, I could smell his delightful scent. He has an incredible ability to reduce my body to jelly and, not for the first time, I wondered if I were falling in love with him. As I smiled at that possibility, I collected my dirty dishes and carried them to the sink to wash up. After that, I changed into my pajamas and crawled into bed. The muscles in my body rapidly unraveled, and as I rolled onto my side and pulled my knees up to the fetal position, I let lovely images of Henry drift across my mind like in an old-fashioned 8mm motion picture.

* * *

My alarm woke me at four-thirty, and I rolled over to turn it off and stretched my arms above my head as I yawned. I crawled out of bed and dragged myself into the shower. Although it took a little while to wake up, once I focused on what adventures I could look forward to in the next couple of hours I was re-energized. I washed and blow-dried my hair, then ran the curling wand through it for a little pizzazz. At the mirror, I applied just the right touch of makeup, not too much that Memphis shone through, but enough to compliment my complexion, cover my freckles, and darken my lashes.

Happy that I still looked like Jane, I moved to my closet. What to wear? What to wear?

I decided on my white jeans that I rolled up twice at the bottom. This would ensure my sexy Christian Louboutin stilettos, the ones that practically yelled at me for attention, would be easily seen. The shoes had a fascinating orange, chocolate, and cream-colored crocodile skin that crossed over my toes and curled around my ankle, and killer eight-inch heels. I tied in the orange in the shoe with a Michael Kors tote and a pair of dangly earrings. I decided on my knitted caramel top that was prone to gliding off my shoulder all the time, and for this reason I abandoned wearing a bra.

I turned to the mirror. It was perfect, for me, the Jane me, and Henry.

With a genuine smile planted on my face, I grabbed my bits and pieces, shoved them in my bag, and strode out my door.

All my worries from this morning were long gone, and as I rode the elevator up to the ninth floor, I was pleased by my reflection in the mirror. Anticipation had colored my cheeks, and my eyes had a cheeky mischievousness about them.

The doors pinged open and I strode to Henry's penthouse. Before I even knocked, the door opened, and there stood my suave tutor.

"Good evening." He reached for my fingers, brought them up to his lips, and kissed the back of my hand.

I giggled at the lovely greeting. Dressed in a navy suit with a white shirt underneath with a couple of buttons undone, Henry was all class.

He stepped aside and with his hand on the small of my back, guided me into the room as the door shut behind us. "I thought we'd take advantage of the wonderful view upstairs."

"Sounds perfect."

He led me to the spiral stairs. "After you."

Halfway up the steps Henry cupped my bottom. "Hey." I giggled. "That's a bit cheeky."

"It's the perfect amount of cheeky if you ask me."

I laughed now, and he laughed with me. Henry had me glowing inside and out.

At the top of the stairs, I stepped into the glassed-in room and admired the spectacular view that spanned the dark blue ocean as far as I could see. Henry led the way through the glass door and held it open for me to pass through. A stainless-steel ice bucket with a metallic-topped bottle inside nestled alongside the spa that was bubbling away with a low hum.

Henry curled his arm around my waist, and we walked together to the glass wall that allowed us to see an enormous stretch of beach. As if they had a mind of their own, our fingers entwined and we stood side by side taking in the glorious panorama. The sun was already hidden behind the abundant high-rises, but its long rays cast between the buildings to layer the beach in alternating gold and dark stripes. White caps on the waves rolled into the shore, crashing over hundreds of people still swimming in the shallows.

We stood for a while just taking in the view, and I felt so comfortable with this gorgeous man at my side. It was easy to be fooled into thinking we'd known each other forever. I sighed with contentment. "It's so beautiful."

Henry positioned himself behind me, put his arms around my waist, and I tilted my head back onto his shoulder, offering him my neck. He lowered his lips and ran delicate kisses up my flesh that had delicious pulses running through me. "You're beautiful."

I turned and looked into his eyes. Henry was the epitome of tall, dark, and handsome. He was easily movie-star material. His features were fine and perfectly symmetrical, from his elegant nose to expressive blue eyes that were framed with thick, dark lashes.

The way he looked at me had me believing that all my dreams had come true. Henry was the one who was beautiful, but as he'd taught me many times over I simply said, "Thank you."

"Do you fancy a dip in the spa?"

"But I didn't bring my bathers."

"Exactly."

I giggled. "Oh, yay." The prospect of finally seeing my suave tutor naked had my insides dancing.

He curled his hands under my knitted top and glided his fingers up my waist. My nipples hardened as I waited for his reaction to me not wearing a bra. And what a reaction it was. As he cupped my breasts, his eyes widened and his pupils grew enormous. His groin grew too, and I reached down and rolled my fingers over his pants.

Henry removed my top, and as I stood there, naked from the waist up, he stepped back and his chest rose and fell as he devoured me with his gaze. His tongue lashed out, gliding over his lips and when our eyes met a delirious sense of knowing crossed between us. He stepped forward, caressed my breast, and bent over to glide his tongue over my nipple. Just when I thought that delicate bud couldn't get any harder, it did.

Henry pleasured my breasts, first my right, then my left, taking his time with each and building layer upon layer of lust inside me. I drove my fingers through his thick hair and pulled on a handful as he sucked my nipple over and over. "Oh, Henry." His name felt so perfect whispered off my lips, and when he pulled back to look into my eyes, I knew he'd enjoyed the sound of it, too.

He led me to the deck chair and indicated for me to sit. With my foot up on his thigh, Henry undid the buckle at my ankle and glided my stiletto off. Repeating the move with my other foot, he then rolled his knuckle up my instep. It was both ticklish and delightful.

"You even have beautiful feet."

I giggled, and when he helped me to stand again I decided it was my turn to remove some clothes. I reached for his shirt buttons, and with Henry watching my fingers, I gradually revealed the incredible body I knew was there. As I reached in to run my hands over his torso, Henry bent down and savored my neck again. While he glided kisses from my shoulder to my ear, I ran my fingers around his nipples, drawing them out to rock-hard pebbles.

I removed his jacket and shirt, tossed them onto the deck chair, and stepped back to examine every exposed inch of my gorgeous man. "You're very handsome, Mr. Addison."

His brilliant smile made him even more stunning.

His fingers found the button on my jeans and following his move, I did the same to him. Then, as if perfectly choreographed we both stepped back and took our own pants off. In a flash we stood opposite each other wearing nothing but our underpants. A cool breeze teased my flesh, hardening my nipples even more.

Henry's erection threatened to burst from the navy jockey undies and I stepped forward, ready to release that beast. But Henry stepped back. "Not yet."

"But I want to." I offered my best sad face, and he chuckled.

"Patience."

I so desperately wanted to see him fully naked, but I'd learned two things with Henry. One was that he was the master of teaching me new things, and two was that anticipation was an intoxicating aphrodisiac.

He led me to the spa. "Would the madam like to hop in?"

"Sure." I slipped out of my G-string and tossed it at him. Laughing, Henry clutched the miniscule lace, and as I'd expected, he raised it to his nose. With his eyes closed, Henry inhaled nice and deep, and as I turned my attention to his groin his cock moved beneath the navy fabric.

He placed my underwear on the deck chair and turned his attention to the champagne bottle next to the spa. As the cork released with a loud pop I stepped into the bubbling water. The warmth embraced me, and as I settled onto one of the seats below the waterline he handed me a glass of champagne.

My already purring insides hit a whole new tempo as I waited for the moment Henry stripped completely naked. After placing his champagne at the side of the spa he walked around to the steps. My heart thumped in my chest. I didn't want to blink for fear of missing even one millisecond.

But it didn't happen.

Henry stepped down into the spa.

"Hey, that's not fair."

"What?" He raised his brows as if he had no idea what I was referring to.

"You kept your undies on."

He glided over toward me, and reaching for his champagne, he then sat at my side and raised his glass for a toast. "Cheers."

"Don't change the subject."

He nodded at our glasses, silently insisting that we toast. So we did, clinking the glasses together, and then we both took a sip. As the delicious bubbles slid down my throat and the water in the pool bubbled around me, a random thought scurried cross my brain. What if Henry was embarrassed to show me his penis? I'd never thought about that. Maybe he thought he was too old for me, or too small, or something just as silly. I needed to do something about that.

I put my glass down, then before he could object, I glided toward him and with my hands on his shoulders, I curled my right leg over his hips to straddle him.

The bulge in his groin nestled nicely right beneath my pussy and grinding back and forward, I made sure he knew that I knew he was erect.

"What are you doing, madam?" He grinned at me.

"Pleasuring myself."

He chuckled, and I smiled at the wonderful melody. I continued rocking, moving my hips back and forward, using his hardness to please my throbbing vagina. He locked his eyes on mine and my insides sizzled at both the intensity of his gaze and the wonderful sensations flowing through me.

Henry gulped his drink down and put the glass aside. Then he reached down, and as I continued to rub back and forward, he pressed his thumb against my clit and rolled the hypersensitive bud. I gasped, clutched his shoulders, and tilted my head back, continuing my momentum. His finger drove over my clit and glided into my throbbing hole and I raised up on my knees, giving him room.

Henry placed his hands on my hips and glided me off him. Before I knew it, we were on the opposite side of the spa. He had my hips above the water and as I clutched onto the tiled edge, he lowered his face between my legs.

As the warm water caressed my back, and the cool air teased my nipples to attention, Henry licked his hot, probing tongue up and down my sex. My eyes rolled, and I gasped aloud as he drove a finger into me. His tongue twirled around my clit in perfect timing to his finger that thrust into me. A second finger joined his first, and as he drove them in and out in a slow, twisting motion I hooked my knees up over his shoulders, begging him to keep going.

Every nerve in my body tingled, and as I clawed at the tiles, I curled my back upwards and squeezed my knees, trapping his head between my thighs. Suddenly, there was a third finger, but this one wasn't at my pussy—it was at my anus.

"Hey." I pulled my legs off his shoulders and dragged my bottom into the water.

He reached up to caress my cheek. "You trust me, don't you?"

"You know I do, but I don't do anal."

"Have you ever done it before?"

"No, of course not."

"Then let me show you how it should be done." His pupils were huge as he pleaded with me.

"Henry, I don't know . . ."

"I promise it won't hurt, and if you say stop at any time, I will."

I shook my head. Anal had never appealed to me. Just the very thought of someone penetrating that part of me was horrifying. But this was Henry, my fabulous tutor, who'd shown me more things about my body than any man ever had.

"Jane. Trust me."

"I do, it's just . . . I don't know."

He threaded his hands up and down my inner thighs. "Exactly, you don't know. Let me show you."

"Okay." I could hardly believe it was my own voice that'd spoken. "But you have to let me touch you, too."

"Okay." He smiled a warm, knowing smile.

I blinked at him and, worried I wasn't being specific enough, I decided to elaborate. "So if I agree to this, you'll let me"—oh God, how did I say it—"play with your penis until you ejaculate."

His hands curved right up my thighs, parting my legs more each time. "Okay, I agree. Now relax, and know that if you tell me to stop, I will."

"Okay."

"Relax, Jane. I'm going to show you something truly special."

His words and hands were like an intoxicating spell, talking to my body rather than my mind, and my hips began to move with a will of their own.

He raised my hips and as I clutched the sides of spa, he lowered his head and glided his tongue up and down my pussy again. His fingers returned to my vagina, working their incredible magic to bring my arousal right back to where it'd been just moments before. His fingers twisted in and out, plunging deep inside me as his tongue, hot and hard, played with my clitoris.

Just when I thought he'd abandoned his plan, his hand glided over my bottom and his finger nudged at my anus. I clenched in response, and he drew his finger away and returned to my pussy to continue drawing out my unbridled arousal. Moments later his finger was there again, gently touching my uncharted hole. As he continued to lick and finger my pussy, his other finger glided around my anus, gently rolling over and over until it no longer felt weird.

In fact, it felt okay. I relaxed my bottom, and tried not to think about what was he was doing. It wasn't hard—with every lick of Henry's tongue I was taken to another world. And then it happened. Gently, gently Henry pushed his finger into my anus. I gasped at the intrusion and he halted his probing, but continued everything else.

A couple of heartbeats later, he pushed again, driving his finger farther into my anus, all the while continuing the tongue lashing and the twisting thrusts into my pussy. It was exquisite and weird. It was thrilling and shocking. It blew my mind.

It pleased my body.

I clawed at the walls. I cried out and parted my legs, letting Henry know that whatever he was doing he could go right on doing it. And he did. Licking, probing, and plunging both my holes. I was in heaven. I screamed as every nerve in my body erupted into a mind-blowing orgasm that shot me right off the roof of the Hot Horizon Hotel and sent me to the stars.

Rolling waves of joy threaded through me over and over and over, and when I could come no more, I lowered my hips and opened my eyes. Henry's fingers came out, leaving me with a weird throbbing sensation in my bottom.

His smile was magic, and before he had a chance to renege on our agreement I went to him. With my hands on his shoulders I pushed him to the far edge, glided my hands down his waist, put my thumbs into his underpants and tugged them from his body. I tossed them aside and went straight to my prize.

With one hand around his penis, I used my other hand to raise his bottom. Seconds later, my suave tutor's cock bobbed above the water like a ship's mast. It was magnificent—perfect in length, perfect in width. The pink crown, swollen with excitement, glistened in the discreet lighting. I lowered my lips to that glorious specimen and sucked him into my mouth.

Henry moaned, deep and guttural, and I glided my lips down his shaft and sucked his cock into my throat. I moved one hand to cup his balls and with my other hand around the base of his shaft, I glided up and down in time to my sucking.

His balls sucked upwards, and as I rolled my lips down Henry jerked beneath me, drove his fingers through my hair, and cried out. A heartbeat later his hot fluid shot into the back of my throat.

I continued to glide my hand up and down his shaft as I swallowed his juices. He softened in my mouth, and I pulled my lips up for the last time and ran my tongue around the tip of his crown, ensuring I'd lapped up every last drop. I licked my lips as I pulled back, genuinely enjoying the taste of him.

"Wow." His voice was shaky.

"Wow." I nodded in agreement. Once again, Henry had shown me something extraordinary about myself and I'd be forever grateful.

"Are you okay?" He reached for my hand and entwined his fingers in mine. Was I? Whilst my mind wanted to deny it, my body was saying the opposite. Henry had introduced me to anal sex in a way that had made it gentle, interesting, and undeniably erotic. That orgasm had been unlike any other—without a doubt, it'd been extraordinary. Finally, I nodded. "Yes, I'm fine."

"I'm glad." He reached for the champagne bottle, topped up our glasses, and handed one to each of us. "You're extraordinary, Jane."

I sipped my bubbles. "As are you, Henry."

"Thank you," he said, and we both laughed.

We sipped our drinks in silence and I noted once again how comfortable it was with him. As I processed through my brain what he'd just done to me, I wondered what he was thinking. "Have you done that before?" I wanted to slap myself at my nosiness. "Oh sorry. You don't have to answer that."

"It's okay." He touched my arm. "You can ask me anything."

I gulped back a big sip of wine.

"When my wife and I first got married, we had amazing sex. She was adventurous, just like you."

Sensing he wanted to tell me more, I put on my therapist's hat and sipped my drink in silence.

"As the years went by, Helen lost her confidence. She was constantly worried about how she looked. But I didn't care—I loved her. I loved her body, and after she had our beautiful children I loved her even more."

"What happened?"

"She started to push me away. Always worried about her weight and the stretch marks that came with childbirth. If we did make love it'd be with the lights off, and it was always me driving the passion, never her. She fell out of love with me and I have no idea why."

"Oh, Henry." My heart crumbled at how forlorn he looked.

"We went for months without sex, then it became years."

Knowing how amazing Henry was with a woman's body, I couldn't imagine what her reluctance was.

"One afternoon, she was out with her girlfriends—well supposedly—and on a whim, I decided to drive around to my mate's place with a six-pack of beer. He didn't answer the door, but figuring he was out on his boat, like he usually was, I went around the back. And that's when I saw them. Caught them right in the middle of sex."

"Oh Henry. How horrible." I squeezed his hand and felt every bit of his agony. "I know exactly how painful that must've been. And probably still is."

"It was . . . until I met you. You taught me how to feel again. I'd become stone cold inside. Blocked out my ability to feel love and passion."

I leaned over and kissed his cheek, and he curled his arm around my shoulder and drew me next to him. The warmth of his body was like a familiar blanket. I rolled my head into his shoulder and as I listened to his breathing, little stars slowly dotted the evening sky.

"Your story is almost exactly like mine."

"Really?" He shook his head.

"I caught Alexander with my best friend having sex in his car."

"What's wrong with these people?"

"You know what the worst thing was?"

"Worse than that? What?"

"They tried to say it was my fault that he'd slept around. We had a huge screaming match during which he went on to tell me all the other women he'd had sex with while we were engaged. Apparently every one of them was my fault."

Henry curled his hand to my cheek and drew his lips to mine. The kiss was sweet and delicate. "It was never your fault."

"I know that now. It took me a long time to believe myself though. This year has helped."

He smiled at me. "You're one of the most erotic women I know."

"Why thank you, Mr. Addison."

"I mean it, Jane. Too many women are worried about their appearance to truly let their bodies take over."

I nodded, absorbing his words.

"I'm more interested in a woman's open mind than how flat her stomach is."

"No offence, but you're not like most men."

"I'll think you'll find I'm exactly like most men."

I huffed, not entirely sure if I agreed with him.

"Here's some words of wisdom for you. Everybody gets old. Your body will wrinkle and sag with age. That's inevitable. But your mind is what keeps you young." He placed his hand on my knee. "Retain your sense of adventure. Do things spontaneously. Prance around naked and have sex on the kitchen counter. Those sorts of things will keep you young and make you feel much more alive than any Botox needle will."

I entwined my fingers into his and breathed a contented sigh as I committed his words of wisdom to my brain. The water bubbled away around us, the stars twinkled above us, and as the handsome man beside me held my hand, I tried to memorize everything about this truly exquisite moment.

It was an eternity before Henry unhooked our fingers. "Come on. You need to get ready for work."

"Oh bugger." It was a rotten realization, but nonetheless, I let him lead me from the spa. He handed me a towel and I dried myself off and redressed. Carrying the ice bucket and glasses, we made our way back downstairs.

At the kitchen counter, I smiled at him. "Thank you for a wonderful evening."

He stepped over and kissed me, just a gentle, brief kiss. "Thank you too. Now off you go. Don't want you getting into trouble."

I huffed. "That's true."

"Oh yeah. Was everything alright this morning?"

"Yes, it was fine." I decided against enlightening Henry to what had happened after he left.

We said our goodbyes and I made my way back to my room. By the time I'd showered and dressed in my clothes for work I had just over an hour until I needed to head downstairs to start my shift.

Aware of my growling stomach, I set about cooking salmon for dinner, taking particular care to make sure it was still dark pink in the middle, yet the skin was nice and crispy. From the fridge I pulled out a crunchy salad that came in a packet and took about six seconds to toss. My stomach practically barked at me as I carried my dinner onto my balcony to eat.

Crispy-skin salmon was by far one of my favorite meals and lucky for me, it was quick and easy to make. The first mouthful was heaven, as was every one after that. Within minutes, I'd devoured the whole lot.

A cool breeze floated off the ocean and I went inside, grabbed a jacket and my diary, and returned to my seat.

I turned to the 23rd of September, and at the top I wrote *Mr. Henry Addison Room 52*, my suave tutor. In intimate detail I described what we'd done in the spa and more importantly, how it had made me feel. I didn't hold back and wrote down everything from feeling uncomfortable about the experience to how incredible it'd been. As I noted how Henry had taught me yet another way to explore the intricacies of my body, I wrote *Uncharted Waters* beneath his name.

I closed my diary, and as I sipped a glass of water and stared out to the millions of stars across the inky black sky, I wondered how many more lessons I could learn before this year was over.

27TH SEPTEMBER
MARATHON MAN
Room 45 - Hot Horizon Hotel

At the end of my shift, I'd had every intention of going to my room and crawling into bed for a long sleep. However, once I stepped onto my balcony I changed my mind. The weather was magnificent.

I dressed in my workout gear, pulled on my Nike runners, grabbed a hat and sunglasses, and headed back out my door. Ignoring Needledick as I crossed the lobby, I stepped through the sliding glass doors and was eternally grateful for my decision to go outside, because walking up toward me was one of the hottest men on the planet.

"Jane." His deep voice perfectly suited his musclebound physique.

"Corben." Unlike last time we'd greeted, I was in control of my emotions.

"You heading out for a run?"

"I was about to. Would you like to join me?"

We met on the middle step. The urge to reach up and kiss him was a powerful magnet, but I couldn't risk the chance of Needledick seeing it. Corben grunted and shook his head. "Wish I could. But my shift starts in half an hour, so I have to keep moving."

"Pity. I was gearing up to whip your butt." I couldn't believe I'd said that and swallowed back the cheekiness.

He cocked his eyebrow at me. "Really? You can whip my butt later if you like."

My insides did a little flip. "Maybe I will."

Corben placed his hands on his hips and made his bulging biceps bulge even greater. "You're getting a bit cheeky."

I chewed on the inside of my bottom lip.

"Today's your day off, isn't it?"

"Yes, it is."

"Right. Well, I'm taking you out tonight. Unless of course you had plans?"

I blinked up at him. *Taking me out? Me and Corben out on a date.* My knees wobbled at the wonderful prospect. "No. Just so happens I'm free tonight."

"Lucky me." His voice was smooth, in control.

"Lucky me too."

He grinned, and the transformation in his usually stern features was startling. "I'll meet you right here at eight-thirty."

He leaned over, smacked my bottom, and then carried on up the stairs without waiting for my response. I blinked after him, unsure whether I should be happy or annoyed with his forthrightness, but my bubbling insides answered that question. Happiness was going out in public with a man like Corben.

The spring in my step had me on the beach in no time, and I made my way to the sand that was nice and firm from the outgoing tide. I turned with the sun on my left-hand side and started jogging parallel to the shoreline. As I found my stride and pumped my arms back and forward, my head tumbled over a zillion questions about my evening with Corben.

Where was he taking me? What should I wear? Was this our first official date? And if so, were there many more to come?

The way I was feeling right now, I hoped the last question would be answered with a big fat yes. Ten months ago, the idea of an evening with a hunk like Corben had seemed ludicrous. Now, though, it wasn't just a possibility—it was a certainty.

With the sun on my cheek and the gentle breeze drifting off the ocean to lick the sweat off my neck and chest, I inhaled the crisp ocean air. I didn't think I'd ever felt this alive before.

I tried to clear my mind and concentrate on my stride, but it was impossible. Thoughts of Corben dominated every second of my workout. Lucky me.

My energy levels were at a record high, and I carried right on past the surf lifesavers' club for another ten minutes. It was only when my breathing became ragged that I slowed down to a steady jog and then stopped altogether.

Two men with surfboards walked toward me. They'd peeled their wetsuits down to their waists, allowing their finely toned bodies to glisten in the sun.

Their dazzling smiles and casual swagger added to their already stunning appearance.

They flanked me, one on either side as they walked past, grinning.

"Good morning."

"Hi there. Great day for a run."

Like a dazzled virgin, a hot flush blazed up my neck and cheeks as they each spoke to me. "Yes, hi, and yes it is." My squeaky voice was that of an awkward teenage girl. The man closest to the shore turned to look over his shoulder and winked at me. Despite all my resolve, I couldn't stop my jaw dropping.

He laughed, and they carried on walking.

My already amazing day just got a whole lot better. I turned in their direction and as I followed their tight little butts, I began my return journey home. The shorter of the two men shoved the other man in the shoulder, and he stumbled slightly before he gained his balance and then turned to walk back to me.

I continued my stride but with every step we closed the distance between us, it became harder to breathe. I'd convinced myself that the guy was going to walk straight on past, but when he stopped a couple of paces before me and turned his board around so he was facing the same direction as me, I thought my lack of breath would have me passing out.

"Hi again."

"Hi." I grinned at him.

"I'm Tom."

"Jane. Nice to meet you."

He ran his free hand through his curly sun bleached hair. "Are you here on holiday?"

I could hardly comprehend that this sexy stranger was actually talking to me. The Jane me. "No. Are you?"

"Yes, just up from Adelaide for a week."

Our strides were matched perfectly, and as I tried to sneak glances at the man beside me I was grateful for my dark sunglasses. "You've had incredible weather."

"Yes, we have. Anyway . . ." He cleared his throat. "It's my last night here tonight. Would you like to go out with me?"

I choked on my own tongue, and we stopped as he patted my back.

"Are you okay?"

"Sorry, sorry, it's just, wow. Really?"

He laughed a glorious, manly, contagious laugh that had me relaxing. "Yes really."

I was seconds away from saying yes when I remembered Corben. Never in my whole life had I needed to choose between two men, and my thoughts spun around at the wonderful gloriousness of it.

Quick as a flash, I compared my two suitors. Both were stunning representations of the male species. While Corben was a hunky Mr. Universe, Tom was slender with lean muscles in all the right places. In the end, my decision was easy. I knew I'd have a wonderful evening with Corben, whereas this young man was an uncertainty—a sexy, fascinating uncertainty.

I curled a lock of hair that'd escaped from my band behind my ear. "I'm sorry, I'm so flattered, but I already have a date."

He huffed. "Bugger. Oh well, if he turns out to be a dick, we're hanging out at the Surfers Paradise Beer Garden later. Come and find me." He winked at me, and then jogged ahead to catch up to his mate.

My wonderful day had just shot into spectacular, and it took all my might not to break out into a few cartwheels. I was the luckiest woman in the world. Turning toward the ocean I spread my arms wide, breathed in deeply and screamed, "Woohooooooo."

Grinning like a crazy woman, I strolled back toward my hotel and my mind skipped from one lovely thought to another. People walked along the beach with me, all looking equally as happy as I was. A young couple who couldn't be any older than seventeen swung their clasped hands back and forward, and the girl's pretty features reminded me of Chelsea-Lea.

My ex-best friend had been one of the most beautiful girls at my school, if not the most beautiful. Unlike me, it was nothing for her to be asked out two or three times a week. Sometimes in the same night. My mind flashed to her standard response. "Piss off, creep."

We'd giggled at that a few times, but now, as I recalled the forlorn looks on those young boys' faces, I was deeply saddened that I'd taken joy in their embarrassment. It occurred to me that I had no idea if she'd had her baby, which was a timely reminder to call Aunty Ann and catch up on all my home town gossip.

Before I left the beach, I paused and turned to the ocean, making a point of taking in the entire panorama and confirming for the hundredth time that I lived in one of the most beautiful places in the world.

I deliberately avoided glancing at Needledick as I crossed the lobby, and fortunately, he didn't attempt to converse with me either. At my room, I had a quick shower and dressed in my cotton pajama shorts set. I made peanut butter on toast, matched that with a hot coffee in the cow mug Henry had given me and with my phone in my pocket, I carried my breakfast out to the balcony.

As usual, the simple breakfast was yummy, and I devoured it in about ten seconds flat, then I picked up the phone and dialed Aunty Ann.

"Well hello. How's my gorgeous niece?"

"I'm excellent, Aunty Ann. How are you?"

"Same-o, same-o. Not a lot going on in my life I'm afraid."

"Are you going to Dad's sixtieth?"

"Of course. I can't wait to see you."

"You too. I miss you. Did you know Alexander is going?"

She sucked the air in between her teeth. "No I didn't. Your mom never mentioned that to me. Why would they invite that bastard?"

I pushed back and hoisted my legs up onto the other chair. "Apparently Alexander and Dad are great friends. They go fishing together."

"What? No. I can't believe that."

"That's what I said."

"After everything he did to you."

"Yep. I'm so glad you're on my side, Aunty Ann."

"I'm going to ring your mother and give her a piece of my mind."

I was two seconds away from objecting when I changed my mind. Maybe Mom would listen to her sister. "Thank you, but I doubt it'll help. Hey, tell me what's happening with Chelsea-Lea?"

"Oh yes, you should see her. She's the size of the Goodyear Blimp." Aunty Ann's coarse laughter rumbled down the phone, and I chuckled with her. Her laugh became a rugged cough, and as I waited for her to breathe again, I tried to picture Chelsea-Lea looking like that.

Aunty Ann cleared her throat. "You know how pregnant women usually have this glorious glow?"

"Yeah."

"Well, she doesn't. She's really let herself go. Her hair's all frizzy, and she has a skunk stripe because she hasn't had it colored. You won't even recognize her."

"I can't wait to see what she looks like."

"She'll have the baby by then."

"I know. So do you know who the father is?"

She huffed. "Word is it could be any number of guys. Nobody wants to own responsibility yet. So there'll be a few paternity tests once the poor little munchkin is born."

I whistled. "Holy cow."

"Yep, your friend has got herself into a right mess."

"Not my friend."

"Thank god. She was a bitch."

"Who got what she deserved. It's just a shame there's an innocent baby involved now."

"True. So tell me about you. Got a man in your life?"

I smiled as I wondered which one I should mention, then I decided there was no harm in the truth. "As a matter of fact, I have several, and would you believe two men asked me on a date just this morning?"

She burst into fits of laughter again. "You go girl! Oh, I can't wait to hear all about them. Make sure you fit in time to come and see me when you're

here. I mean, without your parents around, too. I want all the juicy details."
I chuckled. "Okay, I will."
"How about you come over for tea on Saturday morning? I'll make one of my pineapple upside-down cakes."
"Oh, that sounds just perfect. It's a date."
"Wonderful."
"Anyway, I'm going to get some sleep. I need to be ready for my hot date tonight."
"Okay, sweetheart. Give that boy a jolly good root for me, will you?"
We burst out laughing together, and I waited out the barking cough that followed.
"Bye. I love you." Her voice was a croaky whisper.
"Love you too."
I glowed with love as I put the phone aside and gathered my dishes to carry to the sink. It seemed so unfair that a beautiful woman like Aunty Ann didn't have children while someone as undeserving as Chelsea-lea did. Life could be so cruel.
As I crawled into bed, I wondered what I'd look like when I was pregnant. Hugging my pillow, I closed my eyes and the one image that stood out was how happy and glowing I'd be.

* * *

I woke several hours later, and when I rolled over I was surprised to see it was after six o'clock. I'd forgotten to set my alarm. I stretched out, rolled off the bed, and headed to the bathroom. My hair stuck up in all directions, and I had sleep creases down my cheek. It was lucky I still had a few hours before I needed to be ready for Corben.
I was undecided on whether I should eat or not. Corben hadn't mentioned we'd be going to dinner. My grumbling stomach forced my decision, and I made two slices of Peanut Butter on toast and decided to have it with a glass of Sauvignon Blanc.
Out on the balcony, I ate my snack, sipped my wine, and watched the world go by for an hour or so. It was a beautiful night. The moon was nowhere to be seen, but a million stars dotted the blackness. Down on the beach, a bunch of teenagers looked to be having a party. Thumping music drifted up from the sand, and several girls still in bikinis danced to the rhythm.
It made me wonder where Corben was taking me. He didn't strike me as a fancy restaurant type of guy, so I pictured somewhere more casual. He wasn't the chatty type either, so a venue with a bit going on would be ideal, like a bar, or maybe the casino. I grabbed my dishes, headed inside and washed up.
After a long hot shower, I did my hair and makeup and then stood at my

closet, hoping for inspiration. I decided on my jeans, and rolled them up at the bottom to show off whatever shoes I chose. It was the perfect night to wear a pair of shoes that hadn't had an outing yet—something sexy was called for. On my knees, I leaned into my closet and scanned my extensive shoe collection. Right at the back I plucked out a pair of navy suede stilettos. They had a thin strap that went over my toe, an enclosed ankle that did up with a back zipper and a lace strap that wrapped around and around my ankle. Best of all, the heel wasn't too high—only about five inches. They were perfect, and I smiled as I realized these little beauties were about to get a wonderful memory to go with them.

Using the navy as inspiration, I matched it up with a navy linen button-up shirt that had little flaps which I used to secure my sleeves that I rolled up at couple of times at the cuff. Tying it all together, I draped my long fake pearls around my neck twice and put on matching pearl earrings.

I looked in the mirror and turned to inspect my butt to ensure my lacy G-string wasn't visible. With ten minutes to spare, I grabbed a black tote, tossed in my essentials and then strode out my door. I utilized my time in the elevator to apply a touch of my favorite Bobbi Brown Retro Red lippy.

The middle-aged gentleman who did my shifts during my nights off was behind the counter. He was an aloof man whom I'd tried unsuccessfully to chat with a few times.

I waved at him; he waved back, and that was the usual extent of our communications. Not that I minded—I was just grateful that his presence allowed me to have every Wednesday off work.

Corben waited for me on the middle step, just as we'd arranged. He looked like a rock star in dark denim jeans, stylishly torn in a few places, a white T-shirt that failed to hide the bulging pecs beneath it, and a black leather jacket that looked both expensive and well worn. When I stepped up beside him, he smiled and leaned in to kiss my cheek.

"Are you Jane or Memphis tonight?"

I blinked at him, wondering which one he wanted me to be. Then I smiled. "I'm both."

"Good." He nodded with conviction and led me to a taxi that was waiting in the drop-off zone.

He opened the door and I slid in. Seconds later he slipped into the back seat beside me, and I assumed Corben must've already told the driver our destination as the car pulled out into the evening traffic.

Corben smelt divine, an intoxicating mix of cologne and leather.

He turned to me. "Hope you've got your dancing shoes on?"

I glanced at my shoes and cringed. The last thing I'd thought Corben would suggest was dancing. "Well, they're not as high as some of my shoes."

"Good."

We drove the opposite direction to the casino and headed toward Surfers

Paradise. About ten minutes later, we pulled into a taxi zone near Cavill Avenue. Corben gave the driver twenty dollars and we stepped out at the same time.

Walking side by side, we strolled up the crowded mall. Despite it being a Wednesday night, people were everywhere. I shouldn't have been surprised—Surfers Paradise was a party hotspot, no matter which night of the week it was.

"Hungry?" Corben asked.

"Of course."

"Good."

He put his hand around my waist and led me over to a hotdog stand. I nearly chuckled. Was he joking? My head did mickey flips as I realized he wasn't joking.

"Hey Johnno, how you doin'?" Corben leaned over the counter and he and Johnno shared some kind of ritualistic handshake.

"Corben, how's my man?"

Corben turned his attention to me. "Johnno here makes the best hotdogs on the Eastern seaboard."

"Oh, good." I searched my date's eyes, almost anticipating him to burst out laughing and declare this as a big joke. But he didn't.

"So, what would you like?"

"Ummm . . ." As I scanned the blackboard menu, totally bemused by this weird turn of events, Corben stepped up to the counter.

"I'll have the usual." He turned to me. "I can recommend the grilled bratwurst and the smoked Kransky, and Johnno makes his own ketchup."

"Excellent." I hoped I didn't sound too sarcastic.

Deciding I had no other option, I studied the menu more extensively. If I was going to do this, I was going to do it properly. Maybe Corben was testing me, seeing how I'd react to this rather unconventional dinner choice.

"Okay, I'll have the Magnum PI."

Corben raised his brows. "It's spicy."

"I noticed."

"Okay then."

He turned to Johnno and ordered my meal.

"Extra bacon please." I touched Corben's arm for his attention. "And a water."

"Roger that."

Ten minutes later, carrying our dinner, Corben led me to a bench seat in the middle of the mall and we sat opposite each other.

I needed both hands to pick up my hotdog, and right from the very first bite I was sold. The brioche bun was fresh, the sausage was just the right amount of spicy, the smoked ham and fresh pineapple added nice twists, and the homemade ketchup was to die for. We ate in silence, sharing our glances between our food, each other, and the crowd around us.

"You surprise me, Memphis Jane."

"Oh, why?"

"I dunno. I just thought you'd cringe at a meal like this."

So it had been a test. I did a silent jig that I'd passed with flying colors. "I love my food."

"I can see that." He glanced down at my empty plate.

"Best hotdog I've had in years." It was the truth, too.

"You're a fascinating woman."

Was that good or bad? By the twinkle in his eyes, I decided it was good, and instantly wondered what other tests he'd planned.

We remained seated for a while making idle chitchat about the passing crowd. Every once in a while he'd glance at his watch, and I had a sneaky feeling he was waiting for something, though I resisted asking what.

The crowds grew thicker and noisier as the evening rolled on, and it was ten-thirty before Corben finally stood up and tossed our rubbish into a nearby bin. "Come on then. It's time to work off some of those calories."

Oh god, I didn't like the sound of that. Unless of course it involved wild, crazy sex—then count me in.

Ten minutes later I acknowledged that no, it didn't involve wild, crazy sex, as he led me up a long set of stairs to the entrance of Incognito dance club. Here we go—test number two.

Corben and the bouncer did what looked like a well-practised secret handshake, and we were admitted without paying the ten-dollar cover charge.

My first assaulted sense was my hearing. The music was loud, and the heavy beat vibrated through my chest. Corben led me to a small round table in front of the bar, and he slipped the reserved sign into his pocket as we sat down on the stools.

The loud music, required him to lean into my ear to speak. "What do you drink?"

I shrugged. "Wine."

He pulled back and frowned. "White or red?"

"White please, Sauv Blanc."

"Okay, back in a sec."

Corben must've had an express lane through the throng at the bar as he was back moments later holding a large wine glass with a tiny slosh of wine in the bottom. He in turn had a crystal tumbler with an amber liquid over a couple of ice cubes. Handing me my glass, we chinked ours together, and then I took a sip. It wasn't Shaw & Smith, but it was acceptable.

Talking was impossible, so as I drank my wine, I alternated my gaze between my hunky date and the dance floor. Corben was a man who commanded attention, and by the constant glances I observed from passing women, he sure did get it.

My first wine went down very easily and before I knew it, Corben had bought me another. I made a mental note to buy the next round.

It was my kind of music. Not too heavy or techno, and it was easy to move to the beat. Before I knew it I was wriggling in my seat and wondering when Corben would actually ask me to dance. With my second drink gone, I reached for my bag and leaned over to him. "What are you drinking?"

"I'll get it."

"No you won't." I was more forceful than I'd intended, but I wanted him to know I meant it.

"Okay." He shrugged. "Canadian Club on ice."

I wiggled to the bar and ordered two Canadian Clubs on ice. Corben smiled at me on my return, and once again we chinked glasses and I sipped mine. It was sweet and spicy and really yummy.

One of my favorite songs came on, 'Cake by the Ocean', and before I comprehended what I was doing I pulled my tote up to my shoulder, jumped off my stool, grabbed Corben's hand, and dragged him to the dance floor.

With my hands above my head, I clapped out the funky beat as Corben stepped from side to side with a cheeky grin on his face. I sang the lyrics loud, knowing full well that nobody could hear me. I had all the moves and felt so good showing them off. Stepping forward, I glided my hands down Corben's chest, treating him as a dance pole. He rolled his head back and laughed, confirming that I'd just passed his second test.

Many people glanced at Corben—women, mostly. Why wouldn't they? He was the hottest man in the club. And he was all mine. My hands had a mind of their own and groped his bountiful muscles as I gyrated to the rhythm. It was so much fun, and I couldn't stop laughing as I broke out all my funky moves.

When the song finished, Corben led me back to our table. As I sat, he went back to the bar and returned moments later with two almost-black drinks in martini glasses. The top of the drink was a thick froth and nestled in the middle were a couple of coffee beans.

"Oooh, what's this?"

He leaned into my ear. "Espresso martini."

"Yummy," I said, even though I'd never had one before. I tipped it up and sipped, and to my delight it was strong yet delicious.

A couple of songs later, I finished my martini and dragged Corben to the dance floor again. He'd loosened up a bit, and it was his turn to shake out a few moves. We were in sync, taking the groovy beat to a whole new level. After a couple of songs, he led me back to the table, and this time when he returned from the bar he had a couple of shot glasses, with a salt shaker, and two lime wedges.

"Oooh, what are these?"

He frowned at me. "Tequila. Haven't you had it before?"

"No."

He laughed and leaned in. "Follow what I do."

"Okay."

He rubbed the lime on the back of his hand near his thumb and sprinkled the salt on the wet spot. Then he held the lime wedge in the salted hand and the shot glass in the other. Corben raised his hand to his mouth and in a truly erotic display, he glided his tongue over the salt, then tossed the drink into his mouth, and bit into the lime. He slammed his glass onto the table, and tossed the lime skin into it, signifying the end to the ritual.

Rubbing my hands together, I was eager to give this a try. Corben's eyes dazzled in the flashing lights as he watched me apply the salt. Then I put the lime wedge in one hand and picked up the shot glass. He wriggled his eyebrows, and I made a show of curling my tongue over the back of my hand, then I tossed the clear liquid into my throat and gasped at the potent onslaught. I shuddered as the fiery liquid coursed through my body.

"Quick, suck the lime," Corben yelled, and I bit into the citrus, grateful to eradicate the tequila taste.

I stuck my tongue out. "Oh god, that was terrible."

He put his arm around me, pulled me in for a hug, and kissed my forehead. "You'll get used to it."

I could easily get used to him caressing me in public like this.

The night carried on like that. We danced to several songs, and he entertained me with a different-colored drink each time he returned from the bar. I lost all track of time, and it was wonderful to be out celebrating the nightlife with Mr. Universe. But my pussy soon commanded attention and with each drink I consumed I groped him more, becoming increasingly adventurous each time.

Eager to taste my hunky spunk, I slid off my stool, sidled up beside him, wrapped my arms around his thick neck, and planted my lips on his. At my probing tongue he opened his lips, and as our tongues danced together I glided one hand over his thigh and between his legs.

He laughed as he pulled back. "Alright, lady, it's time I took you home."

I wriggled my eyebrows and glided my finger from his left nipple to his right. "Okey-dokey."

It seemed like only seconds before we were in a cab. Somehow, we got out of the taxi and magically appeared in the elevator at the Hot Horizon Hotel. I shoved Corben back against the wall, forced my tongue into his mouth, and drove the palm of my hand over his groin. My pussy pulsed as if still moving to the nightclub beat. I stepped back and yanked my shirt apart sending buttons flying.

Corben's jaw dropped and wanting to capitalize on the shock factor, I handed him my tote and yanked my top off. As his eyes bulged and his smile broadened I reached behind my back, unclipped my bra, and swung it around in my hand. Tossing it onto the floor, I clutched onto Corben's shoulders, jumped into his arms, and wrapped my legs around him.

Our mouths were locked together as the elevator dinged open, and he carried me to his room. Once inside he had my back against the wall and his hand around my breast, squeezing and twisting my nipple until it was close to hurting.

I gasped and pulled back. "Owwweee."

"Sorry, babe."

Babe! Okay, he's forgiven.

I slipped off his hips, dropped to my knees, and fumbled with his jeans zipper to remove the beast I knew was there. In a flash, his pants were around his ankles and his cock was in my mouth. Damn, he tasted so good. I glided my tongue around and around the head of his penis and drew that long, fabulous length into my throat.

Corben drove his fingers through my hair and as I remained still, I allowed him to drive his cock in and out of my mouth. I groaned, and he moaned as his erection grew even greater. He stepped back and pulled me upright, and next second he practically tossed me onto the bed. His hands were on my feet, and as the room spun around in warped circles he removed my stilettos.

His hands were warm and eager as he worked on undoing and removing my jeans, and before I knew it, we were both naked. I spread my legs and glided my hand over my sex to touch my clit.

"I'm ready." I barely recognized my own voice.

"Oh, I know you are." He tore open a condom packet that I hadn't seen him get.

Corben flipped me over so I was on my hands and knees. His cock nudged my vagina and as his hands dug into the flesh at my hips he rammed it into me. It was fast. It was shocking. It was so fucking good. So good, in fact, that an orgasm ripped through me, wild, explosive, and incredible.

I fisted the sheets and hung on as Corben thrust into me again and again and again.

He was a machine, in and out, over and over, to the point where I thought this was never going to end. And I meant never. I was exhausted. Enough was enough. My arms couldn't hold me a moment more, and I face-planted onto the bed.

Corben rolled me onto my back, and I let him manipulate me. He hooked his hands under my knees and dragged me toward him, aiming his cock for my pussy, and once again he was in me. As I gazed up at the muscle god who was thrusting his enormous jackhammer into me, I felt like I'd slipped into some kind of magical dream. The room gently spun around. My eyes rolled as I tried to keep up with it, and then everything went black.

* * *

I woke with a start, blinking at both the golden blaze streaming in through the window and the thumping pain behind my eyes. Without even looking down, I knew I was naked—the only thing covering me was a white sheet wrapped around my knees and my string of pearls draped over my breasts. The room was familiar, yet it was different. When a rumbling noise shattered the silence, I eased up on my elbows and stared at the man beside me. Corben was naked, flat on his back, his jaw ajar as he snored loud and deep.

Oh *faaaaarrrrk*. I'd stayed the night.

As I ogled him, I tried to piece together what'd happened. My furry tongue reminded me of the different drinks we'd had. I recalled dancing. Laughing. The sex up against the wall. Bits and pieces came back to me, but there were so many blank spots.

Trying not to wake him, I rolled off the side of the bed. The room whipped around, and as my eyes tried to keep up, my stomach lurched. I made a dash for the bathroom and just managed to reach the toilet before I threw up.

Oh god. I forced back tears as I heaved over and over.

When the contents of my stomach were gone, I stood and leaned on the bathroom sink. My eyes were as red as one of the cocktails we'd drunk last night. I filled a glass with water and gulped it down. Poking my tongue out, I cringed at its ghastly gray color and drank another glass of water.

The rumbling noise coming from the bed confirmed Corben was still asleep. I decided this was my chance to sneak out of there. I tiptoed from the bathroom and set about looking for my clothes. I found my G-string and jeans and pulled them on, but my bra and top were nowhere to be found.

My feet froze to the floor as the shocking realization of where they were hit me. I'd torn them off in the elevator. I didn't know whether to laugh or cry. Corben let out a loud gurgling noise, and I braced for him to wake up. I watched mesmerized as his muscles bulged and flexed and he rolled onto his side to face away from me. I now had a fine view of his broad muscular back and his perfect derriere.

I pranced to his closet and pulled open the doors. There wasn't a single item of clothing hanging in there. Feeling like a petty thief, I went to his overnight bag and lifted the lid. A singlet was at the top. With a sigh of relief, I pulled it out and tugged it on. I just about burst out laughing at the absurdity of it. The arms on the singlet were so low that each of my boobs poked out of them.

Yanking it off, I rummaged through the rest of the case, but it was pointless. He only had two singlet tops in there and a scrunched up work uniform. I was tempted to take the uniform but then realized he might need it today. Squeezing my temples, I begged my brain to think. Short of attempting a topless streak to get to my room, I was out of options.

Realizing I was at the point of desperate measures, I fished in my bag for my phone and sent a message to Lolita.

'Fancy rescuing Memphis again?'

'HAHA, hell yes.'

'Thanks. Come to my hotel, room forty-five, but don't knock. Text me when here. And bring me a shirt. Please.'

'Cryptic, yay, b there in 20.'

The twenty minutes were more like twenty hours, and each time Corben's snoring hit a new crescendo I expected him to wake. By the time my phone vibrated to announce Lolita's arrival, I was a nervous wreck.

I opened the door a couple of inches and poked my head out. "Hey, thank you."

"Let me in."

"Shhhh." She had no idea how loud she was. "I can't."

"Who's in there?"

"It's Corben."

"Mr. Universe? Come on, I want to see."

"No. Give me the shirt."

"Awww, not until you let me see."

"Lolly," I hissed at her. "That's blackmail."

"No." She wriggled her head. "It's girlfriend code."

I cocked my head. "Can I have the shirt please?"

"What the fuck are you girls doing?"

My stomach threatened to hurl again at the sound of Corben's deep voice. Next second, Lolita pushed on the door and winked at me as she strode past. I watched wide-eyed as she strode right up to my naked Corben and held out her hand.

"Hi, I'm Lolita. Jane's best friend."

Corben glanced at me, then without covering himself, he shook Lolita's hand. "Did Jane invite you over?"

Lolita made a show of checking Corben out, and he didn't seem to mind one bit. "Well, sort of. She asked me to bring a shirt—apparently she can't find hers."

Corben chuckled. "That's because she tore it off in the elevator."

Lolita jiggled from foot to foot and clapped. "Ha, that's gold."

As Corben sat up and planted his feet on the floor, Lolita mouthed 'wow' at me. I stifled a giggle as the most surreal moment of my life unfolded. Corben stood up, and a flush of embarrassment blazed my cheeks as Lolita boldly let her eyes travel over his body.

"'Scuse me for a sec." As Corben strode to bathroom, both Lolita and I watched the glorious spectacle that was his physique.

"Holy shit, babe, you've hit the fucking jackpot. Literally."

"Shhhh." I put my finger to my lips as I giggled. The sound of Corben peeing was just as embarrassing, and I tried to ignore it as I pulled on the ridiculously tight t-shirt Lolita had brought for me.

Corben flushed, and moments later he emerged from the bathroom with a towel slung low on his hips.

"Anyway, thank you for a wonderful night, Corben." I hooked my tote over my shoulder. "We need to get going before Needledick gets on the prowl again. Especially if he found my bra in the elevator."

"Needledick?" Corben frowned.

"Her boss," Lolita volunteered. "He's caught her a few times."

"Yeah, I remember him. That's how I met Jane."

"Ahhh, she told me about that. Hey, oh my god." The bulge in her eyes and elevation in her voice had me dreading what Lolita was about to say. She clicked her fingers. "I have a brilliant idea."

I groaned.

"No. Trust me, babe. You're going to fucking thank me big time." She strode toward me. "We're going to your room for a bit. Corben, you stay here. I'm going to need you."

He shrugged. "Sure."

Lolita hooked her arm into mine and next second, we strode out the door. "This is going to be so good."

My head was already a clouded fog, and I wasn't sure if I wanted to hear her brilliant plan. I moaned in response.

"Jeez, babe, how much did you drink?"

I shook my head and instantly regretted it. "I don't know."

"Ha. I love it."

"I don't." With her arm hooked into mine, we made it to my room unscathed. She dragged me to the bathroom and turned on the shower taps. "Strip, woman. You need a shower."

I groaned again, but knowing it was pointless to argue, I undressed and hopped under the cascade. As the tumbling water pummeled some breath back into my weary body, I spied Lolita through the shower screen rummaging in my makeup kit.

By the time I'd turned off my taps and stepped out, she had a thick layer of makeup on, my purple contact lenses in, and my crazy black wig that scrambled in all directions on her head. I burst out laughing despite it hurting like hell. "What're you doing?"

"You'll see." She tossed me a towel. "Now I need you to go for a walk or something, but you have to come back at exactly"—she glanced at her watch—"nine-thirty."

Knowing full well she wasn't going to give me any more info, I rolled my eyes. "Okay."

I toddled to my bedroom and dressed in jeans and a T-shirt.

"This is going to be such a hoot." Lolita emerged from the bathroom wearing just a G-string, showing off the perkiest boobs ever. "Now, off you go. But remember, you must be back at exactly nine-thirty."

"Yes, boss."

"Ewww, don't call me that."

I grabbed my sunglasses and bag, and she pulled me in for a hug. "Go get yourself a bottle of water, okay?"

"Okay."

In a thick haze, I rode down the elevator and was grateful Needledick was busy with customers as I made it outside the Hot Horizon Hotel. I crossed to the beach and sat on the park bench for a bit. Glancing at my watch, I noted I had twenty minutes up my sleeve, and went in search of that bottle of water and something to eat.

At the Blue Haven Café, I devoured a macadamia and white chocolate muffin and drank two bottles of water before it was time to leave again. "Here we go," I mumbled under my breath as I stood and pushed my chair in.

I arrived back at the hotel two minutes early and waited on the bottom step for a bit. Then, with a huge breath to calm my racing heart, I did as I was told and re-entered the hotel at exactly nine-thirty. The lobby was quiet, and unsure exactly what I was supposed to do, I headed toward the elevator. Halfway across the room, Needledick caught my attention by waving something around. I gasped as I realized it was my bra. "Did you lose something?"

My feet froze to the floor and my mouth fell open.

With perfect timing, the elevator doors pinged open and Lolly and Corben strode from the elevator arm in arm. She was in my Poison Ivy green satin corset, my black lycra workout pants that looked totally hot on her, and a pair of my killer black stilettos. The wig was huge, the makeup eccentric, and Lolly pulled it all together like a true performer.

"Hey." Damn she was loud. "There he is. That's the guy who grabbed me."

Together, Corben and Lolly strode to the reception counter. I, however, remained dumbstruck in the middle of the lobby.

"Hey, that's my bra, you creep." Her voice echoed about the marble expanse.

Corben stood with his feet apart, his fisted hands making his award-winning biceps bulge even further. "You been touching my woman?"

Needledick looked from me to Lolly, his jaw ajar, his eyes bulging. "I arrrr . . ."

I had to get a closer look and convinced my feet to take me to the counter. "You what?" Corben sounded evil.

"He's the one who grabbed my arm." Lolita pointed a long fingernail at Needledick. "That's when I kicked him in the balls."

"You're lucky I don't kick you from here to Perth. Never touch her again. Understand?"

"Yes." Needledick shook his head so fast it was a wonder it didn't fall off.

"Give me that." Lolly launched over the counter and grabbed my bra. She screwed her face up at Needledick. "Asshole." Lolly hooked her arm into Corben's. "Come on, honey, let's get outta here."

They strode past me without glancing in my direction and halfway between me and the glass doors, Lolly reached around and squeezed Corben's butt cheek. It took all my might not to burst out laughing.

I turned to Needledick. "Looks like you found Memphis."

His shoulders slumped, and he splayed his hands on the counter as if he needed it for support.

I folded my arms across my chest. "You thought it was me, didn't you?"

He shook his head. "No."

"You need to get a life. Asshole." I turned on my heel and strode to the elevator.

By the time I was in the mirrored cube, I couldn't hold back my laughter a moment longer. I giggled all the way to my room and was still laughing when I flopped back onto my bed. I grabbed my phone.

'God I love you.'

'That was so much fun.' Lolita's response came in a flash.

'He should leave me alone now.'

'I know. Told you it was perfect.'

'You were right.'

'OMG, babe. Corben's a total hottie.'

'I told you.'

'I want all the details on Tuesday—got it?'

'Of course.'

'Luv ya.'

'Love you too.'

I put my phone on my beside table and picked up my diary. I turned to the 28th of September, and at the top I wrote *Mr. Corben Benson Room 45*. I detailed our night out, everything from the yummy hotdogs to dirty dancing in the nightclub.

I detailed the sex and wrote how Corben seemed to be able to go on forever, so long in fact that, for me, it was too long. Maybe it was because I'd been terribly drunk. I didn't know—it'd seemed like an eternity. Maybe it had only been a minute or two.

At the top of the page I wrote *Marathon Man*. I giggled at that, and after I closed my diary, I slid off the bed and headed into the kitchen.
I needed food. Eggs and bacon. Lots and lots of bacon.

Keep turning the pages for a sneak peek at the next book in this series.

ABOUT THE AUTHOR

Kitty Kendall is a bucket list achieving, junk jewelry collecting, hopeless romantic who loves great wine and a good adrenaline rush from time to time. She also collect classy shoes and expensive perfume. But her greatest thrill in life is writing romance and the steamier the better.

Bring It On!

She's travelled extensively, some 37 countries and counting and she's addicted to experiences that make her scream… white water rafting, scuba diving with sharks and hang gliding are just a few. Her stories reflect her sense of adventure and her love affair with her very own hero.

Kitty also writes romantic suspense under the pen name of Kendall Talbot. She's won numerous awards, including Romantic Book of the Year, and several of her books are Amazon bestsellers. Check out www.kendalltalbot.com to find out more.

Read more at www.kittykendall.com

Keep turning the pages for a sneak peek of the next book in this series.

ACKNOWLEDGMENTS

I couldn't have written the Rise of Memphis series without my husband. His willingness to help out with the necessary choreography was commendable. But seriously, I wouldn't be an author without his unwavering support. He entered my heart more than thirty years ago, and I'm crazy lucky to have a man like him at my side.

Writing a book is never a solo effort, and I wouldn't have survived this series without my wonderful editor Lauren at McStellar Editing. Lauren's tough love helped me polish the rough drafts until they were shimmering diamonds.

Along this journey I started a secret Facebook group - Cheeky Memphis, and although I've never met any of the women who joined me there, I want to thank them for making this journey so special. Without their very intimate details and stunning pictures of totally hot men, this Memphis project would've been a very lonely one.

So in no particular order, special thanks goes to:
Brandi Warhank, Dawn Viertlbeck, Revva, Janet Ross, Sarah Frost, Raven Johnson, Vikki Clay, Michelle Harris, Jay Epiha, Ronda Thayer, Sunny Lane, Kathy Allred, Jennifer Kennessey, Tina Whitley, Sam Young, Evelyn Lazenby, Romana Purkiss, Maria S, Nicole Holt Sexton, Nicole Betalon, Vickie, Amanda Petersen, Gayla File, Angela Davisson, Babel of Literaria, Michelle R, Christina Conrad, Barbara Laarhoven, Lala Poara, Debbie Schrum, Emily Maynard and Marita Lightbody. I hope I didn't miss anybody, but if I did I apologise from the bottom of my heart.

I'd also love to acknowledge my writing buddies who are all incredible authors too. For more than a year they've had to hear me bang on about Memphis, and this journey has been made much more enjoyable knowing that they've been there with me. Special thanks to: Tania Joyce, Noelle Clark, Isabella Hargreaves, Anthea Jones, Matt JX and Claire Austin.

And finally and most importantly I want to thank you—my readers. I wouldn't be living my dream of being an author if you didn't support me along the way. I hope my stories take you on an emotional journey that fills you with joy, makes you laugh, and helps you to believe in true love.

You can write to me any time at kitty@universe.com.au.

Rise of Memphis Tame Me

This three book box set contains:

Rise of Memphis October Chronicles
Rise of Memphis November Chronicles
Rise of Memphis December Chronicles

KITTY KENDALL

7TH OCTOBER
MY MAGIC ELIXIR
Room 28 - Hot Horizon Hotel

"I still can't believe you've been holding out on me." The fact that Lolita could even talk, despite running at a frightening pace, was a testament to how fit she was.

I frowned at her. "What?" I spoke between breaths. "No I haven't."

I was pretty certain she was still punishing me after making her eat that cheesecake a couple of weeks ago. Even though it'd only been about five mouthfuls, I'd learned my lesson. Never force-feed Lolita.

"You never told me Corben was that hot."

"Yes I did."

She played with the buttons on her treadmill, and the spinning tread raised to its highest elevation. The crazy woman was running at maximum speed and maximum elevation yet she could still talk as if she were merely taking a stroll on the beach. I loved and hated her right then.

"You said he was hot. That doesn't even begin to describe him. Now that I've met both Billy and Corben, I know you're holding out on me."

"No I'm not."

"Your descriptions fall way short of the mark. I mean, Corben was a total fucking babe. Either you give me all the details"—she waggled her finger at me—"or photos. You choose."

I just shook my head; it was impossible to speak anyway. After a couple more seconds, I decided I'd had enough and jumped off the spinning tread. "I'm done."

"No you're not. Get back on there."

I turned to her and cocked my head. "Nope." That was the first time I'd ever defied Lolita, and she scowled at me.

"No cake for you this morning then."

"Watch me."

She gasped, then burst out laughing. How on earth she could laugh and run at the same time was beyond me. I turned off my treadmill and wiped the sweat off my forehead with a towel. As I sipped my water and waited for Lolita to finish her run, I summarized everything we had to talk about this morning. By the time she jumped off, I decided I'd need a large piece of cake to get through all the topics.

A quick glance in the mirror confirmed my cheeks were as flushed as they felt. Lolita, on the other hand, looked like she could do it all again. We grabbed our things from the lockers and headed to the Blue Haven Café.

Spring was out in all its glory with the sun blazing as a white ball, high over the ocean. The red and yellow lifesaver flags were far apart today, indicating the ocean was behaving itself, and based on the amount of people in the water, I assumed it was fairly warm, too.

While Lolly sat at our usual table, I went inside to check out the cake selection. My mouth salivated as I glanced from one delectable to the next. In the end it was the chocolate Jaffa cake that spoke to me the loudest.

I returned to the table and sat so I could see both Lolita and the beach.

"How's Needledick been?"

"Weird, as usual. It's like he still doesn't believe what happened but has no choice. I don't care anymore; I'm over him."

"Good. He doesn't deserve your attention anyway."

"True."

Matt arrived, and we placed our orders. The second he left, Lolita tapped her fingernail on the table. "So tell me all about Corben. He's fucking hot."

I giggled. "I know." As we waited for our meals I detailed the unusual date I'd had with Corben. I started with what I wore and moved onto his choice of meal.

"A hotdog stand?"

"I know, weird huh? It was yummy though."

She scrunched up her nose. "Of course you'd enjoy it."

"I had fun. We sat in the middle of the mall, and as we ate our hotdogs we watched the people go by. I didn't mind it, and you know what? It suited Corben. I couldn't imagine him doing fine dining."

A frown drilled across her forehead, then she squinted at me. "I think you like Corben. A lot."

Matt arrived with our food, and as he placed our dishes on the table I thought about her comment. There certainly was a lot to like about Mr. Universe. But was he the man for me? I didn't know.

"So do you think he's the one?"

I stabbed my cake with the fork. "He's the one for now."

Lolly burst out laughing. "Ha, you're a riot."

"Thank you." The Jaffa cake was everything I'd hoped for—moist and delicious with hints of fresh orange complementing the rich dark chocolate. Every forkful was a party in my mouth.

"So who else are you really keen on? What about Billy?"

I sighed as I thought about my hunky cowboy. "He's really lovely. They all are. Every one of the men has been amazing in their own way."

"Okay, which ones are at the top of your list?"

"What? Out of all of them?"

"Yeah. Which were your favorites?"

"Okay, well at the top of the list is Henry."

She cocked her head. "The old guy?"

"He's not old."

"Whoa, calm down. It's my way of remembering these dudes. Okay, so he's not old. Why do you like him so much?"

"Well . . . he's incredible. His body is amazing. He's smart, funny, suave, and oh my god, does he know how to please me."

"What'd he do this time?"

I cringed at the thought of telling her and instantly regretted it.

"What? Tell me." She reached forward and clutched my arm.

Knowing full well I had no choice but to divulge the details, I closed my eyes and hated myself right at that very moment. "Stuck his finger up my . . ." I cringed, unable to say it.

"Holy shit, babe, you really are stepping out. Did you like it?"

I shrugged. "It was weird."

"But you liked it, didn't you?"

I felt the need to clarify why I liked it. I leaned forward, and with my voice barely a whisper I described in intimate detail exactly what Henry did to me. Lolly barely uttered a sound as I explained how Henry brought my orgasm to a whole new level. When I finished, I leaned back and attacked my cake again.

Lolly fanned herself. "Holy smokes, babe. He sounds fucking amazing."

I grinned at her. "Told you."

She pointed her finger at me. "From now on, that's exactly how you're going to tell me about these romps. No more glossing over the details. I tell you what though—I need to grab Calvin and get me some anal sex going on."

My jaw dropped, and cringing, I scanned the café, hoping like hell nobody had heard her. To my surprise, it seemed she'd gone unnoticed. I turned my gaze to her as she pushed back and stood up. She came to me and wrapped her arms around my shoulders. "You're amazing, babe."

I had no idea why. But adhering to Henry's advice I nodded and said,

"Thank you."

She threw her bag over her shoulder. "Calvin better answer his phone or I'll have to get my Venus Probe out."

I had a good idea what the Venus Probe was, and thank god she'd looked away or she would've seen the shock on my face. Lolita jogged off, and as I watched her non-existent ass disappear into the crowd I thought about her choice to own a vibrator.

I'd never used one myself. Maybe, that was because prior to this year, sex hadn't even been close to amazing. Now, though, I understood just how incredible it was. But still, once I had a man in my life, like Lolita did, I couldn't imagine the need for a vibrator. I chuckled as I hoped that the man who I did fall in love with enjoyed having sex, because he was going to be getting a hell of a lot of it.

As I smiled at that wonderful thought, I put a twenty-dollar note under the salt shaker and stood up to push my chair in.

Back in my room, I showered and crawled into bed. After the workout I'd had, sleep came quickly.

* * *

The evening shift started slowly and didn't get any better as the night rolled on. Until, that was, just after eleven o'clock, when a handsome stranger strolled through the lobby doors and enchanted me with his beauty. In a flash, my boring shift had become a hell of a lot better.

His skin was creamy white, with a touch of rose to his cheeks. It was obvious that he hadn't been exposed to Australia's harsh sunshine for long. His blond beard was full, covering the lower half of his face, but it was his eyes that drew me in. Fierce, cornflower blue eyes that grabbed me and wouldn't let me go.

He was younger than me I'd say by at least three years, and his strong, confident stride was that of a man who'd figured out the mystery of the universe. He struck me as someone who had an excellent work-life balance. But from the second I glanced into his intense eyes, I was ready to tilt that balance way over to the life side. At least, that was the plan.

"Good evening." I cleared my throat. "Welcome to the Hot Horizon Hotel."

"Hello, I'm Maxximus Diederik. I've booked for one night." His European accent was strong, sexy.

Dragging my eyes away from his, I stepped to the back counter and after a quick flick through the check-in cards I removed his.

"Here we go, Mr. Diederik. Do you have your identification there?"

As he fished around in a leather satchel over his shoulder, I took the opportunity to explore his body.

He wore a navy T-shirt that showed off the fine tone of his arms, and his hands were exquisite—smooth tanned skin with perfectly trimmed nails. His only jewelry was an interesting silver ring with unusual engravings around the outer edge.

As he handed his passport over, it took all my might not to accidentally-on-purpose touch him. I flipped to his photo and quickly noted his age; this fine young man was indeed younger than me by four years. As I took a photocopy of his passport I decided it was time I explored some younger flesh, and my insides did a dizzying flip at my naughty decision.

I turned back to him, and my breath caught in my throat at his side profile. The discreet down lighting captured the golden tones of his slicked back hair and his beard was thick and bushy, adding length to his already strong chin.

"What brings you to the Gold Coast, Mr. Diederik?"

His smile was extraordinary, and as I blinked at him, I realized Maxximus could be Bradley Cooper's twin. "Please . . . call me Magic."

My eyebrows shot up with a will of their own. "Magic?"

"Yes, Magic Maxx. It's my professional name. I'm here for the Evolution International Yoga conference."

Yoga with Bradley Cooper. Count me in. "Oh wow." I started undressing him with my eyes, peeling off layer after layer to review the body sculpted by the art of yoga.

"Do you do yoga?"

"Oh, ummm no." *But I'm ready when you are.*

Thank you for reading.

Hopefully your sneak peek has left you wanting more.

Books in this series

Rise of Memphis Box Sets:

Rise of Memphis Touch Me (January, February, March)
Rise of Memphis Tempt Me (April, May, June)
Rise of Memphis Tease Me (July, August, September)
Rise of Memphis Tame Me (October, November, December)

Rise of Memphis Monthly Chronicles

Rise of Memphis January Chronicles
Rise of Memphis February Chronicles
Rise of Memphis March Chronicles
Rise of Memphis April Chronicles
Rise of Memphis May Chronicles
Rise of Memphis June Chronicles
Rise of Memphis July Chronicles
Rise of Memphis August Chronicles
Rise of Memphis September Chronicles
Rise of Memphis October Chronicles
Rise of Memphis November Chronicles
Rise of Memphis December Chronicles

www.kittykendall.com

Printed in Australia
AUOC02n0707270417
285145AU00001B/2/P